MW01230380

Praise for Grumpy Old Man ....

There are shocking plot turns springing from the character's background that lead to a solid ending. - *Kirkus book review*

The plot here is solidly engaging with unexpected development, alluring characters, and unique details throughout! Reminiscent of the work of Carl Hiassen. An original murder mystery. ***** 4 Star Book Life review*

Mr. Lyons writes in a lively, satirical, manner that echoes the idiosyncratic nature of the characters. ***** 4 Star Publishers Weekly review*

I would really like to read more about Palmer Doyle and his motley crew of investigators. The story is far from simple and takes many interesting turns. ***** 4 Star Book Sirens review*

Grumpy Old Man is a fast-paced satire with quirky characters and solid plot that is entertaining, interesting and has an unexpected ending. ****** 5 Star Reedsy book review*

There's plenty of action, drama, and plot twists that make Grumpy Old Man a page turner until the very end. ****** 5 Star Dana's book review*

Grumpy Old Man reminds me of Ove in – a man called Ove – by Fredrick Backman. ***** 4 star Goodreads review, Virika*

Grumpy Old Man by Tom Lyons

A spirited whodunit with an amusingly discontented detective. – *Kirkus book review*

Lyons' lighthearted mystery teems with vibrant characters. – *Kirkus book review*

This sympathetic gumshoe (Palmer Doyle) incessantly, and humorously, complains about everything in the State of California, earning his titular grumpiness. – *Kirkus book review*

<u>Books by Tom Lyons</u>

The Complete Realtor – 2007

Putt like a tour professional – 2010

Shark in the water – AKA – Family – 2014

Psychopath Chronicles – 2015

Grumpy Old Man - 2022

Dedicated to my mother,

Edna Jean Lyons

1925-2020

Thank you, Mom

Also, to my wonderful wife,

Amelia

Grumpy Old Man

A Palmer Doyle P.I. murder mystery

By Tom Lyons

Copyright @ 2021 by Thomas Lyons

June 2021

When he woke, not for one second did Ramsay Marshall think that today would be the day he'd die.

But dying he was. And there was nothing that he or his fifty-million-dollar fortune could do to save him. Unable to control his bodily functions, he peed through his silver silk pajamas—a ridiculous-looking Hugh Hefner outfit—then he shit himself before continuing to bounce and twitch uncontrollably in a dance-of-the-zombie that his body was now performing.

An hour earlier, he had wolfed down sushi and avocado toast for breakfast, feeling great. How could he not have? Sushi was his favorite food. His fifty-foot SeaBreeze cruiser, "Lucy in the Sky," sat moored in twenty-five feet of clear blue water near Sand Harbor Beach on the Nevada side of Lake Tahoe.

The water was so clear; he could see jagged rocks and white sand on the bottom. It was a Tahoe postcard summer morning: a cloudless, cobalt-blue sky, the sun rising over Squaw in the east, warming the air but doing little to heat Tahoe's frigid waters. Ramsay leaned on the side of the boat and took a deep breath. A scent of pine carried on the breeze; overhead, red-tailed hawks flapped and screeched while scouring the water for fish skimming the surface. Ready to swoop down.

Ramsay was not a boat person, yet he'd decked his yacht with the latest technology, and he'd sprung for twin inboard diesels for long trips, like for cruising to Cabo, his favorite excursion. The boat had solar panels powering all electrical needs: the Sub-Zero fridge, for Ramsay's five-hundred-dollar bottles of Chardonnay Wi-Fi; satellite radio; and a fifty-six-inch widescreen TV, mounted over the circular bed in the master suite. Her double fiberglass V-bottom hull made "Lucy" easy to handle in choppier waters than one would normally find here on the lake. Ramsay was not a fisherman—fish slime disgusted him, the smell turning his stomach—but he'd made sure that they installed the latest Garmin CHIRP sonar technology fish-finder. Now he could see thousands of those "slimy little fuckers" at the push of a button. Plus, sportfishing had grown in popularity since the pandemic had started. *The Tesla of boats.* Ramsay boarded Lucy for all his "excursions," where he'd be safe from the jealous eyes of his third wife, Jojo, a bleached blond forty-five years his junior.

Ramsay had recently turned seventy-five, but he looked ten years older. His lizard-like skin, sun damaged with liver spots, had long since ripened with wrinkles, deep creases embedded in his face and neck, as if he had been lying in midday summer sun, covered in cooking oil, his entire life. Decades of heavy drinking had mapped red canals of broken blood vessels on his nose. Reminded one of Rudolph the red-nosed reindeer. He was thin, emaciated looking, with two-day-old white stubble trailing down his turkey-jowl neck. A multiple decades' old biker tattoo adorned his left calf. Ramsay knew that his tattoo looked asinine.

Nothing looks as foolish as an old person with one stupid faded tattoo.

His most notable feature, besides his red bulbous nose, was his mid-back-length, stringy white hair that, this morning, he had banded in a pony. He hadn't washed it in a week, its foul odor like that of an unwashed dog. If he'd let it hang loose around his face, he would have looked like a medieval dungeon keeper. Pencil-thin legs

7

poked from the bottom of his Hefner robe. Ramsay fancied himself a playboy, but truth be told, he looked ridiculous—a septuagenarian Bozo the clown.

A few steps down from the rear deck, a beautiful twenty-five-year-old woman with an hourglass figure lay face down, naked and asleep on the large circular bed.

"What an incredible ass," Ramsay mumbled to himself, leering at her with his lecherous old man's gaze. Plucked her from the website, specifically for the pictures of her rear end.

Worth the twenty-five hundred.

She called herself Panama; said she was born and raised there. Exotic looking with perfect skin and dark brown almond-shaped eyes. *Must be some Asian in her lineage.* Panama had a bountiful bosom, thin waist, and that absolutely world-class feminine ass.

Probably Mexican. Jumped a fence somewhere to get into the States. Passing herself off as something more exotic.

The alcohol they had consumed robbed him of his memory of the previous evening, but the sweet soreness he felt told him that there'd been a happy ending, at least for him.

Two R95 respiratory masks—the kind that hospital workers use for personal protection equipment, or PPE— lay on the table next to the breakfast dishes.

The best money can buy. That stinkin' Chinese virus can't live up here in the Tahoe.

As he took in the incredible views over the lake, he noticed that something in his body didn't feel quite right. *What did she give me last night?* He tried to shake his

8

head clear. Music might help.

"Alexa, play Ella Fitzgerald." His tongue wasn't working right, catching on his last word. Hair of the dog, he thought.

"Playing 'Blue Skies' by Ella Fitzgerald," Alexa said.

> *Blue skies, smilin' at me*
> *Nothin' but blue skies do I see*
> *Bluebirds singin' a song*
> *Nothin' but blue skies from now on*
> *Never saw the sun shinin' so bright*
> *Never saw things goin' so right ....*

Ramsay tried to fix himself a Bloody Mary, but the fingers of his right hand felt stiff. They wouldn't move. He tried with his left hand; that hand felt frozen too. Like trying to snap his fingers and missing.

"Hmmph?" His tongue felt swollen, as if ballooning in his mouth. His jaw felt numb.

Ella sang on.

Tingling started in his shoulders, then snaked its way down both his arms. The tingling turned into numbness, like the injection of Novocain before a root canal. Soon he could not move his arms; they lay useless, pinned to his side. Forget his legs. They wouldn't work right at all. Bouncing now, he started the dance of the Zombie. This didn't feel like a heart attack—he'd already had three, so he knew what a heart attack felt like. Doctors had put stents in. No, this didn't feel like a heart attack at all. Ramsay had heard about the things that supposedly run through your mind when you realize you are about to die.

That your entire life passes before you, as if you are watching it in 3D with surround sound on an IMAX screen.

Ramsay had no such thoughts. Instead, he raged.

What's happening to me?

He tried to walk below deck, but, with his body stiff as an ironing board, the twitching and bouncing held him in its grasp. He spun like a top, arms pinned to his sides, pin balling off the boat's safety rails; Bozo the clown performing the Zombie dance. The paralysis traveled to his lungs. He couldn't breathe. He felt dizzy, lightheaded. His face twisted into a scary Halloween mask, his body ready to go full tilt. His sense of smell, however, remained intact. The stench of his own shit and piss hit him full on. His stomach lurched, and he vomited, emitting retching sounds like a cow giving birth.

He tried to yell, through the open doorway to the bedroom, to rouse Panama; a little gurgle and frothy, bloody bubbles were all that escaped his mouth. She lay asleep, on her belly, oblivious to his cartoonish thrashings. The curve of her marvelous ass was the last thing he saw. His brain, somehow still working full speed, thought, *Shit. All that Viagra I just bought is gonna go to waste.* He felt himself getting an erection. He pinged one final time off the railing at the rear of his boat.

"Fook muh," he managed to gurgle.

Ramsay Marshall toppled like a jerking stone statue, erection intact, and pitched from his beautiful yacht into the frigid waters of Lake Tahoe.

Boats at their moorings, more boats than usual, crowded the lake, but nobody heard or saw Ramsay tumble into the water.

Overhead, hawks flapped their wings and screeched.

"Play more Ella Fitzgerald?" Alexa asked.

1.

"Ah. This is more like it." Palmer Doyle took a sip of hot black coffee from his thermos. He refitted his hook with a fresh salmon egg and cast with his right arm, towards the reeds that stood near shore, out of the morning sun glare. "Peace and quiet."

Las Vaqueros, a man-made lake a quarter mile wide and two miles long, sat between parched golden hills just northeast of Livermore, California. Buddy, his six-year-old Malinois, the Belgian version of a German shepherd, sniffed the morning breeze. The Malinois was considered to be one of the smartest breeds in the world; many of them trained as military dogs and could carry out a string of commands, such as run and hide, stay under cover, sniff out the bomb, or disarm the perpetrator. Some had earned medals like the Distinguished Service Cross or Purple Heart.

That was not the case with Buddy. Besides sit—and that he would only do if a treat was involved—there were no other instructions that Buddy seemed to understand. Plus, unlike others of his breed, Buddy had the attention span of, well, a dog. Buddy sniffed the lone tiny bass flopping in a pail at the boat's bow, then scampered to the rear where Palmer sat, nuzzling his nose under Palmer's hand.

"Okay boy, I get it. Gotta throw the little guy back. Almost time to go. Let's enjoy this a little longer. Okay?"

Buddy was off-kilter today.

Palmer craved peace and quiet. Nothing would suit

him better than to leave the hustle and bustle of living in the East Bay of the San Francisco Bay Area and move to a place in the Sierra foothills, like Camp Connell or Twain Harte or Arnold, where there weren't as many people around.

Palmer and Becky had been married for twenty-five happy years. They had raised a wonderful daughter, Francesca. Though, Francesca was now twenty-three and living in London with her girlfriend. She worked as a nurse at the Royal London Hospital. With the nest empty, Palmer wanted to pack up and head for the hills; Becky didn't. It was simple as that. They argued.

"I'm not going to leave Dublin while Francesca is young." Dublin was an East Bay city of almost eighty thousand people, located at the crossroads and exhaust fumes of two major freeways.

"She's an adult."

"This is her home. You know how young adults are. They move around. Suppose something happens and she needs to come home?"

"She lives in London."

Palmer remembered when Francesca had brought her "friend" Lena, home. Palmer had shaken his head. *Daughters. There's always more to worry about with daughters.*

"My parents, they need me," Becky had said, adding to her list of excuses. Her parents, in their seventies but healthy and active, lived in San Ramon, the city nearest to Dublin, five miles to the north.

"Need you? They don't need you," Palmer had retorted. "They were on cruise ships nine months of the year before many of the cruise lines went bankrupt. Every day that they're home they go dancing. They don't

13

need you." He didn't bother to mention that if they did move to the foothills, it would only take a couple of hours to drive to Becky's parents' house. It was not like they were moving to the far side of the earth. "They can take care of themselves."

"They're getting older. Someone needs to take care of them." Then she'd added how she really felt. "I don't want to move away from here. This is my home."

She'd never be ready. Women put down roots. Now that Palmer and Becky had raised their daughter, they had different ideas about how and where they wanted to spend the rest of their lives. No harm, no foul. Rare is it that couples who had spent years together raising children would agree on what to do next once the kids left the nest. Her not wanting to move had made him mad. More than once he had lost his temper discussing where they would live.

Palmer made a mental note to buy her flowers, pink roses being her favorite; he owed her an apology.

It was noon by the time Palmer had traveled the six miles south on Vasco Road. Though it was the middle of summer, when there was usually less traffic, as he entered the freeway heading west towards Dublin, traffic had come to a dead halt. Six lanes. Stopped. Gridlock. Except, of course, the toll lane. *I'm not going to pay money to drive any freaking freeway.* Cameras captured license plate info and whether or not a car had the required "FasTrak" placard visible on the front dash patrolled overhead. Took about a week before a hundred-dollar ticket arrived in your mailbox. *Big brother is watching.*

The other five gridlocked lanes were littered with trucks—sixteen wheelers, container trucks, freight trucks, trucks hauling new cars, trucks hauling totaled

14

cars, trucks transporting construction materials, U-Hauls, and old jalopies carrying fruit or cows or horses. Plus, of course, all the Amazon Prime trucks carrying thousands of next-day deliveries. Dutifully, Palmer pulled his car behind a rig carrying strapped-down sewer pipe materials and worked his way over to the left, where cars were inching along at five miles per hour. The truck drivers were poorly trained, inconsiderate, or both. They sped up to switch lanes, oblivious to anything in their way.

Driving in California, you had to pay attention. The twenty-first century version of Darwin's theory of evolution, Palmer mused, was survival of the fittest on California freeways. *Who would have thought?* Eleven miles to go till Dublin. At this rate, it would take two hours. *I could walk there faster.* And the potholes. *Why can't they fix the potholes? Because they're spending money on the wrong things, that's why. Like on health care for all the Mexican women who cross the border into the States illegally, so that the good ole U.S. of A. can pay for the birth of their babies and all associated hospital costs.*

What's the matter with us?

And traffic only grew worse as each day went by. *Because there are way too many people living in the area. Too many people moving into the area.* Home builders were building—no, jamming—in thousands of new two- and three-story homes on zero-sized lots, and the city officials in Livermore, Pleasanton, Dublin, and other East Bay cities were allowing thousands of these homes to be built without plans to upgrade the infrastructure, like schools, parks, and freeways where Palmer's car was now stopped cold. *Why are we allowing this to happen? Because the builders are lining the pockets of city politicians, lining the pockets of City Council members to get this bat shit high-density housing approved. That's why.*

Palmer stewed. He noticed a fender bender off the side of the freeway: some lady driving a new Lexus had rear-ended another woman driving a Tesla. Traffic slowed even more, though it hadn't seemed possible. Buddy stuck his nose out the open passenger-side window and sniffed.

"Gotta be a complete idiot to rear end another car," Palmer said to Buddy. "Follow too close, brake late, don't pay attention to the road. Who knows? The idiot might have been texting."

Tail wagging, Buddy turned and started to lick Palmer's face.

"Easy, boy, easy," Palmer said. "I know. You're impatient too. You want to get going. You know I gotta get to the office? Gotta be a complete idiot to rear end another car."

For a moment, Palmer felt himself longing for the shelter-in-place times when few had driven the Northern California freeways. He dismissed that thought.

Strange times.

And why were all the builders building so many new houses? Because of Asians? Asians were everywhere in California—not that Palmer had anything against Asians. Those he knew were lovely, well educated, considerate people. But the people from Asia had discovered California with its wonderful weather, great lifestyle, good schools, and abundance of fun things to do. In the beginning of the nineteenth century, the United States had put immigration restrictions in place for the number of Asians allowed to migrate to the States. From the 1880s until the mid 1950s, few had been allowed into the country. That had changed after World War II;

immigration rules loosened, and Asians moved to the States in increasing numbers, finding ways to sneak family members into the country under the noses of immigration officials.

Palmer had met some of his Asian neighbors at a block party Becky had forced him to go to last Labor Day weekend. Well, she'd bribed him to go by making a big batch of the potato salad that Palmer loved so much, the recipe with garlic and chives, a little vinegar mixed with mayo, and a dash of Grey Poupon. Begrudgingly, Palmer grabbed the patriotic red, white, and blue paper plates, napkins, and the potato salad, not about to let that dish out of his sight. He trudged on down to the picnic tables set up in the middle of the street at the rear of their court.

One of his neighbors, new to the neighborhood, had moved there from India. Must have been about twelve of them, six or seven adults. *That's why there are so many cars in front of their house.* The men dressed in American fashion, while the women wore colorful saris. Only one of the men spoke English, the rest smiling and nodding their heads at the holiday conversations. They seemed like nice people, and their children dressed neatly and were well behaved. Another new family on the street was Chinese, also a large family with at least a dozen members, including parents, kids, grandparents, and possibly one great grandmother. They were all pencil thin. The driveway and front of their house was littered with cars. *No wonder the freeways are clogged. Six or seven drivers living in each house.* The Chinese family also seemed nice, but they spoke little English. Palmer made the best of the situation, though, by drinking several glasses of Vodka on the rocks as he smiled at his new neighbors. And when Becky wasn't looking he had helped himself to several large servings of potato salad.

Vodka and potato salad, that's the life.

Palmer had no issues with his Asian neighbors, but not all Asians got along. The Chinese hated the Japanese and vice versa. For centuries, well before the documented atrocities committed by the Japanese during the Second World War, the Chinese had hated the Japanese. Koreans hated the Japanese; Taiwanese hated the Chinese; and Filipinos hated the Chinese, Japanese, Koreans, and the Taiwanese. People from Thailand, Laos, Cambodia, and Vietnam moved into their own little pockets of various neighborhoods in California, and their young adults joined different gangs, often gunning each other down.

No one trusted Indians—not even other Indians, India being a country with dozens of caste systems, each with their own idiosyncrasies, prejudices, racist views, and rules. Few Indians got along while living in their native countries and the same was true after they migrated to the States.

And there were so many of them. 1.4 billion Chinese, 1.4 billion Indians, almost four billion Asians total. And a billion is a *thousand* million. A big number. The population in California was forty million, maybe fifteen million Caucasians. Asians in the world outnumbered the Caucasians living in California by one hundred to one. *Just a matter of time before they owned the entire state. Hell, just a matter of time before they owned the entire country. It's already happened; it just has to play out over time. Soon you won't see a storefront sign in English.*

Palmer Doyle wanted to move to the hills.

He didn't have anything bad to say about Asians. Just that there were so damn many of them living here, and they all seemed to have cars.

Twenty minutes passed; he had inched forward three miles on 580 West, surrounded on two sides by trucks, a midget among giants, both hands gripped so firmly on the steering wheel that his knuckles turned white.

It was clear that he was going to be late meeting with his three p.m. appointment. Meghan, his ever-vigilant office manager, picked up on the second ring.

"Good afternoon, it's a great day at Doyle International. How may I help you?"

His investigations company was located in Dublin, a city with over a hundred thousand souls, located in the East Bay of the San Francisco Bay Area. Lately, his services were in high demand. His firm handled insurance fraud claims; the burgeoning business of DNA identification and forensic genealogy; missing persons, especially missing children; criminal investigations, the oft committed crimes of identity fraud and identity theft; and the moneymaker for the firm, fidelity issues—or digging up the dirt on cheating spouses, and Doyle had learned to pay special attention when one of the spouses was wealthy. All of his business came from referral, law enforcement agencies, or attorneys needing to prove their cases. And thanks to Palmer's previous life in the service, uncovering the identities of lost servicemen from their remains was a big part of his firm's business. Palmer didn't advertise; he did not want the general public to know about his firm. He preferred the anonymity.

"It's Palmer, Meg." He held the phone next to his right ear.

"Hi, Sarge." Old army nicknames die hard.

"What's going on?" he said, half grumbling to himself.

"Tough day, Sarge?" Meghan asked, picking up on his

Grumpy Old Man by Tom Lyons

mood.

"Took me sixty minutes to drive nine miles on five-eighty today."

"Sorry, Palmer. Roads are a mess."

"Tell me something I don't know." Still grumbling. "Can you believe that? Sixty minutes."

"Sharkie has news on the Pauly case. Wanna talk to him?"

"Sure."

"Sharkie," or John, the younger brother of Palmer's wife, Becky, was a licensed PI. He was the worst private investigator in the history of the world, in Palmer's opinion. Big and dumb with a shaved head, he walked around like he had the handle of a broomstick shoved up his rectum. His stomach looked like it was made of blubber; it flapped over his smaller waist and short legs. He was a big man, well over six feet tall, and he weighed somewhere north of two-fifty. He walked like a walrus might if a walrus could stand on its tail, toddling from side to side. His voice reminded Palmer of Patrick the Starfish from SpongeBob SquarePants.

No one called John Sharkie to his face, only behind his back. How he'd obtained his nickname had little to do with his lack of mental acuity and more to do with two unsightly characteristics: first, his incisors and two front teeth were triangular and came to sharp points, like shark's teeth; second, he had tiny black shark-like eyes set deep in his fat face. On top of all that, he had a dark, odd-shaped mole on his right cheek. Strange looking man.

Needless to say, Palmer never would have hired him if his wife hadn't pleaded with him.

It took a while for John to pick up. "Hi, Sarge," he finally said.

"Hey, John boy. What's going on with the Pauly case?" Palmer thought he heard Sharkie chewing something on the other end.

"Well, she sent us a check."

A big check, I hope. "Great. Good job."

Palmer couldn't shake the image of a giant pink starfish wearing green shorts out of his mind.

"What'd you find out?"

Simone Pauly thought that her husband Paul—yes, his name was Paul Pauly—had been cheating on her, so she'd hired Doyle's firm. There was nothing earth-shattering about standard PI work like this. Follow the husband, go where he goes, put a tail on him. Nowadays, a PI would also put a GPS chip on his car, bug and track his phone, and tap his computer. Access to a cell phone and personal computer just about guarantees everything about the subject's life will be presented on a silver platter. Turns out that Paul was simply going to the country club to play golf every day. But because Simone thought he was cheating, she made sure to have sex with him every morning and every evening, so that he would be too tired to get it in with his "mistress".

"He kinda walks bowlegged, like he's sore down there," Sharkie told him. "All he does is play golf. Then he gets hammered at the club. Gin. A miracle that he never gets pulled over and arrested on the drive home."

Palmer waited, sensing that John, resuming his strange chewing sounds, had more to say.

"He complains to his friends that his wife won't leave him alone. Has to have sex with him every day. She doesn't trust him. Poor guy is in his late-fifties. His friends just laugh and say how lucky he is and how they wish that they had his problems. Getting a piece of ass twice a day."

"Anything else?"

Sharkie continued: "Turns out, she is the one screwing around with the pool guy, this little Mexican dude with Oakland Raider tattoos on his calves. Fucks him once a week. Each time he comes to the house to service their pool. But that's not the strangest part."

Sharkie fell silent and even the chewing stopped.

"Well?" Palmer asked impatient.

"It's kind of weird, boss. After she fucks the pool guy, she goes upstairs and takes a nap. Around then, Paul is just starting his first drink at the club, double Beefeaters on the rocks, so there is plenty of time for her to catch forty winks."

"The weird part?"

"Well, she has this male mannequin that she takes to bed with her, you know, the kind of mannequin that you might see dressed up in a Macy's store window?"

Palmer remained quiet.

"She goes to sleep hugging the mannequin."

Nothing wrong with Paul. Simone's the one who's screwed in the head.

"She dresses the mannequin in her husband's golf clothes. And that's not all."

"Okay, I'll bite."

"Well, the mannequin's an anatomically correct one— you know how you can go into a sex shop in the Castro district in San Francisco and buy one of those female mannequins that have a vagina and round mouth and full lips with red lipstick on?"

Palmer had never stepped foot in the Castro district.

22

"Simone's mannequin has a penis. Hair down there too. Pubies."

A not-so-pretty picture appeared in Palmer's mind. Was the mannequin manscaped? Could it have an erection? Or was it limp? Or always erect? He thought he might know the answer to that question but decided not to ask.

"Check clear?" Palmer finally asked. *A wife will spend a fortune, even if she doesn't have one, to find out if her husband has been cheating on her.*

"Yeah, boss." The image of a pink starfish in green shorts planted itself in Palmer's head, again.

"Great job, John. Patch me back to Meg, will ya?" *Not like Sharkie to tie up a case into a neat little package. Dollars to donuts he screwed up somewhere.*

"Sure thing, boss."

"Meghan? Push my three o'clock with Sophia Mueller and her stepfather. Can you call them and push it back to four?"

Palmer glanced at his withered left arm, the missing muscle mass like a phantom limb. His left arm had never worked right since the blast. The arm was much thinner than his right and riddled with scars. He had plenty more scars on his left ribcage and hip. He'd been born a lefty but after his injury, he'd had to learn how to use his right hand to perform everyday tasks.

Sophia. My guardian angel.

Haven't heard from her in fifteen years.

When Meg interrupted his thoughts, Palmer imagined she could read his mind from miles away and over the phone. "She called too, Sarge, to push back the

23

appointment 'til four."

"She did?"

"Caught in traffic."

There you have it.

"Meghan? Do me a favor and pick up a dozen red roses for me?"

Silence on the other end of the phone.

Palmer pictured Meghan Tully's lips tighten into a pinched smirk, her eyes narrowing into slim almonds of judgment. He didn't know why Meghan clammed up when he discussed his wife.

"Never mind, Meg. I just remembered. I have to pick up a few things. I'll get the flowers." Palmer could spare Meghan the trouble, while figuring out how he was going to apologize to Becky.

"Okay, Sarge." Meghan replied. "And Sarge? Do me a favor, please?"

"Sure thing, Meg. What?"

"Before you get here, take off your fishing hat."

Palmer felt his head and sure as shit he still had his fishing hat on. Just a simple wrinkled old hat, the same one Palmer had worn for the past few years. The hat had ripened in age with white sweat stains around the brim, and a couple of fishhooks were stuck in its sides. It smelled of power bait and worms.

"Took it off before, Meg," Palmer lied.

"Okay, Sarge."

How did she know that?

Twenty minutes later, Palmer arrived at a strip mall near his office. There was a Starbucks, a florist, and a post office within sight. A Black Angus steakhouse on the corner. *Perfect. I'll just zip in and zip out.* He realized he wouldn't be so lucky, as he drove around the lot, looking for a spot to park. *Nada.* Other cars hurried up and down the lanes. Drivers cut off other drivers, blaring their horns, some nearly running over pedestrians in their frenzy to claim the next open parking spot. *When did finding a parking spot in a strip mall become a free-for-all?*

Many of the storefronts in the strip mall were empty. The remainder of tenants had been sit-down restaurants, sandwich shops, retail stores, and a nail salon. During the height of the pandemic, they had gone out of business.

Palmer circled the lot several trips before finding a space. Once parked, he put Buddy on a leash, then headed towards the coffee shop. Palmer Doyle stood six feet tall, but his lanky arms and big hands made him look taller. He walked with an athletic gait, a certain readiness in his movements. His full head of brown hair was now speckled with grey, and his bushy eyebrows needed trimming. Palmer's big nose was flattened against his face, like a boxer who had lost too many fights, and it was starred with burst veins from too much liquor over the course of his lifetime. And he certainly felt his age catching up with him: now, at fifty-nine, his knees crackled and popped until loosening after several steps.

Palmer could smell the foul odor of five-day-old-fish wafting off him. Suddenly aware of his disheveled appearance, he glanced down at the rumpled fishing clothes: brown shorts smudged with power bait residue, a faded Golden State Warriors long sleeve that hid his withered left arm. He always wore long sleeve shirts to hide the scars.

Except for the high blood pressure pills that he took daily, he was healthy. He had taken all the required fifty-years-old-plus medical tests that doctors recommend, with the exception of his colonoscopy. *Something not natural about that.* And, of course, like most fifty-plus-year-old men, he got up several times a night, like clockwork, to empty his bladder. Benign Prostatic Hyperplasia, whatever the hell that was.

Some days he forgot to take his blood pressure meds.

He had to pee right now.

Once inside, Palmer ordered coffee, black, and a chocolate chip cookie for a mid-day sugar fix. Palmer enjoyed nothing more than a good cup of Joe. He drank half a dozen cups a day. He knew that was too many, all that caffeine spiking his already-jumpy nerves.

"Ei twi fi," said the young woman at the register. She was tall and shapely, dark skinned, and her auburn hair was held in a bun with what looked to Palmer like some kind of dog bone.

"What?" Palmer replied.

"Ei twi fi," the young woman repeated, tapping her foot on the floor.

"What?" Palmer snapped at her.

"Think she means eight dollars and twenty-five cents, sir."

Whipping around to see who'd spoken, Palmer met eyes with a young man, wearing a face mask with an Oakland Athletics logo.

Why does everybody call me sir? Palmer looked back at the young woman whose eyes were fixed on his big nose, as if he was the dumbest man on the planet.

"She's from Tasmania," the young man added,

26

thinking this information would clear things up.

"We think she's an Aborigine."

That might explain the bone in her hair.

Doesn't anyone speak English?

After grumbling, Palmer took his coffee, grabbed Buddy's leash, and headed towards the post office. Along the way, Buddy sniffed everything. His daughter, Francesca, had asked for several books that she wanted to read, so Palmer planned to post them. In the package, which he carried in his right hand, Palmer included a check for one thousand dollars. *She could probably use the cash.* He made a note to plan time off and take a trip across the pond to visit.

Inside the post office, twenty people waited in line. Most looked angry or impatient, standing with folded arms, tapping their feet. Behind the counter stood one small Asian woman who moved at a snail's pace. She wore a R95 face mask. Looked like she was in a very bad mood. Only one person to service all these people. No wonder the term "going postal" originated in a post office. From 1986 through 1997, forty people were gunned down in US post offices around the country in twenty separate incidents.

A United States government office. Our tax dollars at work.

I'll come back later. Palmer slinked out but not before eyeing each person in line for a possible hidden weapon.

Getting a dozen pink roses for Becky was easy. The florist was, thankfully, still open. When he headed into the parking lot, he saw that someone had left an empty shopping cart directly behind his car. The place to put empty carts was less than twenty feet away from the discarded cart.

What's the matter with people? Couldn't this person have pushed the shopping cart another twenty feet?

Backing out of his parking space reminded him of the chaos of a war zone. Vehicles whizzed by behind him in their frenzy to get to wherever they were going. He broke into a sweat as the now familiar flashback hit him once again; he was sitting in a mud hut within the walls of a compound located in Kunar, Afghanistan, dodging bullets. To the east, capped with snow, were the sharp-ridged Hindu Kush mountains. Though he felt as if he could reach out his hand to scoop the snow off the peaks, the temperature in the hut approached one hundred and twenty.

Just as quickly as it had arrived, the memory faded. He backed out and turned to put his car into forward when his front bumper was clipped by a car whose driver was rushing to park in the spot he had just vacated.

Enraged, he jumped out of his car, a cramp in his left calf slowing him only slightly. His car's left front light housing and bumper was damaged. The hood of his car was bent.

Five thousand, from the looks of it.

It was hot, the July sun's heat radiating off the concrete. Buddy whined, stuck his snout out the window, and sniffed. Palmer realized that his muzzle had turned grey; distracted, he found himself mentally counting the years and months, then the number of days that he and Buddy likely had left together.

The other car was a C-class black Mercedes, and Palmer did a double take as he watched a female driver emerge. She was angry. Asian, but which kind Palmer could not discern because of her clothes. Her head was covered with a wide-brimmed hat. She wore sunglasses and a white surgical face mask.

Who knew that wearing face masks would be the new normal?

She wore what looked like winter clothes, though the temperature was in the upper nineties. She popped open one of those silver umbrellas that block the sun's UV rays. She looked like a walking mushroom. Though Palmer could not understand a word she was speaking, as she raged, he realized that she thought the accident was Palmer's fault. She was small, about a foot shorter than Palmer. She didn't speak a lick of English, only pointed her finger at him menacingly while she spoke in her native tongue.

"Do you have a driver's license?" Palmer heard himself growl back at her. He should call the police and file a report. His nose beaded sweat in the heat. *There goes my four o'clock with Sophia.*

The woman didn't respond to his question, but she kept ranting in her high-pitched screech. She scrunched her nose when she got a whiff of him, now standing merely two feet apart. People nearby pulled out their phones and started recording.

"My name Sammi," she said.

"Driver's license? Insurance card?" Palmer growled.

Sammi reached into a shopping bag. Out came what looked to be a license. It was not a California driver's license but rather some kind of laminated official-looking card issued by the Chinese government. Not a single word of English on it. Just a bunch of indecipherable Chinese characters and a picture of a woman who may, or may not, have been standing in front of him. He couldn't tell, with every square inch of her covered in winter clothes. *Fuckin' great.* She probably had no idea that she

29

couldn't drive legally in California without a California driver's license. She probably had no insurance either, Palmer thought. Plus, the name on the ID was Ming Lee Wang, not Sammi. Resigned to his fate, Palmer ignored the woman and limped back to his car. He massaged the cramp in his left calf as he called the police and waited.

Palmer had nothing against Asians, no beef at all. It just seemed that Asians were involved in a shitload of the minor traffic accidents in the Bay Area. Many did not have a valid California driver's license from what he'd heard. Having a Chinese license did not cut the mustard.

So many lousy drivers.

Time to head for the hills.

With time on his hands, Palmer looked around to figure out why a nearly empty strip mall had so many cars in the parking lot. Many of the cars had people sitting, or sleeping, in them. Those cars were littered with personal belongings. *People are living out of their cars.* Observing further, he noticed that some of the empty storefronts had blue tarps and sleeping bags lying around inside. Squatters.

This strip mall is becoming a homeless encampment.

Two hours later, roses in hand, Palmer walked up a crushed stone path to the top of a hill. His calf felt better, but he still felt angry about the episode at the shopping center. *Have to get a rental car while my car is in the shop. Gotta pay the deductible. May have to pay the entire amount of the repairs if Ming Lee Wang doesn't have auto insurance and if my insurance company won't cover it.* It was an inconvenience he didn't deserve, his time wasted.

At least Meghan had been able to reschedule Sophia and her father for the following morning.

"I think she felt relieved, Sarge," Meghan had said. "They were still stuck in traffic."

Figures.

Buddy ran on ahead, sniffing the ground; he knew exactly where to go. Gravestones of different heights and colors dotted the hillside. Crosses of varied heights faced the setting sun. *Everyone has a nice view here.* When Buddy arrived at a familiar marker, he lay on the ground, splayed out next to the gravestone. He wagged his tail, turned his head around, then whimpered.

Elizabeth Doyle
Born 3/18/1965
Died 4/01/2021
Wife
Mother

Dead one year now.

His Becky.

Coronavirus.

"You know she's here, don't you, Buddy?"

Palmer removed the wilted roses that he'd placed last

week and arranged the new flowers before sitting on the ground. Several plastic markers with one word on each stuck out of the ground near Becky's grave.

Hero. Wife. Mother.

For her entire adult life, Becky had been a nurse, a health care worker, helping sick people get healthy. It had been her life's calling. At forty-eight, she'd beaten breast cancer, but as it turned out, her being a cancer survivor was one of the underlying conditions that made her more susceptible to COVID-19. She was one of the first health care workers in California to succumb to the virus, well before most understood how underlying conditions made a person more vulnerable to the disease. She'd known she had the virus, known that she'd caught it from a patient in the ICU.

She'd quit work. Her fever hadn't gone away. She lost her sense of smell and taste, had zero appetite, dropped twenty pounds. She had no energy, then the virus found its way into her lungs. She was admitted into the same hospital where she worked. Breathing became difficult. Watching his wife struggle to breathe was more than Palmer could bear. She was placed on a ventilator. Palmer was not allowed into the hospital to visit. Their visits were restricted to Facetime calls. So, he drove his car and circled the hospital where she lay. Day after day. Trying to figure out a way in. So he could see his Becky. Hold her hand. But security at the hospital had been tripled, so Palmer simply continued to circle the hospital. In the end, like thousands of others infected with the virus, she died alone. Palmer could only imagine how horrible that must have been for her.

"I'm sorry, honey. I know you never wanted to move.

Sorry I lost my temper."

I'm so sorry that you had to die alone. You must have been so scared.

Each time he came to visit her, he started the conversation with these same apologies. Each day as she'd battled the virus, a piece of Palmer had died too. "I'd like to sell the business at the end of the year, Becky. I don't want to do it anymore." *Not without you here.* "I'd turn it over to your brother, but I think you know how that would turn out." He'd run it straight into the ground.

"Remember Blue Lake Springs in Arnold?" He paused to look at the sun setting over the East Bay hills in the west. A beautiful sunset. "You liked it there too. Well, I found a cabin with a deck on the back that looks out over the forest. I was thinking of moving. What do you think?" Palmer looked at his wife's headstone. "I'll move you up there too. Find a nice spot with a view that you'd like. Okay?" In the end, all their little squabbles seemed so meaningless. "Gonna take a week off and go see Francesca too." All he could dwell on was that his wife had died alone. And how scary that must have been for her.

Buddy snuggled next to Palmer. "I know what you're thinking, but I don't think it's too late to make a go of it with Francesca, you know, mend those bridges." Palmer pulled Buddy into a one-armed hug. "I know that I've been a lousy father, but she's my daughter." Buddy licked Palmer's face. "Okay, buddy, time to go. Anyway, Becky? Think about it, will you? Let me know how you feel about us moving. We can talk about it when I see you next week. Okay?"

Palmer cocked his right ear towards his dead wife's gravestone.

"What's that honey?" he asked.

"Yeah, you're right. I'm drinking too much."

He cocked his head again.

"I know what you said. I remember. You're right. I'll try to cut back."

Palmer then rose to his feet. "Love you, honey." Funny, it was at that moment that Palmer pictured Becky before she had become sick: tall, blonde hair, blue eyes, always in a good mood, regardless of what life threw at her. She'd had this smile that had melted him every time she flashed it his way. He could see her, as clear as a recent photo, in his mind's eye. Though Palmer knew that her body was gone, he figured that Becky's soul was nearby, listening.

Eventually, he knew, the memories of a healthy Becky would be those he would remember. But, a year after her death, the wound was still too raw. And he was still too angry about her death. In his sleep, he often dreamt about his wife, the loneliness of her absence cutting him to his core.

With Buddy leading the way, Palmer trudged back down the hill.

2.

Early the next morning, an hour before their monthly staff meeting, Palmer sat at his desk and called his auto insurance company, All-American Insurance.

"Please listen closely, as our menu options have changed," a computerized female voice said. "Press one to enter your account number. Press two to obtain your current balance."

Shit. Great. "I'd like to talk to a real person," Palmer said.

Damn you, Sammi. Or Ming Lee Wang.

"Press three to make a payment. Press four if you are paying by check. Press five to pay by credit card." A soothing computerized female voice at that.

"I'd like to speak with a real person, please," Palmer said, tapping his foot. Last night, like most of his nights in the past year, his bedtime companion was insomnia. After five Ketel Ones on the rocks, he finally slipped into a nightmare-riddled sleep. *Why did I argue with her about trivial things? I should have taken better care of her. I used to get mad at her because she rose from bed so much earlier than I did in the morning; she often woke me and I couldn't get back to sleep, then I'd yell at her for waking me up. Now I'd give anything to have her wake me early in the morning. Why did I make such a big deal out of such trivial stuff?*

"To speak with a representative, please stay on the line."

Finally.

Meghan walked into the office, wide-eyed and ever-so-alert for so early in the morning. She was showing off her shapely figure by wearing a tight short black skirt, a form-fitting white lacy blouse, a pearl necklace, and two-inch pumps. Meghan Tully was a pretty red-haired, freckle-faced Irish girl. She flashed a megawatt smile and waved at Palmer when she saw him sitting at his desk, phone to his ear.

Another seven minutes passed, and then Palmer finally heard a click, followed several seconds later by a live voice.

Meghan stuck her head inside Palmer's office. "Coffee, Sarge?" She had a sultry, Lauren Bacall kind of voice.

You know how to whistle, Steve, don't you? You just put your lips together and blow.

That famous line from *To Have and Have Not*, the famous 1944 movie in which
Bogart and Bacall meet and fall in love, jumped into Palmer's mind.

Palmer heard a click on the phone, followed by a dial tone. Disconnected.

"Fuck!" he bellowed.

"I've got donuts too," Meg said. Palmer loved donuts.

After filling Palmer's coffee mug with black coffee, Meghan ducked back out of his office.

What the fuck is the matter with these companies?

"Sorry, boss," Meghan said a minute later, reentering his office. "Is that a call I can make for you?" Palmer looked up before she could shake a look of disappointment from her face.

"Nah, some woman clipped my car yesterday. I'll take

care of it."

Meghan noticed how Palmer was dressed this morning. Freshly ironed slacks, polished brown shoes, a crisp clean-looking royal blue golf shirt. He had two-day old stubble; he seldom shaved more than twice a week.

"Sleep well last night?" she asked.

"Like a baby."

"Eat a good dinner?"

Who does she think she is? My mother?

"As a matter of fact, I did. Made myself a fresh chicken pasta salad with avocado."

"Nice." Meghan's eyes widened.

"Garnished with Cilantro," Palmer added. Frozen Kirkland-brand microwavable fish sticks washed down with Ketel One was more accurate, Palmer thought. He redialed All-American Insurance.

"Please listen closely as our menu options have changed."

"A live fucking person, please!" Palmer yelled into the phone. "Immediately!" he added, taking a bite out of a donut.

Nine minutes passed as Palmer listened to the same elevator music loop again and again. Another heavily English accented voice finally answered. "How may I help you?"

"I'd like to report an accident."

Several seconds passed. Palmer heard a clicking sound.

"Accident?"

"Yes."

Another several seconds passed before he heard, "Where are you located, sir?"

"Dublin, California."

"Zip code, please?" Another several seconds passed before a question registered in Palmer's mind.

"Where am I calling?"

No response.

"Where is your office located?"

No response.

"Zip code is nine four five six eight. Now, what country are you from?"

The voice on the other end responded, "Mumbai."

"Mumbai?"

"Yes. Mumbai, India."

"You mean to tell me that I'm talking to somebody in India?"

Not a surprise in this day and age.

"Yes, sir," the voice said after another click and several more seconds had passed.

"India," Palmer repeated, growling. "Well, well. So, customer service for All-American Insurance is located in India."

How ironic is that?

"Not all of our customer service offices are located in India, sir, but your call was forwarded here."

Palmer felt like he'd been slapped in the face. *All-American Insurance has its customer service department located in India.*

Yeah, I get it. It's all about the profits: they can pay

Indian people low wages, and they're happy to get it. They can buy a month's supply of food for their entire family for the same amount of money that it costs here to buy a Starbucks latte. Satellite phone systems carry the calls, hence the delay and clicking sounds.

Time to shop for another insurance company.

Palmer grumbled. He hung up the phone.

Meghan came back a minute later and topped off Palmer's coffee mug.

"Just got a call from the Muellers," she said.

Palmer kept mumbling to himself, so Meghan moved around to speak into his right ear.

"Just got a call from the Muellers," she repeated.

"There's nothing wrong with my hearing, Meg," Palmer said. "How many times do I gotta tell you that?"

"Sorry, Sarge."

"And don't look at me like that. I know what you're thinking. I am not being grumpy."

"Got it, Sarge."

"What was it about?" he demanded. He noticed Meg's mood written across her face, then added, "Is that a new outfit?"

A thought took seed. *She's young enough to be my daughter.*

"Oh! This old skirt and blouse?" Meghan pirouetted like a runway model and beamed her pretty Irish smile Palmer's way. "No, it's not new. Don't think I've worn it in a while, that's all." Meg couldn't wipe the smile from her face. "Sophia and her stepfather rescheduled for tomorrow."

"She give a reason?"

"Something about a medical issue."

Meghan filled Palmer's coffee mug and floated out of his office.

The words "medical issue" carried Palmer back thirteen years, back to that awful day and back to the recurring nightmare he'd been having since.

He felt dizzy, nauseous, as he oscillated in and out of consciousness. Was he lying down on a cot? Or was it a hospital bed? He tried to turn his head to vomit and noticed IV needles hanging from his right arm. But he couldn't turn his head; it felt like it was secured, or strapped, to the bed. He vomited all over himself. He didn't feel pain—morphine drip? A pneumatic tourniquet hung high on his left shoulder; Palmer could hear the air pump wheezing, tightening. He could fell the added pressure on his upper left arm. He was able to turn his head that direction to take a look. Hamburger meat. His arm looked like goddamned hamburger meat.

How didn't he feel any pain? He then saw a big needle stuck out of his left elbow. A nerve pain block? The entire left side of his body felt like it had been run through a meat grinder. His vision was blurry as he glanced around. Human shapes stood there, speaking, but he didn't hear anything, just a loud ringing, a constant, annoying, painfully loud ringing. His sense of smell had remained intact, though. The stench of blood, body fluids, a strong disinfectant . . . ammonia, maybe? And sulfur? The smell of sulfur from gunpowder assaulted his senses.

A nurse appeared, an angel it seemed to Palmer; was that a halo over her head? Her mouth was moving, but Palmer couldn't hear a word of what she was saying. Just a loud incessant ringing in his ears. What about the little boy? he asked her. What about the little boy? The nurse, to Palmer, looked like a young Kim Basinger, the film actress, leggy and blonde with blue eyes and a beautiful, angelic face. Yet, somehow, she looked vulnerable, like Basinger often looked in her movies. What's your name? he asked her. Her lips moved, but Palmer couldn't hear her. She pointed to her name tag. Sophia M, registered nurse, Kandahar Trauma Hospital. So that's it. I'm wounded. Kandahar? Still deep in Taliban occupied land. His mind flashed the image of a desolate mountainous countryside near a city. Was that the name of the city? Kunar?

He moved to look at his body and assess his injuries. He couldn't remember what had happened, how he'd been wounded. His mind drew only a blank canvas, his memory erased. Was he concussed? But he remembered a little boy. He seemed to remember that this little boy, maybe six years old, was crying as he ran up to him and Corporal Thompson. Probably separated from his parents. Who knows what happened to the parents. What happened to the little boy? he asked Sophia. She leaned over and touched his right arm, no doubt saying soothing words, but he couldn't hear what she said. He turned to her: Please, please, don't let them cut off my arm. Please. Then he passed out.

He always awoke at this moment, his clothes soaked with sweat, checking to see if his left arm was still attached to his body.

3.

"Come on, people," Palmer said, sitting in his large conference room. "As infrequently as we meet, can you all please do me a favor?" He scanned his computer screen through the Zoom app, alternately looking at Meghan, John, then towards the other investigator on his staff, Dakota Thompson. "Can you please do something about those cells phones?"

All meetings these post-pandemic days happened via Zoom, with no one coming to the office, except for Meg. Palmer had suggested that she, too, work from home but she refused to.

Though Palmer had a smart phone, and he knew how useful the technology was, he couldn't help but be a little bit annoyed by them. At first, all three of his staff had their noses buried in their respective phones, even on a conference call. As if nothing else in the world existed. *As does everyone these days.* The constant aggravating sounds annoyed him to no end: the different ringtones for incoming calls—the twinkle, the old phone, the wave; a tri-tone ring for voicemail; a bell sound for email notifications; a swoosh or several bells chiming, for text messages. Some phones beeped on every sports or news update, or to signify bedtime, or time to wake up, and even when you took your ten thousandth step for the day. But the real kicker—an alarm for when it was time to meditate.

Then Dakota, who was late as usual for the Zoom meeting, had set even more annoying custom tones for all of her social media accounts. Plus, she had set seventies disco music for her ringtones.

"At least put them on silent, so I don't have to listen."

Meditate? An alarm goes off when it's time to meditate?

Begrudgingly, his staff complied.

He watched as Meghan mouthed into her screen, "He's grumpy this morning."

John looked pained as he wiggled in his chair, his Gumby face contorted as if he had cramps. Though wearing mandatory face masks to help contain the coronavirus was no longer mandatory, John still wore his, even when he was home alone in his own house. His was light green fabric printed with turtles. Palmer made a note to himself not to get too close to Sharkie next time he saw him in person.

Meghan, still floating on air from Palmer's comment whispered, "Hemorrhoids."

Palmer had already drunk five cups of black coffee this morning.

"I'm not hard of hearing, Meg," he grumbled. "And I heard that." He hoped that he hadn't given her the wrong idea earlier by noticing her outfit. *You would've thought I'd told her that she looked gorgeous, or that I wanted the two of us to start picking out curtains together. All I said was "Is that a new outfit?"*

Women. Always hearing something different than what you said.

"Okay, who wants to start? And for the record, I am not grumpy."

"I've some updates on cases we've been considering," Meg offered.

"Okay, shoot."

"The brown is the new green file?"

43

Palmer scrunched his face.

"The possible class action suit against various landscaping companies?" Meghan started. "Cities cut water usage to homeowners because of the drought. Remember those companies that would spray paint your dead lawn green, so it looked like a normal lawn? Instead of brown? There was some kind of chemical in their spray that killed all the grass, killed everything in their yards to boot, even in areas that weren't sprayed. So now there are close to a thousand homeowners in the Tri-Valley with dead lawns; their yards look like the surface of the planet Mars. We've been collecting all the info with hopes of filing a class action. Looks like the companies that did the lawn spraying were owned by this one Mexican guy. Fernando Valenzuela. He set up about five different companies under five different business names. And he just disappeared, probably just skedaddled across the border back to Mexico."

"Fernando Valenzuela was a pitcher for the Dodgers in the eighties, Meg," Palmer said.

"Well, lots of Mexicans have the same name. Probably not the same guy."

No one commented, so Meg continued. "Same with that roofing company."

"Roofing company?" Palmer asked.

"Yeah. Company called Roof Doctors. They'd target homes with old wood shake roofs 'cause they'd catch fire in an instant. Entire houses burned down before the fire department could get there."

In the seventies and eighties, thousands upon thousands of Northern California homes were built with wood shake roofs. As the roofs aged and the wood dried under hot California sun, they could ignite like tinder

44

doused with lighter fluid. *Poof.* House and roof were gone.

"Issue is that the roofs they replaced the shake roofs with were sold to them as concrete tile shingles, but they were made with a papier-mâché product. They only looked like concrete tile shingles. But when the first winter rain hit, the roof tiles just sort of melted."

"The roofs melted?" Palmer repeated. *Does Valenzuela own the roofing company too?*

"Yeah, Sarge," Meghan continued. "Over nine hundred homeowners who paid big money for their newly melted roofs signed up to go after this company, but then Roof Doctors disappeared too."

"Imagine that," Sharkie mused. "Can't get blood out of a turnip."

"Thanks for the input, John," Palmer said. He noticed that John's shirt had dampened under the pits. "Nothing there as well. Can't win a class action suit for any sizable amount of money if you can't find the bad guy."

"We do have somewhat of a case against this Nigerian prince email scam," John continued. "The perp has been targeting older women in retirement communities. Promises them big money, in British pounds, directly deposited into their bank accounts, as if they just inherited it. All he asks for is a bank account number so he can wire funds."

"Ahh."

"The prince was nice enough to attach his picture. Wanna see it, Sarge?"

Palmer took a look. "John, this is Eddie Murphy, the actor."

Unbelievable.

45

"Can I see it, Sarge?" asked Dakota. Dakota took a look and fidgeted with her phone. "This is a publicity shot from the movie 'Coming to America.' In the movie, he plays an African prince looking for a bride in America. Even has his crown on in this photo."

"You know what they say about black men," John added. He moved his green face mask to the side and flashed a shark-toothed smile.

Meg and Dakota shivered at John's off color comment.

"None of the old women recognized him from the photo?" Palmer asked.

"Guess not," John said. "Once a woman responded to his email, he'd ask for bank account and credit card info. Some of the women gave that info to him. Imagine that? Even in this day and age, with all the safeguards built into the system, he was able to withdraw money from some banks, make charges to some of the credit cards. We've got over two thousand women who said they lost money, so they signed up to go after this guy, once we find him."

Lot of lonely women out there.

"Good luck with that" Meghan added. "It's probably just a guy posing as a Nigerian. Probably operates out of a foreign country. You'll never find him. May even be the same guy who's been killing all the lawns, Fernando Valenzuela."

Are there any honest people left in this world?

"Meg's probably right, John," Palmer said. "Probably another dead end."

Business is not as good as I thought.

"How about our core business items, people?" Palmer continued.

How about any missing person cases? The bread and

butter of a PI firm.

"I've got updates on the coronavirus scam cases we've been working on," Meg said.

You know. Like a missing wife, child, or business executive. A missing girlfriend maybe?

"Good. Let's save that for later. How about you, John? Got anything more for us?"

Beneath his mask, John's face contorted with discomfort, his mouth twisted like a clown's. Meg and Dakota shared a look, both trying not to giggle.

"Remember the woman who disappeared after a Tinder date?" John started. "The family hired us to find her." He looked at his notes.

"And?" Palmer asked.

"Well, last week while walking her dog, a neighbor found a woman's arm and a right foot. Dog sniffed them out."

I don't like where this is going.

"Police set up a recovery area and turned up her entire body. In separate pieces."

Palmer remembered the news headline: TINDER DATE ENDS IN DISMEMBERMENT.

"Family owes us a check. Technically it was not us who found her, but that part of the case is solved," John concluded. "Technically we can build a case that we did find her."

Everyone took a moment. Palmer shook his head.

There are a lot of screwed up people out there in this world, John being near the top of the list.

"Let's put that one on the back burner for now, John. Anything else?"

Good grief.

John scrunched his face, a studious look, as sweat dripped from his forehead. "I've been thinking about this 'me too' stuff, boss. You know. All the famous people who've been caught with their pants down, like Bill Cosby, Matt Lauer, Harvey Weinstein. You know."

"They haven't been caught with their pants down, you moron," Dakota said. "They've raped and sexually abused women. And now they are being brought to justice for their crimes."

"Don't call me a moron." John shot her a furious look, though his anger didn't seem genuine coming from beneath little green turtles. "I went to college."

For about two weeks, Palmer remembered. "Dakota? Please."

"Sorry."

"Suppose we get the goods on someone famous. Go and start digging around more in the entertainment industry, in politics, say. Gotta be thousands more women who this happened to."

"Where are you going with this, John?" Palmer asked.

"Dunno. Say we get the goods on someone really famous. Say someone like Bob Hope?"

Dakota looked towards the ceiling. Meg stared at John over her computer screen, seemingly at the dark raised mole on his right cheek.

"Bet a guy like Bob Hope would pay big bucks to keep something like that quiet," John said, in his squeaky voice.

Dakota threw up a little in her mouth.

"Good thinking, John boy," Palmer finally said. "Let's

you and I talk privately later, okay?"

"Okay, boss."

Not one missing person's case. What about a juicy infidelity case? Everyone loves hearing about them. Especially those cases where a guy has two different sets of wives and kids, living in different cities. And one family has no idea about the other.

"Anything else?" Palmer glanced from one employee to another on his computer screen. "Dakota, you're up next. But first, how about a bathroom break?" When he sat for too long, Palmer's prostate crushed his bladder.

Everyone reached for their phones.

"I'm working on a couple," Dakota started after a ten-minute break.

Normally Palmer didn't like tattoos, or rather people with tattoos. He didn't see the point of putting yourself through so much pain, nearly torture, to sit still while some Harley-driving greaseball stuck you thousands of times with a sharp needle just to inject bright, multicolored ink under your skin. The tats itched, skin turned red and inflamed from infections, and special salves and lubricants were needed to keep the skin soft and the colors vibrant. As you aged, the tattoos aged; the colors faded, the images wrinkling like aging skin. But for Dakota Thompson, Palmer made an exception. She had a shitload of arm and neck tattoos, but on Dakota, her skin a caramel color, the tats looked okay. Graceful even.

And he turned another eye towards her pierced left eyebrow and the gold ring protruding from it. Tall, thin, and wiry, she was strong, her muscles more robust than they looked at first glance. Dakota had black curly hair, dyed in spots a weird shade of purple. Palmer guessed her age to be thirty.

There was no denying her smarts and her credentials. Besides her master's in family genealogy, she was a computer expert; she could crack any computer no matter how good the password protection and firewalls were. Palmer had heard a rumor that she had spent time in prison for the white-collar crime of identity theft, which you had to be a computer expert to be any good at. That fact didn't bother Palmer. *To catch a thief, you've got to be a thief.* In the investigations industry, there was some truth to that. *Besides, I made a promise to Jimmy.*

Dakota twirled her hair with a finger, avoiding eye contact as she spoke.

Guess her anxieties are kicking in this morning.

"Remember that law firm, the River Law Group? The one that contracted us to help them stop all this robocall bullshit?"

It seemed that everyone these days received a dozen computer-generated phone calls, or robocalls, a day; when you answered your phone, a live person would be alerted, coming on the line a couple of seconds later. Each day Palmer blocked six to eight new numbers robocalling him, trying to sell him something of absolutely no value to him.

"Yeah, I remember. We cashed a decent retainer fee from them."

"Guess how they get a ton of their clients?"

"What do you mean?" Palmer rubbed his temples, feeling the beginnings of a headache coming on.

"I visited their site the other night. Turns out they have a computerized robocall system set up in their back room." Dakota gestured her arms in excitement as she spoke.

"What?"

"That's how they find their clients. They robocall them. When someone picks up the phone, they explain to the person what they do, and then they slam them for a retainer fee to represent them in a class action suit."

"So," John began. "The 'stop the robocalls' law firm uses robocalls to find its clients? Am I getting this right?"

"Correct," Dakota answered.

What's the matter with people?

Palmer refilled his coffee mug, still rubbing his temple. "One question, Dakota. What do you mean that you visited their site the other night?"

John snorted.

"Never mind, Dakota. I don't think I want to know the answer to that. Anything else?"

"I'm still working on Duke's final-final for the inheritance."

"Great."

The Duke, or Leonard McDougal, had been a famous concert pianist, flaming gay like Liberace, and he died at the young age of forty-eight from a combination of a prescription drugs overdose and excessive alcohol consumption. Turns out, he was just another celebrity who didn't know what kind of drugs and booze he was putting into his system. And like many multi-millionaire dead people, he didn't leave a will.

"How many people have put a claim into his estate so far?" Palmer asked.

"Eighty-seven," Dakota replied. When a person died "intestate," or without a will, then any Tom, Dick, or

Harry could file a claim stating that they were related to the deceased, and that they deserved a piece of the pie.

"Eighty-seven," Palmer repeated.

"All but three I've eliminated by the DNA results."

Eighty-four of them are crooks.

"Sixteen of the claimants were black, though Duke was a lily-white Scotsman. Those sixteen people didn't think that was odd, and they claimed to be related by family. Two people incarcerated in prison claimed to be long-lost relatives. And one ninety-year-old Asian woman claimed to be his aunt."

"His aunt?" John repeated.

"But as I said, DNA results, plus a detailed family tree, eliminated all but three people. Looks like the Duke had two half-siblings and one sister. They'll probably split his estate."

"Then they get to run the family business for the next fifty years," John added. "Dead celebrities make a lot of money."

"Family business?" Palmer shook his head. "How much did he leave?"

"About sixty-five million. And they figure about two million a year in royalties in the coming years."

"Future royalties?"

"Record sales, sales on memorabilia, tee shirts, that kind of thing."

"Great job, Dakota," Palmer said. *Finally, a paycheck.* "Anybody else have anything?"

"I'm working on two infidelity cases," Dakota added. "You know, the-wife-fucking-the-tennis-pro-at-a-hotel-near-the-club and the-husband-bending-his-secretary-over-his-desk kind of thing."

"Wish I could make so much money as a dead celebrity," Meghan interrupted.

"Me too," John chimed in. "Elvis made near fifty million last year."

"How do you know that?"

"I follow him on Twitter; we're Facebook friends too. Elvis tweets several times a week about all the money he makes."

Palmer was losing interest.

"Michael Jackson makes more money," Meghan replied.

"That's a lot of tee shirt sales." John chuckled. "I've got something else that I've been working on, boss."

Palmer could hardly wait to hear.

Meg then raised her phone to take a selfie, apparently still pleased about Palmer's comment on her outfit.

"Meg! Please!" Palmer snapped.

Meg froze.

Dakota took her hands off of her phone.

"Please don't tell me you are going to post that on Facebook. This is a business meeting."

"Sorry, Sarge."

"There's a pharmacy that's licensed to do business out of Canada, and they sell prescription drugs in America," John started. For such a large man he had such an odd voice, Palmer thought.

"People in the States use these Canadian pharmacies because they can get drugs without an actual doctor's prescription. People can get drugs like Xanax, Vicodin, Ambien," John continued. "The popular drugs."

As if there weren't enough drugs out there.

"This particular pharmacy is based out of India."

"What?" Palmer asked. "They're based out of India?" *Like All-American Insurance.*

"Shipments are postmarked from there. And on their marketing materials, they say that they are headquartered in New Delhi."

"But they are licensed in Canada?"

"Yeah, Sarge. They're called Global Pharmacy."

"Okay. Got it."

"They sell Viagra too. It's their top seller."

Small wonder.

"They target older men in fifty-five-plus communities and even older men in active and assisted living communities. Anyway, we got a couple of calls from an active adult community in Brentwood, which is about an hour's drive from here."

"And just how is this possible business for us?" Palmer asked. He had almost called him Sharkie before catching himself.

"Well, the calls were from guys who'd ordered Viagra. They sent in their money and waited, but they never got their pills. So, I conducted a survey. Turns out that hundreds of old dudes haven't gotten their little blue pills, and when the company did send out some pills, they sent the old guys Aleve instead of Viagra."

With this, John sat back in his chair, looking quite satisfied with himself. When no one responded, he added, "Don't you get it? Because Aleve and Viagra look alike—

they're the same color blue. So, how is this possible business for us, Sarge? We email blast every elderly community in the state. Gotta be thousands of old guys who want their daily boner. Baby boomers and all of that? Probably tens of thousands of old guys who ordered from this pharmacy, and since they never got their little blue pills, none of them can get the woody they deserve."

Meghan and Dakota were speechless.

"Let's sign up thousands of these poor, horny old guys and take it to a law firm who files the papers for a huge class-action suit. Guaranteed to bring us a windfall. Don't you think so, Sarge?"

Palmer rubbed both temples now.

Didn't Sharkie realize that they wouldn't be able to chase down the people responsible for this? That they'd just disappear into the woodwork, like the Mexican landscapers who killed lawns, and the roofers who installed roofs that melted in the rain? How could they make people based in India pay damages for medications not delivered in the States?

Please, Becky, please, give me some kind of sign so I can fire him.

"Think about it, Sarge," John continued. "We could use Mail Chimp. Blast the entire country. Think about how many old guys aren't getting their Viagra. Gotta be a million of them. Big bucks."

On camera, Palmer watched John pause to scratch his crotch, his face melting in relief, like a guy holding his urine for hours until finally he could pee. Palmer looked at Meg, who was smart enough not to return his look lest she burst out laughing.

At least Dakota knows what she's doing. She's a good investigator. The cases she's working on are more of our core business.

"How about the coronavirus scams we're working on?" Meg said. "Want updates?"

"You bet," Palmer said. *Hopefully something solid.*

"Well," Meg started. "Whoever set up those websites about getting your stimulus checks?"

"The government stimulus checks?" John asked.

"Yes. Once you visit their website, they ask for your bank account number and info so they could 'deposit' your US government stimulus check money."

"Let me guess," Palmer continued. "Once you give them your bank account info, they clean out your account."

"Yes," Meg said. "At last count, there were approximately one hundred websites set up. All with the same scam. We've gathered info on four hundred and ten people who've been scammed."

"That's a lot of money stolen," Palmer noted.

"Yes. But whoever it was up and vanished, took down all the sites, and our best efforts at tracing them. The websites originated somewhere in Tajikistan."

"Tajikistan?" Dakota asked.

"A country of nine million people in central Asia, surrounded by Afghanistan and China."

"Great," Sharkie scoffed.

"Let's forget that one and move on," Palmer grumbled.

"Well, the two Cuban brothers who started the 'disinfect your house from the virus' scam are behind bars."

"What's their story?" Palmer asked.

"They promised to disinfect your house from coronavirus," Meg started.

"People believed that?"

"Several hundred did. They forked over seven hundred and fifty dollars each to have their homes sprayed inside and out." Sharkie chimed in. "With a solution of water and lemon juice."

"One easy payment of two-hundred-and-fifty dollars a month, for three months is what they advertised. How they got people to sign up."

"Continue," Dakota said.

"And instead of getting rid of the virus, their houses just smelled like lemon meringue pie," Sharkie said.

"Or a Vodka gimlet," Meg added. "And, of course, no one can find any of the money the Cuban brothers stole."

"Another bloodless turnip," Palmer added, regarding his staff on his computer screen. "Let's move on." He reached for his coffee. "Any other scams from the virus that you guys are working on?"

"Well, there's the fraudulent charities scams, the spoof government programs, plus all those companies claiming to be able to ship face masks and ventilators, that kind of stuff." Scammers fleeced people to the tune of thirty-seven billion dollars a year, by most estimates. God knows how much more money they were making while preying on peoples' fears during the pandemic.

"The US government, the FBI, is handling the coronavirus scammers," Dakota added. "To date, they've uncovered more than five thousand scams."

Crooked people who will do anything to make a buck.

"I've one other item that I've been working on," Sharkie said.

Good grief.

"Remember when our illustrious president claimed that injecting disinfectant might get rid of the coronavirus?"

Of course. That news had gone viral quickly.

"Well, after his comments, hundreds of people across the country either swallowed or injected themselves with disinfectant," Sharkie continued.

"They chugged Lysol?"

"You know what they say," Sharkie added. "A spoonful of Clorox a day keeps the doctor away." He flashed his shark-toothed smile beneath his turtle print face mask.

"One guy sold thousands of doses of his toxic COVID-19 'cure' through his church in Florida. Touted it as a miracle cure," Meg began. "Said it cured Alzheimer's, autism, AIDS, and cancer. As well as COVID-19, of course. All for three easy payments of ninety-nine dollars each. Hospitals were swarmed with people who needed to have their stomachs pumped," Meg recalled. "Several died."

"Almost as pathetic as the Tide Pod challenge. You know how fucked in the head Floridians are."

"That's enough, John." Palmer's tone was firm.

"How about we track down all those people and file a class action suit against the ex-president?"

"I said that's enough, John," Palmer snapped.

If he wasn't so good at breaking and entering businesses and houses to plant microphones, cameras, and other stuff, he'd be long gone.

"Besides, you can't sue the president. Let's wrap this up, shall we?" Palmer was growing impatient, his bladder already turning on him again. "Anyone have any leads on missing person cases?"

"Not really, Sarge," John answered.

How did he get so good at breaking and entering? Don't think I want to know the answer to that.

"Not me," Dakota chimed in.

Meg simply shook her head.

"Not good, people."

Before he finished speaking, both John and Dakota had exited the Zoom chat. No one had the patience to sit through more, even though it was a remote meeting. Out came all the smart phones, Palmer was sure of it.

Meg's phone buzzed.

Dakota: Boss looks good this AM. Wassup?

Meg: Think he's meeting with a female client later. A business meeting. I think they know each other.

Dakota: Old flame?

Meg: Dunno.

Dakota: He doesn't look hungover.

Meg: Visine, probably.

Dakota: You know everything that happens here. Keep me in the loop?

Meg: K. No problemo.

Palmer settled in with a fresh cup of coffee.

We've got a bunch of Mexicans who kill lawns, take peoples' money, then leave the country. Got another group of Mexican roofers who install defective roofs that melt in the rain. They, too, take people's money, and when their scam in discovered, they, too, leave the country. The scams may, or may not, be headed by Fernando Valenzuela, the ex-Dodger pitching great.

A Prince from Nigeria, who sends out publicity photos of Eddie Murphy wearing a crown, is scamming thousands of old women out of their money. Then, a company supposedly doing good deeds by trying to stop those God-awful robocalls actually uses a robocall system to attract its clients.

And old guys all over the country are blaming an Indian pharmacy based in Canada for their inability to get an erection because they are being cheated out of their daily dose of Viagra. And, to add to all of that, hundreds of fake companies and criminals around the world are scamming people out of their money using the fear created by the coronavirus pandemic.

And, oh yeah, I've got an investigator on my payroll who thinks that Bob Hope is still alive. And he wants to sue the ex-president of the United States, to boot.

Business was not as good as Palmer had hoped. He rubbed his temples. It was time to take Buddy for a walk. He hadn't pooped yet this morning.

Buddy suffered from separation anxiety, so when Palmer closed his office door for the Zoom meeting, he left him a bison bone stuffed with peanut butter to keep his doggy mind off of his doggy troubles. Palmer wagered he needed to poop by now.

I need something to keep my mind off of my troubles too.

He had just the thing. Vodka. It was only eleven in the morning, but Palmer was looking forward to having a

Ketel One on the rocks. He was starting to think about Becky.

4.

Palmer often wondered why so very few of his life's happenings actually played out as anticipated, or as planned. The events of the following morning provided no answers, only confirming the question.

He was scheduled to meet with Sophia and her stepfather, and like yesterday, when they were originally scheduled to meet, he spent more time on his appearance. Clean, freshly ironed pleated pants paired with a laundered polo shirt that nearly matched. The only part of his appearance he paid less attention to was his face: a two-day grey stubble stared back at him in the mirror. He drank less the night before, having only three stiff Vodkas; he didn't want to appear hung over. But just to make sure he looked presentable, he squirted a couple of drops of Visine into his eyes.

Buddy was riding shotgun, his head sticking out the window, sniffing; he was always sniffing. He thought of yelling, "bad dog" again, for what had happened yesterday, but he knew that Buddy would never make the connection. When he'd arrived home yesterday, he found that Buddy had performed a chewectomy on Palmer's favorite bed pillow. Thousands of down feathers floated softly around Palmer's bedroom, as he'd left his ceiling fan on. It looked like someone had just shaken a snow globe. Buddy and his doggy separation anxiety again— the dog didn't like it when he was left alone. It took Palmer over an hour to clean, never mind the trip to Target to buy another pillow.

"Bad dog," Palmer grumbled, anyway. But Buddy just kept sniffing, head out the window.

Palmer finally got the dog to poop, finding that Buddy

had suddenly developed the habit of pooping in private. Off he'd go, hiding his butt under a leafy bush before squatting to do his business. When he finished, off he'd run at full speed, happy and relieved as if he didn't have a care in the world. "Good grief" was all Palmer could say when he realized that Buddy wanted his privacy, just like a person closing the toilet closet door.

The drive from his house to his office usually took no more than ten minutes, even with the crazy morning rush hour traffic; he was running a couple of minutes late, so he was driving a bit faster than usual down the freeway. He'd just found out that Ming Lee Wang hadn't had her car insured, and he was not completely sure his insurance carrier, All-American Insurance, with their customer service department located in India, would cover the cost of the damages. Probably not.

About five grand.

With his mind was elsewhere, he paid little attention to the road, and his front left tire ran over a huge pothole. The impact was so jarring that he felt his jaw clench.

Now what?

Next minute, he was driving on the rim. He pulled over to the side of the road to inspect the damage. While getting out of his car, he noticed that his left arm was throbbing. His left arm always hurt; his daily routine of alternating heat and ice treatments and downing Advil hadn't proved as effective in alleviating his pain this morning.

Flat tire, and the wheel rim may be damaged too. My spare is also almost flat.

His frustration only grew when he pulled out his phone to let Meg know that he was running late, and he discovered that his older model iPhone was locked, and for the life of him, he couldn't remember his passcode.

Why does everything have to have a freaking password?

And why can't anybody take care of the freeways in California? There's plenty of money to keep building all of these goddamn houses. Plenty of money for more shopping centers, more outlet stores, but the freeways in California are a mess—badly in need of repairs, re-surfacing, and widening. By God, the freeways around here need to be wider to accommodate all the fucking cars on the roads. Why can't they fix the freeways?

After several more attempts at guessing his password, the old phone locked him out.

Phone, computer, TV, bank account, all my credit card accounts, email, Facebook, everything else in this world. Passwords, passwords, passwords. Why does everything in life need a password?

Palmer walked to the nearest business, a 7-Eleven, so he could find a payphone to call Meghan.

"The Muellers are already here," she said when he finally reached her. "And your password is Francesca."

My daughter's name. Figures.

"I'm running about thirty minutes late, Meg. Apologize to them for me too, will you?"

"Want me to call you an Uber? Get you here in about fifteen."

"What's an Uber?"

As Meghan explained Palmer rolled his eyes, though no one could see him. *What ever happened to good, old-fashioned cab rides?*

"If you had a newer model iPhone, that wouldn't happen Sarge. You can use your thumbprint, or face, to unlock your phone."

"Really?"

"No shit, Sarge."

"Okay then. Thanks, Meg."

Then maybe I won't have to be an Einstein.

While waiting for his Uber to arrive, Palmer noticed a large white sign a couple of hundred feet away. Looking closer, he saw it was a courtesy notice from the City of Dublin, stating that they'd received an application to build forty-four hundred homes on the land. He knew that once a developer applied to build, the city was required to post a sign informing people in the area that homes, if approved, were going to be built. Behind the sign, several blue tarps, strung up on poles, were hidden. *More homeless people.*

Forty-four hundred homes? On one hundred acres of land? That's over forty homes to the acre. Are they crazy? What are they going to be—four- or five-story houses built on small lots? Five-story apartment buildings? The people who run the city and approve this nonsense are nuts.

Palmer knew that developers lined the pockets of city officials to guarantee said "officials" would approve their super high-density building projects. The more homes the developer built, the more money they would make; the more homes the City of Dublin allowed to be built, the more money the city would receive in tax revenue. Win–win for the city and the developer. A complete loss for the common man.

Has anybody given any thought to how many cars this

would add to the local roads? Each home has four to six drivers, four to six cars. Multiply that by forty-four hundred? That is about twenty-six thousand cars.

No wonder so many people are moving out of California.

Palmer imagined the hundreds of new potholes that would ravage the roads, potholes that he'd constantly have to dodge.

Though his day had barely started, he already felt aggravated.

Very few of life's happenings actually played out as anticipated, or as planned.

His left arm ached.

5.

It had been fifteen years since Palmer had last seen Sophia Mueller, when she'd been thirty years old. She looked like she hadn't aged a day—no crow's feet or deep circles under her eyes, and it didn't look like she'd had facial cosmetic surgery. Still the young Kim Basinger look-alike, she had her blonde hair pulled back in a pony, with those distinctive whiskey-colored eyes gazing out from soft features. Sophia was dressed demurely in a white lacy blouse, black slacks, and a red blazer, but her clothes couldn't hide her feminine curves underneath. She wore little makeup, just a bit of rouge and a nude lip gloss. Sophia also had a small mole just below the right side of her lip. The mole reminded Palmer of something, or someone, but he couldn't place it.

When she stood close to Palmer to shake his hand, she flashed her smile. When she stared at him with those whiskey-colored eyes, Palmer felt something inside of him jump.

"How long has it been?" she asked. She was tall; Palmer remembered her telling him years ago that she'd trained to be a ballet dancer as a youth, taking years of lessons before giving up her dreams of dancing ballet professionally when she grew too tall.

"Fifteen years, give or take," Palmer answered. "I was still in the hospital when you were transferred out. Back to Germany, I believe."

"Yes, that's right. To the Landstuhl Army Medical Center, near Stuttgart." Sophia smiled at him. "You have a good memory. How's your arm?"

Palmer felt his stomach twist as if he might get sick.

He was wearing his customary long-sleeve shirt to cover the scars on his left arm. "Ah, you know. Good days and bad days. But I'm very glad that I still have it. The arm, I mean."

Sophia stared at him but dropped the subject. "Palmer, this is my stepfather, Martin. Martin Mueller." She turned to the man standing next to her. "Martin, I'd like you meet an old friend of mine from my days as an army nurse, Palmer Doyle."

Often well-educated with master's degrees, army trauma nurses provided acute care and surgical nursing. They worked close to the battlefield, as badly wounded soldiers needed treatment quickly. They had to stabilize, and sometimes resuscitate, soldiers, many of whom were just boys with horrific life-threatening injuries, from machine gun fire, shrapnel, bombs, grenades, IEDs, and more.

Palmer extended his hand. "Not quite an old friend. I was her patient."

Martin looked to be about seventy-five years old. He was thin, frail almost, with a cane hanging from his arm. His face was chalk white. He wore an R95 surgical mask. Surprisingly, his handshake was strong.

"This is Buddy," Palmer said, nodding towards the dog lying on a big fluffy dog bed in the corner of the room. Palmer had to resist giving Buddy a scolding look.

"Malinois," Martin said from beneath his mask. "Smartest dog breed in the world, they say." He spoke perfect English with just a trace of a German accent.

"Not Buddy," Palmer said, sighing. Buddy picked his head up at the mention of his name, sniffing the air. Then he rose to his feet, spun in two complete circles, and lay

68

down in exactly the same spot in exactly the same pose as before. "He's the dumbest Malinois in the world. But there is one thing he is smart about."

"What's that?" Sophia asked.

"He likes to poop in private."

Sophia and Martin looked at each other. Neither said a word.

"Malinois dogs can be trained to carry out a string of commands," Martin continued. "Some can memorize as many as twenty, then do them one after another without prompting."

"About the only thing Buddy knows how to do is sit. And that's if a treat is involved." After a moment, Palmer added, "He's a rescue dog," as is that explained everything. "I got him three years ago."

"There are schools that you can send him to," Martin said, with the cadence of a German who had a need for precision.

"When did you move to the States?" Palmer asked, getting back on point.

"Two years ago," Martin said. "After my Helen died."

"My mother," Sophia offered. "And living here has been good. Closer to MD Anderson."

The famous cancer treatment center in Texas. That explains why he looks so frail. A senior citizen who has cancer—just the kind of person that coronavirus kills quickly.

Palmer felt bad for Sophia, first having lost her mother, and now having to care for a sick stepfather.

"They've been treating Martin for two years, and we were just told that he is in remission. A clean bill of health."

Doesn't look healthy to me.

After a moment, Sophia added, "Well, it looks like you are doing well and that your arm is doing well, too, Palmer."

As she spoke, Palmer's mind drifted back to the Kandahar Trauma Hospital in Afghanistan, fifteen years prior.

Where did you get these? Sophia asked, pointing to scars on Palmer's right side.

Sophia was changing his dressings, which she did daily. First, she would remove the old bandages, which were crusted with dried blood, pus, and other bodily fluids. Next, she'd clean the wounds. Look for infection. Apply medicinal salve. Reattach the morphine drip and IV. Push his bedpan closer to his bed. Apply fresh bandages.

It hurts, Palmer told her, wincing. Can you give me more of that stuff?

Now, you know I can't do that without checking with the doctor.

Please? he pleaded, nearly crying. How about some Vicodin?

Too addictive, Sophia answered. So, no.

How bad is it? Palmer asked.

It's beginning to heal.

Liar.

The left side of Palmer's body was a mess. Hamburger meat. He'd been hit forty times by shrapnel. Shrapnel traveled fast. Nails, ball bearings, and pieces of small sharp metal had hurled towards him faster than detonation speed. He'd been concussed, and the ringing in his left ear refused to go away.

Sophia cleaned the left side of his body from shoulder to waist: his left hip, left leg. When she finished, she kissed his forehead.

She noticed a quizzical look on his face.

Why are you looking at me like that?

Just wondered why you kissed me.

Dunno. After what you've been through? You guys

deserve the best.

You're a kind person.

Kind? Maybe. If you only knew how many proposals I get from wounded soldiers I treat. I'm only trying to be nice to you guys.

I didn't propose. I just wondered why you kissed me, Palmer said. I was in a firefight two weeks after I got here. And to answer your question from earlier, I took a bullet to my right shoulder, was bayoneted in my side. Happened six months ago.

Hand-to-hand combat. My God. How awful, Sophia said. Looks like they've healed nicely, though.

She took care of him, nursing him back to health. His own guardian angel.

He'd already seen her wedding ring.

You're married, He said. A statement.

Yes.

Where do you live?

Germany.

How does a US Army nurse come to live in Germany?

Now, Sergeant, Sophia started. I'm not here so you can flirt with me about my personal life. I'm here to make sure that you get well.

I'm not flirting with you, Palmer said, an impish grin on his face.

Now, Sergeant.

An admonishment.

Thank you for saving my arm, Palmer said. And not letting the surgeon cut it off.

I didn't do a thing, she replied.

Not sure I believe that. Palmer searched her eyes.

Sophia shrugged. Just told the doctor what you told me. That you didn't want it cut off. I don't know if that made any difference.

Well, thank you anyway. And just so you know that I wasn't making a pass at you, I'm married too. Happily married.

When she had finished her work, she rose to leave but first leaned over to kiss his forehead, again.

Do you kiss all your patients?

Just the heroic ones.

I didn't do anything that any other soldier wouldn't do. What happened to Aakrama?

Who?

Aakrama. The boy. Afghan families give their children names that are important to the family. Aakrama means companion to Muhammad. Do you know what happened to him?

No, Sophia said. But that's a conversation you should have with your CO, don't you think? A twinkle in her eye. He felt she might be flirting with him. Or was she just being a girl?

Palmer and Corporal Jimmy Thompson had befriended the little gap-toothed boy of seven. He was always smiling, his long black hair glinting in the sunlight. Palmer and Thompson had made it a point to give the boy some food when he came around. Oddly enough the little boy didn't like chocolate. What little child doesn't like chocolate? Instead Aakrama had a craving for peanuts, so both men made sure that they had plenty to give him, because he shared them with his little sister.

Palmer had a soft spot for the children of Afghanistan.

73

Truth was, he had a soft spot for all children. Children here were innocent victims of a brutal war. Blameless, most didn't understand what was happening. Innocent victims. All they knew was that they were hungry. Palmer's own daughter, Francesca, was eight years old and in third grade back home in California, and he shuddered when he considered how scary it would be for her to be caught in a war zone like this.

So, Palmer did what he could do to help.

Thinking of the boy, he spoke to Sophia: All I remember was that Jimmy and I saw Aakrama walking towards us. He was holding his sister's hand. A black-haired little girl, about five, maybe. She was smiling, but she was shy, her eyes looking at the ground. He let go of her hand, smiled at Jimmy and me, and walked over the get his peanuts.

Palmer's eyes widened as his mind pulled him back into the memory.

Then what? Sophia asked.

There was an explosion.

Sophia leaned over closer and held his good hand.

I don't remember anything after that. Just the explosion.

I'm a nurse, Sergeant. I'm not privy to what happens on the battlefield. Best to ask your CO.

What happened to Jimmy? Corporal Jimmy Thompson? Was he wounded too? Jimmy was Palmer's best friend in the service. Both were the same age, around forty, and both had served in the Gulf War in 1991, when they were in their late twenties. Both had reenlisted and volunteered after 9/11.

Best to ask your CO, she repeated. My guess is that he'll check on you soon. And for the record, my husband is an army doctor stationed in Germany. That's why we live there.

She rose to leave. See you tomorrow.

Oh. Thanks, Palmer said.

6.

Now, fifteen years later, Sophia sat in his office. Looking into those eyes of hers, Palmer felt his heart thunder in his chest. She smelled great, too, like mangoes, her hair freshly shampooed.

"We're here because we need your help, Palmer. We'd like to hire you to look into something for us." Sophia gestured gracefully as she spoke.

"Did you hear about the death of local businessman Ramsay Marshall in the news?"

"Can't say that I have."

Sophia handed Palmer a copy of a newspaper article.

San Jose Mercury News
Susan Rogers
6/29/2021
San Jose, Ca.

The body of local businessman Ramsay Marshall, 75, was recovered last night in Lake Tahoe by a local fisherman who goes by the name "Tahoe Bob."

Marshall, who had a history of heart trouble, was found in 25 feet of water off Sand Harbor, Nevada, near Incline Village. He had been vacationing in the Tahoe area. Ramsay owned Sunrise Village, a mobile home park, in San Jose. The Washoe County Sheriff's office believes that Marshall had a heart attack and fell off his boat, "Lucy in the Sky."

He is survived by his third wife, Jojo Ramsay, son Brad Marshall, and daughter Sophia Mueller.

A celebration of life will be held on 7/16/2021 at 11:00 a.m. at Callaghan's Mortuary in Livermore, Ca. Marshall will be interred at Queen of Heaven Cemetery in Lafayette, Ca.

"He died three days ago?" Palmer asked.

"Yes," Martin answered.

"He was your father?"

"My biological father," Sophia said, tears welling.

"I'm sorry." Palmer felt for her.

"My wife, Helen, was Ramsay's first wife," Martin explained. "We married five years after they divorced."

A quizzical look came over Palmer's face.

"When mom and Ramsay divorced thirty-five years ago, Mom took me to Germany with her, where she was born and raised. I was maybe nine years old then. She met Martin shortly after," Sophia explained.

"Ramsay married Jojo five years ago," Martin added.

"Article says that Jojo was his third wife?"

"Yes. Mary Bartholomew was his second wife. She is Brad's mother," Sophia said. "She died years ago, when Brad was a teenager."

"I see." Palmer turned his head, not far enough that they would notice, but enough so that he could listen with his right ear.

"Ramsay liked his women young," Martin explained. "Got rid of them when they got too old."

Nice guy.

"So, you and your brother Brad have different mothers?" Palmer asked, still trying to get his bearings.

Sophia nodded. "Brad is my half-brother."

"Got it," Palmer said. "Sunrise Village?"

"Dad owned it. A mobile home park in San Jose."

This guy owned a mobile home park on acres of land in San Jose? Smack in the middle of Silicon Valley?

"How many spaces in the park?" Palmer asked, already doing the math.

"Six hundred and fifty."

Six hundred and fifty homes at an average rental space fee of fifteen hundred dollars per month times twelve months. That comes out to almost twelve million dollars a year in annual revenue.

"He owned the land?" Palmer asked.

"Outright," Martin offered. "No mortgage."

Probably about fifty acres to support over six hundred homes. This guy was filthy rich.

"Then there's this." Sophia handed Palmer another document. A death certificate.

"Says here that the attending physician was a Doctor Schultz from San Jose." Palmer started. "How did he get involved?" With a somewhat suspicious death, the local coroner would have been the first one to investigate.

"Once my father's body was recovered, Brad immediately had the body flown to San Jose."

"That's odd," Palmer said.

"We thought so too." Sophia tilted her head in his direction.

"The local authorities in Nevada didn't autopsy the body?"

"Not that we know of," Martin replied. "We didn't find out about Ramsay's death until the following day."

"How was Brad able to accomplish that? Transfer the body to California without an autopsy, I mean."

"My family has money, Palmer," Sophia said.

Makes sense, Palmer thought. Not the first time that money passed hands for a favor from the local police. "It says here that myocardial infarction was the cause of death."

"Yes. His fourth heart attack. Because of that, Brad declined to have an autopsy performed. He didn't think it necessary."

That's odd. Autopsies are almost always performed following an unexplained death unless waived by next of kin.

"Well, that is unusual," Palmer said.

"Brad can do that without consulting others. He's the executor of Dad's living trust." Sophia said.

"He's being buried at Queen of Heaven Cemetery?"

"Yes."

That's the cemetery where dead celebrities are buried. Located high on a hill in Lafayette, with views of the hills and San Francisco Bay. Dead rich people would have great views.

"And this is the police report." Martin handed Palmer another piece of paper.

It was a standard report. When Ramsay did not respond to his third wife's phone calls, the Washoe County Sheriff's office sent a police boat to investigate.

They found Ramsay's yacht empty. At Brad's request, they began searching the bottom of the lake. No luck. The following day, "Tahoe Bob," a local fisherman with long white hair, found Marshall's body wedged between two rocks in twenty-five feet of water.

Lucky. Lake Tahoe is over sixteen hundred feet deep in its deepest parts. If Ramsay's body had not been caught between rocks, chances are, the currents would have swept his corpse into deeper waters. Each year, hundreds of people drown in the frigid waters of the giant lake, and their bodies are never found.

The report noted the officers involved and their badge numbers, as well as the exact date, time, and weather conditions at the scene. The officers spoke with "Tahoe Bob," including his statement in the report, which noted that there was clothing scattered about, leftover food containers, and cigarette butts with lipstick on the filters left in an ashtray.

"So why show me all of this?" Palmer asked, even though he knew where this was headed.

"I think Brad killed him—or had him killed—to get his money," Sophia said, her voice steady.

Those eyes.

"Let me start from the beginning." Sophia took a breath. "Since I moved back to the States two years ago, my father and I had become much closer. We talked every week. For the first time, I got to know him better. I discovered that he was not this ruthless businessman that people thought he was. He was not this womanizing bastard that everyone believed."

"Okay."

What about the red lipstick on the cigarette butts found on the boat?

"I grew to like him. He treated me fair. And that was not always the case when he left my mom and me. Two weeks before he died, he confided in me. He told me that he was scared of Brad. He told me that if something happened to him unexpectedly, well, that Brad might be behind it."

"Did he give you any reasons why?"

"Yes," Martin interjected. "Last month, Brad asked Ramsay for a loan of four hundred thousand dollars."

"A lot of money."

"Brad is a gambler, an addict. He had markers due with several casinos. They wanted their money. Brad was long overdue with his payments. And Brad didn't have money of his own. He'd lost all of his gambling."

"How do you know that for sure?"

"Dad told me," Sophia said. "Can you believe that? Even though he already gets fifteen thousand dollar a month in trust fund income."

"So, he got angry," Martin said.

"He's a psychopath," Sophia added. "One time when dad refused him money, Brad threatened to kill him. He actually tried to choke dad once too."

"Strong word," Palmer said. "Psychopath."

"Dad was scared of him," Sophia said. She held her voice steady, but Palmer could sense anger brimming under the surface.

Martin continued: "He got angry when Ramsay told him no. And do you know what he did? Ramsay had this wonderful house with this marvelous backyard. He loved his gardens with trees, flowers, plants. Over an acre. He'd been keeping his own yards and gardens for years, and they were immaculate. He even entered some of his flowers and other plants in local fairs. Won ribbons. Brad knew this; he knew how much those gardens meant to his father. When Ramsay told him no, Brad few into a rage. He took his motorcycle, rode it through Ramsay's yard, and destroyed his gardens. Destroyed everything in a fit of rage. All because his daddy wouldn't pay his gambling debts. And Brad is a thirty-seven-year-old man."

"A psychopath," Sophia added again.

Palmer considered the definition of psychopath. Smart, brilliant even, highly organized, ruthless, narcissistic, with absolutely no empathy for anyone, or anything else, except themselves. This Brad didn't seem to quite hit the mark, with his juvenile petulance.

Palmer's mind drifted back to a case about ten years ago, in nearby Pleasanton, California. The Country Club murders. A son, thirty years old, had snuck into his parent's house, which was located in a gated country club, and had bludgeoned his father and mother to death, all because his parents would not give him his inheritance money early, so he could gamble it away with his new young stripper girlfriend in Las Vegas. The police investigators had caught him by tracing gasoline receipts back to a Bakersfield gas station, which was located next to a sporting goods store, where he had purchased the baseball bat that he used to club his parents to death. That guy was in San Quentin, on death row, awaiting a lethal injection.

Palmer knew what a person addicted to gambling was capable of.

After a moment, he spoke: "Something like that could happen, but didn't Ramsay have a history of heart trouble? It's not unreasonable to believe that his weak heart was what killed him."

"Dad had had several surgeries over the past five years. He'd had a couple of stents put in." Sophia paused to consider. "Yes, he had a couple of heart attacks, but the damage to his heart was minimal. And with clean arteries and valves, you could build a medical case that this heart was healthy."

She's a nurse.

"Think about it," Martin said, the wrinkles on his face deepening with concern. "Ramsay refuses Brad the money to pay his gambling debts. He has no money of his own. The only way he can get the money he needs is if his father is dead. Then he gets his share of the inheritance."

Sick or not, this guy is stressed out.

Palmer watched as Buddy rose and slowly circled in the corner, sniffing the ground.

Not now, Buddy, please.

"That's why I came to you Palmer. I'm not sure what to do," Sophia pleaded.

"We're prepared to offer you a substantial retainer just to look into this for us." Martin waved a check in front of Palmer's face.

Fifty thousand dollars.

"If you find that we are wrong, if Ramsay did die from a heart attack, then we can put this to rest."

Palmer took a moment to collect his thoughts. Maybe Ramsay Marshall died from a heart attack. Maybe he was murdered. And if he was murdered, wasn't there potentially other murder suspects? Business enemies? Ex-wives? Others who might want him dead?

A fifty-thousand-dollar retainer.

He'd have to talk with Becky about this.

He thought of Sharkie. He had a private investigator on the payroll who thought that Bob Hope was still alive, offering to earn the firm money by finding out whether or not Bob Hope had, recently, sexually abused women.

"I'll look into it," Palmer said, pushing the check back towards Martin. "I'll do some prelim, but I don't want your money now. If something turns up, then we can discuss a retainer."

"Do you want us to leave these reports for you?"

"Not necessary." One of Palmer's strengths was his memory, which was almost photographic. More than once, his memory had helped solve difficult cases. He'd read each report just once but committed each to memory.

"Okay then." Almost imperceptibly, Martin's shoulders seemed to loosen.

Buddy rose, circled, and sniffed.

"Buddy!"

The dog froze, rear leg half in the air.

"Well, we'll leave you now," Martin said, eyeing the dog. "We've stated our case, I think." Martin had to use his cane to help him to stand.

"Thank you so much, Palmer," Sophia said, taking his hand in both of hers as she regarded him. "It was great to see you again."

Her touch sent shock waves through him.

"I'll be in touch."

After Sophia and Martin left, Palmer took Buddy for a walk behind his office building. Meg was waiting for him when he returned, hands on hip.

"You don't really think that her dad was murdered, do you?" she asked. "You're not going to take her case, are you, Sarge? I'm not sure about her."

"Not now, Meg. Not now." Palmer led Buddy to his snack dish in the corner.

How did she know what we were talking about?

Palmer's mind raced. There was a lot to do. First, no autopsy had been performed on him, although technically, he'd died a suspicious death. A red flag. Palmer would have to find out why no autopsy was performed—had Brad really bought off the police? And the death certificate. The attending doctor was under no obligation whatsoever to talk with Palmer about his findings, but it might prove helpful to see what he had to say, if Palmer could persuade him to talk.

Ramsay Marshall was worth a lot of money, maybe as much as fifty million dollars. Fifty million reasons to kill someone. Palmer had to divide the workload between himself, Sharkie, and Dakota. He'd have to find out more about Ramsay's son, Brad. But what about Ramsay's wife, Jojo? Had to add her to that list. And had the guy had any business enemies? Palmer had to find out about that, too.

Palmer remembered that the police report noted that they'd found cigarette butts with lipstick on them on Ramsay's yacht. Yet, it was Jojo who had tried to call Ramsay and then alerted the police when Ramsay didn't reply. So, she hadn't been on the boat with him. If the woman on the boat was not his wife, who was she?

It made sense to check on Sophia and her stepdad, Martin, make sure that they, too, were on the up and up. There was a lot to do before he could decide if there was a case here.

Meghan returned to the conference room. She was wearing form-fitting white pants and a red blouse that fit snugly across her chest.

This time Palmer thought twice about complimenting her attire.

"Here, Sarge." She handed Palmer a phone. "I got you an iPhone 10."

"Gee, thanks, Meg. You didn't have to do that."

"I charged it to the business."

"Oh. Good thinking. Okay, thanks."

"If you want, I can help set it up for you. You can use your fingerprint or your face as your password."

"Great. That'll help." It sure would. No more embarrassing I-forgot-my-password situations, like he'd had this morning.

"Sure, Sarge, no problem." Meghan turned to walk away. "Oh, and I got your flat tire fixed. Your car is in the lot outside."

"Oh. Thanks again, Meg."

Palmer found himself observing her figure as she walked away. Then he took a bite out of a donut. Meg made sure that there were always fresh donuts at the office.

"Come on, Buddy. Wake up." He shook his dog. The pup was having a doggy dream, his hind legs racing as if he was running after something. A rabbit, perhaps, his favorite thing to chase. "Time to go home."

A vodka on the rocks was waiting for Palmer. Oddly enough, Palmer didn't feel grumpy right now. But then he realized that he'd have to spend some time setting up that new iPhone.

That thought made him feel grumpy.

Part two

Gamblers Creed:
"I hope that I break even today. I need the money."

1.

"Now, Ms. Petula, don't be jumping on Barney's back like that. Can't you see he doesn't feel well today?" John Babbitt said in his squeaky voice. "Gertrude? You too. Please leave Barney alone."

John sat in a plastic lounge chair in the front yard of his rented home, which was on a quiet tree-lined street in an older section of Tracy, California. Yeah, it was a long drive to the office each morning in Dublin. Bumper-to-bumper traffic all the way most days, a simple forty-minute drive turned into a three-hour nightmare. But rent was affordable in Tracy, plus John had little disposable income these days. He had already spent a lot of his money on pain medication. And like tens of thousands of others these days, he could work from home.

On the lawn, just a couple of feet from where he sat, were two blue plastic children's pools, each a foot and a half deep and eight feet wide, the kind you get at Walmart for about seven bucks each.

The pools were filled with a shitload of turtles, six to eight in each, swimming and flailing as they tried to claw their way up the smooth plastic walls and out of their toddler's pool prison. John's collection was not the majestic giant sea turtles that pervade the equatorial waters of the Pacific, but merely common snapping turtles, found mostly in freshwater ponds. If he got one of his fingers too close, one of his "pets" would snap and leave a nasty wound.

"Good job, Clyde. Nice going, Heathcliff," John said as he watched each turtle try to scamper up the sides of the pool, only to fall back into the murky green water after each attempt. John was wearing his green turtle print face mask.

I should change their water one of these days.

John had named each of his turtles. They were easier to take care of than dogs or cats, which is why he preferred them as pets. Once they finished their morning pool-climbing exercise ritual, John would carefully pick each one up from behind, avoiding the snapping jaws, and drop them in one of the two large tanks he kept in his living room. He lived alone, and all he wanted to do after work was sit, relax, and relieve his itchy rectum. Then he'd watch his turtles slosh around and snap at each other in their grimy fish tanks.

"What's the matter, Barney?" he said, looking at the lethargic turtle sitting listlessly at the bottom of the pool. John noticed a green slimy substance oozing from Barney's nostrils and from the holes at the side of his head that doubled as ears. "Uh oh. That doesn't look good."

John had given Barney a mixture of castor oil and vinegar on his morning breakfast of lettuce, which was the health concoction that John's mother had given him as a child whenever he was sick, but that didn't seem to work for the turtle. All it did was make Barney ooze more puss and green slime from his orifices.

Two things were bothering John this morning. First, he had that constant dull headache that had plagued him for the last couple of weeks. It made him feel woozy, forgetful. It sometimes made his eyesight blurry. For the umpteenth time, he wondered if all the concussions he'd suffered as an offensive lineman for his high school football team had anything to do with it. Or maybe he had contracted coronavirus?

And, of course, those damn hemorrhoids—external hemorrhoids because they stretched outside his butt. As the day progressed, his butt would leak.

This morning, the hemorrhoids itched; they hurt like hell, and as luck would have it, he was almost out of the Vicodin that he took every day. Amazing how Vicodin helped relieve his rectum itch. His prescription for the narcotic had run out, and he was out of refills. Most mornings, after his morning turn on the throne, he'd simply take a pill and pack his butt with a combination of Vaseline jelly and toilet paper. Though the pandemic had ended, old habits die hard, and he kept over a year's supply worth of toilet paper stashed in his closets. John went through a lot of toilet paper. That combination of Vaseline and TP would normally get him through the day with little bother and also helped with the smell.

No way would John consider getting his hemorrhoids lanced again. Too painful. Last time they lanced them in the doctor's office. John lay on his stomach, butt cheeks spread, while the doctor injected a local anesthesia with a needle. That hurt like hell! Then out came the longer, thicker lancing needle. Talk about real pain—John had seen stars. He screamed, at the top of his lungs, more than once. He could still feel, even today, the pain, that long needle pushing deep into the skin inside his asshole. Even thinking about it now made his rubber face twist in agony. That day he could barely drive himself home, as his butthole bled. He'd had to lie on his stomach for a week. After four days, his butt stopped bleeding, and he could finally shuffle around the house to fix his food and take care of his beloved turtles.

So, no way would he get his hemorrhoids lanced again. He'd have to get more Vicodin. The other day he'd ordered some from that Indian Pharmacy, Global

Pharmacy, the one based in Canada. But like the thousands of old men who'd ordered Viagra that never arrived from Global, robbing the old dudes of their treasured boners, John figured that they'd ripped him off too. Just took the money and never sent him his Vicodin.

"How're the turtles today, John?" his next-door neighbor Henry asked.

Henry was ninety years old and had stroked out. Yet, each morning, he held onto his walker with the little black wheels and took a turn around the block. Took him well over an hour to walk about three hundred yards. He now stood in front of John's house.

"Fine, Henry. Fine. Thanks for asking," John said, amiably.

Henry would shuffle his feet forward a yard or so, then push the walker forward. Shuffle his feet forward a yard, then push the stroller forward again. To John, it was like watching paint dry. Took him five minutes to cross the fifty yards to the house next door. John admired Henry, though—the man was old and in failing health, yet he kept trying.

Henry stopped his walker, slowly turning to face John. "How're the turtles today, John?" he asked again. "Nice face mask you have there too."

"Fine, Henry. Fine. Thanks for asking. Thanks for the compliment too. But Barney's under the weather."

Forgetful.

"Yes, the weather's been really nice lately," Henry replied, this time nearly yelling.

Hard of hearing as well.

Slowly, Henry turned his walker forward; he continued his slow shuffle forward.

"Have a great day, Henry."

John didn't know if he wanted to live as long as Henry, especially if he needed a walker to get around.

He decided to take Barney to the vet.

2.

Licensed to carry a concealed weapon, John strapped on his ankle holster and checked his Sig Sauer P229 9mm handgun.

Bunch of crazies out there these days, with all the business, school, casino, and nightclub shootings. Skinhead Nazis shooting Jewish people and strip joint DJs mailing bombs via US mail, trying to kill politicians and movie stars.

You can't be too careful. And all those crazies who've come out of the woodwork since the pandemic started?

Look what happened at the United States Capitol building last January? Too many crazies out there.

He loaded Barney into his Walmart-brand aqua culture pet carrier, which was half filled with water and had an air hole up top so Barney could poke his little head out for a breath of fresh air, if he cared to.

On his way to the vet, he thought of his deceased sister, Becky. He hadn't always gotten along with her— she didn't think highly of him, and she hadn't been afraid to let him know it. *You're a few fries short of a happy meal,* she'd often said, her favorite way to give him the needle. But he had her to thank for getting him his private investigator job. It was the best job he ever had; it was certainly better than his previous one, which had been cleaning out Porta Potties at construction sites.

Nothing worse than cleaning out —fecal matter, urine, vomit. And the smell! Sticking that hose down there and sucking up all the shit. Yuck!

Being a PI made him feel that maybe, just maybe, he wasn't that stupid after all.

After the last team meeting, John had discovered that Bob Hope had died in 2003 at one hundred years of age. He decided he wouldn't say anything to anybody at work about his miscue, hoping that maybe his coworkers hadn't noticed.

Traffic, as usual, was heavy; he seemed to catch every red light on the way. While stopped at one, he noticed an elderly woman driving a new Mercedes Benz slow down near the cross intersection. Right behind the old gal, a young woman, driving a newer model Toyota, was busy looking down at her phone.

Texting.

A moment later, the Toyota slammed into the back of the Benz.

The driver's side door swung open, and out flew the young woman, screaming a string of obscenities in Spanish at the old gal who still sat in her car, somewhat in shock.

"Que carbon! Joder! Tonto del culo!"

John took out his iPhone and recorded the exchange. The young Spanish-speaking woman had a pretty face and a nice ass. Her voice seemed to pierce right through John, as he watched from a distance.

John, who'd never had any luck with women, thought maybe he could morph into her knight in shining armor and help her out.

The old gal finally climbed out of her Mercedes. About seventy years old and somewhat matronly, she yelled at the young woman in Russian. John noticed that she was wearing a face mask adorned with a picture of the Kremlin.

"Schas po ebalu poluchish suka blyad!"

She didn't appear to be hurt.

"*Cono!*" yelled the girl, spitting at the ground.

Does that mean what I think it means?

"*Ty che blyad?*" the Russian woman yelled back.

"*Que te folle un pez!*" screamed the young woman, determined to have the last word, whatever that word meant.

John did a quick Google search on his iPhone.

I don't know much Spanish, but did she just say "I hope you get fucked by a fish?"

John knew the young woman was at fault for the accident. She had been texting while driving before she rear-ended the older woman's car after she had slowed for a changing light. But the young one didn't see it that way, apparently. John figured that there could be up to twenty thousand dollars' worth of damage between the two cars. Easily. Not to mention that both women would see enormous increases in their car insurance premiums. The old woman's insurance would increase, too, even though she was not at fault.

John continued to record the exchange, the young woman screaming in Spanish and the old woman screaming back at her in Russian. He wondered whether he should do the right thing as a witness and involve himself. Should he call the police? Try to make peace between the two?

John watched the two women glare at each other, each now pulling out their own phones to record their exchange.

Since John knew little Spanish, except for a couple of words (among them *cunt*, *fuck*, and *fish*), he didn't think that he'd have much of a chance with her. He took another look at her butt.

Nah.

Nobody gives a shit these days.

Off to the vet's, he drove.

Not once Had John considered why he had no luck with women. In his way of thinking, it shouldn't matter that he was obese and that concussions had dulled his brain and that some mornings he smelled weird. That his favorite hobby was watching his turtles. That when he spoke, he sounded like a popular cartoon character who had just inhaled helium. And then, of course, there was the big black mole on his right cheek.

John treated every woman he met poorly. He believed that women were meant to carry his seed; he was quick to go for the gold. What man wouldn't? he reasoned.

Hell, I don't even have any luck with hookers.

Last year, after one particularly long spell without female companionship, John had looked online at an escort service and found a nice-looking Chinese girl. He texted her first, and she texted him back semi-nude photos of herself. He called to hear her voice, to make sure that the pictures were really her and not of some famous Chinese movie star.

"Me love you long time," she had said to John on the phone. "You have a happy ending. Two pops, you likey?"

John rented a cheap motel room. God forbid one of his nosy neighbors saw a strange Asian girl coming out of his house.

"What's your name?" John asked when she arrived. She was definitely the girl in the photos: slim, black-haired with pretty almond eyes, small boned with tiny hands and big boobs. Just what the doctor ordered.

My lucky day!

"Chastity."

Imagine that, a hooker named Chastity.

"How much?"

"You got five hundra dolla?" Chastity asked.

John flipped through his wallet. "I've got three hundred," he said, dejectedly.

"Okie dokie then. I give you fifteen minutes."

John handed over the money.

"Ga."

I think that means good.

"What do you do for a living?" Chastity asked him.

"I'm a private investigator," John said proudly, thinking he might impress her.

Instead, she scrunched her nose. "What's that smell?"

John realized that the smell was emanating from him. From his rectum.

"Excuse me a second." He crow-hopped to the bathroom to wash his privates. "I'm working on an important case," he added, talking through the closed door, trying to impress the girl further. He washed himself, pouring talcum powder down his shorts.

That should do it.

"Can you tell me anything about what you are working on?" She had the voice of a songbird.

"Nah," John said, pulling up his pants, rushing to finish. "Boss swears us to secrecy. Sorry."

When he came out of the bathroom, the room was empty. John did a double take. The girl had skedaddled, leaving him high and dry. Took his money and ran.

John opened the motel room door. Looked up and down the hallway. Nothing. Ran to the parking lot. Nothing. Chastity was gone.

Disappointed, John walked back to his room. He decided to stay the night since he wasn't smart enough to have rented the room for a couple of hours only, an option that many hotels offered for the "afternoon delight" crowd. He'd paid for the entire night.

I couldn't even have sex with a hooker.

One thing he was good at, though, thanks to Sarge, was disarming home security systems—not the newer kinds with real-time video feed, but the older models, the ones with a keypad somewhere near the front door of the house, the ones with motion sensors on windows and on each floor of the house. All he had to do was to unscrew the cover, disconnect a red wire here, connect a green wire there, and voila! The alarm was off.

Sarge had called to give him an important job on a new case that the team was working on. Five people whom Sarge wanted tabs kept on. Easy peasy. First, John had to put a GPS tracker on each car; then he'd know exactly when they were on the move and where they were going. Then, he'd break into each person's house and hide a couple of tiny cameras and microphones, each smaller and thinner than a dime. You could find out a lot of neat stuff about people that way, the things people do in the privacy of their own homes.

People do weird shit.

First on Sarge's list was Brad Marshall, son of the dead old guy named Ramsay Marshall. And Brad's wife, Aiko. What kind of name was Aiko? *Japanese?* John remembered the name his grandfather, a World War II veteran who had served in the Pacific, had not-so-endearingly called the Japanese. Mary Bartholomew, who was Brad's mother and wife number had died years ago. *Probably nothing to check there, but ex-wives are always offing their ex-husbands.*

Next, Jojo Graham-Marshall, a real looker from the picture Sarge gave him was wife number three, Ramsay's current wife. She'd once tried out to be an Oakland Raiders' cheerleader. *A trophy bride.* About thirty-five years old, she was a tall blonde stunner. John's money was on her. He bet she found him hiding his old, wrinkled sausage in the wrong bat cave, and instead of cutting it off, like Lorena Bobbitt had twenty-five years ago, perhaps Jojo hired somebody to kill him.

And, like all great investigators, Sarge wanted to know more about the woman who had hired him, the old dead guy's daughter, Sophia Mueller. She wouldn't be the first person to hire a private investigator to throw off the scent. John was also tasked to check out Martin Mueller, Sophia's stepfather.

More than likely, since he'd had three heart attacks before he died, the old guy had just suffered another ticker killer and had keeled over.

No payday for the firm there.

But Sarge signs my paycheck. I gotta do what he says.

Sophia would get a GPS tracker attached to her car and a couple of cameras and microphones hidden in her house. John would try to put a camera in her bedroom too. Imagine what must go on there, he thought, with a looker like her.

"My turtle is not feeling well," John said to the receptionist at the vet's office, an older, heavy-set woman dressed in a floor-length, form-hiding flower-print muumuu. Her nametag read "Ruby." Ruby wore a yellow flower-print face mask.

Oh, Ruby, don't take your love to town.

Songs often popped into John's mind seemingly out of nowhere, though he doubted that this portly Ruby had taken her love anywhere recently.

She looked at John closely, giving him the up-and-down, from behind black-rimmed glasses hanging off the front of her facemask. She took a long look at the turtles on John's face mask.

"Give him here," she said finally, grabbing Barney's Walmart-brand aqua culture pet carrier. "Please fill out these forms. Do you have medical insurance?"

"For a turtle?"

"Well, few people insure their turtles, but you can. Here's a pamphlet."

"You can get health insurance for a turtle? Is it expensive, Ruby?"

There was that song again.

"How would I know? Do I look like Flo from Progressive to you?"

Maybe how Flo might look like in another thirty years.

"No. No insurance," John said, eyes trained down. Sweat dripped from his forehead.

"Fill out these forms. I'll bring your turtle back to the vet."

John watched as the woman struggled to get out of her chair and waddled through a closed door. He looked around. It was an older office, built thirty years ago, John guessed. Wood-paneled walls, single-pane windows, dog-scratched parquet floors. It smelled like a wet dog. He eyed the security system: one older camera perched high in the corner of the reception area and one sensor over the front door. Old system. A veterinarian office probably had pain medications somewhere. Opioids, steroids, horse tranquilizers. Did pets get hemorrhoids too? Turtles? He didn't think so, and when he thought it through a bit, he didn't know where a turtle's butthole was, anyway. The seed of an idea took root inside his head.

A young woman dressed in green scrubs entered the room. "I'm Doctor Foreman," she said, extending a perfectly manicured hand and carrying Barney's Walmart-brand aqua culture pet carrier in her other hand. She wore a medical-grade R-95 facemask.

"How's my Barney?" John asked.

After Doctor Foreman studied John's face mask for a moment, she looked him in the eye. "I'm afraid he was dead when you brought him in." She handed him the pet carrier. "Didn't you notice?'

John put his eye into the air opening on the carrier.

Yep. Barney was dead all right.

His rubber face twisted into the forlorn face of a two-year-old child demanding ice cream from parents who just told him no.

John cried, his face hidden behind his mask.

3.

"Zeus! Zeus!" Dakota shouted. Her dog had started his day by humping the brown recliner in her apartment. "C'mon, pup, give me a break, will ya?"

But Zeus would have none of that.

Zeus was a two-year-old, two-hundred-and-sixty-pound English Mastiff who had not been fixed.

"My recliner is not a girl dog," she said. "Not any other kind of girl, either."

Dakota didn't believe in having dogs fixed. *It's not natural.*

Impatiently, Dakota worked at her computer, quickly tapping keys. She wore Apple AirPods Pro in her ears, listening to her favorite music, disco from the seventies. The walls in her room were covered with Wonder Woman posters.

Zeus was enormous, closer to the size of a bear than a dog. He was eight feet long, from the tip of his nose to the tip of his tail, and forty inches tall when standing on all fours. He had a massive square black head, a head the size of a bison. Bred to be territorial and protective of their owners, the majestic English Mastiff roamed the castles of England in the 1800s, a medieval security alarm system. Thieves would think twice about robbing the lord and family if they saw a couple of frothing two-hundred-and-fifty-pound dogs charging at them.

Protective of Dakota, Zeus was twice her size. He ate four meals a day. A sloppy eater, cleaning up after he ate was a nightmare; dog hair and drool coated everything. And cleaning his poop? A rhino's crap was roughly the same size, thought Dakota. And the smell? But she was a dog person. Ever since her father had given her a chocolate lab puppy for her fifth birthday, she had loved dogs. But because she didn't believe in having dogs fixed, Zeus incessantly humped everything he could get his massive paws around.

As Dakota's recliner, which weighed over one hundred pounds, toppled over under the dog's weight, Zeus let out a deep-pitched yelp, rolled over, and began licking his privates.

"Serves you right," Dakota said. "Bad boy." Her house always smelled like dog. She upped the volume on the song "Kung Fu Fighting".

Tall, lean, with long dark hair that she usually kept tied in a pony, Dakota had the angular face and high cheekbones of a runway model; her ancestry analysis had discovered Cherokee blood in her lineage. Her father, she knew, was part Cherokee. She eschewed makeup, wearing only her tattoos and piercings proudly. she had a silver ball tipped stickpin in her left eyebrow that she was particularly fond of. Most mornings, she did nothing to get ready except brush her teeth and pin back her hair, before rushing to the gym.

Dakota was freakishly strong, stronger than most muscular men, with arm and back muscles as defined as a young Schwarzenegger, thanks to her twice daily three-hours-long exercise routine lifting heavy weights. This morning, she wore a grey sweatshirt with the arms cut off, showing her massive biceps and colorful tattoo sleeves running down each arm.

Dakota's tattoos were a collage of the life she'd lived for her thirty years on earth. On her left arm were dozens of broken red hearts, with tiny, shattered pieces of the hearts running down to her wrist. Tattoos of the archangels Gabriel, Michael, and Raphael, with their mythical powers of healing and protecting, adorned her right arm. Not wearing makeup didn't stop the gym boys from buzzing, but boys always wanted to move too fast, and Dakota never had been comfortable jumping into a relationship—or a bed—with a stranger. She just swatted them away, which was not a problem. She would not let any man hurt her again.

Most of the men she met were assholes, anyway; Dakota enjoyed the companionship of women more these days. She found herself attracted to women.

In her mid-twenties, she had won several state-level women's fitness championships, blowing the competition away. But when she'd entered a national-level contest held in Atlantic City several years back, it had left her with an unpleasant taste. By far, she'd been the best contestant, her body the strongest, her muscles the most defined; she had starved herself the week before on a no-carb diet, drinking gallons of water for her sinewy muscles to shine, yet she had lost to a girl who was clearly not her equal, only to find out later that the girl was the daughter of the pageant owner.

What a fuckin' rip-off.

Angry even now, as she thought of the injustice of the pageant, she pounded her computer keys until her phone rang. *Meg from the office.* She turned her AirPods off.

"Well, they met at the office, and I think Sarge is going to take the case," Meghan said.

"Who met?"

"Sarge and that woman with her stepfather."

Dakota was silent.

"You know. The case Sarge is thinking of taking?"

105

Meghan reminded her.

"What's she like?" Dakota was multitasking, working on a project for Sarge while talking to Meg. Though she had the fastest Internet speed available, she typed so quickly that she was always waiting for the screen to refresh. Her right foot tapped the floor.

"Sophia."

"Is that her name?" She was feeling antsy now, the screen refresh failing to keep up with the speed of her brain, her attention deficit disorder kicking in big time.

"She's fucking gorgeous," Meghan said, an edge to her voice. "You should've seen Sarge. Clean shaven. Freshly pressed clothes. She could have led him around by a ring in his nose."

Zeus chose that moment to hump Dakota's refrigerator.

"Zeus!"

"What's he doing?" Meg asked.

"Nothing," Dakota said, embarrassed. "Gotta go."

"Wait," Meg said. "One thing first. Do you know if anything is wrong with John?"

"No. What do you mean?"

"Well, he was in the office earlier this morning," Meg started. "Moping around. He looked depressed."

"Don't know. I haven't talked to him in a couple of days."

"Hummph. It was almost like he was grieving. Or something." Meg waited a beat. "Talk to you later."

"Okay."

Dakota had to do something with Zeus. Humping furniture and stainless-steel kitchen appliances was not acceptable. But the enormous dog just sat there on his hind legs. Even while sitting, he was almost as tall as Dakota. He raised his massive paws, placed them over her shoulders, and with his sandpaper tongue that was larger than Dakota's head, he licked her face.

Dakota used her strength to fend him off. "Bad dog!" she yelled. "Bad dog."

With that, the huge mastiff rolled over, laying on his back as he stuck his feet in the air in a submissive posture. Dakota cracked a smile when he stuck his massive tongue out of his bison-sized head, showing off his tusk-like teeth.

Good grief.

A former smoker, Dakota felt the urge to light up. She took deep, slow yoga breaths until the urge passed.

Sarge had given her five names to check out. While waiting for her computer screen to refresh, Dakota chuckled remembering her job interview with Sarge last year.

"How do you break into other people's computers?" he had asked her.

"Easy. One way is to send a malware program, via email, to the person's computer that you are trying to hack."

"What's that?"

"You know all those emails that you get? From people you supposedly know, asking you to click on a link in the email?"

"Yeah. I get dozens of them every week."

"I hope you don't click on the link. If you do, you could

be fucked."

"I don't click on them now. I might have in the past when I first started receiving them, though," Palmer had replied. "Didn't know better."

"Well," Dakota had started. "When you click on the link, a program hidden inside that link loads inside your computer. Worms its way into your computer. And you don't know it's happening."

Though it had been a warm summer day, Dakota had noticed that Palmer wore a long-sleeve shirt.

Palmer had sat taller in his chair. His left arm lay still in his lap.

"In your computer, you keep all of your sign-in information and all of your passwords. Correct?"

"Yes."

"Your computer saves all of those, so that you don't have to remember them. When you go to sign into, say, your bank accounts or brokerage accounts, your sign-in and password info load automatically."

Dakota remembered realizing the light bulb go off in Palmer's eyes.

"So, this malware, or computer bug, captures all of your sign-in and password info?" he'd then asked.

"Correct." She'd noticed Palmer tilt his head slightly to the left, towards her, almost as if he was trying to listen with his right ear.

"Fuck," Palmer had said. "People are fucked when that happens."

"Right again. In minutes, I have all of your most important personal and financial information. Bank accounts, balances, history of deposits and withdrawals, who you wrote checks to. I can take money from the account any time I want. Brokerage accounts, credit card accounts and info. I can charge anything I want to your credit cards."

"You say it, Dakota, like you've done this before." Palmer had phrased it like a question.

"Er . . . No. I'm just saying what could happen. If I was dishonest. Which I'm not."

Dakota let her words sink in.

"And that's not all. I can access medical records, info on family members and friends, all the social media info I want."

Palmer Doyle had never understood social media. He knew nothing about it, and he didn't want to know anything about it: Facebook, Twitter, Instagram, or any of that stuff. "Social media? How can that be useful in an investigation?"

"Ah!" Dakota had replied. "This stuff is gold. Facebook info, posts, Facebook friends. Suppose a married woman has conversations with several men on Facebook. What might that suggest?"

"Ah."

"Instagram, Snapchat, Twitter, LinkedIn. All kinds of interesting things are happening on these platforms."

"I see," Palmer had said. "You could find out about cheating spouses and such."

"Exactly And if the person stores info on the Cloud, you can also access all their records. All of their call information—who they made them to, the date, time, and duration. You can even find out if a person has one or two cell phones."

"You can store information up there in the sky?"

Palmer had asked.

"Not that kind of cloud, Mister Doyle."

"Oh. I see. Why is that stuff important?" Palmer had asked.

Dakota remembered that Palmer had probably known the answer to that, and that this was probably a test.

"If a person has a second phone, they usually have something to hide from their spouse or significant other. One phone is for work and family. The second is the mistress phone."

"Correct," he'd said. "You can get all this information about a person if they click on a link in an email?"

"Yes. And there're other ways to break into a person's computer too."

"Such as?" Palmer had asked.

"Change the computer's boot order, replace the utility manager with a command prompt, create a new user account remotely. And so on."

"Ah." Palmer had a blank look on his face.

"Straight men are the easiest to steal information from. Just send them an email with a picture of a naked lady, ask them to click on her picture to see more. Soon as they click, they are looking at more naked ladies, or porn. While they're thinking about getting their rocks off, I'm mining their most important personal and financial information, since I coded an encrypted Trojan underneath the pictures."

"Trojan?"

"A Trojan horse, Mister Doyle. Not the Trojan you're thinking about."

"Oh. Please call me Palmer, or better yet, Sarge."

110

"Breaking into Windows computers are the easiest. Most don't have firewalls. Like taking candy from a baby. Mac computers are more difficult to crack, but you can phish them, keep sending them Malware, or a 'Wanna Cry Worm', and sooner than later you'll get in."

"How did you learn to do all of this, Dakota?" Palmer had asked.

Dakota remembered shifting in her seat. She shrugged. "Computers have always fascinated me. Always wanted to learn more about them."

But that wasn't quite the truth. While in college, she had used her skills to break into other people's computers. At the time, she was broke and needed money. But she'd thought she was bulletproof, that she couldn't be caught, and that had proved to be her undoing. She was caught going to the same well, or the same online clothing store, one time too many. An on-the-ball police investigator had knocked on her dorm door one day. Convicted of identity theft, she had spent three months in a women's minimum-security facility. That was information she was not planning on sharing with Palmer Doyle.

Palmer had hired her on the spot. He gave her the title "Director of Cyber Security". "You have the perfect skill set," he had told her. "When can you start?"

Something told her he already knew about her identity theft conviction.

After she had been working for Doyle International for a week, Palmer had stopped by her desk.

"You have a degree in family genealogy. Tell me about that."

"I have a master's degree in family genealogy," Dakota had corrected him. She knew—and she knew that Palmer knew—that the combination of DNA research and family genealogy would change police work, crime solving, and private investigation work in the future.

"Have you read about how murders and rapes and violent crimes committed years ago are being solved today? That the guilty parties are being brought to justice?"

"Yes. In our line of work, you stay current."

"There's been a surge in people wanting to track down long-lost relatives. For example, a mom who gave her daughter up for adoption fifty years ago, when she was a crack addict and didn't have the money or wherewithal to raise and support a child. But now she's curious about her, what kind of life she's led. Or maybe a little boy was sent to a foster home thirty years ago because both his parents had been arrested, and now he wants to know who they are."

"I know. Lots of horrible stories," Palmer had replied.

"With violent crimes," Dakota had continued. "DNA was taken from suspects years ago, but because of lack of evidence, since we had no way to test DNA, those suspects were never charged. But their DNA remained in the system. But now, companies like Ancestry.com and others have collected DNA samples from millions of people."

"Go on," Palmer had said.

"Today, DNA programs that didn't exist years ago now look for similar markers in the DNA. They can now find people who have similar markers, who may be family members or relatives to a suspect who may have committed the crime years ago. Investigators can narrow the search without the suspect's knowledge, track them, or get new DNA samples from them—for instance, from a napkin that they left at a fast-food restaurant. Then they match the present-day DNA to the DNA taken when the crime was committed years ago."

Palmer had nodded. "That's how they caught the Golden State killer."

"Exactly."

The Golden State killer, a serial rapist and murderer, had killed at least thirteen people and raped over fifty women in California between 1974 and 1986. The crimes went unsolved for over forty years until modern DNA technology identified the man through similar DNA markers with his siblings.

The crime-solving implications for investigation firms like Palmer's were staggering.

"We'll put that to good use," Palmer had told her.

But Dakota had a different reason for studying family genealogy, the same reason why she'd trained in weightlifting to become so strong. She had a different motive for accepting a position with Doyle International. For the time being, she was going to keep her reasons to herself.

After she had finished researching the five people that Palmer wanted info on, she jotted down closing notes and shut her written file.

Interesting stuff, especially about the dead old guy's son, Brad Marshall. He's a real tool.

Zeus let out a whimper—if you could call the sound a two-hundred-and-sixty-pound dog made a whimper.

Dakota logged onto her computer and read an article

113

about a guy named Donor #2757. A sperm donor who had fathered forty-five kids, at last count.

Lucky guy. Gets paid to jack off.

Some of the sperm donor kids wanted to find out who their siblings were, where they lived, and if they were still alive, so they could have a "family reunion".

DNA research had made all of it possible. Impatiently, her fingers skimmed across the keyboard, searching for more info.

Zeus barked. He smelled. He needed a bath. Dog drool ran from his mouth to the floor. Dakota took care not to go near or he would slime her. Zeus didn't like water. When she brought him to the dog baths at Pet Food Express, it usually took two or three people, each with a choke chain on Zeus, to hold him in place under the water hose.

Running him through an automated car wash might work better.

"What is it boy?" she asked, as she looked at her Apple watch. Five p.m. Time to eat. That's why he was barking. He was hungry. "Jeez, boy. You can tell time now?"

Dakota turned her Airpods back on, listened to the song "Me and You and a Dog named Boo", mouthing the lyrics along the way.

4.

*Watch out Sarge! Corporal Jimmy Thompson screamed;
he jumped in front of Palmer, shielding Palmer's body with
his own.*

*Palmer could still see it playing out like a slow-motion
video. Aakrama, six years old, gap-toothed with black
bushy eyebrows and a prominent nose, was smiling,
walking towards them. Palmer was holding out his hands,
which were filled with peanuts, the boy's favorite. Then
Aakrama's face changed. Fear overtook him as if he had
seen or heard it coming too.*

*Palmer had felt the shock wave, the pressurized,
compressed air particles, hurtling at him faster than the
speed of sound before he heard the explosion.*

*Jimmy lay on top of him, his torso and head twisted at
an unnatural angle, like a broken doll. Palmer's head hurt.
He had trouble opening his eyes. He couldn't focus. The
ringing in his ears was deafening. People were running,
shouting, rushing around, but Palmer heard nothing save
the ringing in his ears. Smoke filled the air. The smell of
gunpowder was everywhere. He had difficulty breathing;
something had sucked the oxygen out of the air. He sensed
more bodies lying around him on the ground, writhing in
pain. The entire left side of his body felt numb, paralyzed.*

*Jimmy had rolled off of him, his mouth moving, but
Palmer couldn't make out what he was saying. Jimmy
moved his hands frantically as he tried to pack his
intestines back into the open wound that had once been his
stomach. Dark red arterial blood poured from him as he
looked down at his wounds.*

I'm okay, Sarge. It just nicked me.

Palmer did a quick assessment. You're gonna be just

fine, soldier.

Embrace the suck, right, Sarge?

Embrace the suck, Jimmy. Embrace the suck.

I'd die putting foot to ass for our country anytime, Jimmy had said. A quiet minute passed before Jimmy added, I'm not going to make it, Sarge. Am I? His voice was almost a whisper.

Sarge couldn't hear him. Medics are coming; stay with me.

A blank look came over Jimmy's eyes; he stared skyward. Promise me? he asked.

Stay awake, goddamn it, Corporal! Stay awake. That's an order! Palmer screamed. But he couldn't hear his own words.

Thompson's body relaxed. He no longer tried to push his guts back into his stomach. Promise me?

A quizzical look crossed Palmer's face. Thompson reached into a silver locket that hung around his neck on a silver chain and clicked it open.

Inside was a picture of his teenaged daughter.

Sergeant Palmer Doyle nodded towards his friend. I'll take care of her. I promise.

The horror of seeing Thompson with his guts spilling on the ground would never leave him. It was one thing to kill the enemy in battle; it was another thing to watch one of your brethren, your friend, bleed out and die.

When he woke, he felt dizzy, nauseous, as he oscillated in and out of consciousness. Was he lying on a cot? Was he in a hospital? It was hot, humid; the air was dry in here. At least he wasn't choking. He tried to turn his head to vomit.

IV needles hung from his right arm, his left shoulder, his stomach. He couldn't turn his head; it felt as if his head was strapped to the bed. He vomited. He didn't feel pain, though—morphine drip? A pneumatic tourniquet hung high on his left shoulder. Palmer could hear the air pump wheezing, tightening; he could feel the pressure on his upper left arm. A big needle stuck out of his left elbow. A nerve pain block? The left side of his body felt like it had also been run through a meat grinder. His vision was blurry. Around him people were speaking, but he heard nothing, just the constant ringing in his left ear. There was nothing wrong with his sense of smell, though. The stench of blood, bodily fluids, a strong disinfectant . . . ammonia, maybe? And the smell of sulfur, from gunpowder, filled his nose.

He felt scared. He thought, I know how you felt, Dad, when you were wounded in Vietnam.

Suddenly, as if his dream moved on fast-forward, he knew where he was: the army trauma hospital at Kandahar, near the Afghan city of Kunar. He felt relieved when he realized his left arm was still attached to his body.

What had happened to Aakrama? Was he okay? Or was he injured or killed in the explosion? And what had caused the explosion? An IED? A truck running over a roadside bomb, maybe? Enemy fire? Mortar fire? Was the explosion real? Did it even happen? Or was all of this some kind of sick dream?

His mind fast-forwarded again to see his nurse walking in. It was nighttime. She had been nursing him back to health for a week now. He looked down again to see that his left arm was still attached to his body. Relief flooded him. Instead of the constant ringing in his ears, he could

117

now hear what she was saying out of his right ear.

My hero, she whispered, as she came over to his bed in the dark and disconnected several of the IV lines. She washed him with a wet sponge. The lukewarm water felt good on his injured body. Her hair smelled like peaches. He couldn't help but get aroused. She must have to noticed, but she didn't say a word.

You take care of yourself, Sarge, you hear? she said. After she reconnected his IV line, she walked away.

The next day, a pretty, freckled-faced young nurse with red hair stopped by to change his bandages. The following day, the same freckle-faced girl attended to him again. Palmer guessed that she wasn't a day over twenty-one years old.

Where's Sophia? Palmer asked her.

Oh. Didn't you hear? she said. They transferred Nurse Mueller.

Oh. No, I hadn't heard.

I'll be taking care of you now. The young nurse smiled. My name is Wendy.

5.

Before he dressed, Palmer stood in front of his bedroom mirror, performing his daily arm exercises. He extended his scarred left arm up over his head, stretching the arm into wider and wider circles. Then, fifty slow circles with his arm stretched in front of him. He picked up a seven-pound dumbbell and repeated the exercises. Slowly, the scar tissue loosened, and his range of motion increased. He grimaced in pain as he worked into the curls, presses, and lifts while holding the weight.

Not feeling too bad this morning.

It was time for an icepack.

After the explosion, Palmer had spent three months in army hospitals. Several arm muscles had been severed by flying shrapnel. His biceps were torn in multiple places, and his triceps muscle had been completely severed. Flexor muscles in his forearm had been hit with shrapnel. Army doctors had reattached the damaged muscles as best they could. Palmer had endured the skin grafting and skin tissue flap surgeries. Blood vessels had to be reattached. The pain he felt was numbing, but they attached him to a morphine drip. He'd undergone thirty procedures on his left arm.

But his arm was still attached to his body.

Initially, he couldn't use the arm. It just hung at his side. The swelling, numbness, and purple black bruising took months to go away. And, damn, it was painful; it felt like his entire arm was being stabbed with razor-sharp knives. Vicodin became his best friend.

On to another army hospital, he'd gone for four

months of rehab and therapy. He'd accepted his Purple Heart with his right hand.

After rehab, he had regained twenty percent mobility and ten percent of his strength in his arm. It was still almost completely useless, hanging bent at a weird angle. That was when depression and post-traumatic stress disorder kicked in.

Took him several years, with help from army psychiatrists, to conquer his depression, and it took another year to kick his Vicodin addiction. Nowadays, instead of popping Vicodin to numb his pain and senses, Vodka took its place. Palmer Doyle's army days were over.

Now he had about fifty percent mobility in his arm and one-third of his strength. The kicker was that he had been a lefty; his left arm had been his strongest. He'd had to learn to do most basic everyday tasks like eating, tying his shoes, washing himself, and combing his hair with his right hand and arm.

Good times.

After fifteen years, the scars still looked hideous, so he wore a long sleeve shirt every day.

Palmer took extra care with his appearance today; he was meeting with Sophia and her stepfather to go over his team's initial findings. He felt tired, not having slept well. His enlarged prostrate hadn't allowed him more than two and a half hours of continuous sleep before waking him to pee.

"What do you think, Buddy?"

Buddy, sitting on his hind legs close by, looked up.

Palmer inspected the mirror.

120

"Still jowly," he said, patting his cheeks. He put on glasses and took a closer look at his neck.

"Turkey neck too. Attractive."

Buddy sat there, looking at Palmer. Palmer enjoyed talking to his dog.

"Fuck. Getting old," he said, feeling grumpy.

Buddy's anxieties had kicked in this Monday morning; the dog practically hung onto Palmer's leg as he prepared to leave. After taking Buddy on his walk the other day, watching him sniff every blade of grass on the trail, Buddy had pooped in private behind bushes, in the same spot that he pooped every day. After, Palmer had caught Buddy chewing on a rock. It crunched against his teeth— not smart behavior from the supposedly smart Malinois breed. When the dog bared his teeth later, Palmer saw a couple of chipped front teeth. Buddy looked like an old man who had never gone to a dentist.

"That's a good look, Buddy," Palmer said. "Jump in the car. You can come with me today. I don't want you chewing up the furniture."

The dog wagged his tail, bared his crooked gravestone smile, and jumped into the car.

Palmer's car was back from the collision repair shop. The cost to repair his Chevy Volt came to forty-five hundred dollars. Ming Lee Wang, the crazy Chinese lady who'd clipped his bumper outside the coffee shop, did not have insurance, but fortunately Palmer's insurance covered the entire cost, minus the deductible. The most frustrating part of the process for Palmer had been dealing with the All-American Insurance customer service department. Pleading his case to a rep in India had fried Palmer's patience.

Working with the local collision repair shop had been a headache too. The perky receptionist was new to the job and poorly trained, always connecting Palmer to the wrong person or disconnecting him entirely.

Why does all this shit have to be so difficult?

He felt increasingly mad just thinking about the delays—the time wasted simply trying to get anyone to answer his basic questions.

His daughter, Francesca, who lived and worked as a nurse in London and was shacking up with her lover girlfriend, had recently emailed Palmer, inviting him to visit in London.

My lesbian daughter.

Though he had known about Francesca's sexual preference for years, he still didn't understand or approve.

It's not natural.

Since his wife Becky had died, he had felt a strong desire to reconnect with Francesca to make sure that she was okay, to see how she was handling the grief of losing a parent.

But staying in the same house with Francesca and her lover? That didn't sit well with him. What if, behind closed bedroom doors, they were loud? Palmer couldn't help but visualize what might happen in there: the exotic oils they might use, the lubricants, the vanilla-scented candles. Using female vibrating stuff and all of that. It made his skin crawl.

Yuck.

If he visited Francesca in London, perhaps he'd rent a hotel room nearby.

6.

"All the leaves are brown, all the leaves are
brown
And the sky is grey, and the sky is grey,
I've been for a walk, I've been for a walk
On a winter's day, on a winter's day
I'd be safe and warm
If I was in LA."

Traffic on the freeway was lighter than usual, as Palmer listened to his favorite soft rock station. Buddy was riding shotgun with his head stuck out the window, sniffing air. Palmer noticed a new billboard next to the sign informing folks that forty-four hundred new homes would be built on the huge plot of vacant land just north of the freeway. The thought of all of those new homes— and all the people and cars they'd bring to the area—still made him mad. Blue tarps housing the homeless sat in the billboard's shade.

They're turning the Bay Area into the LA basin.

Billboards these days were not like the billboards of old, when only one advertiser had appeared. Nowadays, a billboard was a revolving electronic changeling, rotating through up to seven different ads, increasing the owner's ad revenue seven-fold. Palmer glanced up to read this one.

COME MEET THE MESSIAH!
THE HOLY ONE—RAJI GUPTA

APPEARING ONE DAY ONLY!
THIS COMING SATURDAY FROM 1-4 PM

The ad showed a picture of an Indian man with a black beard, wearing a turban, next to the lettering.

Palmer chuckled.

Since when does the messiah hail from North India?

That was news to him.

He wondered what had happened to the California dream. It had disappeared. What had happened to this great state? Retirees and others who could afford to move were leaving the state, taking the money from the sale of their overpriced houses to pay cash for houses in Reno, Vegas, Oregon, Idaho, Arizona. They were getting the hell out. Who could blame them? The cost of living in the state was ridiculously high, the highest in the nation. The urban areas were overcrowded, but builders kept building new homes, and traffic on the freeways grew suffocating. Most roads were badly in need of repair. The state's bridges were crumbling. Most of the new homes being built had solar panels on the roofs to help lower energy costs, an idea Palmer certainly approved of. But he knew the majority of those solar panels were built in China. Most things came from China these days. The richest company in America, Apple, manufactured iPhones, iPads, watches, and laptops in Chinese factories.

The ethnic makeup of the state was changing. Palmer had read a news article recently alleging that forty percent of Californians did not speak English in their homes. Asians were buying the houses that Caucasians were selling. Asians were buying up businesses; Chinese and Japanese were buying restaurants; Indians were buying gas stations, the 7-11s, Subways, and pizza

125

parlors. His Italian sausage pizza was now probably being made by someone wearing a turban. In San Francisco, police looked the other way when the homeless committed crimes. What good would it do to put them behind bars, anyway? Some of the homeless preferred to be put in jail, where at least they'd have a roof over their heads and three square meals in their bellies every day.

What happened to California?

Not that Palmer considered himself racist, or close-minded, or anything like that. These were just the facts.

A real estate agent who specialized in Palmer's neighborhood, and who had become Palmer's client, had filled him in on what was fueling the ethnic changes in the East Bay. The agent's name was Max Miller, and his wife's name was Maxine. They advertised themselves as "Max and Maxine—The Spouses Selling Houses!"

One day, Max had walked into Palmer's office and hired him, suspecting Maxine of having one too many male clients. Turned out that Maxine had been showing men vacant houses and having sex with them on the newly installed beige carpeted floors. She hadn't sold many houses but always had an abundance of showings. After the divorce, Max and Palmer remained friends.

Months later, Max had stopped by Palmer's house and filled him in on realtors' secrets about who was buying all the houses. Max was overweight, a voracious red wine drinker, and originally hailed from Holland, having lived in the States for only five years. He spoke in staccato English.

"In China, a person cannot own da land like they do 'ere in da State, da governmant, or da collectives, own da lan. A person only has da right to use da lan in China. So, Chineee families group together and pool da money to

126

buy, often sight unseen, California properties. They buy da singel-family houses, da duplexes, apartmants, apartmant buildings, vacan lan, da wineries, vineyard lan, centars da hold weddins and parteys, and virtually every udder kind da lan or property that dey can get," Max had said. After his divorce, Max had sold an uncanny number of houses.

Guess his clients understand what he is saying.

Remembering the conversation with Max made Palmer angry.

He wanted to get the hell out of the state. Palmer now thought that was a better idea than moving to the Sierra foothills in California. He laughed despite himself. He was Caucasian, and he was upper middle-aged. He fit the profile.

Palmer Doyle did not consider himself a racist, but people liked to live among their own kind. People of the same ethnicity had been living close together in the same neighborhoods since the country's inception. One just had to look at names of ethnic communities within any city. In New York, in years past, there had been Germantown, Little Italy, Chinatown, Little Guyana, Koreatown, and Little India, to name just a few. Cultural differences such as cuisine, goods for sale, religions, and languages had set these neighborhoods apart. The same is true in most American cities.

Birds of a feather flock together.

Palmer's phone rang. Usually he would check the number first before answering, but since he was driving and couldn't see the phone number calling, he simply answered.

Someone speaking Chinese spoke on the other end. Palmer realized it was a robocall. A Chinese-speaking robocall.

Good grief.

He had to laugh. The call reminded him that he should check in with Dakota on that case about the law firm leading a class action suit against robocalls—the firm that was actually using a robocall system to solicit clients for their lawsuit.

Can't make this stuff up.

Palmer made the mistake of falling in behind a construction truck carrying landscape gravel just before the truck hit a pothole. As if in slow motion, Palmer saw the rear gate of the truck open and close at the jolt of the impact, for just a second. Gravel and rocks spewed out, bouncing like handfuls of marbles towards Palmer's car.

There was nothing he could do to get out of the way in time. Flanked by trucks, he couldn't change lanes. Buddy, too, saw the mess unfold. He focused his eyes on the bouncing rocks, baring his chipped teeth as he barked, trying to swallow the debris as they flew past Palmer's car.

Shit.

This can't be happening.

Not again.

Furious now, Palmer loudly hummed the classic rock song, "California Dreamin'" by The Mamas & the Papas.

**"California dreaming, Cal-i-for-nia dreaming
On such a winter's day."**

7.

"Foa nie fi."

Cranky and tired, Palmer figured another cup of coffee might help wake him up. He'd already had three cups this morning. One more wouldn't hurt. He stopped at his regular coffee place. He didn't like leaving Buddy in the car, alone and locked up; the dog sat obediently on his hindquarters outside the coffee shop front door, watching with unblinking eyes every move that Palmer made.

"What's that you say, Ester? Four ninety-five?" He cocked his head to listen with his right ear.

Palmer had settled into an easy truce with the young Tasmanian Barista, who spoke her own indecipherable brand of English. Her auburn hair was pinned up in a bun atop her head with the same dog bone Palmer had seen a couple of weeks ago.

"Ya. Dat's wha I sed. Foa nie fi."

"Okay then." Palmer fought his surly mood.

Outside, an odd-looking stranger wheeling a broken down baby stroller approached Buddy.

"How's everything with you Ester? Okay?" Palmer asked.

"Fiin. Dings 'r fiin. Danks fer aksin," Ester replied. "Wit yu?"

"Couldn't be better," Palmer said, scooping up his latte and heading outside. As soon as he'd swung the door open, the smell of the approaching man assaulted him. The stranger must have gone unwashed for months. Palmer guessed he was about sixty-five years old, obviously homeless. Palmer had recently read an online news column about how homelessness, since the pandemic, was exploding in California. The state was now home to twenty percent of the nation's homeless population.

The bums are moving into California because of the glorious weather.

The truth was depressing. An obsessive reader, Palmer had versed himself in the coronavirus pandemic and what it had left in its wake. The pandemic had put multiple industries out of business. The restaurant industry was kaput; no one wanted to gather in crowded enclosed places, even to eat. The airline industry would have gone belly-up if the government hadn't bailed out the companies. Hotels and motels imploded since travel had virtually come to a halt. Retail stores and malls had shuttered across the country. Companies that owned and managed shopping malls declared bankruptcy. Millions had lost their jobs, the skills they had gained over years while working in their respective jobs and industries no longer needed. When they couldn't pay their bills or their rent and mortgages, the real estate industry spiraled. Banks that held mortgages offered no relief, and eventually evictions soared too. Many who had the option moved in with family. People who didn't have the luxury of moving in with others either lived out of their cars or became the new and highly educated homeless. But homeless, nonetheless. So, parking lots filled up with people living inside their cars. Thousands set up camp as squatters, moving into the empty stores where thriving businesses once sold their wares.

The odd-looking stranger dressed in filthy, ragged army fatigues. An ungroomed long beard, red but graying and stained brown, hid much of his weathered, ruddy face.

God knows what might grow in that beard.

Palmer spotted a chew of tobacco in the stranger's bulging right cheek.

Explains the brown stains.

He wore a captain's hat, similar to what a fishing boat captain would wear, except his hat had one long black feather angled out of its side. In his broken-down stroller sat an older but content-looking German Shepherd. In the bottom pocket of the stroller, Palmer eyed greasy cooking utensils, discolored dinner plates, and a dog-eared cookbook titled - "The Paleo Diet Cookbook".

"Fine looking dog you have, Mister Doyle," he said, looking at Buddy. He had a deep baritone voice and spoke as if he were English royalty.

Who does this guy think he is? Captain Jack Sparrow? And how does he know my name?

"Allow me the opportunity to introduce myself," the old man said. "My name is Jonesy. And this is my companion, Mister Peabody." He nodded toward the big dog. Mister Peabody wore a face mask that covered his long nose. The face mask had a picture of a dog on it.

Is that a picture of Rin Tin Tin?

Mister Peabody was panting with his long tongue hanging out of his mouth. Hanging across his back was a blanket that may have been cream-colored at one time but was now mostly muddy brown.

Palmer turned away, unable to stomach the stench.

"Palmer Doyle," Palmer said, saluting but not extending a hand. Last thing he wanted to do was touch this guy.

"Yes, yes. I Know who you are, Mister Doyle," Jonesy said. "Your reputation precedes you."

To Palmer, he sounded as if he'd played the part of a footman in Downton Abbey. "My reputation?"

Buddy hung close to his side.

"Why, yes. You are the famous private investigator. Are you not?"

"Well, I don't know about famous."

"Now, now, sir. No need to be modest." Jonesy pulled off his captain's hat, ran a filthy hand through his filthier long white hair, and held the hat over his heart. "I plan on earning your trust, sir." Jonesy held his gaze with a serious look. "You see, I think I can help you. I believe that I can be an effective investigator for you."

Palmer stifled a guffaw. "Why do you have those?" he asked, nodding towards the filthy kitchen utensils and plates in the stroller.

"Why to cook healthy meals," Jonesy said, pointing to his Paleo cookbook. "Of course."

"Of course," Palmer said. He tapped the side of his head with his hand, as if to say - *How could I be so stupid?*

He felt like handing Jonesy twenty dollars and sending him to the YMCA to take a bath. Palmer was sure Mister Peabody needed a bath too. As did Mister Peabody's muddy brown blanket.

"Oh, I don't mind that you seem skeptical, sir." Jonesy looked off into the distance, staring at nothing.

This guy speaks perfect English. He's educated.

"But, like I said, I plan on earning your trust, sir. If you will allow me the opportunity. And my—I hope you don't mind me saying—your coffee smells mighty fine." Jonesy

133

stared at Palmer's coffee cup. "I'd gladly pay you Tuesday ..."

"Stop right there." *Who does this guy think he is? Wimpy from the old Popeye cartoons?* "Here. Take my coffee."

"Why thank you, kind sir."

"Don't mention it."

Just then, a cell phone rang. Palmer looked around but saw no one else. He'd heard a different ringtone than the one on his phone.

Jonesy frowned, digging into the pockets of the baby stroller, and pulled out a phone.

He saw that it was an iPhone. *Good grief. Homeless people have smart phones, too, nowadays.*

Thinking about cash-rich Apple once again this fine morning, with their billions of dollars socked away, Palmer grew angrier. How they made all the majority of their products off shore. How they funneled hundreds of millions of dollars in foreign sales profits through Irish-based subsidiary companies to avoid paying the U.S. Government its fair share of taxes. And Apple was an American company! Apple paid so little in Federal taxes, legally, through all those corporate tax loopholes, that it was a joke. It was a travesty, actually.

It's not right. I pay more in sales taxes here in California each year than Apple pays in federal taxes. Maybe that's a bit of an exaggeration, but it feels like that's the case. As if we don't pay enough in taxes with state income taxes, business taxes, a high sales tax, property taxes, city and county taxes, and gasoline tax. Californians pay the highest tax rate in the country.

"Excuse me, sir," Jonesy said, politely. "Good day,

Madeline." Jonesy held the phone at arm's length as he turned the speaker on. "Yes, I have a moment." Jonesy made an annoyed face at Palmer and raised a finger his way, as if asking Palmer to wait. Jonesy listened intently. "Well, my opinion is in my brief, if you've taken the time. Have you read my brief? Madeline?

His brief?

"Why thank you, Madeline," Jonesy said after a pause. "My regards to your family too."

Who is this guy?

"Now, where were we?" Jonesy said, placing the smart phone back in the baby stroller. Mister Peabody sat there, tongue still hanging out, with a dopey smile on his canine face. "Ah yes, earning your trust. Well, time will tell, Mister Palmer. Time will tell. It was my pleasure to meet you. Time for me to get going now. I've got many, *many* things to attend to. Come along, Mister Peabody."

Busy for a homeless guy. What can he possibly have to attend to?

"Wait," Palmer said, curiosity getting the better of him. "Who are you?"

"Why, I'm Jonesy," the old guy replied, as if that was all the explanation needed.

"No, what did you do? When you worked, I mean." He took another look at Jonesy, doing his best not to get another whiff. "If you ever had a job, I mean."

"Well, sir, I had an outstanding job. A very important job."

Palmer waited.

Jonesy looked at Mister Peabody.

"I was a Superior Court Judge."

"A Superior Court Judge?" *No way.*

"Yes. A Judge, here in Alameda County. I know, looking at me now, it might seem like a bit of a stretch."

"A bit of a stretch?"

"Well, sir." Jonesy looked off in the distance again. Palmer could tell he was looking at nothing in particular but thinking of some odd thing. "I checked out on life for a while, to be honest. But I'm back now." He took a dog treat out of his grimy pocket and tossed it in the air towards Mister Peabody, who snatched it in mid-air, not missing a beat. "I'm back now and eager to serve you."

Not if I can help it.

"Well, it was nice meeting you," Palmer said, gathering up Buddy, who was reluctant to let Mister Peabody out of his sight. "Take care now," Palmer said, heading towards his car.

"Why thank you, Mister Doyle, and may God bless."

He sounded like Red Skelton. How the famous comedian had ended every one of his TV shows from the seventies.

And may God bless.

Once in his car, Palmer took out his phone to search on Google. There he was. He had his own Wikipedia page: Judge Jonathon Jones, Superior Court, Santa Clara County, California, 1994-2006. Alameda County, California, 2006-2017. Retired two years ago. Graduated from Harvard Law School. Started his career as an Assistant District Attorney for Santa Clara County. After ten years, he had been appointed to the appellate court system, then promoted to Superior Court Judge eight years later. Served eleven years on the top court in Alameda County, handling violent crimes, murder trials, felonies. He dealt with the toughest cases. His Wikipedia page had a picture that must have been taken years ago, before Jonesy had grown his long, shaggy white hair and beard, before he wore army fatigues or his feathered captain's hat. In the photo, he wore clean clothes. No Mister Peabody. Just Jonesy, smiling into the camera.

"Well, I'll be damned, Buddy. I'll be damned."

Buddy sniffed, unconcerned, his head hanging out the window.

"Now he's hanging out in an abandoned strip mall."

He checked out on life for a while.

That sounds good. I'd like to do that. Check out on life for a while. But not in California. Not too sure about living under a blue tarp, either.

8.

Meghan arrived at the office early to make Sarge a pot of fresh coffee. She'd figured that Sarge might arrive early; the Muellers were scheduled to be here this morning. Neither the Muellers nor Sarge wanted a Zoom meeting. They preferred a face-to-face.

She wondered how much vodka Sarge had drunk last night. She had a way of telling, by observing the way he looked, how he moved, how he'd dressed. If he was alert, showered, and shaven, he'd usually had three, or fewer, drinks. On the days he was in a fog, he had drunk himself to sleep the night before.

Meghan had had a busy weekend. Bored with her red hair, she'd visited the salon and had it lightened two shades, then highlighted with blonde streaks. The look softened the freckles on her Irish face, especially the ones on her nose. She had to stay out of the sun; otherwise, with her fair skinned complexion, she'd burn to a crisp. Of course, she had to buy new clothes to go with her fresh look. She chose a pair of beige pants and a yellow blouse, which made her hair look lighter still. A pearl necklace hung from her neck. She wore pearl earrings too. She bought three-inch-heeled pumps; Meghan loved shoes, and more than seventy pairs hung from hangers in her closet. She'd also manicured her nails a softer shade. Then, of course, she had to change her makeup by using a lighter foundation and a lighter shade of lipstick.

She felt good.

Sarge walked in, mumbling. He had paid attention to his appearance this morning: navy blue slacks, freshly ironed, a long sleeve light blue dress shirt, and shiny black loafers. His eyes were clear. Probably two drinks, maybe less.

He shot Meghan a quick look. "Call the mobile auto glass company for me, will ya, Meg?" he said. "Need a new windshield."

Meghan flashed her smile. Her smile was her suit of armor, her protection. When she smiled, people didn't know what she was thinking or how she really felt.

Off Palmer walked to get a cup of coffee.

"Sure thing, Sarge." Her shoulders sagged.

She poked her head out the office window towards his parked car. His windshield had been hit several times, the glass spidering.

9.

"I've invited some members of my staff to sit in," Palmer began. Truth was, this was all of his staff, but there was no reason Sophia Mueller and her stepfather needed to know that. "They did the legwork," he continued. "They can answer any questions you have. To my left is John Babbitt. He's been an investigator with us for seven years."

Sharkie squirmed. His bulky body barely fit in the chair. He looked alert, but he had a sad look on his Gumby face. Palmer thought he looked comical, an overweight man with his too-small-for-his-frame face. In his squeaky voice, from under his turtle print face mask, he said, "Pleased to meet ya." Three fingers on his right hand were covered with bandages.

Wonderful.

Fortunately, Meg had filled Palmer in when John walked into the office this morning. Not wanting John to know they were talking about him, they had exchanged texts.

    Palmer: What's the deal with Sharkie
    this morning?
    Meg: First, he's grieving.
    Palmer: Grieving?
    Meg: Yeah. Barney died.
    Palmer: Barney? Who's Barney?
    Meg: His pet turtle.
    Palmer went quiet for a minute.

Palmer: Something else?

Meg: Well, he doesn't think we know, but we do. He has the Piles and they are bothering him this morning.

Palmer: Piles?

Meg: Yes. The Piles. He's got them bad, takes pain meds. At least his hygiene is decent this morning. He doesn't smell like a sewage plant. But they must itch.

Palmer: What's the deal with all of those bandages on his hand?

Meg: Gertrude bit him.

Palmer: Gertrude? I didn't know he had a girlfriend. Why would she bite him?

Meg: Gertrude is not a woman. She's a turtle.

Palmer: A Turtle?

Meg: Yes. A snapping turtle. He's got about a dozen snapping turtles for pets. He has names for all of them.

Palmer went quiet for a moment, again.

Palmer: More info than I need, but thks.

Good grief. The piles instead of hemorrhoids? Haven't heard that term in ages. Nothing is sacred anymore. Sooner or later, everybody knows everything.

"Thanks, John," Palmer continued. "Thanks for pitching in today. And this is Dakota Thompson. She's been with us for three years."

"Good morning." Dakota said. Not talkative by nature, she gave everyone a quick look before burying her head in her laptop, her foot tapping the floor. Even during the height of the pandemic, Dakota had chosen not to wear a facemask.

"Dakota is our in-house computer guru," Palmer said, proudly. "She's in charge of our genealogy department." Dakota was, in fact, the entire genealogy department. This morning, she wore workout sweats and a muscle shirt cut off at the shoulders, which showed her Schwarzeneggerian arms. The tattoos of hearts on one arm and archangels on the other stood out, visible to everyone in the room. Her arms were burning this morning after bench-pressing three hundred pounds multiple times during her five a.m. workout. Dakota wore her thin gold ring through her pierced left eyebrow.

Sophia Mueller and her stepfather blinked, looking at each other, but neither said a word.

"And this is Meghan," Palmer continued. "My office manager."

Meghan was, in fact, the entire office staff.

She put on her most cheerful face. "Good morning! I'm pleased to meet you."

"A bit of medical business before we begin," Palmer continued. "I'm guessing everyone has gotten their vaccine?"

Sophia glared at him.

She's a nurse, of course she has.

All of Palmer's staff, except John, had received their vaccinations. Two shots each.

"Meg is going to test for oxygen levels and temperatures."

The new normal.

Meg took her oximeter and placed it on Sophia's pinky. The oximeter measured a person's body temperature, pulse, and oxygen levels in the blood, which were a reliable indicator of whether a person might have coronavirus. A good medical tool for seeing if someone was sick.

"It works better if you put it on an index finger," Sophia said, a bit sarcastically. She glared at Palmer again.

As a backup, Palmer had installed a body heat temperature scanner, which looked like a pair of binoculars mounted on a broomstick. The scanner also tested each person for fever.

"Looks like Wall-E," Meg had said when Palmer had first installed it at the entrance door.

"Who's Wally?" Palmer had asked.

"You know, the cute little space robot that thinks he's a teenage boy. The movie."

"Haven't seen it, Meg."

"Sure, you have, Sarge. Everyone has. Don't you remember? Came out about ten years ago. From Disney, I think. Wall-E falls in love with a girl robot and chases her all over the galaxy."

"Haven't seen it, Meg," Palmer had repeated while checking that he'd correctly installed the scanner.

And with no one having to say anything to enforce it, they all practiced social distancing.

As usual, Sophia Mueller looked great. Her blonde hair had been styled and highlighted with soft blond curls that hung from the right side of her head.

Like Kim Basinger in the movie LA Confidential.

Today, she showed off more of her curves by wearing a blue blazer over a tight-fitting top with an open neckline and a short skirt revealing thin hips and toned legs.

"I'm guessing you have interesting things to tell us this morning." Sophia smiled.

"That's what I'm good at," Palmer answered, maintaining eye contact with her. "Finding out things." He turned to her stepfather. "How are you doing today, Martin?"

"Feeling well. Thanks for asking, Mister Doyle." Martin's voice sounded weak.

"Please, call me Palmer."

Martin Mueller did not look at all well. Tall, pencil thin, his once erect posture now had him hunched over like a question mark. A cane rested by his side. Though he claimed that his cancer was in remission, he looked ill. He had the chalk-white facial coloring of the seriously ill; Palmer had noticed his pallid complexion when he'd entered the conference room this morning. Martin looked feeble when a raspy cough overtook him.

Nearly broke him in half.

"Shall we get started?" Palmer asked.

Below his black face mask, Martin gave him a tight-lipped smile.

Buddy, curled in his dog bed in the corner, eyed Martin and Sophia, never taking his eyes off of them.

10.

"First thing I did was research your father, Sophia," Palmer began. "I wanted to know more about him, what he was like. His life, his work, his habits, things he did. If he was an upstanding citizen, good family man, well then, maybe no one would have had motive to harm him."

"He was a sanctimonious little prick!" Martin growled.

An electric charge zigzagged across the room.

Sophia's eyes widened. "Ah, Dad."

"Don't 'Ah, Dad' me,," Martin said.

"He was a crook, his father was a crook, and his son is the worst one of all. Brad's a freaking psychopath."

"More coffee, anyone?" Meg asked, trying to lighten the mood.

"If you did research on Ramsay," Martin continued, "then you'd already know this."

"If I may," Palmer continued. "Ramsay inherited the Sunrise Village Mobile Home Park in San Jose, California in 1973 when he was twenty-five years old. His father, Warren, left it to him when he passed."

"What did he die from?" John asked.

"Myocardial infarction."

"What's that?" John asked.

"Heart attack, John." Palmer gave Sharkie a look. John was sweating through his shirt.

"Dakota?"

Dakota looked up from her computer. "Warren Marshall started The Sunrise Village Mobile Home Park in '43, during World War II." She spoke authoritatively.

146

"Last year. it generated approximately \$1.2 million a month in income, or about \$14 million a year.

John whistled. "That's serious dough."

"Yes, it is. You have more?" Palmer asked.

"I do. Last week, I visited the City of San Jose offices, planning to get more information about Warren Ramsay and the origins of his trailer park."

"Why do that?" Sophia asked.

"To research the title, deeds of trust, things like that. If there are clouds on title that may have happened during Warren's lifetime, well, someone may still have had a bone to pick with Ramsay about that."

"Ah," John said. "Makes sense."

Martin and Sophia said nothing.

"I got lucky," Dakota continued. "The City of San Jose incorporated in 1850, and they've been keeping records on all land, parcels, businesses, and home sales since." Dakota tapped the floor with her right foot.

"And?" Martin said, somewhat impatiently. "Why does that matter?"

"Well," Dakota continued. "In June of 1942—"

"Seven months after the attack on Pearl Harbor," Palmer injected.

"Yes, seven months after, Warren purchased fifty acres of farmland, an orange orchard, from the Nakatomi family."

"Japanese?" Sophia asked.

"Yes, Japanese," Dakota answered. "Warren paid them one hundred dollars an acre for the land."

"Why, that's fucking highway robbery!" screamed Martin. "I told you Warren Ramsay was a fucking crook! I told you!" He flared his nostrils again. "Why, even way back then, that land was worth fifty times that!"

Palmer took over. "We believe that the Nakatomi family was sent to an internment camp in early 1942."

"An internment camp?" Sophia repeated.

"Yes. After the bombing of Pearl Harbor, the government took actions based on the belief that Japanese Americans living in the States couldn't be trusted. Many citizens believed that they were planning on helping Japan win the war. They were rounded up, thousands of them, and sent to these camps, which were prisons. They were forced to stay there under US Army guard for the duration of the war."

"Wow," John said. "Talk about a raw deal."

"Yes. But legal, at the time. President Roosevelt's executive order made it so," Dakota said.

"That's not all. Most had all of their belongings, savings, cars, and land they owned taken from them. They were treated like criminals. They could only take what they could carry on their backs to the camps. If they tried to reclaim their property, or if they questioned authorities about their belongings being taken from them, many were shot."

"Shot?" John asked.

"Shot," Palmer answered. "Yes."

"Well, I'll be damned," John said.

"Where was the Nakatomi family taken?" Sophia asked.

"We believe they were sent to a camp in Lodi, California. In the San Joaquin Valley. But we have no proof of that. We are still checking."

While Dakota spoke, capturing the Muellers' attention, Palmer studied the room.

Why is Martin so upset?

He watched Dakota, her eyes wide, foot taping the floor.

Her attention deficit disorder is in full bloom this morning. But she is handling her part. Any fool can see that the Mueller's are put off with her appearance.

Sharkie was squirming in his seat, trying to get comfortable.

Becky? Please! He implored his dead wife. *Send me a sign. Does he still think that Bob Hope is still alive?*

No one on his staff had reported anything unusual about the Mueller's. They seemed to be on the up and up. The only time they'd ventured out over the past week was to hop onto a plane to fly to Houston, probably to visit the MD Anderson Cancer Center.

Palmer glanced at Meg, who was smiling as she refilled coffee cups. He noticed her new hair color, her new outfit.

Dakota continued. "Warren Ramsay owned an adjoining parcel of ten acres. But then he had sixty acres of land, and he turned the Nakatomi orange orchard and his ten acres into a mobile home park. I have a copy of the zoning change permit, approved by the City of San Jose in 1943 right here." She passed out copies. "Warren was in business after that."

"I told you he was a fucking crook," Martin repeated, his brow furrowing deeper.

"Unbelievable," Sophia said. "What about after the war? When the Nakatomi's were set free? Did they try to reclaim their land?"

"Yes," Palmer continued. "However, the family patriarch, Ikatsu Nakatomi, or Joseph, as he liked to be called, passed away while interred. His heirs took Warren to court. They lost. After the war, predatory land speculators had no problem shooting Japanese Americans when they tried to get their belongings or properties back. Many years later, the United States Government made some reparations to the Japanese American families that were interred during the war."

"Like the American Indians now, with their casinos," John interrupted. "Because we killed all the Indians, then gave them white man's diseases. They dropped like flies from all that, and then we stole their land."

"Well, I don't know if I'd use that comparison, John," Palmer said, glaring at Sharkie. "But the Nakatomis' fifty-acre property was no longer theirs. Sold to Warren Ramsay."

"A fucking crook," Martin Mueller said again.

"We raped all their women, too, before we killed them," John added in his squeaky cartoon voice. "Their casinos are everywhere." His Gumby face contorted in a weird rubber-faced smile.

"Okay, John. Thanks." Palmer snapped at Sharkie.

Please, Becky? Please?

"Can I freshen anyone's coffee?" Meg asked again, her suit of armor smile plastered on her face.

150

"The apple doesn't fall far from the tree," Martin said, now calmly. "Warren was a fucking crook. And Ramsay learned how to be a crook from his dad. And now Brad, Ramsay's son, is a crook, learning his trade well from his father and grandfather. Maybe it's hereditary in this family.."

Palmer said nothing.

"What did you find out about my dad?" Sophia asked. "Was he as bad as his father? I didn't know anything about his business dealings, except what I read in the news. He shared none of that with me."

"Dakota? John?" Palmer asked, nodding to his investigators.

"Over the last twenty years, income from Sunrise Village exploded. With the local real estate boom in Silicon Valley, Ramsay could increase the space rent fees every year. He made a killing," Dakota explained. "But about fifteen years ago, Sunrise Village needed work. Deferred maintenance. Roads within the park needed to be repaved, the roof on the community center was shot, common area grounds needed paint, road work, upkeep, etc. So, Ramsay hired contractors to do the work. But he didn't always pay them what they agreed upon in the contract."

"What do you mean?" Martin asked. "How did you find this out?"

"A title search that detailed several mechanics liens against the property. When Ramsay failed to pay, the contractors put liens on Sunrise Village. This info is readily available from public records."

Martin and Sophia shared a look.

"At the time of Ramsay's death," Dakota continued, "there were several unresolved lawsuits against him and Sunrise Village to the tune of about $1.2 million dollars."

"He was trying to cheat people out of their money, wasn't he?" Martin asked.

"We don't know that for sure." Palmer interjected. "We don't know the outcome of these lawsuits, who is to blame, who owes who how much money. We will not be quick to judge until the legal system and cases play themselves out in court."

"He was a fucking crook. Just like his father," Martin said again.

This guy is wound as tight as a top.

Sophia said nothing.

"John?" Palmer grimaced at Sharkie. "You have info for us on Ramsay?"

Sharkie's face twisted, as if he had just choked down a too-large oyster. He cleared his throat. "He married three times. Helen Schmidt, when she was twenty-five."

"My Helen," Martin said.

"My mother." Sophia nodded.

"Yes. He divorced her when she was thirty-five and married Mary Bartholomew three years later. She, too, was twenty-five years old when they married."

"Brad's mother," Sophia added.

"Correct," Sharkie continued. "Divorced her thirteen years later. Both divorces were ugly."

"Water under the bridge," said Sophia.

"He remained single for several years, until he married Jojo Graham, who was working as a bikini barista at a coffee shop when they met."

"Let me guess." Martin rolled his eyes. "She was twenty-five years old, too, when they married."

"Bingo."

"He liked them young. He must have been about seventy when he married Jojo?"

"Seventy-one," John replied.

"Nice guy," chided Martin. "Got rid of his wives and girlfriends when they got too old. And too old for him were women in their mid-thirties. Apparently."

"Just presenting facts," Palmer said. "Not making judgements."

"Nice guy," Martin repeated. "Fits the mold. You said the divorces were ugly?"

"Yes," Sharkie continued. "As you probably know, since you later married Helen, all she wanted was a fair shake, what was legally hers, which was alimony and child support."

"For me," Sophia added. "Child support for me."

"But Ramsay refused. He hired the best divorce attorney to fight her tooth and nails."

"Cheap bastard," Martin added.

"My mom was a beautiful person," Sophia said. "She was a figure skater, a wonderful skater and a professional athlete. She made the German Olympic team for the '68 Winter Olympics held in Grenoble, France."

Palmer sat straighter in his seat. "That was the Olympics that Peggy Fleming won the gold medal for figure skating."

Meg and Dakota had blank looks on their faces.

Before their time.

"Mom finished eighth," Sophia said.

"Well," John continued. "Once the divorce was finalized—"

"Of which my mom didn't like the outcome," Sophia interjected. "She packed up, and we moved to Germany. She met Martin soon after."

Martin looked lost in thought.

"Like I said," Sophia added. "Water under the bridge. This happened almost forty years ago. And father and I mended those broken fences a long time ago."

Sharkie was not finished. "When he divorced Mary, he hired the same divorce attorney again."

"He might have been trying to protect his interests," Sophia said.

Palmer wondered why she was defending her dead father after all he'd put her mother through. The two exchanged a look.

"Maybe," Sharkie added. "But Mary died almost twenty years ago."

"Brad's mom?" Martin asked.

"Yes, Dad," Sophia said. "Remember? I told you about that."

Martin plowed ahead. "So, Ramsay died before he could divorce Jojo?" His question had a tone of malice.

"Now, Dad," Sophia chided.

Palmer stood. "Our investigation into Ramsay Marshall tells us that there are people out there who might have a motive to harm him. Shall we move on?"

Martin nodded.

Sophia gave Palmer a smile.

"Not a nice man," Meg said under her breath, watching Sophia smile at Sarge.

"You mentioned to me previously," Palmer addressed Sophia, "that your dad had a living trust. And that Brad was the executor?"

"Yes," Sophia said. "We're equal heirs, the two of us. We split his estate except for a lump sum amount to be paid to his third wife."

"I see."

Palmer sat back in his chair. There were a number of people who had motive to kill Ramsay Marshall: his wife, Jojo, for starters; his son, Brad, for sure. As his father's living trust executor, Brad Marshall was responsible for distributing his father's estate according to the provisions in the trust. As executor, he had certain advantages over the other beneficiaries in the trust. But he couldn't change the contents of the trust without a court order.

Ramsay hadn't been the most honest of businessmen, dealing dishonestly with many people. All of those businesses and people who had a gripe with Ramsay could be added to the list of who would have had a motive to harm him.

Martin seemed to read Palmer's mind. "You want to take that retainer now?" he asked.

"Yes."

Martin reached into his pocket and handed the check to Palmer.

Fifty thousand dollars.

"Thank you."

"Excellent."

"I'll need a copy of Ramsay's living trust."

"I'll see that you get one," Martin added.

    I'll have to go over it with a fine-tooth comb.

"And by the way," Palmer added. "Where is Ramsay buried again?"

"Queen of Heaven cemetery," Sophia said. "The one with the views of San Francisco Bay."

"That's right. You mentioned it to me before."

The dead people have splendid views there.

"Why do you want to know that?" Martin asked.

"Just curious."

11.

"Hit me." Brad Marshall sat at third base, his favorite position at a blackjack table. At third base, a BJ player could watch all the cards played by players ahead of him before deciding what to do, which gave even a player like Brad an advantage. Plus, Lumpia, the Filipino dealer whose table he sat at, had a proclivity to miscount card totals, a rarity at any casino. Another rarity was that she occasionally and unknowingly showed her hole card while looking at her hand, which gave Brad an advantage, one that even bad blackjack players had trouble screwing up.

Hitting a hard fifteen against a dealer eight face card.

"Six," Lumpia said. She was so short that she stood on a foot-high wooden block so she could better survey the table. "Showen leven," she said to Brad in broken English. She had a high-pitched voice, like a squeaky mouse.

"Stick."

Twenty-one.

Lumpia turned over her hole card. *Eighteen.*

"Winnaa!" she said to Brad, smiling as she handed over five green chips.

Five hundred dollars.

Brad was at the Hekawi Indian Resort and Casino, in the Sacramento foothills. The Hekawi was an indigenous gaming casino surrounded by a championship golf course. Brad was here on a stay-and-play package, which allowed him a one-night stay and two rounds of golf on the championship layout.

Inside the entrance of the casino was an enormous fifteen-foot-tall marble statue of Jay Silverheels, the indigenous actor who played Tonto in the popular Lone Ranger TV series of the 1950s. People gawked at the statue of the famous Indian, which brought in more business to the casino, gambling being the big moneymaker.

Never mind that Silverheels, who died over forty years ago, was not a Hekawi from Northern California but a Mohawk, born and raised in the Six Nations Grand River area of Canada. No one seemed to notice. Or care.

The Hekawi claimed tribal sovereignty over their lands, which allowed them and hundreds of other American Indian tribes, like the Hekawi, to build casinos on their lands in retribution for the past crimes committed by the US government. After all, the government had killed tens of thousands of indigenous—women, children, and old people alike—raping the women first before killing them, then stealing their lands, then herding them like cattle onto small reservations located in a hot desert, where they plied them with cheap liquor and gave them a myriad of white man's diseases, such as smallpox, chickenpox, measles, as well as deadly malaria, typhoid fever, and the bubonic plague. These diseases killed tens of thousands more American Indians.

"Winnaa!" Lumpia squeaked again, as she busted in four cards after Brad had doubled down and pulled a thirteen. This time, she handed over ten green chips.

If this keeps up, I'll be able to pay some of my markers.

The name Hekawi, which no one else seemed to notice, was not the real name of the tribe that owned the land and resort. In fact, it was the Miwok, whose tribal leaders had figured the Hekawi name, which was the

158

ame of the fictional American Indian tribe featured in the '60s hit comedy series "F-Troop", might attract more people and bring in more revenue.

"Winnaa!" Lumpia shouted again. Another five green chips.

I wonder if she knows that her name, Lumpia, is the name of the popular Filipino food appetizer?

Brad Marshall was thirty-seven years old, eight years younger than his half-sister Sophia. He was tall, fit, with his black hair permanently glued down in wavy layers by a dippity-do-type hair gel. A hurricane-force wind couldn't blow his hair out of place. His two front teeth were oversized, like a rabbit's, and coupled with an overbite, his grin resembled a two-hundred-pound version of the Cheshire Cat. He was a good looking man, though he hadn't gotten his good looks from his father. Ramsay Marshall was many things, but good looking he wasn't. Brad had received his good looks from his mother, Mary, Ramsay's second wife, who'd been quite the looker when Ramsay had married her when she was twenty-three.

Brad liked to dress in black slacks. Today he wore them with a gold-trimmed black cowboy shirt. He looked like a cross between California Governor Gavin Newsom and singer Johnny Cash. Addicted to Viagra and always wanting to be ready for the ladies, Brad made sure that he had the drug in his system 24-7.

Brad had hoped to play golf today, but he'd forgotten to make a tee time, which in the past would not have been a problem. But the golf course was so crowded that he couldn't get a tee time to play, so he sat at the blackjack table all day long.

During the coronavirus pandemic, overcrowded golf courses had become the norm. Golf, an outdoor sport which provided natural social distancing, suddenly became enormously popular. There were millions of new golfers.

Hackers.

Brad was subjected to six-hour rounds instead of the normal four hours because the hackers didn't know proper golf etiquette. They took way too long to play. Some even played in flip-flops.

Flip-flops?

There are no flip-flops in golf!

I didn't get sick, yet the fucking state dictated that I had to stay home. Now, a year later, I can't play golf because of all these new fucktard golfers who took up the game because of this damn virus.

I can't do the things I love to do.

In Brad's case were, these things were, in no particular order, gambling non-stop, though he was bad at it; playing golf poorly; drinking stiff Manhattans and having sex with numerous women who were complete strangers. The pandemic had made engaging in his favorite activities much harder.

Damn pandemic.

And the sports book at the casino was now closed. Gambling on team sports had disappeared because of the pandemic. Brad had always liked to relax by sitting at the sports book bar and sipping a Manhattan while he bet big on sports teams. Getting about a dozen bets going at once is what held his interest, though most times he lost nine out of twelve bets. And the ponies too. He liked to bet on the ponies. Some had said that most of the ponies he bet on were still running towards the finish line several days later. That had been taken from him too. Real horse racing was kaput, replaced by virtual horse races.

Virtual horse races? What the fuck?

"Winnaa!" Lumpia squealed again. Brad was winning big, perhaps twenty to thirty thousand dollars, but he didn't like to count his chips. He considered it bad luck. For once, he had a large stack of chips to count. Usually, his chip pile disappeared quickly. The cards he was pulling were so good, he felt himself getting a hard-on.

He had come to the Hekawi resort alone. His wife, Suzie, had stayed home. She didn't like to gamble; she didn't like it when Brad gambled either and she hated golf. When they first met, she'd wanted to learn how to play golf so they could spend time together. She had asked him to teach her. But Brad only wanted to play with the guys, so he could gamble while playing; you can't gamble with and take money from your wife, so he kept teaching her the wrong things, like handing her a one iron to hit most golf shots. A one iron is the most difficult club to hit in golf, so difficult that most touring professionals no longer use one. A one iron is almost extinct. But Brad kept handing Suzie a one iron.

"Here you go, honey," he'd said while handing her the one iron, plastering a smile on his face. "Try this one again."

She couldn't hit the ball ten feet, never got it airborne. It didn't take her long to get frustrated, quit the game, and then declare how much she hated golf.

Mission accomplished.

"Another Manhattan, sir?" the cocktail waitress asked him. Attractive, in her thirties, with long black hair, she wore customary casino cocktail server attire: a short tight skirt showing shapely legs, a low cut, frilly white top that showed off the tops of ample sized breasts.

"Sure thing, sweetie," Brad said, tossing a green chip on her tray.

"Thanks!" She flashed a saucy smile.

Brad watched her butt as she sashayed away.

Who knows? Maybe? A bit too much junk in the trunk for me, but I'd do her, no problemo.

Thank God his father had finally died. It was about time that the old fucktard kicked the bucket.

How many heart attacks had it taken for him to finally die? Three? Four? How does an old fuck-tard like him survive so many heart attacks?

Whack! Whack!

The seeds of Brad's dislike of his father had been planted years ago. Brad was two when his father had first slapped him; though it had happened thirty-four years ago, he remembered it as if it had happened yesterday. He could still feel the sting of his father's hand and could still summon the feelings of humiliation that flooded back with that memory.

Brad had been playing in the living room of their house, happily and carefree.

Whack!

"I told you to be quiet and not to bother me," his father had said. "I'm trying to read the newspaper here. Can't you see that?" Though it was barely nine in the morning, Ramsay had reached for his Schlitz beer.

Brad had been knocked silly; his head hit the corner of a white marble coffee table that was exactly the right height for a two-year-old head to smash into.

Brad's mom, Mary, gasped, covered her mouth with her hand, but had said nothing. She leapt to Brad's side to inspect the red lump blooming on his head. She ran to the kitchen for ice.

"Why are you crying? I barely touched you."

From that day on, Brad knew to stay away from his dad whether or not he'd been drinking. The only time Brad had felt he could approach his father was when he was working in his garden. It was then that Ramsay became calm.

As Brad grew through childhood, he acted out, doing destructive things like shooting his neighbor's pet dog with marbles launched from his slingshot. He'd throw rocks through neighbor's windows to feel the joy of seeing them smash. Once he half strangled a neighbor's kitten because the cat kept coming around looking for milk. When he'd let go of its neck, it took the stunned cat several minutes to regain its senses. Each time Brad did something bad, he knew that he would face his father's wrath. Eventually, when Brad was seven years old, he punched a neighbor's four-year-old daughter in the nose, drawing blood, when the little girl had tried to kiss him. While waiting for his father to return home from work to dish out Brad's punishment, Brad began to develop a nervous twitch in his left eye.

Ramsay left Brad and his mother, Mary, when Brad was ten years old—the age when a young boy needs his father most. Someone to play catch with or shoot baskets together. Someone to teach him how to fish or even just hang out with. When Brad allowed himself to feel the pain of the emotional wake his father left, his leaving hurt the most. The pain of abandonment.

He was probably fucking around with a twenty-one-year-old, Brad surmised now.

When Ramsay left, Mary slowly drank herself to death. Years later, when Brad was a teenager, Mary died after mixing too many sleeping pills with her rum. And even when she was gone, Ramsay wanted nothing to do with his son. He sent Brad off to live with his maternal grandmother after setting up a trust account for him.

Gave me money to get rid of me. Paying me off so he didn't have to spend any time with me.

Brad hated his dad. For years, he'd been hoping for and plotting his demise. He would have done something more drastic to his father, and sooner, if it hadn't been for the intervention of his wife Suzie.

One day, he and Ramsay had had a bad argument over Brad's monthly trust allowance. "I need more money!" Brad had demanded of his father. "I have expenses."

"What?" Ramsay had answered. "You can't live on your fifteen thousand dollars per month? What the fuck is the matter with you, boy?"

The two had almost come to blows, with Suzie having to separate them.

"If you don't like it, go out and get an actual job, you ungrateful little prick!" Ramsay had said, raging.

Brad was livid. So livid that he wanted to punch him. "You old fucking bastard. I'll see you d—." But Suzie had grabbed him, yanking him away before he could finish his threat.

"Brad. Sweetheart. Drop this for now. He's your father."

Brad had backed down.

"Let's talk later," she had whispered to Brad.

"California has Slayer Statute laws," Suzie had told him later, when they were home. "When he dies, if they can prove that had anything to do with his death, these laws prevent you from inheriting his lands, property, cash, whatever."

"Really?" Brad had answered, remembering the conversation clearly. "Fuck me. Better mind my Ps and Qs."

"Yes, really," Suzie had said. "Darling, there is a better way to get what we want."

Get what we want?

Instead of getting into arguments or fights with his dad, he chose instead to do things that would aggravate the hell out of him.

Give him another heart attack.

Brad's favorite trick was to do wheelies on his father's prized yards and gardens with his motorcycle. Ramsay had spent hundreds of hours working on his manicured property. So, when Ramsay had once again refused to pay for Brad's gambling markers he decimated all Ramsay's flower beds in the middle of the night, when everyone was asleep. The destruction had given Brad great joy. He let his old man guess who did it, as if he hadn't already known. But the old fuck couldn't prove it. Brad just cleaned his bike afterwards, putting on a fresh set of tires. Different size tires too, with different threads. The old fuck had called the police, but after visiting Brad at his home, they couldn't prove a thing. The anguish it must have caused his old man. Hundreds of hours of work in his garden, all for naught. Destroyed in a heartbeat. Brad lived for that feeling.

But somehow, the old fuck survived heart attack after heart attack.

But now it didn't matter. He was dead. *I finally did it.* His estate would be settled. Brad and his half-sister had been giving the banks, the brokerages, the insurance companies all the information they needed to move forward. Death certificates, copies of the trust; they filled out and signed all the silly papers that were needed. In a couple of weeks, he'd have all the money that he'd ever need. More than he could gamble away.

Finally.

Now he just had to figure out what he was going to do with his half-sister, Sophia.

"Winnaa!" Lumpia called again as Brad hit fourteen and pulled a seven. Twenty-one to the dealers twenty. Her squeaky voice grated on him. He wanted to punch her in the mouth.

Sounds like a fuckin' mouse.

"Another Manhattan, sir?" The pretty cocktail server again. Smiling at him. This time the white blouse she was wearing was pulled down a smidge more, allowing the tops of her breasts to poke out at him.

"Please, sweetheart," Brad said, this time slipping another green chip onto her tray along with a piece of paper he'd scribbled his room number and a smiley face on. "What time do you get off?"

"In an hour." The waitress smiled as she walked away.

"Great." Brad said, flashing a toothy smile.

He barely knew his half-sister; he didn't give a shit about her. Sophia had been eight when he was born, and, soon after, her mother had scooped her up and moved them to somewhere in Europe. In his lifetime he'd only see her a handful of times, usually when his father had felt nostalgic, or guilty, and had gathered his two legitimate children around him at the holidays or on Ramsay's birthday.

One of the times he saw Sophia stuck out in his mind. He didn't remember the reason they had gotten together. All he remembered was that they were at a resort in Cabo when Brad was about twelve, and Sophia nearly twenty. Brad was swimming in the resort pool, making believe that he was diving for treasure at the bottom of the pool. He tried to hold his breath as long as possible while underwater, a game for him. Sophia had jumped into the pool wearing a string bikini. He hadn't seen her for about seven years, back when she'd had the body of a little boy. But now at almost twenty years old?

Holy shit!

She had huge boobs that bulged out of her bikini top, slender hips, and long legs. Looked like a supermodel. She was so fucking hot that Brad ran to the bathroom to jerk off.

At forty-five years old, she was still beautiful.

I'd do her now. I just don't want to give her any of Dad's money.

Best he could figure was that Ramsay's estate was worth somewhere in the $45 million dollar range. They were equal heirs. Ramsay's third wife, Jojo, had been written into the trust as well; she was slated to receive a million dollars for the two years she was married to Ramsay. Brad shivered when he thought about Ramsay and Jojo having sex.

A couple of million dollars was liquid. He couldn't stop Sophia from getting half of that. The principal part of the estate was tied up in the mobile home park in San Jose. Fifty acres of prime Silicon Valley land. No mortgage. Monthly rent income from the six hundred fifty mobile home spaces. One million dollars per month of rental money coming in. A cash cow.

Cha ching!

Sophia wanted to sell the park, get her half of the money that way.

Why the fuck would anyone want to sell a great income producer like that?

Made no sense to Brad. His guess was that if she wanted cash so badly, she would be open to being bought out. Brad could put a mortgage on the place, get it appraised, and give her half the money that way. He chuckled to himself over the thought. Sophia probably didn't know that since the pandemic had hit, real estate values had fallen off about thirty percent from their highs the previous year. High-tech workers in Silicon Valley no longer had to work close to the offices in San Jose. Meetings now were almost all remote, via Zoom. People could live anywhere. The appraisal would come in low. Then he'd buy her out and pay her off. In a couple of years, real estate values would appreciate. They always did.

I win, Sophia loses.

Brad hated the thought of giving his half-sister any money. The thought left a bitter taste in his mouth. Like chugging vinegar. He felt no compassion towards her.

Perhaps there was another way to make sure she didn't get the money?

At blackjack table, the cards turned bad. Brad figured it had to happen eventually.

"Cash out," he said to Lumpia, pushing stacks of green chips her way. It was rare when Brad actually won at blackjack. For once, he didn't chase his money and lose big.

"Color change!" she screamed at her pit boss.

God, I'm getting pissed off at that voice of hers.

"For you, honey." He pushed a green chip Lumpia's way. The pretty server should be off duty by now.

"Tank you, kin sir," Lumpia replied.

If only I had a knife.

Good thing Suzie isn't around.

She's so fucking jealous.

I'll shower several times before I go home to get the server's smell off of me.

Brad remembered an incident from one week after they had returned from their honeymoon in Tahiti. He had just bedded a redhead that he'd met that morning at the gym.

And people thought me crazy for having a little Viagra in my system 24-7.

"You smell like sex," Suzie had screamed, spitting her words out as she twirled a pair of scissors in her hand. "Where the fuck were you? Who the fuck is she?"

"Honey, please," Brad had cried, arms extended towards her, palms up in conciliation. "Are you kidding me? We just returned from two weeks in Tahiti where we had sex two to three times every single day. I'm still so sore that I can't move."

"I can smell her on you." She twirled those scissors, pointing them at him, raging. It looked like she was ready to go Lorena Bobbitt on him.

"Sweetheart," Brad had said, involuntarily covering his shriveling privates with his hands. "I was at the gym." Well, that part was true. "I forgot to take a shower after." That part was not true. "That's all."

Finally, Suzie seemed to relax, but Brad took careful note of her jealous nature.

Which was only another reason Brad liked to take these two-day golf trips without her. Leaving the BJ table, he headed for the elevator, past the statue of Jay Silverheels, his hard-on still intact, to go fuck the pretty waitress silly. A young couple sharing the elevator shuffled to the side to distance themselves from Brad. A carry-over from pandemic times, he surmised.

Suddenly a dry, hacking cough overcame him, his head shaking violently. It sounded like a smoker's cough, except that Brad had never smoked. To the young couple's horror, Brad had neglected to cover his mouth. They turned away from him and shrunk in disgust.

"What the fuck?" the man said, covering his female companion's nose and mouth with his hands. "What the fuck is the matter with you?"

"Sorry," Brad said, flashing his oversized Cheshire Cat smile their way. Not one hair on his head moved out of place, but his erection shriveled.

Buzzkill. Damn.

12.

Black crows were everywhere. They sat on rooftops. On the docks, they perched on the masts of harbor boats, alongside seagulls. They swarmed together on telephone pole wires like clay targets in a shooting gallery. There were hundreds of them, maybe thousands. Usually, crows cawed non-stop. But Suzie didn't hear one peep from any of them. They only looking at her as if she were lunch.

Normally this wouldn't bother Suzie, except that she was now in Bodega Bay, California, which was the site where the famous Alfred Hitchcock masterpiece *The Birds* was filmed in 1963. In the movie, thousands of black crows, and other birds pecked numerous people to death before the last scene, when the movie's stars, Rod Taylor and Tippi Hedren, quietly tiptoed their way out of town before being pecked to death.

Aiko Tanaka lumbered out of her car, her movement restricted by the outfit she was wearing, and she looked at the Fishetarian, a fish market. She was here to buy fresh raw fish for her sushi restaurant, "Fuk Mi Sushi Bar," located one hundred miles south in San Jose.

When shelter-in-place orders had loosened, many restaurants had already gone out of business. Relying on takeout orders and app delivery companies like Door Dash just didn't bring in enough business, even with good Yelp reviews. Nor did requirements limiting the number of patrons that could sit inside. The only way for most restaurants to keep their doors open relied on full-capacity dining, as well as a fully stocked bar. The Fuk Mi Sushi Bar was no different. Through good word-of-mouth, Suzie had kept the doors open, but barely. Thousands of other restaurant employees had permanently lost their jobs, since many restaurants had shuttered.

Normally the drive would take about three hours, but today it took almost six. Tent cities of homeless people, thousands more added in the past year because of the continued economic fallout from the pandemic, now clogged city streets in San Francisco, making automobile traffic come to a standstill. Aiko had to change her route. She had read, in some newspaper, that since the beginning of the pandemic, the number of homeless people in San Francisco had grown by three thousand percent.

Holy shit.

Now the homeless were gifted with government-issued military tents. Some, reportedly, had central air and heat. In the center of one of the larger tent cities now stood a huge military tent once used as a field hospital, but now used as a sort of shopping center for the homeless, complete with twelve-foot-high ceilings and ceiling fans. It even had a Starbucks coffee shop inside.

Like many Japanese women, Suzie was small: thin, small-boned, with tiny hands and feet but long waisted with skinny legs. Her skin tone was pale, almost porcelain-like from a lifetime of staying out of the sun. Her hair was jet black, pulled back into a pony with a pink scrunchie. Underneath all of her Covid-protective gear, she wore a red floral kimono dress belted at the waist. She wore light foundation to cover her freckled nose, eye makeup to accentuate her almond-shaped eyes, and red lipstick. Suzie was thirty-two years old.

Beautiful and delicate, she looked like a modern-day geisha.

Suzie smelled fresh; this morning she luxuriated in her daily hour-long, steaming hot scented bath, while she picked at a veggie breakfast. It was only when she exited the freeway as she arrived in Bodega Bay and saw what awaited her there that she started to sweat underneath all of her gear.

There was a security gate and temporary wood building at the bottom of the exit barring entry into the town. As she approached, a man opened the door from the building and approached. He was dressed in full hospital personal protective equipment: an R95 facemask, black rubber gloves, vinyl booties, and a hazmat suit. Belted outside his suit were a rubber baton, a taser stun gun, and a revolver.

"Please state the nature of your business in Bodega Bay," he said.

"I'm here to buy fish."

I'm in a broken world where millions of people have overreacted to this damn pandemic.

"From where? And for what purpose?"

"Headed to the Fishetarian, maybe five miles north of town. I own a sushi bar and restaurant in San Jose. I drive here to purchase fish."

"Name?" asked the man. "ID please." His demeanor was pleasant.

Just then, thousands of feet up in the air, a passenger jet passed overhead. The man cocked his head and watched, forlornly. "Sorry," he said after a long moment.

"Wish you were up there flying away somewhere?"

"No," the man answered. "I used to be a pilot for Am Air."

174

"Ah."

"But you can't fly empty airplanes. Like many airline companies not on the government doll, we went out of business."

"Sorry," Suzie said, empathizing.

"Pilots, flight attendants, baggage claim workers, ticket sales people, maintenance workers, travel agents, airplane manufacturers. You name it. The list of workers who lost their jobs and their livelihoods is staggering. So now I work here as a security gate guard."

Jeez.

"Not many planes in the air anymore." The guard gave her a long up and down look. "The ones that do fly are half empty."

A busy airline industry was a thing of the past; even a year after the end of the pandemic, many people refused to get on an airplane. You could add shopping centers and department stores to the list of extinct-as-a-dodo-bird-businesses, as well as restaurants. Which was one reason why Suzie made the long drive. Since her restaurant was allowed to reopen at only half capacity, she had to make extra sure that the meals she served were the best in town. Otherwise, the people who ventured out to eat these days would go elsewhere, and she would be forced to shut her doors. The airline, shopping, and restaurant industries had almost disappeared, and tens of thousands of people had lost their jobs and careers.

Talk about tough times, Suzie thought. She empathized with this guy.

Surely all of this will improve someday. Soon I hope.

"Name?" the ex-jet airplane pilot turned security gate guard asked again. "And ID."

"Oh, sorry," Suzie answered. "Aiko Tanaka." She handed over her driver's license. "I mostly go by my married name, which you see on my license. Suzie Tanaka Marshall. Please call me Suzie." She bowed.

"Please fill out this short questionnaire." The guard handed her a four-page form.

Everyone has their own set of regulations. It seems like there are ten thousand different coronavirus rules.

After perusing, the security guard clipped her finished form onto his clipboard.

"Okay, Suzie Tanaka Marshall. I clear you to go into town. But you have to wear this protective equipment." He handed her a bag labeled "Acme Industries—Your Coronavirus safety equipment!".

Am I in a Looney Tunes cartoon now?

Inside the bag were an N95 mask, foot booties, rubber gloves, and a strap-on, clear plastic face guard. All top shelf. Suzie didn't need the Acme protective equipment, as she had brought all of her own PPE stuff with her. Though coronavirus vaccines had been in use for over a year now, she took no chances. She was not afraid of getting sick herself, but rather she was afraid of being a carrier and passing it on to her parents, or God forbid, her revered grandmother who was still alive at ninety-five years old.

"At all times when in town, you are required to wear these. Failure to do so may result in your arrest." He gave her another long look, then scrunched his face. "But I see you're wearing your own stuff." He looked closer at her equipment. "Your stuff is better than mine." He scrunched his face one more time. "You're good to go."

Suzie was wearing a silver full hazmat suit, which was duck taped shut at the ankles and wrists so no air could penetrate inside. She had on black combat boots and blue latex gloves. She wore a glass full-faced helmet like the kind the robot in the old TV show "Lost in Space" wore.

Danger, Will Robinson!

Under the helmet she wore a face mask. Oxygen pumped into her helmet from a tank strapped to her back. She looked like an astronaut might look before stepping out of a landing craft to explore the surface of Jupiter.

"And that will be twenty-five dollars please," the man then said, taking a credit card reader from his hazmat suit pocket and shoving it in her face. "And I'm not allowed to take, or touch, cash. Please insert your credit card here."

I have to pay for this too?

"Here is your receipt. Thank you."

Ten minutes later, Suzie pulled into the parking lot at the Fishetarian, where she was greeted with a sign. As she read it, crows watched her every move.

Despite what you may have seen on the local news, we are not a Chinese Wet Market! We do not kill dogs, cats, or other domesticated animals, then sell them to the public! We sell fish!! You cannot catch the Chinese virus here!! Promise!!

A scroungy looking man with matted hair that likely hadn't been washed in several months stood at the entry, wearing his PPE.

Though she couldn't see his face under his mask, Suzie was sure that he looked fresh off the boat, like someone from "Tuna Wars". His voice was hoarse, as if he'd been inhaling smoke from all the California wildfires. She felt certain that under the mask the guy was missing teeth. A scruffy grey beard twisted out from under the mask.

"Afternoon, ma'am. Have an appointment today?" By the sound of his voice, Suzie knew she was right about the missing teeth. The words kind of whistled out of his mouth, as if he was talking through a harmonica. He did a double-take at Suzie's outfit.

"I'm here to see Doctor Strangelove, the owner. I've an appointment at three, but I'm early."

"I'm Strangelove."

Yikes.

"What can I say?" He continued. "My parents were Stanley Kubrick fans. They legally changed their last name." he said, as if that was the only explanation necessary.

"You're a doctor?"

"A fish doctor. In other words, an aquaculture veterinarian. Got a license."

"Ahh," Suzie said, then fell silent for a moment. "Suzie. I'm Suzie Marshall. Pleased to meet you." Suzie made sure not to get too close to him. "Can we please go inside now?" she asked, watching the black crows look at her.

Now I know how Tippi Hedren felt.

"Well, right this way, Suzie Marshall." Doctor Strangelove motioned with his arm. "You have a list?"

He smells like week-old fish.

"Yes." She handed over her order, which included a dozen different types of fish: ebi, or shrimp; buri, a yellowfish; chutoro, from the belly area of tuna; salmon, or sake; hirame, a whitefish fluke or flounder; and fugu, or blowfish. "Right here."

"Fugu?" Doctor Strangelove asked, eyebrows raising while attaching her list to his clipboard. "You certified to handle fugu?" He looked over her hazmat gear once again.

"Yes. I've had several years of training."

"I see." Rubbing his chin, he whistled his words. "You know that fugu is more poisonous than cyanide? Two hundred times more poisonous, you know."

"I know how to prepare it to get rid of the poisonous parts."

Fugu, or blowfish, contained tetrodotoxin, a potent neurotoxin. Since 2010, more than fifty people in Japan and hundreds of people around the world had died from eating poorly prepared fugu, hence the three-year training requirement and certification needed for sushi chefs to handle and prepare the fish properly. The tetrodotoxin lived in the fish's guts, intestines, liver, eyes, ovaries, and skin. Besides gutting the fish and its poisonous parts, a person needed to wash and clean the blowfish after gutting.

"And as you know," she continued, "Once rid of the poison, it has a distinctive taste and texture that many of my clients prefer."

My husband, Brad, being one of them.

"Yes, yes, I know all about fugu. Lucky for you we have some fresh blowfish."

"I know. I talked with you on the phone just yesterday."

"Ahh. Yes. Of course." Clearly, Doctor Strangelove didn't remember. He stroked his grey beard with a rubber-gloved hand.

"Right this way."

Twenty minutes later, pushing a hand truck with fish packed in boxes and ice, Doctor Strangelove asked, "Your car has something to keep these fish frozen?"

"My van is outside. I've a freezer in the back."

"Nice."

"Yes. Long drive back to San Jose."

Loading the van, Doctor Strangelove noticed the name stenciled on its sides—"Fuk Mi Sushi Bar".

"That's the name of your place?"

"Yes."

"Alrighty then," Doctor Strangelove said, half whistling through his teeth. "I'll get you loaded up."

Suzie slowly climbed into her van, being careful not to damage her Astronaut suit. She made sure the windows were shut before the fish doctor started loading. She got out her hand-held UV light wand, turning it on. Purple light ran up and down her body.

"What's that?" Doctor Strangelove asked through the closed car window, while scratching his nether regions.

"Germicidal ultra-violet light." Not wanting to get another whiff of him, Suzie chose not to roll down the car window as she replied.

"Does it work?"

"Supposed to get rid of all bacteria."

"But does it work?"

"Dunno. There's no scientific evidence that it actually destroys Covid."

"Ahh. Then why use it?"

"Can't be too careful these days," Suzie replied. "Can you?"

"So, you don't really know if it's working or not then."

"Well, I don't have Covid. Do I?"

"Well, no, I guess you don't. I can't see any Covid getting inside that outfit you're wearing."

"So, you can't really say that the UV light is not working. Can you?"

"I guess not. Sounds like solid logic to me. Where'd you get it?" Doctor Strangelove asked. "I'd like to get one for myself."

"Amazon. Where else?"

"How much?"

"Costs around four hundred dollars."

"Sounds like a rip-off. Or a scam. But maybe I can get rid of any last remaining Covid shit around here and get myself a good suntan at the same time. Kill two birds with one stone."

"Good thinking."

"Thanks. I thought so too," Doctor Strangelove said. "Won't be the first, or the last time, I've been scammed."

As she drove away, she felt the eyes of thousands of black crows hanging from trees and overheard wires watching.

My husband, Brad.

If there was one word to describe how Suzie felt about her husband, that word would be *reprehensible*.

He was dishonest, and he was a lecher—Suzie knew about his exploits.

What wife doesn't know what their husband does?

His selfish habits, his gambling, his womanizing all turned her stomach. And the way he had dishonored his own father? While he was still alive? All she could do was shake her head in disgust.

In Japanese culture, respecting the elderly, and especially your own parents, is an ancient imperative, what sociologists call "filial piety". Parents are revered, listened to, respected, and always taken care of.

Since the day she met Brad, she had ignored all of his shortcomings. First on her agenda was to get him to marry her. By the use of techniques and skills passed from generation to generation—from her grandmother to her mother, and then down to her—Suzie had learned how to be a *yujō* geisha, a Japanese term to describe a prostitute. In America, they had a silly saying that the way to a man's heart was through his stomach.

Hogwash.

The way to a man's heart was through his *ochinko*.

His penis.

Though not all men might be this way, Suzie knew that this certainly was the best way to win Brad Marshall over.

After three months of daily carnal activity, offering herself to Brad wherever and whenever, using her skills, she found it easy to get Brad to propose marriage.

The times when she had waved scissors in her hands, threatening to cut off his balls because of his endless infidelities? Acting jealous?

All a ruse.

As a Japanese woman, Suzie was an expert at putting her mask on and not letting anyone know what her true feelings were.

She just wanted him to think that she cared about him.

13.

John Babbitt's hemorrhoids itched so badly that he chose not to go to one of his favorite places—the Thursday night TikTok competition at the newly reopened – 'masks on, clothes off' gentlemen's club in downtown Fremont. Besides not having to worry about catching Covid, the masks-on concept offered John another plus. The club was not known for hiring the prettiest women; with their face masks on and most of their clothes off while they danced their way into gentlemen's wallets, John didn't have to have his fantasies compromised by looking at, in his opinion, too many ugly women's faces as they lip synced and pole danced their way through the latest TikTok routines.

His rectum burned, not the best sensation, and his doctor no longer would refill his Vicodin prescription. And Vicodin was the best drug to alleviate the pain, the itching, and the burning. Dealing with the smell was different. There was no way he could sit at a wooden barstool; the itching would be unbearable. John had gone online to try to order the Vicodin from Global Pharmacy. But no go. The pharmacy had alluded to something about the ongoing opioid epidemic in giving John a reason they wouldn't authorize his pain pills.

To add to his misery, Sarge had called.

"Be ready to leave at ten tonight," Sarge had said. "Wear old work clothes, heavy boots, stuff you're not afraid of getting dirty."

"Where we going, Sarge?" John had asked.

"You'll find out. I don't want to spoil the surprise," Sarge had said, tension in his voice. "And bring a couple of good strong shovels, will ya, please, John?" He didn't wait for John to reply before he said, "Thanks."

John had moaned, just like he did when he was on his feet walking too long. Sweat beaded down his forehead.

Where we are going? At ten at night?

By the time John had gathered his remaining turtles, minus the now-dead Barney, and placed them in their little blue plastic wading pools sitting on his front lawn, he had decided.

Gotta break into the vet's office and get pain meds.

"How are the turtles today, John?" his ninety-year-old neighbor Henry asked as he passed by again, slowly pushing his walker on his hour-long tour of the block.

Slowly I turned, step by step, inch by inch...

"Fine, Henry," John answered, looking at the dirty green pool water. *Gotta change the water.* "How are you feeling this morning?"

"Looks like a little rain today," Henry said. "Doesn't it? Bet your turtles won't mind a little rain, will they?"

Good grief.

Turtles bothered by rain?

"No. They won't mind. Have a great day, Henry." John watched Henry shuffle past. "Where's your face mask, Henry?" He added, noting that Henry was not wearing one. But Henry didn't turn around to reply.

Must be really hard of hearing.

John scratched his butt and let out a little moan.

Sarge had given John important tasks. He didn't want to screw them up. The last thing he wanted to do was lose

185

this job. Being a PI was the best thing that ever happened to him; and he didn't want to go back to his previous job. He shivered when he imagined the smell of those Porta Potties.

Some things you never forget.

Or some smells.

John realized that people in his office might laugh at him; after all, everyone else knew that Bob Hope was long dead. John had heard snickering. All he wanted was to impress people by doing a good job. He didn't want anyone laughing at him behind his back. The thought infuriated him.

Ramsay's family was first on the list. Brad Marshall's mother, Mary, had died almost twenty years ago; John could scratch her off the list. Tracking Brad Marshall's whereabouts was easy. First, John placed a GPS tracker on his Tesla Model S performance car. He shook his head when he checked to find that the base price on the Tesla Model S started at $120,000.

One of the only places Brad went to was his private country club, in San Jose, to play golf. After golf, he'd do whiskey shots, then speed home, weaving in and out of traffic but never getting pulled over by police. Or he'd drive to Reno, often exceeding one hundred miles per hour on the drive, to visit one of his favorite casinos. Occasionally, he'd hop a flight out of San Jose and jet to Vegas to gamble. Once every two weeks, instead of taking the drive to Reno or jet to Vegas, he'd take a shorter drive to one of the many local Native American casinos that dotted the Bay Area. All Brad did was drink, play golf, drink some more, and gamble. He usually lost.

Not a good gambler.

Last week, John had followed Brad when he drove to Ramsay's widow's house, Jojo, Ramsay's third wife. He'd emerged from his car, after checking his Gavin Newsom haircut and his big-toothed smile in the rear-view mirror. Brad had been wearing a nice navy-blue suit and maroon tie, and he was carrying a briefcase.

Ahh, nice guy.

Guess he's going over estate settlement stuff with the grieving widow.

On the way back from Jojo's house, Brad had stopped at the drive-in window at Starbucks, where twenty-five cars waited in line ahead of him.

Still not letting people inside.

Sarge had received the phone records on Ramsay's cell phone courtesy of Sophia, Ramsay's daughter. The phone records would be of help in tracking Ramsay's whereabouts, his contacts, and his conversations during the last days of his life. It was John's job to find out all he could about the phone records.

The day before Ramsay died, he had made several calls to a Tahoe-based escort company named "Poker-In-The-Rear".

Perhaps that explained the mystery woman who was on his boat?

"I'm in the Tahoe area today," John said when he called the number. He was really at his home in Tracy. "And I'm looking for some company." Trying a different tack.

"We offer companionship only," a female answered in a nasally voice.

"I'm not a cop."

"We still offer companionship only." A bored nasally voice.

"Well, I'm looking for a specific girl."

Silence.

"A friend of mine was in Tahoe a couple of weeks ago. Met this girl from your service. She met him on his boat. On the lake, if that rings a bell?"

"All our girls are over eighteen."

"My friend said that she was a splendid companion. I'd like to book her if I can."

I wonder if female companions wear face masks these days?

"Hey, I'm just the messenger here. All I do is forward your contact info to our girls. After that, I have no idea where they go. They are all adults."

"Don't you keep records?"

"Records?"

"Yes, records. You know—who goes where? With whom."

"You're shitting me. Aren't you?"

"I'd like to find this specific girl, if I can."

"Wouldn't we all, Mac," the woman said. The line went dead.

Dead end. Can't even get laid from an escort service. Good grief. Reminds me when Chastity, that hooker, took my money and skedaddled.

"Ms. Petula!" John yelled, watching his turtles in the little blue plastic pools. "Stop that! What are you doing? Gertrude! You stop that too!"

John's turtles were rather lethargic this morning. He wondered if they might be sick; after losing Barney, he didn't want to take any chances.

Can turtles get coronavirus?

But the turtles quickly snapped out of their lethargy when Ms. Petula mounted Gertrude from behind.

"You're both girl turtles. What the fuck?"

Clyde and Heathcliff were in the same pool as the two female turtles. Pretty soon they were going at it.

Girl turtles having sex with girl turtles? Boy turtles having sex with boy turtles?

"Come on, you guys. Cut it out. What if the neighbors see you?"

The turtles made little barking sounds, like week-old puppies chirping for mama.

That's enough.

John reached into the pool to grab Ms. Petula. She snapped, nearly catching his finger in her jaws.

"Ms. Petula!"

Horny little fucker. I wonder if Rocky's turtles act like this.

John had once seen a recent picture of Sylvester Stallone standing next to the two turtles that were in the original *Rocky* movie, filmed in 1976. The turtles were still alive forty years later. If having turtles as pets was good enough for Rocky, then it was good enough for John. But for now, John had had enough. He took his garden hose, turning it on full blast. Still, it took a while for his snapping turtles to stop their screwing.

After John had cleaned up, put his turtles back in their tanks, where they then appeared to be sleeping it off, he felt his rectum flare back up, so he gave himself a good scratch and let out another moan.

In his opinion, this was a wild goose chase. John believed that Ramsay, who'd had three previous heart attacks, had died from the fourth one.

How many heart attacks does it take to kill an old dude?

He made a mental note to Google the answer.

Next on John's list was Brad's wife, Aiko. She owned a sushi restaurant in San Jose named "Fuk Mi Sushi Bar".

Am I lost in an Austin Powers movie?

Since restaurants had reopened after the pandemic, there had been many changes in the industry. Some restaurants, in conjunction with city officials, were allowed to provide outdoor dining. Suzie's restaurant fell into this category. To appear more crowded, and to adhere to social distancing guidelines, Suzie placed cardboard mannequins at every other table. At one table, there'd be a young cardboard couple laughing while they shared a drink. Two tables over, a cardboard family, complete with two cardboard kids playing a video game, sat at a larger table. All of her mannequins looked like Asians.

Asian cardboard mannequins?

The Fuk Mi Sushi Bar was struggling. Through his digging, John had found out that Suzie was months behind on her rent. On top of that, several food supply companies had taken her to small claims court for nonpayment of supplies. She had laid off more than half of her staff.

Suzie didn't work at her restaurant around the clock; she spent much of her time at her parents' house in San Jose. Both of her parents were alive, healthy, and in their seventies. Checking the property tax rolls, which were public domain, John had found out that Suzie's paternal grandparents had previously owned the house.

Passed down from generation to generation.

Suzie's grandmother, now ninety-five, lived at the house, but Suzie's grandfather had passed years ago.

Doesn't look like Brad and Suzie spend a lot of time together. Shit, if she was my wife, I wouldn't let her out of my sight. She's a looker.

Business enemies? Shit. Ramsay had plenty of those; he had been a ruthless business owner. He'd stiffed contractors, painters, roofers, and handymen who hadn't had the resources to take him to court. One termite extermination company had threatened to dump "a truckload" of termites on Ramsay's personal home when Ramsay had refused to pay the contracted amount for tenting the mobile home park's community center, which was made of plywood, a termite breeding ground.

"Check this guy out, John," Sarge had instructed, giving him a name. He was referring to Arnold Schuck, the owner of Pavers-R-Us, a company that specialized in brick paver systems for residential homes. Wanting his prized garden to look even better, Ramsay had contracted Pavers-R-Us to install a decorative paver retaining wall in his yard. But true to form, Ramsay had claimed that the installed pavers were not to his specs. Then he paid a less-than-contracted price to the enraged

Mister Schuck. Schuck had returned to Ramsay's house, digging up and removing the pavers, and when Ramsay had complained, Schuck had threatened Ramsay with his shovel. The following month, with Schuck sneaking in at night, more pavers in Ramsay's yard had disappeared. On more than one occasion, Schuck had knocked on Ramsay's door, demanding payment and threatening Ramsay with bodily harm if he didn't pay up.

"Sure thing, Sarge," John had answered. "How'd you find out about this?"

"It was in the papers a couple of years ago. And get this—last time he threatened Ramsay, he showed up brandishing a tire iron."

"Okay, Sarge."

When a tenant moved out of their mobile home at the park, Ramsay had cited some silly excuse, like "you damaged my hardscape" to refuse to return their security deposit. To get it back, that tenant then had to take Ramsay to small claims court. It was standard operating procedure for him.

Each year, Ramsay shorted the City of San Jose its normal mandated transfer fees and taxes.

The list of people that Ramsay had cheated out of money went on and on, but John knew exactly what Sarge would say about that.

Did anybody else threaten him? If so, who? Get me some proof, will ya?

John's favorite person to follow was Ramsay's widow, Jojo. Less than half his age and a bottle blond, Ramsay had met her when she was working at 'Bottoms-Up Espresso,' where she worked as a bikini barista, parading around in a caramel-coffee-colored thong bikini, bending over in front of customers while steaming fat-free milk for an all-male clientele. Bottoms-Up, however, had remained in business for only six months before city officials yanked their business license, citing that the bikini-clad female baristas were providing "additional" services.

Ramsay didn't like his new wife showing off her new boobs, which he had paid for, to anyone other than him— but especially not to strange, coffee-guzzling men, so off he whisked her before the city shut the place down.

Jojo was busy grieving Ramsay's death. Everyone grieves differently. Once a month, Jojo had a bikini wax, and twice a month, she hit the tanning salon. Every two weeks, she got her nails done. Five mornings a week, precisely at ten, she was at the gym working with her personal trainer, who took extra care to make sure that none of the exercises Jojo performed made Jojo sweat.

Taking care of her hair was number one on Jojo's grief recovery list. Born with mousy brown hair, she made regular salon visits to maintain her perfect blond locks. Her favorite stylist had moved from California to Arizona. Jojo had not been in Tahoe when Ramsay died; she was in Arizona getting her hair done.

Jojo didn't seem to be the kind of woman, at least in John's mind, who'd sit around eating bonbons all day, waiting for her hubby to come home. Maybe that was why she'd been certified as a Peloton riding instructor. Or maybe it was because of the way she filled out her bicycle shorts.

Lastly, John had to figure out whether Jojo believed she should have received more money from Ramsay's estate. She was slated to inherit one million dollars in a lump sum payment. Most might consider that a fair settlement for over three years of marriage. But did Jojo believe that?

Based on all the money she'd spent while John was tracking her daily activities, he reasoned that she'd need a lot more money than a measly one million dollars.

By the end of the day, John was soaking comfortably in a warm bubble bath. His hemorrhoids had gotten the best of him.

Ahhhh . . . Wish I could soak all day long.

Like my turtles do.

He was excited to see the strippers at the "masks on, clothes off" gentlemen's club at next Thursday night's TikTok competition. He glanced at his schedule. If his butt felt better, he'd be able to go.

Sunday night, I'll go to the vet's office.

Get me some of those animal pain meds.

His butt felt better just thinking about it.

Maybe for once I might get lucky?

Part three

**"You don't get to tell me what to do. You are not
my dog."**

1.

"Zeus! Heel!"

Though she had a pronged choke chain around his neck, it took all the strength in Dakota's Schwarzeneggerian arms to control her massive dog.

Like trying to teach a hippo to walk by your side.

Zeus sat. He turned his massive head towards Dakota and stuck out his huge tongue, dribbling dog slop.

Good grief.

It took strength, discipline, and determination to train any dog, let alone one as massive as Zeus. You had to show the dog who was in charge. Zeus thought that he was in charge, and his was not an easy mind to change. A couple of sharp yanks on the choke chain sometimes got Zeus's attention if the prongs dug deep enough, but when that didn't work Dakota had to use all of her strength to upend Zeus. Then she'd place her knee on his neck, cutting off his air supply until she got his attention.

It was cool this morning in San Ramon, California. Dakota, gliding along on rollerblades, was cruising the Iron Horse trail, a popular thoroughfare running north to south for twenty miles, or the entire length of Contra Costa County in the East Bay. Her dark hair was pulled back in a bun, and she wore no makeup. A baggy blue sweatshirt hid her muscles and tattoos. Air Pods in, "Copacabana" by Barry Manilow blasted in her ears.

The trail was crowded, many riding bikes, most wearing face masks. Dakota was amazed at the number of cyclists who were overweight.

Fast food nation.

The pandemic had brought many changes to modern day life; one of which was that many people now rode bikes. After the shelter-in-place orders were eased, bike sales quadrupled. People drove cars less often, and most worked from their homes, so the need to drive to the office had all but disappeared overnight. Peddling a bike became the preferred way to exercise, to travel, to get outside for fresh air.

Except that this morning, there were hundreds of cyclists out and about, which made it difficult for Dakota and Zeus to get out of the bicyclists' way. Bike bells rang. Zeus didn't move out of their way, so they had to weave around Dakota and her massive dog. Several young men riding by gave whistled at Dakota.

When she stopped for a moment to read a text, Zeus's massive wiener suddenly protruded, the lipstick phenomenon. Zeus jerked on the chain and ran to the side of the trail, pulling Dakota behind like a rag doll. Furiously, he started humping a tree trunk. The bottom of the trunk was covered in green leaves.

"Jesus fucking Christ, Zeus!" Dakota yelled, pulling on the dog's choke chain. "I hope for your sake that's not poison oak you're humping! And that bush has thorns, for God's sake."

Two small women wearing face masks rang their bike bells to let Dakota know they were trying to weave around her and her horny, tree-humping dog. She pulled her headphones off.

Ring ring. Ring ring.

"Ba dag," one woman said. "*Huai gou.*"

Oriental.

"Ba dag!" the woman repeated.

"Sorry about that," the other woman said. "My mother doesn't like dogs. And her English is a bit rough."

"Ahhh."

"*Huai gou!*' the older woman repeated as she rang her bike bell again, peddling on.

Though Dakota didn't believe in neutering dogs, she thought maybe she should make an exception for Zeus.

Zeus tried to hump everything.

And that smell?

Time to give the big guy a bath.

Dakota turned from Zeus, slung his leash over her shoulder, and like a powerful weightlifter pulling a car, she managed to get her dog to disengage from the tree.

I'm tiring of this.

Earlier that morning, she had spoken with Sarge.

"You were able to break into all of their computers?" he had asked.

"Piece of cake," Dakota had begun. "Sent them several emails on topics I thought they might be interested in. Each had an attachment or a link. When they clicked on the link or opened the attachment, my little worm went to work."

"What have you found out?"

"Getting into Brad's computer was the easiest. I just sent him stuff with naked women attached. He clicked on all of them."

"Really?" Sarge had said. "That easy, huh?"

"Yep. His browser history was just about what you'd expect. Visits PornHub every day, plus he has accounts with online gambling sites. Loses a lot of money. He just bought a book from Amazon Get this—it's a book about how to win money at roulette."

"Didn't know you could do that. I mean, it's a spinning wheel with thirty-six numbers on it and a little ball. Completely random."

"Well, don't tell Brad Marshall that. He thinks there's a system to beat the wheel."

"Really? Stupid. Winning at roulette is dumb luck."

"Yes, it is."

Sarge didn't seem grumpy this morning.

"And get this, boss. Each month, his bank account gets a direct deposit for fifteen thousand dollars from his trust fund. By the end of each month, the account is empty. Spends it all. Like clockwork, every month. His credit cards are maxed out."

"How many cards does he have?" Sarge had asked.

"Like ten of them," Dakota had replied. "Several casinos contact him daily. Best I can tell, he owes them close to five hundred thousand dollars."

"What Sophia told us is true."

"Yep. He's a gambling addict. In debt. Has no savings. Doesn't have a penny to his name. Stands to inherit half of Ramsay's fortune. Plenty of reasons to off the old man. One other thing about him."

"What's that?" Sarge had asked.

"He's ordered just about every male penis enhancement product that's out there."

"Jeez. Really?"

"Yep. He's tried them all. And you should see this guy primp around the house, boss."

"How are you able to do that?"

Sarge is in a good mood. Hyper, though. Must have had an entire pot of coffee today. I guess nothing bad has happened to his car lately.

"I control the camera on his computer. I watch him. You should see it, Sarge. His movements are so deliberate; he rehearses them. And that toothy smile. He watches himself in the mirror, like he's performing in front of an audience."

An image had flashed in Dakota's mind. She pictured the old Walt Disney Chip and Dale chipmunk cartoons, both of the little animals with their toothy smiles.

"Brad's wife, Suzie's browsing history is also interesting."

"How so?" Sarge had asked.

"Last night she was researching Gambian rats."

"Gambian pouched rats?"

"Yeah. Giant rats. Mostly found in Africa. Some can grow to three feet long."

"Yuck. A rat the size of a golden retriever. Why would she do that?"

"Well, this is a kick. Rats live off of what we throw away in garbage dumps. They pitch their tents near restaurants, where, before the pandemic, leftover food went into the dumpster. Now get this. Since many of these restaurants are closed, the rat's food supply has been cut off. So, they've become more aggressive. They attack people, looking for food. Turns out that there's a rat family living out behind Suzie's sushi restaurant in San Jose. I checked out her restaurant. My guess is that she's got a rodent problem, and now she's researching how to get rid of the little fuckers."

"Jeez. Giant rats that attack people? Sounds like a movie from the 1950s. You know, giant mutant rats terrorize the town of Topeka, Kansas. Or something like that. If it were me, I'd shoot them."

"Well, I think she's looking into something a little less violent. Like finding the best way to kill them off."

"Poison will do the trick. Anything else?"

"Here's the best part. Does the name 'Nakatomi' mean anything to you?" Dakota asked.

Sarge thought. "Isn't that the last name of the family who lost their land to Warren Ramsay during World War II? Weren't they sent to an internment camp somewhere?"

"Bingo. They had a one-hundred-and-fifty-acre orange orchard taken out from under them because they were Japanese American at the wrong time in our history," Dakota said. "They were sent to a camp in Lodi, California, where they stayed until the war ended. Hundreds of other Japanese Americans had their lands confiscated, too. In John Nakatomi's case, he sold the land to Warren Ramsay, Brad's grandfather, for a song. Warren used that land to start the mobile home park."

"The same park that Brad and Sophia stand to inherit today."

"The one and the same," Dakota said. "Brad's wife's legal name is Aiko Tanaka Marshall. And she goes by Suzie. But guess what? Tanaka is her father's family name. Wanna take a stab at what her mother's family name is?"

"Nakatomi?" Sarge asked, half-heartedly.

"Bingo."

"You mean . . ."

"Suzie's mother's maiden name is Nakatomi. She's the daughter of John Nakatomi. And follow this: John's wife, whose first name is Aima, Suzie's maternal grandmother, is alive and well. Ninety-five years old and she lives with Suzie's parents in that little family house in San Jose."

Silence crisscrossed wireless phone lines.

"Well," Sarge finally said. "What a coincidence. And this woman married into the Marshall family."

"Yep."

"I don't believe in coincidences."

"Neither do I, Sarge," Dakota said. "Neither do I."

2.

"Great work, Dakota!" Sarge had slapped the desk.

Dakota thought.

Let's see. Suzie married Brad Marshall. Her grandparents had fifty acres of prime land in San Jose, California stolen from them. Suzie must have deliberately married Brad, knowing who he is. To get revenge for her family? To somehow get their family's land back? After such multigenerational treatment, it makes sense. It would take years to get their proper revenge. How? First, the old man had to die. Then Brad would have to die, too, right? But first, Suzie would have to make sure that her family trust was written in such a way that she'd inherit Brad's full share, rather than it all going to Sophia. The land would then pass back to Suzie. And then back to her family. Well, one half of the land, anyway. Sophia would inherit the other half.

Fits like a glove.

Fits better than that glove fit O. J. Simpson.

"Thanks, boss," she said, finally.

I wonder if Sarge came to the same conclusion.

"I sincerely hope that you don't break into my computer," Sarge said, jokingly. "Hate to think what you might find there."

"I'd never do that, Sarge. Never came to mind."

But, of course, she had thought of it. She had already broken into Sarge's Mac desktop and his iPad. She'd broken into Sharkie's computers as well.

Palmer Doyle's browsing history was what you might expect from a fifty-nine-year-old widower.

He had joined online dating sites, like Match.com and eHarmony, but he'd never filled out his personal profile, so none of the ladies could find him.

Sounds like he's not quite ready to date.

He'd also looked at several dog rescue sites.

Perhaps looking to get a companion for Buddy?

I thought Malinois were supposed to be smart?

He'd visited plenty of sites about the best places to fish in the Sierra Nevada mountain range. He'd looked at fishing poles, fancy reels, fly-fishing reels, the best bait to use, the correct tackle and hook size, and so on. And he'd liked to look at real estate sites like Zillow and realtor.com, searching for homes and cabins in mountain towns like Angels Camp, Sonora, and Pioneer in Northern California.

Thinking of moving, maybe.

And he'd searched numerous times for anger management programs, seminars, and books by the most popular self-help authors.

Why is he so angry? He didn't seem angry. Grumpy, sure. Always has an edge. But angry? No. But maybe he's angry about Becky dying?

Poor Sarge, Dakota thought. She knew that Sarge and her deceased father, Corporal James Thompson, had served in the army in Afghanistan together. She also had guessed that before her father had died, Sarge had promised him he'd watch over her.

Some kind of warrior's creed bullshit. Or Band of Brothers *crap.*

She reasoned Sarge had hired her to monitor her. For that, she felt grateful. He treated her like a daughter.

She was often protective of him as well.

"You need to wear your face mask, Sarge," she'd often told him when the pandemic was at its peak. He often forgot to wear one.

"Yeah, I know," he'd say.

"Not only does it protect you from getting covid," she'd explain time and time again, as if talking to a child. "But it protects all those around you, as well. And you know that I don't have to tell you how important it is for older people to mask up."

"Sorry, Dakota. You're right," he'd admit.

But Dakota didn't need anyone watching over her. She'd made sure of that by becoming just about the strongest female on the face of the planet. Three-hour workouts, twice daily, seven days a week, over a six-year period will do just that.

Her father had been killed in Afghanistan when Dakota was thirteen years old. She had never known her birth mother, who, according to her dad, had left both of them when Dakota was an infant. Finding out who she was, and whether she was still alive, was at the top of her agenda.

Corporal Thompson and Dakota had bounced around from army base to army base, and they'd been living in Fort Dix, New Jersey at the time of his death. One of her father's superior officers, a Lieutenant Bill Jenkins, had befriended her, helping her deal with the loss of her father.

As soon as her female curves had filled in, Lieutenant Jenkins had raped her one night when soused on bourbon.

She thought of it all now—the emotional pain in the aftermath of that assault, the humiliation it had caused her, how this man had violated her against her will, how he'd driven her to get stronger than any person alive.

For a couple of years after, she'd had trouble shaking the depression.

Shit like that will never happen to me again.

After her father had died, Dakota wanted to find her birth mother. That became an obsession, which fueled her interest in genealogy. The advances in the genealogy field were astonishing. By submitting her own DNA sample, she hoped to find her mom, or at least find a sibling or a close relative of her mother's. What if her mother had given birth again after having Dakota? Perhaps Dakota had a brother or sister.

As for Lieutenant Bill Jenkins, years later, when Dakota was an adult, she had tracked him down. He'd retired from the service and was living in a condo in Myrtle Beach, South Carolina. His jaw had hit the floor when he opened his front door to find a buffed-out Dakota Johnson grinning at him with a smile that didn't reach her eyes.

She overpowered him, hog-tying him to his bed. She cut off his genitals, then stuffed them in his mouth, duct taping his mouth shut.

"How does that feel? Fucker."

Then she left.

3.

Sharkie's computers contained nothing that Dakota hadn't already expected. He was a strange one with odd hobbies. His browsing history contained searches for different reptile species. He kept snapping turtles as household pets, but he also considered purchasing other reptiles: snakes, lizards, iguanas, geckos, and rainbow lizards. He bid on the reptiles on websites, but he never actually bought any other reptiles besides turtles.

Another popular search of his was "How to make money like dead celebrities do". Apparently, Elvis Presley's estate had made over thirty million dollars in 2019, and Michael Jackson's had made twenty million.

Still studying dead celebrities, I see.

In the last two weeks, he had tried unsuccessfully to purchase pain killers online, Vicodin mainly.

Jojo Marshall, Ramsay's widow, had even more revealing browsing history. Easy-peasy getting into her computer, since she routinely clicked on any email that contained info on beauty products, such as exfoliation methods, Botox injections, and how to get an apple-shaped booty.

"And get this, Sarge," she had said to Palmer. "She's got profiles on sites like cougar.com and adultfriendfinder.com."

"The grieving widow," Sarge had said sarcastically.

"She's sent emails to her stepson Brad." Dakota hung air quotes on the word "stepson".

"Isn't he older than her?"

"Yep. The emails are kind of flirty in nature, though she doesn't come right out and say, 'come fuck me right now' or anything like that."

"What does she say?"

"Stuff like 'I need a favor' or 'could you stop by, Brad, when you get a chance, please'. Stuff like that."

"I see," Sarge had said. "What else?"

"The week after Ramsay died, she started Googling sites on how to contest a living trust."

"Ah."

"She clicked on different lawyers' websites. Turns out, you *can* contest a living trust."

"I didn't know that."

"You can, Sarge. A trust can be dragged into court by the trustee, the beneficiaries, or by someone disinherited under the trust. The most commonly used grounds to invalidate or challenge a trust?"

"What?" Sarge had asked.

"Lack of capacity, fraud, or some problem with how the document was signed, or enforced."

"So, I guess a lump sum payment of one million dollars is not enough money for our former bikini barista turned trophy wife."

"Could be."

Might be a motive.

"You know, Sarge, none of what I do on this case is illegal."

"Do tell?"

"I'm a certified, ethical hacker."

"Is there such a thing?"

"Sure as shit. I'm a certified hacker. Banks, insurance companies, and other specialized entities use them all the time. People hack into systems, many from Europe, Russia, or Africa, to break in and steal important info," Dakota had said, remembering headlines of past years when millions of people's private information had been compromised. "Companies need to know who broke into their supposedly secure systems. That's what a certified hacker does. We find out who breaks in. Then we fix the problem—stick our finger into the dike to stop the leak, so to speak."

"Never thought of it that way," Sarge had answered. "Makes sense How about Sophia and her stepfather, Martin?"

"Martin was a builder back in Germany. Built high-density housing in the Stuttgart suburbs. Two- and three-story homes on small lots. That way, the builder can cram a lot of houses into a smaller space, making more money. Turns out, he's been looking at the building codes and land planning practices here in California."

"Interesting. Know why?" Palmer had asked.

"Dunno, Sarge," Dakota had said. "I'll find out more. He's been researching several sites on cancer cures, alternative healing methods, shit like that." Dakota remembered how frail Martin had looked last week. "But I had trouble getting into Sophia's stuff. She's computer savvy. She didn't click on any emails with attachments. Had to worm my way into her computer by creating a remote new user account."

"Ahh."

He doesn't know what that is.

"She's been looking at a lot of info about coronavirus."

"She's a nurse."

"Yes. Normal that she'd research the virus. But she hasn't been looking at any sites with cancer info."

"What do you make of that?"

"Dunno, Sarge," Dakota had said again. "On one hand, you'd think that because her stepfather is sick, she'd be researching those sites, educating herself. But she may have been watching over his Martin's shoulder while he was looking at his computer. I don't know."

Palmer remained quiet.

"Turns out that she's not much of a computer user anyway, Sarge. She doesn't spend much time on it."

4.

As Dakota and Zeus finished their walk, Zeus took off towards a garbage can near the side of the trail. Even using all of her strength, Dakota couldn't slow Zeus down. Zeus mounted the garbage can, wiener out again in full-lipstick mode.

"Fuck!" Dakota screamed. "Now stop that!"

Twice in one hour?

"C'mon, boy. Give me a break. Will ya?"

Ring ring! Ring ring!

The two Chinese women on their bikes . . .

The garbage can was no match for Zeus. Zeus, frenzied, knocked over the can, then tumbled alongside it on the ground, resulting in a loud clang. Unluckily for Dakota, the can, filled to the brim with garbage, spewed over the ground. A breeze picked up paper scraps and flung it around the trail.

"Zeus! Heel! Stop that this instant." Dakota reared back and slapped the dog hard on his massive head. Zeus wouldn't break stride, Dakota's hand throbbing from the impact.

"*Ba dag! Huai gou!*" yelled the older Chinese woman.

"I'm so sorry," Dakota said, rubbing her hand.

That's it. I've had enough.

When Zeus finished his business with the garbage can, he took off, with three quick steps in one direction, before shooting off the other way, then zigzagging back the opposite direction. Dakota noticed the floppy smile on his face.

"He's got the Zoomies," she explained to the women. She felt an urge to light a cigarette.

"Zoomies?"

"Yeah, you know. He's a puppy. Only two years old. Has lots of energy. He zooms this way, then zooms that way. You know, the zoomies." With that, Dakota extended her arm forward and air whistled, feigning speed.

The older Chinese woman shook her head.

The younger one asked, "Have you tried accumpumsure?"

"Excuse me?"

"You know." She looked skyward, searching for the right word in English. "accumpumsure." With that, she mimicked sticking something sharp in her arm.

"Acupuncture?" Dakota asked.

"Yes. Fo dog."

Acupuncture for dogs? Stick Zeus with dozens of needles? How could you possibly get a dog to stay still for that?

"For what purpose?" Dakota asks.

"To help with his soosies." With that, the younger Chinese woman extended her arm forward and air whistled, feigning speed just as Dakota had. The older woman shook her head in agreement.

"Think I'll pass." Dakota offered a measly smile. "But thanks for the idea."

The two women peddled away, waving as they went.

Zeus squatted and dropped an enormous poop, the size of a rhino's droppings, in the middle of the trail. He zoomed off again. When he finally stopped, he sat back on his hind legs by the side of the trail and dragged his butt along the ground, as if using the ground as toilet paper. When Zeus finished, another smile plastered on his face, he bounced to the side in a shuffle, almost as if he were dancing to fiddle music.

That's it. Tomorrow I'm calling the vet. Time to get Zeus's balls cut off.

Thankfully, the urge to smoke a cigarette had passed.

5.

"You drive like a fuckin' old lady."

"Shut up, John," Palmer said, a scowl on his face. He sported a three-day-old beard.

They were in Palmer's beater pickup truck driving west on Highway 24 near Walnut Creek. At midnight, the roads were nearly empty.

In six hours, this freeway will be gridlocked.

"Well, it's true. The speed limit is fifty-five here, and you're doing fifty. Barely."

In the past few weeks, his car had needed a new bumper, new tires, and a new windshield. Thanks to a lousy driver with no car insurance, nails on the roads, and gravel rocks that had bounced merrily like marbles from the back of a truck.

You bet I'm being careful.

Up ahead a car was weaving, barely staying in its lane. Palmer changed lanes, giving the car a wide berth when he passed.

"Is that a woman wearing a burka?" Palmer asked John, looking over as he passed the car. "She's from somewhere in the Middle East?"

"Yep. Texting," John answered. "The burka counts as a face covering, Sarge." John pointed to the same green turtle-print face mask he always wore. "You should wear yours."

"People are idiots," Palmer said, irritated. "What's the matter with people these days? And I will not wear a face mask. Had my vaccinations."

He remembered how Dakota, just recently, had called him and "old person". Then she'd stressed to him how important it was for old people to mask up. Though it was true, Palmer had taken offense at being called "old".

"Better safe than sorry. You know that. You know what happened to Trump. He caught the Covid bug."

"Got over it quick though."

"Where are we going, Sarge?" John asked, peering into the back of the pickup. "What's that? A medical stretcher?"

Palmer looked straight ahead.

"And why are you so grumpy?" John pestered.

Palmer knew better than that; wearing face masks slowed the spread of Covid. Everyone knew that. Since the COVID-19 vaccine had become available in sufficient quantities to end the pandemic, wearing a face mask was no longer deemed mandatory. In a world with eight billion people in it, the challenge was producing enough doses. That took time. Palmer had grown tired of wearing a face mask. To Palmer, all he needed to do to stay safe from the virus was to use common sense, mainly avoiding indoor crowded places where the virus spread like wildfire. Plus, wearing his face mask made his nose itch. He couldn't stop sneezing when his mask was on.

"We need to pick up something heavy," Palmer explained. "And I'm not grumpy. Idiot drivers. Imagine that. In the middle of the night. Texting on their phone."

Loaded in the back, beside the stretcher, were a pickax, two large shovels, and a large black garbage bag. Buddy, leashed in the back of the truck, stuck his nose up and sniffed.

"Where are we going, Sarge?" John asked again, this time with a bit more squeak in his voice. "And why are you running this like a military operation?" John stared at Palmer's large, flat nose.

"Maybe because I'm a retired army staff sergeant."

"Funny, Sarge. Why is Buddy here?"

"He's a good watchdog."

"What do we need a watchdog for?"

"We're almost there," Palmer said as he exited the freeway at the Orinda exit. "And what are you looking at, John?"

"Nothing, boss," John replied, but he was thinking about boxing great Mike Tyson's famous line while looking at Palmer's enormous nose.

Everyone has a plan until they get punched on the nose.

Before he picked up John, Palmer had taken the time to stretch his left arm, which hurt like hell. He also took a Tramadol, but that didn't help with the pain. Palmer Doyle felt grumpy.

Gonna need the arm tonight.

Palmer didn't trust John; there was something about him that just didn't sit well with him. He was always looking for the easy way out, taking too many shortcuts. Something just wasn't right. Those shark teeth only worsened his appearance that already made Palmer shudder. John was addicted to painkillers; he just didn't think anyone knew about it. If it weren't for the promise that Palmer had made to his dead wife, Becky, to take care of her younger brother, Palmer would have let Sharkie go eons ago.

216

Then a car driving close to one hundred miles per hour zoomed past Palmer's pickup.

"What the fuck?" Palmer screamed. "What the fuck is the matter with people? You see that John?" *Crazy drivers on the roads these days.*

"What's the problem?" John asked. "Probably late for work."

"At midnight?"

"Night job, maybe?"

"But driving one hundred miles per hour?"

"So?"

Palmer couldn't believe that Sharkie did not see an issue with driving that fast on the freeway when the posted speed limit was fifty-five miles per hour.

Another car zoomed past, also driving around one hundred miles per hour.

"The freeways are full of crazies," John said. "God, I hate the freeways. Either you're stuck in gridlock or people are whizzing by you like you are standing still."

The new normal for driving on freeways in the Bay Area.

Driving up Charles Hill in Orinda near the Caldecott Tunnel, Palmer shifted into low gear. He parked in a dirt parking lot near the top of the hill and turned off his headlights, but not before John caught sight of the "Queen of Heaven" cemetery entrance gate.

"What are we doing here, Sarge?" he asked.

"Grab the shovels, John. Put them on the stretcher. Give me a hand with this stuff, will ya?"

"I've got a bad feeling about this."

It was past midnight. The sky was clear except for a crescent moon, which dimly lit the cemetery's entrance. A breeze whistled through the trees.

"This is fuckin' creepy."

Palmer unleashed Buddy, who immediately jumped from the truck, ran to a nearby tree, sniffed for a moment, then lifted his leg.

Palmer could almost see the tiny mouse running on the treadmill in John's mind, turning the wheels, albeit slowly.

"You hear something?"

"Just the wind, John."

"Oh, no!" John shrieked. "Fuckin' no!"

"What? Come on. Let's get moving."

"We're going to dig up the old dead guy, aren't we?" John asked.

"Maybe."

"What the fuck for?"

"To do an autopsy."

"Autopsy a dead guy who's already buried? What the fuck are you talking about, Sarge?" John was nearly in tears. "It's illegal to exhume a body. You have to have the family's permission. Do you?"

"Sort of," Palmer said.

"Sort of?" John shrieked. "What the fuck does that mean?"

"Well, half of the family gave me the go ahead."

"Let me guess," John said. "Sophia's half."

"Something like that. Ramsay's been in the ground for two weeks. Perfectly okay, medically speaking, to perform an autopsy after that amount of time." Palmer quickly walked towards the locked gate entrance and disabled the security camera. Buddy stuck to his side like glue.

When Ramsay died, Brad had chosen not to have an autopsy. As the executor of his father's estate, it was his prerogative. An autopsy was almost always performed for an unusual or sudden death, such as Ramsay's case. Since Sophia believed that Brad or someone else might have had something to do with Ramsay's death, Palmer thought an autopsy must be done.

"Bad luck, Sarge. This is bad luck." John shook his head. "Five years of bad luck. That's what I'm gonna have." He continued to shake his head while pacing back and forth, legs spread wide. "And did you know that today is Friday the fuckin' thirteenth?" His pace quickened.

Palmer watched him stride back and forth.

He's moving funny.

Palmer made a note not to get too close to him.

Probably smells awful.

"I don't want to do this, Sarge," John complained again.

"Embrace the suck, John," Palmer said. "Embrace the suck."

"Embrace the suck?" John screamed. "What the fuck does that mean?"

"Army slang."

"Army slang? You haven't been in the army for fifteen years. What the fuck?"

They walked through the cemetery, carrying the stretcher loaded with the pickax, shovels, a toolkit with a couple of rolls of duct tape inside, and the black bag.

"Must not step on any of the graves," John said, weaving his way around headstones. "Must not. Bad luck. Bad juju."

Palmer could tell John was in a bit of discomfort, walking with his legs spread wide, letting out a little whimper now and then.

"I can't do this, Sarge. I can't," John pleaded.

"What a beautiful night," Palmer said, looking at the dark silhouette of the hills ahead and the twinkling lights of the city of Orinda the other direction, down the hill. "Delightful views here. No wonder why people pay big bucks to have their loved ones buried here."

"They're fucking dead!" John yelled. "Dead! They don't give a shit about the views. They can't see them."

"Calm down, John. This won't take long. We'll be outta here in a jiff."

"I don't like this one fucking bit," John said. "Bad juju. I can't do this. I won't do this, Sarge!"

"Do you want to go back to your old job and suck the shit outta Porta Potties, John?" Palmer yelled. "Well, do ya?"

Palmer watched John's nose twitch as if he could smell the insides of those Porta Potties. Palmer raised his eyes to the heavens.

This is asking too much of me, Becky. Too much.

"If it weren't so big and flat already, I'd punch you right in the nose, Sarge."

Palmer guffawed, a big hearty laugh. "Good one, John. Down goes Frazier! Maybe I won't send you back to cleaning Porta Potties after all." Then he added, "Well?"

"Okay. Let's make it quick though."

"That's better."

It was early August. A strong, chilly breeze whistled through the trees, adding to the eerie calm of the graveyard at midnight.

Palmer remembered what Mark Twain had once said about San Francisco in the summer: *The coldest winter I ever spent was summer in San Francisco.*

Buddy gave a little yelp at the wind tail between his legs as he nestled close to Palmer.

"Some watchdog you got there, Sarge," John joked nervously.

Soon, they were in the vicinity of Marshall Ramsay's grave. The graves here were laid out facing east to west.

"I guess they can watch the sunrise and the sunset better this way," Palmer mused.

"They're fucking dead, Sarge," John repeated. "This fucking place is haunted." John took great care not to step directly on any person's grave. "Very bad juju."

"There's no such thing as ghosts, John."

"Says who?"

A moment later, they stood in front of a freshly chiseled gravestone.

Ramsay A. Marshall
9/2/1946 – 6/24/2021
Father, Husband, Philanthropist

"Philanthropist?" John squeaked. "What a bunch of shit."

"Did you want it to say 'crook and adulterer' on there instead, John?" Palmer asked. "How would that look?" He rolled his eyes, though John could barely see him. "Let's get to work."

Palmer removed red faux flowers that had been laid at the gravesite.

Both men donned gloves, turned a flashlight towards the grave, and started digging. Since the grave was freshly dug, the dirt was easy to move. Still, it didn't take long for Palmer's left arm to give out.

"I need a break," he said to John as he sat next to the grave, scowling as he rubbed his aching arm. Meanwhile, Sharkie kept digging.

Twenty minutes later, Sharkie jumped out of the hole, sat next to Palmer, and guzzled a bottle of water. "What's that?" he asked, watching a flashlight headed their way.

The light snaked its way to where Palmer and John sat. Palmer made out the shape of a huge man pushing a what looked to be a baby carriage. As the stranger walked closer, Palmer made out a ragged red beard sprinkled with white and gray. The man wore a brown bearskin coat and a boat captain's hat with a feather sticking out of the side.

He looked like a cross between Attila the Hun and Grizzly Adams.

"Well, hello Mister Doyle," the stranger said, coming to a halt as he set the brake on the baby carriage. "It's me, Jonesy."

Palmer cocked his head and tilted his good ear towards Jonesy.

"Who the fuck is Jonesy?" John asked.

Jonesy ignored the question. "And you remember my dog, Mister Peabody?"

Mister Peabody's stroller was still overflowing with stuff: dirty clothes, garbage bags filled with numerous candy wrappers, dog food in greasy plastic bags, plus one old, worn sneaker.

Buddy trotted over to the stroller. He and the German shepherd sniffed each other's rears, wagging their tails. Mister Peabody, wearing his face mask with a picture of a female dog on it, jumped out of the stroller. The two dogs ran down a hill.

"Best friends already, I see," Jonesy said.

"Who the fuck is Jonesy?" John asked again. "He reminds me of someone, Sarge, but I can't place it."

"This is an . . . acquaintance of mine, John." Palmer didn't want to explain that Jonesy was an old homeless man who had once been a superior court judge in Alameda County.

"What are you doing here, Jonesy?" Palmer asked. "How did you find us?"

"Well, I followed you here," Jonesy answered. "I figured you might need some help." Jonesy motioned towards Palmer's left arm.

Guess the old homeless guy has a car.

"If I may," Jonesy continued. "May I use your shovel, Mister Doyle?"

"Be my guest."

"Must be difficult to have all that military training and not be able to help," Jonesy said. "Well, you know. Not be able to use that bad arm."

Palmer gave Jonesy a look.

Within thirty minutes, John and Jonesy had uncovered Ramsay's coffin.

Strong old fucker.

"Toss me that crowbar, please," Jonesy asked Palmer.

A minute later, he had opened the coffin.

"What a god-awful smell!" John said, pressing his face mask down over his nose.

"Yes. Quite putrid, I'm afraid," Jonesy said. "Please pass the duct tape."

"He almost looks like he's still alive," John said.

"He hasn't liquified yet," Palmer noted. "Maybe in another month. Just bloated and discolored."

Palmer couldn't decide what smelled worse—Ramsay Marshall's corpse, Sharkie's hemorrhoids, or Jonesy's body odor.

Bugs crawled in and out of Ramsay's mouth.

"Yuck . . . that's fuckin' disgusting," John said. "Let's get this over with."

"The duct tape, please." Jonesy got to work and somehow snaked several long stretches of doubled-over duct tape under the body. "Now, gentlemen, if I could have some help, please."

Both Palmer and John jumped down to join Jonesy in the grave. Each wrapped a wad of duct tape around their hands.

Duct tape. Good for anything—apparently including exhuming dead bodies.

"Now, pull!" Jonesy sounded like someone who was used to being in charge.

Ramsay's corpse let loose a sound, like a farting noise, then Ramsay's head jerked upwards several inches.

"What the fuck?" John screamed, jumping, like Bugs Bunny in a Looney Tunes Cartoon, clear out of the grave. "Is he fucking alive? Or what? Did someone put a whoopee cushion in the bottom of that coffin?"

"Gas bloating," Palmer said.

"Normal," Jonesy said. "For a dead body."

"Well, thanks for that, Grizzly Adams," John said. His face was ashen, as if he had just seen a ghost. "Who the fuck is this guy, Sarge?"

Palmer and Jonesy looked at each other.

Both Buddy and Mister Peabody, now without his doggy face mask, had finished their wanderings and were standing on the sides of the grave, both their tails wagging. With Buddy's penchant for pooping in private, Palmer hoped he hadn't gone off and violate some poor dead person's grave.

"You been a good boy, Buddy?" Palmer asked his dog.

John emerged from the hole in the ground, and both dogs tried to sniff his butt.

"Get the fuck away from me, you mongrels," he yelled.

"Lost your face mask again, didn't you, Mister Peabody?" Jonesy said.

Thirty minutes later, with Ramsay's remains safely zipped inside the body bag and secured by duct tape to the stretcher, Palmer, John, and Jonesy were at the cemetery's entrance, where Palmer then re-armed the security cameras.

"I once told you I wanted to earn your trust, Mister Doyle," Jonesy said.

"I remember."

"So that I may become a trusted investigator on your team."

"What the fuck?" John shot a glance at Jonesy. "Yeah. Right. Like that will ever happen. Let's get the fuck outta here, Sarge. Before someone spots us."

"Who's Sarge?" Jonesy asked.

"Army name," Palmer answered.

"I understand," Jonesy said. "People called me 'Your Honor' for years."

"Your Honor?" John said. "Who the fuck is this guy, Sarge?"

"Stuff it, John. I'll explain it later." Palmer turned to the old, whitish-bearded, homeless former superior court judge. "Thanks, Jonesy. You did well. Why did you help?"

"Well, thank you, Mister Doyle." Jonesy extended a large, meaty hand out of his bearskin coat. "Why did I help? To be of service, of course. What higher purpose can a man strive for?"

"What hole did you dig this guy out of, Sarge?" John asked. "What an asshole."

Palmer said nothing.

Jonesy, still ignoring John, added, "And may God bless."

There he is again, sounding like Red Skelton.

But looking like Attila the Hun. Or Captain Ahab.

6.

When John arrived home from the cemetery, he was so wigged-out that he couldn't sleep. He felt wired, as if his entire body was plugged into a 220-volt socket.

The dead old guy farted and moved.

Creeped the hell out of him.

Bad juju.

Then and there, he decided to drive to the Tracy Animal Hospital and get pain killers. His butthole hurt.

It's the middle of the night. When would be a better time?

The Tracy Animal Hospital was an old building built in the mid-sixties. The exterior was painted olive green. John parked behind the building; no other cars were parked in the lot, except for a low rider Chevy Bel Air. Even the alarm system was ancient, as evidenced by the Acme Security Service sign posted by the front door.

I'm in a Looney Tunes cartoon, again.

This time its Wile E. Coyote.

The alarm system was so old that the equipment was located outside the building, in a small electrical box.

Imagine that. An alarm system with wires. Located outside the building, where anybody could access it.

John quickly broke into and disabled it.

There were several night lights on inside and a storage area where different animals lay caged. Most slept, but several small dogs woke at the intrusion and started yapping.

"Shhh! Be quiet," John said. "You little shits."

Better be quick.

Locked in cages were cats, two cockatoo birds, one large snake, several snapping tortoises in another cage, and one container with a small hole for air that contained two pigs. In the corner was an enormous cage that housed a massive dog.

John stopped to look at the turtles, careful not to let his hand get too close. His dead turtle pet, Barney, had drawn blood several times when John put his fingers too close.

Barney's gone.

Tearing up, John thought that he should have buried Barney at the cemetery where Ramsay Marshall was buried; that way Barney could have enjoyed those superb views. Instead, John had stuck him in a black plastic bag and buried him in his backyard.

Stuck him under the compost pit.

"You're Dakota's dog," John said, having seen Zeus with Dakota at the office.

John had worn medical scrubs just in case someone spotted him inside the vet's office he would at least look like he belonged. Of course, he wore his green face mask with the turtles.

Everyone knows you can catch COVID-19 from dogs. Dogs sneeze all the time. They'll spray an entire room with doggy Covid virus goop.

John smelled like wet dirt and a putrid stench from the dead guy. He had halitosis, body odor, plus that dirty butt smell, which did not go unnoticed by Zeus, who leapt to his feet, trying to shuffle around in his cage, which was locked by a plastic zip tie. Zeus raised his massive head and sniffed.

"You're getting your balls cut off tomorrow morning, aren't you, big guy?" John said. "Best of luck with that." He chuckled.

Glad I'm not getting my balls cut off.

Creeping further inside the office, John found the cabinets where the medications were kept. He easily shimmied one open with a screwdriver—child's play. He found what he was looking for.

"Let's see. Buprenorphine, Codeine, Banamine, Paracetamol, Banamine," he muttered as he quickly searched the medications on Google. "Most of these are for horses. But I guess anything with 'mine' or 'phine' in it should be okay." John inspected the labels. "Hmmph. No mention of the ingredients. Different from medicine for people. Guess it's because animals can't read labels."

Meds with "phine" or "mine" in it should contain morphine.

Should be fine.

He stood there, thinking, while scratching his butt.

"Ah. What the fuck," he said, pocketing several meds, but not before cracking open a Banamine, breaking a pill in half and dry swallowing it.

"Ahh. Better," John said, still ignorant of what he had just swallowed.

Gotta get rid of this itch.

230

John beat a hasty retreat. "Better safe than sorry," he said out loud to himself.

Suddenly, he heard a noise in the building's rear where the animals were kept.

John headed to the front of the building. In the receptionist area, he ran into two Mexican men cleaning the office.

Explains the low rider car.

Both men were built like fire hydrants, short, stocky, with bull-sized necks and jet-black hair as if coated in bacon grease.

"I forgot the cleaners were coming this morning," John lied, feigning innocence.

"Señor? What are you doin' 'ere?" The older of the men asked. He had a black Frito Bandito mustache, covering a cleft lip.

"Just getting files ready," John said, thankful he'd worn the medical scrubs and a mask. "Have two operations this morning. I want to be prepared."

"Ohh," the man said. "You must be the new veterinarian?"

"Come again?"

"We heard 'dat 'dere was a new veterinarian hired. That must be you. No?"

The little mouse running on the treadmill that turned the wheels in John's mind raced overtime.

"No. Not me."
"No?"
"I'm the new doggy doctor."
"Ahh."
A moment passed.

231

No one spoke.

John believed they had bought his explanation.

"Well. Good talk. Thanks," John said. "Gotta run." He headed to the rear of the building, abandoning the idea of walking out the front door.

He saw the younger Mexican reach for his phone.

Guess they didn't buy it.

In the rear room, once Zeus had gotten a whiff of John, his zoomies took over.

Back and forth in the flimsy cage he zoomed until it tumbled over. The plastic zip-tie broke under Zeus's weight, and the gigantic dog was free. He shook his giant head to clear doggy cobwebs, then off he ran, John in his sights.

As John reached the rear door, he heard the sounds of the giant English Mastiff paws running across the floor, plus the unmistakable moaning sound of the monstrous dog. Sounded like a charging rhino humming a Motown love song.

"What the fuck?"

John reached for the door, but not quickly enough. He felt the enormous weight of Zeus's paws wrapping around him, pushing him face-down on the floor.

"Zeus! Get off of me! Zeus! Get the fuck off of me!"

It felt like an elephant on his back; the dog was too heavy, his weight forcing air out of John's lungs.

Zeus's bison-sized head sniffed John's butt.

What the fuck?

John felt something rub against his backside. He turned his head to see Zeus's pink wiener burst out of hibernation.

The lipstick was out of its case!

"Oh, no!" John screamed. The only ones who heard him were the men in the other room. They ignored his cries and kept cleaning.

"OHHH. NOOOOOOO!" John screamed again at the top of his lungs.

7.

The gridlock of freeway traffic pre-pandemic had returned. Though he drove in the fast lane, Palmer's speed odometer barely topped five miles per hour. He found himself surrounded on all sides by Amazon Prime trucks, their drivers trying to make good on Amazon's promise of next-day delivery. Most people had switched to online shopping for everything these days.

Freeways. If it's not gridlock, during non-commute hours you have idiots driving close to a hundred miles per hour, dodging in and out of lanes and passing other cars as if they were standing still. Freeways are littered with ambulances, fire trucks, EMT vehicles, and police cruisers blasting sirens and flashing lights as they rush to save the lives of those same idiot drivers when they eventually crash their cars in a fiery ball.

I've got to move out of this state.

It was a sunny September afternoon, temperature in the mid-eighties, clear blue skies, no humidity—the type of glorious weather that seduced people from all around the world to move to the San Francisco Bay Area. Based on the freeway traffic, it seemed to Palmer as if most of those people had already arrived.

Palmer glanced at the passenger seat. No Buddy. He missed his pup. When Palmer had walked towards the garage to leave, Buddy had grown excited, wagging his tail at the prospect of a car trip, so he could stick his snout out a window and sniff those wonderful smells.

"Not today, Buddy," Palmer had said, placing a hand on Buddy's head to keep him from running into the garage. "You can't come with me. Sorry." Buddy had wagged his tail while looking at Palmer with a doggy smile on his face. "I'm meeting a client. At a restaurant." Buddy kept looking at Palmer. He cocked an ear. "No dogs allowed at this restaurant. Now stay."

On some level, he felt that the dog understood his words.

His phone rang. It was Meg.

FaceTime? Why would she want FaceTime?

I don't want her to see me.

Instead of cleaning and ironing his old slacks and faded, worn-out shirts, Palmer had purchased a new outfit for today: new beige dress slacks, an expensive long-sleeved white dress shirt, new socks, and new beige loafers.

Palmer answered, making sure he was only visible from the face up. Meg's smiling face appeared on his car's console.

The wonders of modern technology.

"What's up, Meg?" His left arm hung limp at his side.

She looked good. Was that another new outfit? He would not comment on her appearance this time. Palmer had learned his lesson the last time he'd commented.

"The official copy of the autopsy came in. Toxicology report too. Want me to forward to you, Sarge?"

"That'd be great, Meg. Thanks." Then he added. "I'm on my way to meet Sophia and her stepdad." Palmer already knew the results, but having a hard copy would be helpful.

"Just Sophia will be there," Meg said flatly.

What kind of tone is that?

"Said that Martin isn't feeling well."

"Oh," Palmer answered. "Okay. Thanks."

"You bet, Sarge," Meg returned. "How's your arm feeling?"

"It's okay." He nearly snapped at her.

But that wasn't the truth. Though Palmer, John, and the retired-superior-court-judge-turned-homeless-guy Jonesy had exhumed Ramsay's body seven days ago, Palmer's arm was still sore from his efforts at digging; nerve pain ran down his shoulder to his fingers. Debilitating. His arm tingled. It felt paralyzed.

"You sleep okay, Sarge?" Meg asked.

Who is she? My mother? He let it pass. *Was this why Meghan wanted to FaceTime me? So she could check up on me?*

"Slept great, Meg. Thanks for asking."

This also was not exactly the truth.

Palmer's urine had been red this morning. He had pissed red urine every two hours through the night, the aftereffects of getting a large kidney stone blasted three days ago.

The stone, too large to pass on its own, had shown up on an x-ray during Palmer's yearly physical. Before he could schedule the ultrasound procedure that would blast the stone into itty bitty pieces, he had to endure several tests, such as blood work, urine and stool tests, an EKG to make sure that his heart was in good shape, and a CT scan to pinpoint the stone's exact location.

Welcome to the golden years.

He had trouble understanding the nurses and helpers who went over test results via phone prior to the procedure.

236

"How long will I be down?" he had asked one nurse.

"Down, sir? Wha you mein? Down?"

"How long might I be unable to go to work? How long should I take it easy afterwards?

"Doctar Lee say test result okie-dokie."

Good grief.

"Heart okie dokie too."

Never mind.

"Procedure scheduled for tomorrow."

"Thanks." Then Palmer added, "A bunch." He struggled to take the crabby tone out of his voice.

It didn't sound like the blasting would be a big deal. It was an out-patient procedure, so he wouldn't need someone to drive him home after, but the procedure itself was invasive. First, they would center his backside on a table with a circular cutout before placing a balloon-like plastic liner filled with lukewarm water under his naked rear. No anesthesia. No pain meds. Every thirty seconds, they would direct a highly concentrated ultrasound shock wave, a powerful piston-like laser, through the water into the exact spot where the stone was located. Felt like an earthquake being fired through a high-powered rifle smack into his kidney.

Thump! Thump! Thump! Thump!

The procedure lasted forty-five minutes, with Doctor Lee firing dozens of ultrasound bullets into Palmer's kidney. Palmer was bruised purple when he left.

"There might be a little blood in your urine and stool for a day or so," Doctor Lee had said to him as he left. "Just a little."

An understatement.

"The stone is now just itty bitty pieces," the urologist added. "Good deal."

For the past three days, his urine was crimson, though the deepness of the red color had lessened each day. His stool was bloody for two days.

This is a good deal?

Small wonder why he felt so grumpy.

Two days later, he had a follow-up visit with Doctor Lee. But when the urologist entered the exam room, it was a different doctor.

"I thought my appointment was with Doctor Lee?" Palmer said.

"I'm Doctor Lee," the man said. He was clearly not the same man who'd performed the procedure.

"The urologist?"

"Yes."

"I've been talking with a different doctor."

"Oh. Yes. I see."

"Your name is Doctor Lee also?"

"Yes."

"Is there more than one Doctor Lee working here?"

"There are six of us."

"All urologists at this same hospital?"

"Yes."

"Done," Meg said, snapping Palmer's mind back to the present. "Autopsy is in your inbox."

"Thanks, Meg," Palmer said. "I think the Mueller's are going to find the results interesting."

"I do too, Sarge," Meg had replied. "I do too. Please be careful driving."

Palmer read between the lines of Meg's words. With his car first being hit by Ming Lee Wang, then getting a flat tire from a pothole on the freeway, then having his windshield shattered by a rock thrown from a construction truck, Palmer hadn't had the best of luck while driving lately.

He grunted, then hung up.

8.

It was a twenty-minute drive to the restaurant where Palmer and Sophia Mueller planned to meet. Perhaps, he thought, no industry in America had suffered more from the Covid pandemic than the restaurant industry. At last count, Palmer had read that across the country, over 150,000 restaurants had permanently gone out of business.

Horrible.

Palmer arrived twenty minutes early. He considered it rude to arrive to any appointment late. The hostess led him to an outdoor table at Scott's Seafood Bar and Grill in Jack London Square, a popular watering hole for locals in Oakland. The restaurant overlooked the Alameda Estuary, a meandering, mirror-calm river that fed into the San Francisco Bay one mile to the northwest.

He removed his face mask, ordered a Kettle One vodka gimlet, and surveyed the scene. Tables were socially distanced. At the table closest to him, an elderly couple sat. Both dressed in full silver Hazmat suits complete with Astronaut-like silver boots and helmets. Both were double-masked, wearing a face mask under their helmets. Their helmets had a small hole in the glass faceplate where they had inserted a straw to sip their adult beverages.

Jeez.

Both downed their drinks quickly, slurping every drop, before motioning towards the server for two more.

Palmer's hands were shaking. He figured that he'd been drinking too much lately. At his age, blasting kidney stones with ultrasound had taken something out of him. He promised himself not to drink too much today.

Across the estuary, Palmer spotted what looked to be an old houseboat moored at a dock. Made of weathered rotted wood, the houseboat sat tilted as if it was taking on water. It reminded Palmer of what one might see in the Louisiana bayou. On a relatively flat deck on the rear of the houseboat, he spotted several blue tarps, two tattered tents, and clothes drying on a clothesline. Seated on plastic camp chairs were several people, all wearing face masks.

Homeless people.

Wearing face masks. Good grief.

What's next? Upscale homeless housing?

Seeing homeless people on the houseboat made Palmer think of Jonesy.

I hope he doesn't show up here. How does he always know where I'm going to be?

Once seated and waiting, Palmer glanced at his phone to read the news. More than once, he'd found business for his firm this way. Online news journalists were happy to report info on rich and famous peoples' messy divorces, whether or not true. Messy divorces meant claims of infidelity, expensive lawyers, division of assets, opportunities for private investigators to earn their keep. Keeping up with online news media was also a great way to find info on missing persons.

Every day there was interesting news; instantaneously a person could read about anything that was happening in the world in real time.

Today was no exception. The COVID-19 pandemic was still present here in the States, the delta variant having taken hold as vaccines had not totally wiped out the disease. Maybe it would never be wiped out. Three men from California had just been indicted for trying to sell two hundred million dollars' worth of non-existent N95 masks to the Republic of Kazakhstan, a landlocked country in Central Asia that had once been part of the Russian Empire. Palmer marveled at how far scammers had progressed. *But how did they expect to get paid that large of an amount of money without delivering the masks?*

Venmo?

Sophia Mueller arrived fifteen minutes late. She wore form-fitting black pants, a low-cut gold top that glittered as she moved; her blond hair looked like she'd just stepped out of a salon.

"Sorry I'm late," she said as she pinched her knees together and lowered herself into a chair opposite Palmer. A pearl necklace hung from her neck. As she sat, Palmer noticed her loose top sag, revealing her cleavage.

Sophia's earrings reminded Palmer of a fond memory of his daughter, Francesca, who at age three had blurted out, "Diamond earrIngs!" when Palmer had asked her what she wanted Santa Claus to bring her for Christmas.

How did a little girl that age know what diamond earrings were?

Palmer had just talked to his daughter last week when he called to wish her a happy twenty-fourth birthday. She was still living in London and working as a nurse. Francesca's live-in girlfriend Lena had answered the phone. Palmer was learning to accept the fact that his daughter preferred women instead of men.

Francesca was happy to hear from her father, which made Palmer hopeful about the future of their relationship, which had become strained before Francesca had moved abroad.

"How about I pop across the pond for a visit?" he had asked.

"You sound like an Englishman, Dad." Francesca had chuckled.

"Maybe next month?" Palmer continued. "After I wrap up a couple of cases I'm working on right now?"

"Sounds great, Dad," Francesca had said. "Looking forward to it."

Inwardly Palmer smiled, not wanting to show his delight to Sophia.

"Traffic?" Palmer asked Sophia.

"Traffic."

"Sorry to hear that Martin isn't feeling well today," Palmer said.

"Oh. Thanks," Sophia said. "Having a bad day."

Palmer wondered if his cancer had returned. "Hope he feels better soon."

"Thanks."

Palmer looked at her left hand.

No wedding ring.

"I'll have a Chardonnay," Sophia said when the server stopped by their table. "Wente Riva Ranch, if you have it." She flashed the server a smile.

Ruby red lipstick and matching nail polish. A bit of black highlighter on the small mole below her right lip, which somehow enhanced her beauty.

She looks like she just stepped out of a fashion spread for Vogue.

To Palmer, Sophia still looked like a young Kim Basinger; she had the same kind of sensual vulnerability about her that Basinger had had in her movies, especially the kinky mid-eighties flick *9 ½ weeks*. Nowadays, many women, especially actresses, wouldn't be caught dead with a facial mole, given how accessible removing them had become.

Must be a European thing from living in Germany.

The server nodded and looked at Palmer, who pointed towards his glass, showing that he wanted another gimlet.

When Sophia had nursed him back to health in the army hospital in Afghanistan, she had worn a gold wedding band.

It was as if she could read his mind. "My husband died a year ago."

"Oh, I'm so sorry. I didn't know."

"How could you? We were living in Germany," Sophia said. "He was a cardiologist."

"I didn't know that. Again, my condolences." Palmer tilted his head to listen with his right ear.

"When the pandemic was at its peak, he felt a responsibility to help. Germany was hit very hard early on by the disease. He volunteered to work in the Covid wing."

"He caught Covid?" Palmer asked, keeping his hands crossed in front of him so that Sophia wouldn't see his hands shaking.

"Yes. Before, the medical community knew that those with underlying conditions were at greater risk to catch the disease and get seriously ill. Peter was diabetic. Once his symptoms worsened, he didn't have the strength to fight it off." Her voice trailed off.

Unbelievable. I wonder if she knows about my Becky.

He knew what she had gone through; he had gone through the same.

First the Covid diagnosis and those awful symptoms, a fever that wouldn't go away, loss of appetite and sense of smell, vomiting, diarrhea. Those with underlying conditions and the elderly were more susceptible. The virus could travel to the lungs much in the same way that the flu caused chest congestion. But this virus sometimes brought on pneumonia, cutting off the supply of oxygen to the body, choking the lungs, so that you could drown in excess lung fluids. To combat this, doctors' places severe Covid patients on a ventilator, which helped a person breathe better. But first, they'd have to place patients in a medically induced coma so that the patient had a better chance of recovering.

The worst part of this ordeal may have been that the seriously ill were sealed off in a separate Covid wing, where no one but medical professionals were allowed access. Family members couldn't visit. Wives couldn't visit sick husbands; husbands couldn't visit sick wives. Kids couldn't visit their parents or grandparents.

The sick patients were alone. Those that died, died alone, with no one there to comfort them or to hold their hands and tell them they loved them as they passed.

Never for a moment did Palmer think that he might catch the virus. He thought, like many did, that he was bulletproof. For a while, he thought maybe it was a scam that news stories had reported. Then Becky volunteered to work in the Covid wing; each night when she came home, she'd tell him about the awful things that she had seen that day. Then Becky, who had taken every precaution, got sick too. No longer could he think Covid was not real.

Palmer's empathized with Sophia. He wanted to give her a big hug.

But he didn't.

He couldn't. He didn't know her well enough, and besides, this was business. Palmer had an ironclad rule about business: never mix it with pleasure. Yes, he was attracted to Sophia. And yes, he thought that she may be attracted to him. But mixing business with your personal life almost always turned out badly.

Maybe after? After he had finished with her case? Maybe then he'd consider asking her out. Maybe. A man living alone without a wife was a lonely man, and Palmer was no different—drowning his loneliness with vodka, which was a poor substitute to having a wonderful woman's companionship.

He'd have to talk with Becky. To see what she thought.

"I'm a widower," he said. "My wife was a nurse. She was a breast cancer survivor. That was her underlying condition."

"She died from Covid?"

"Yes. She was alone when she died." Palmer looked away.

"Oh. I did not know Palmer," Sophia said, her voice somber. She looked like she was considering the same things that had just run across Palmer's mind. Like she wanted to reach across the table and give him a hug.

"I'm so sorry," Sophia said as the server returned with their drinks.

"Why did you become a private investigator?" Sophia asked, changing the topic.

Palmer was eager to discuss something besides the deaths of their respective spouses.

"A natural progression, I think," he started. "Like cops that go into the security field when they retire. The training that the army provided—the discipline, the patience. It requires a lot of time to solve a case. A lot of work, a lot of patience. If you serve in the military, you come to understand that patience is a virtue. The army teaches patience."

"I agree." Sophia sipped her Chardonnay and pressed her arms closer together to show more cleavage. "Or you don't survive in the army."

"Exactly," Palmer said. "Teamwork is an essential part of daily army life. A PI has to work well with others, has to work well as part of a team to be successful. The army teaches teamwork, and any investigations firm that wants to do well can't do so without good teamwork."

Sometimes Palmer thought the most powerful person in the world was a beautiful woman. A confident woman aware of the power she possessed over men. How she got what she wanted when she wanted it by flashing a smile, raising an eyebrow, or moving her body in a certain feminine way. The power a woman had to entice, seduce, control.

Sophia Mueller was such a woman. Palmer also knew that Sophia knew that she was such a woman.

Sophia had her back to the houseboat across the water, but Palmer, looking over her shoulder, had an unobstructed view of the homeless people on the rear deck. A woman—at least it looked like a woman to

Palmer, though it was hard to tell because of the layers of soiled clothing she wore—squatted like a dog over the side of the boat and defecated into the estuary. When she finished she stood, facing the restaurant. Then she raised her top. Braless, she flashed her boobs while sticking out her tongue and shaking her head from side to side.

Good Grief.

Palmer had recently read that the current governor of California had proposed a solution to the homeless problem. He planned to build "little cities" of "tiny homes," each eight feet by eight feet for sixty-four feet of living space, which would include two bunk beds to sleep two homeless people. The first "little city" in the Los Angeles area would consist of 120 "tiny homes" at a cost of eighty thousand dollars per home. It would include communal showers and bathrooms and a cafeteria-style kitchen for communal eating. For a total cost of $9.6 million dollars.

In San Francisco there was an area named SF Homeless Hotels, hotels that offered rooms and meals to the homeless. Thousands of them. To the tune of $16 million dollars a year. Paid by taxpayers.

Paid out of my tax dollars?

"So why did you join the army?" Sophia asked, drawing Palmer's attention back to her.

"My dad," Palmer started. "He was a warrant officer in Vietnam. Second Battalion, Twenty-Third Infantry, Fourth Platoon. I was seven when he left. During the Tet Offensive in December of '68, his platoon was trapped. The North Vietnamese whittled them to pieces. He took it upon himself to make sure that all the wounded were loaded into choppers."

"Leave no man behind."

"Yes," Palmer said, his left arm hanging by his side.

"Infantry," Sophia said. "Involved in hand-to-hand combat?"

"Yes." Palmer's voice cracked.

"It must have been awful."

"Must have been," Palmer continued. "Anyway, he got out on the last bird. They shot him six times and bayoneted him twice."

"Badly wounded. Like you were."

"Yes, I remember thinking that as I laid on that hospital bed in Afghanistan fifteen years ago. That I knew how my father must have felt when he was wounded."

"Oh, my God. What a horrible thought to have go through your mind. What an awful feeling that must have been."

"They awarded him the Bronze Star. Awarded the Combat Infantryman's Badge and a Purple Heart," Palmer said. "But being part of such a vicious battle was not the worst part. That happened when he got back to the States."

"I read about that," Sophia said. "It happened before I was born."

"Yes. The Vietnam War was unpopular. People didn't believe that we needed to be in the middle of a civil war between North and South Vietnam. Remember the protests on college campuses?"

"Kent State." Sophia nodded.

"Yes. The National Guard opened fire on unarmed students. Four were killed."

"Such a tragedy."

"He was ostracized. An outcast. Ridiculed for being an American hero. Spit on one time while out for dinner with my mom." Palmer's eyes welled up; he turned to the side so Sophia wouldn't notice.

"I'm not old enough to have seen that, but I know it happened."

"So, you ask why I joined the army? To rewrite the narrative. To make my father proud. To show him that American military personnel are, indeed, heroes." Palmer's voice cracked again. "They say that the apple doesn't fall far from the tree. For my father and me, that is truth. I enlisted in '95. I joined the army to make my father proud."

"Is he still alive?" Sophia asked.

"No," Palmer said, tearing up again. "He died twenty years ago. Sixty-three years old. He had nerve damage in his legs from his war injuries, which lead to blood clots. One clot moved into his heart. He had a heart attack."

"Sorry to hear that." This time, Sophia noticed his tears. "You have a Purple Heart too.

"Yes," Palmer said. "Dad saw me complete two tours in Iraq before he died."

"So, mission accomplished then?" Sophia asked. "You made your dad proud. Even if you can't talk to him about it."

"I think so," Palmer said.

I still talk to my father, even though he's gone.

Suddenly, Palmer remembered the connection to Sophia's facial mole, his good memory still working.

Back when Palmer was about six years old, before his father had shipped overseas to Vietnam, he liked to watch a sixties TV show called Honey West. It was a show about a female private investigator, the lead role played by the beautiful blond actress named Anne Francis. She used her feminine wiles to solve cases. Though he was only six, Palmer remembered how safe he'd felt by watching TV in the same room with his father.

"How'd she solve that case, Dad?" He remembered asking his father, some fifty-four years ago.

"Look at her, will ya," his father had answered. "In that tight skirt. Who wouldn't spill the beans to a dame like that? She's the cat's meow."

Anne Francis had the same small black mole that Sophia had just below her right lip.

"So, how is your arm?" Sophia then asked.

"It's fine. A little sore today," Palmer said, as his mind snapping back to the present.

"I can't thank you enough for saving my arm years ago."

"I did nothing," Sophia said. "The attending doctor decided not to amputate."

"But didn't you say something to him about it?"

"If I remember correctly," Sophia began. "You asked me to tell him you wanted to keep your arm."

"Doctor James Bradshaw," Palmer said.

"Yes. That's his name."

"He told me you'd pleaded with him not to cut it off."

"He said that?"

"I'm in touch with him," Palmer said. "When he left the army, he started working at the Children's Hospital in Oakland."

"You're still in touch?"

"Yes. He's a friend. He helped with your father's autopsy," Palmer said.

"He helped with the autopsy?" Her voice rose an octave. "He did an autopsy on my father?"

"Yes. I'll get to that in a minute. I asked my CO about what happened that day in Afghanistan when the bomb exploded."

"You did?" Sophia asked.

"Yes. I don't know if you remember, but my friend Corporal Jimmy Thompson was killed by that blast."

"I don't remember him. I saw a lot of boys die from suicide bombs."

"We were friends. You remember the gal that works for me? She was at the meetings that we had with you and your stepdad?"

"Dakota?" Sophia asked. "Your computer guru? I remember you calling her that."

"Yes. Dakota Thompson. Jimmy's daughter."

Sophia reflected. "You're looking out for her."

"Something like that."

"Remember that seven-year-old boy Aakrama? Jimmy and I used to take care of him. He was an orphan."

"I remember."

"He had the bomb attached to his torso." Palmer's voice cracked. "He was the bomber." Palmer could still smell the gunpowder from the blast.

"I know," Sophia said. "I'm glad you talked to your commanding officer. I couldn't bear to tell you."

"Can you believe they brainwash children, those goddamn fanatics? They brainwash children into wearing suicide vests." Palmer still broke out in a sweat when thinking about that day.

"Absolutely horrible."

"They teach them to hate Americans. They tell innocent children that there is a place in heaven for them if they kill Americans."

"Promises for what might happen in the afterlife are powerful motivators for people suffering in this life."

"Yeah," Palmer said. "Promising them that there'd be one hundred virgins waiting for them in the afterlife."

"I suppose that works for some men."

"They promise the children that if they kill Americans, there will be a place in heaven for their entire family."

"Sad," Sophia said. "Really sick."

"From birth, they teach these poor children to hate. They're brainwashed."

"Awful. But it was not my place to tell you what happened. You understand that?"

"I do."

"Thanks."

They ordered another drink.

So much for watching how much I drink today.

To Palmer, their conversation so far felt more like what he might expect on a first date rather than a discussion about the death of Sophia's father. Time to get back to business.

"Remember that first meeting that we had?" Palmer started. "When we discussed Warren Marshall, Ramsay's father? And how he cheated the Nakatomi family out of fifty acres of prime land in San Jose during World War Two?"

"I do."

"How the Nakatomis were sent to an internment camp in Lodi because they were of Japanese descent?"

"A prison in the middle of nowhere," Sophia said. "Because we didn't trust Japanese people. Even those born and raised in America."

"Correct." Palmer sipped his gimlet and felt a rumbling in his stomach. "And the land was turned into Warren's Sunrise Village Mobile Home Park."

"A shameful time in our past," Sophia said.

"Follow this." Palmer took a breath. "Aiko Nakatomi Marshall is Joseph Nakatomi's granddaughter. Joseph died years ago, but Joseph's wife, Hana, is still alive at ninety-five years old. She lives with Aiko's parents in San Jose, in a house on the plot of land that Warren didn't get."

"Aiko Nakatomi Marshall?" Sophia said, her brows furrowed.

"Aiko goes by the American name of Suzie," Palmer said, carefully studying Sophia's face. "Suzie Marshall. Brad's wife."

Palmer watched a wave of realization wash over Sophia's face. "Holy crap," she said.

"Exactly."

"Damn." Sophia frowned. "Then it's not a coincidence that she married my brother."

"Probably not."

"Does Brad know who she is?"

"We don't know the answer to that yet."

"What's her plan? Her motive? Why did she marry him?" She spoke fast.

"We don't yet know the answer to those questions either."

"Are they happy together?" Sophia fidgeted in her chair. "Or is their marriage a scam?" Her brain now working overtime. "To me she seemed nice."

"You know her?" Palmer asked.

"Met her a couple of times since I moved to the States," Sophia started. "As big of an asshole that my father could be, he liked to have family get-togethers around the holidays, especially Thanksgiving. I talked with Suzie a couple of times. Like I said, to me she seemed nice. We became friendly."

"What about your brother?" Palmer could see how emotional this was for her.

"You know what I think of Brad. He's a narcissist. A sociopath. There's something not right about him, Palmer. He's evil."

"Give me more time to find out what's going on." His stomach churned.

"Okay."

She looked him in the eye. "I trust you, Palmer. I do. Jeez. She didn't marry him by accident. Suppose she means to avenge her family? But after more than eighty years? People have done that—defend their family's honor. I once read about a Japanese man who killed the descendants of the men who treated his ancestors cruelly when they helped build the railroad through the Sierra Nevada mountain range in the late nineteenth century. He wanted revenge for things that happened to his ancestors over one hundred and forty years ago! He killed ten people. With a Samurai sword. And those people had nothing to do with building that railroad. They were only descendants of the people who built it. Those people lived normal lives."

"I read about that. The Japanese guy killed himself just before the authorities closed in on him," Palmer said. "Seppuku."

"Suppose she killed my father? To avenge her family? After getting to know her, I find that hard to believe. You say that you have the autopsy results? What does the autopsy say?" Sophia said, almost hyperventilating.

"I'll get to those in just a minute."

"Brad and I are the heirs. Does she mean to kill Brad too? Her husband?"

"Like I said before, we don't have those answers yet."

"Or suppose—" Sophia said, looking toward the sky, still speaking fast, agitated. Suppose Suzie and Brad are in this together? That might make sense too."

Palmer listened. He wanted to protect this woman.

"Oh. My. God." Sophia looked down at the table, as if searching for answers. "If that's the case, then am I in danger too? What should I do? What should I do, Palmer? Do I need to hire protection? A bodyguard? I need to talk to Martin. He'll know what to do. He always knows what to do."

Scared.

"Now, please, let's not jump the gun, Sophia." He spoke gently, hoping to soothe her. "At this point, we just don't know what's going on. But we're watching the two of them." Suddenly, Palmer's stomach flipped on itself, gurgling loudly, like a swamp flushing down a toilet. Sophia couldn't help but notice.

"There's one more thing that I'd like to mention before going over your father's autopsy. Bear with me—" Then, another loud gurgling sound, followed by a loosening of his bowels.

Of course. The Vicodin that the urologist gave me after he blasted that kidney stone. He told me about the side effects. Upset stomach, dizziness, diarrhea. Be careful. Don't take them unless you absolutely have to. You know how addicting Vicodin can be.

Palmer broke out in a sweat.

"Are you okay?" Sophia asked, a look of concern on her face.

She's a nurse.

"I'm fine," he said, reaching for water. "Just a little tummy ache."

The instructions. They said not to mix them with alcohol. I took one of those pills a couple of hours ago, just before I left to meet Sophia. And now I'm on my third gimlet.

"What's the other thing, Palmer?" Sophia asked.

"Brad's been spending time with Jojo."

"My dad's wife?" Sophia asked. "What for?"

"He's been visiting at her house."

"He's sleeping with her," Sophia muttered. "Such a pervert."

"We're not sure. I've got my best man on it, and he tells me something different." Drinking water quieted his stomach. He drank more water.

My best man? Sharkie? He's my worst man. The big, stupid, turtle-loving jerk.

He's my only man.

"I don't trust him, Palmer. He's a sociopath, he's sick, selfish. He's up to something."

"According to my man, he's been helping her clean up Ramsay's affairs. They had joint credit cards, checking and savings accounts, things like that. To close them, you have to provide certified death certificates, fill out paperwork, make sure the accounts were placed in Ramsay's trust so that the accounts don't go to probate."

"She's twenty-nine years old. Her job before she married my father was to wear a bikini and serve men coffee while bending over to show them her tits. She's got a body like a supermodel. I don't trust Brad. He's a selfish, selfish man. Self-centered. I don't trust him, Palmer. I don't. He's got his own agenda. You need to find out what it is. Please?" Sophia pleaded.

It'd just be like Sharkie to fuck this up, miss the fact that Brad was fucking his dead father's widow.

"I'll take care of it.," he said, his stomach still churning.

"Ok, now hold on to your hat." Palmer started. "I told you that Doctor Bradshaw performed the autopsy on your dad."

"I can't wait."

"I've a hard copy."

"Good," Sophia said. "Martin will want to read it."

"Your father didn't die from a heart attack."

"I knew it," Sophia said. "I knew it! Something else happened! Do you know what it is? Is it in the autopsy? Was my father murdered? He was. Wasn't he?"

At that very instant, Palmer's bowels dropped to his knees. His face flushed red.

"I'll get to that in a moment. If you could please excuse me for a second."

"Are you okay, Palmer?" Her voice sounded constricted.

Palmer didn't answer. He rose to his feet, then duck-stepped to the men's room. He sat on the throne not one moment too soon. He felt dizzy, tears forming in his eyes.

Fuck me.

Once his bowels emptied, he peed red urine until his bladder, too, was empty.

The golden years.

9.

John's hemorrhoids had never felt better; he had no pain and no itching for the first time in months. He felt wobbly, however, as if he had Ambien in his system. The Banamine that he'd swallowed was primarily used to tranquilize horses with abdominal disorders. He thought he had taken a small enough dose so that he wouldn't suffer side effects, but he couldn't shake the dizziness, the fatigue, and the weird buzzing going on in his head.

Better cut the dose more next time.

Hiding his face behind a mask helped hide his shame, the humiliation that he felt after his episode of forced spooning and hiding the salami with Zeus.

He'd gotten away with the theft at least; the cleaners at the vet's office had said nothing. He figured that he'd have to drop a couple of Andrew Jacksons on them, but they declined his money. *Illegals? Maybe?* The alarm system at the office had been installed during the Mesozoic Age so no one was the wiser that John had shut it down for the fifteen minutes that it had taken him to break in find and steal the pain meds, then get sodomized by the giant English Mastiff.

John had just followed Brad Marshall's car to Jojo's house, where Brad had parked. Brad swallowed a breath mint, looked at himself in the car's rear-view mirror, and smiled his phony smile while checking between his teeth for food. Brad's smile made John think of Matt Dillon's fake-toothed smile in the movie *There's Something About Mary*, when Dillon was scamming a young Cameron Diaz to get into her pants.

John had to pee.

He had just come from the bi-yearly physical that was needed to renew his private investigator's license. He had passed the written test with flying colors. At the physical, the doctor had him pee in a cup. John knew the Banamine would show up in the urine test—he was no dummy—but he'd figured out a way to outsmart them. Like boxing great Mike Tyson had once admitted to doing to pass a championship fight drug screening, John had worn a prosthetic penis that he'd purchased on Amazon for thirty dollars. It had a tiny battery-powered pump inside, which he filled with clean urine so that he could pee into the cup without the doctor, who was watching him from behind, getting suspicious.

However, unlike Mike Tyson, John had filled his fake penis with urine from his pet turtles, hoping that the test wouldn't be able to tell the difference between human and turtle urine, though some turtle species pee through their mouths. Filling his fake penis with turtle urine made John think of his dead pet turtle, Barney. Though Barney had passed two months ago, John still mourned him.

But since John hadn't actually peed at the doctor's office, he really had to pee now.

Weeks ago, John hid cameras and microphones inside various rooms of Ramsay Marshall's house, where Brad now sat in its spacious family room. Taxidermies of animal—deer, antelope, and one huge black bear's head—adorned the wood-paneled walls. Clearly, Ramsay had liked to hunt. It was in this room that Brad had helped Jojo sort through the crazy myriad of paperwork necessary to settle Ramsay's estate.

John soon found out that today's meeting was different.

Brad was wearing a black silk bathrobe cinched at the waist.

"Would Daddy like more sugar in his coffee?" John heard Jojo say, out of camera view.

"Depends."

Jojo walked into the family room, wearing a tiny white thong bikini, carrying a tray with a cup of hot coffee and a slice of banana bread.

"Depends on what, Daddy?" Jojo said, bending over at the waist in front of Brad, showing off her fake cleavage, which had been purchased by her dead husband.

Uh oh. What have we got here?

Once a bikini barista, always a bikini barista?

"I was hoping to have me some watermelon sugar," Brad said, reaching for the coffee.

Watermelon sugar?

"Why you naughty, naughty boy," Jojo said, while sitting on Brad's lap, straddling him as she hand-fed him banana bread.

John googled "Watermelon Sugar".

"What's the matter with me?" Brad asked. "I can't taste the coffee. I can't taste anything." Then he coughed, a dry hacking cough that doubled him over.

"Ask and you shall receive," Jojo said, ignoring his cough, while moving her torso up towards Brad's head.

Oh, my god. What?

Turning back to his phone, John discovered that "Watermelon Sugar" was a song sung by the English singer Harry Styles, who became famous while singing in the boy band One Direction, before branching out on a solo career. John queued the lyrics.

Tastes like strawberries on a summer eve

Sounds just like a song

I want more berries and the summer feelin'

So wonderful and warm.

Turns out, 'Watermelon Sugar' was about giving a woman oral sex.

And this English dude wrote a song about it.

Of all the emotions that could have gone through John's brain, thinking about what Watermelon Sugar meant, John felt jealous instead. Then he felt dizzy, nearly passing out.

Goddamn horse tranquilizers.

He took a couple of slow deep breaths, closing his eyes until the dizziness passed.

Guys like Brad get all the girls. I can't even get laid when I pay for it. Sure, he's rich, good looking, in shape.

Plus, his butt probably doesn't reek.

John checked his phone to make sure his cameras were getting the video.

I've hit the mother lode.

At the far side of Jojo's house, John spotted Suzie Marshall sneaking away, hurrying towards her parked car. Her stride looked purposeful, and she gritted her teeth. Once she made it inside the car, John saw her slamming the steering wheel repeatedly, and she was . . . laughing.

Laughing? About her husband and Jojo having sex?

10.

Palmer's stomach had calmed. His bowels had emptied, his eyes were tearing, and he had a headache that felt like part of his brain was being chiseled away. Must be a reaction from the kidney stone blasting meds. It didn't feel like the flu. Covid? No. He'd been double vaccinated as soon as he could get it.

I will not take another Covid test. That nasal swab sticks way too far up your nose. Makes me sneeze.

When he returned to the table, he gulped down a glass of ice water. He sat on his hands to hide the shakes.

Better.

"Are you okay?" Sophia asked with a look of concern on her face.

"Fine, I'm fine." He motioned to the waiter for more water. "I had a procedure done last week, and I had a reaction to the medicine, I believe."

"Oh," Sophia said. "I understand. Happens all the time."

"Want me to get started with the autopsy findings?"

"Did you have any problems exhuming my father's body?" she asked, anxiously.

Besides my left arm giving out, dealing with John being a complete weenie about going into a cemetery at night, and watching helplessly as Jonesy, an old homeless guy, did the brunt of the work?

"No. No trouble at all," Palmer said. "Felt like we taking part in some sort of Halloween horror movie, though." Palmer looked at the homeless people on the houseboat across the estuary, hoping that Jonesy wouldn't show up.

"I understand you can do an autopsy on someone who has been deceased for a while."

"No problem," Palmer started. "Have you heard of Otzi the Iceman?"

"No."

"Otzi's body was found frozen in the Alps," Palmer said. "At first, they thought he was someone who had perished a couple of years ago. A skiing accident maybe. Turns out that Otzi had died over five thousand years ago."

"Wow," Sophia said.

"Wow, indeed. They could do an autopsy. Otzi was about forty years old when he died. Had health issues, frostbite on his toes, gallstones, arthritis in most of his joints, his arteries had hardened."

"Jeez," Sophia said. "Arthritis and arteriosclerosis at forty years old?"

"Hard living five thousand years ago. They looked at the contents of his stomach to determine what he had to eat a couple of hours before he died."

"Amazing." Her eyes widened.

"His last meal was grain, pollen, and ibex."

"Ibex?"

"Mountain goat. Plus, he had worms in his stomach and Lyme disease."

"Modern science."

"They could also figure out that he was murdered."

"Murdered?"

Palmer noticed her eyebrows raise.

"Otzi had a metal arrowhead buried in the back of his shoulder."

"Shot in the back."

"Exactly," Palmer said. "If they can do such an autopsy on a five-thousand-year-old corpse, then performing an autopsy on your dad is not a problem. As I said earlier, someone we both know, Doctor Jim Bradshaw, did the autopsy."

"A good man." Sophia shifted in her seat.

"Yes. He is," Palmer said. "I'll email you a copy but first I'll go over his findings."

"Okay."

"In layperson's terms. So I can explain it easily to Martin."

"Okay. Fine."

Palmer put on reading glasses. "No evidence of myocardial infraction. No evidence of atrial fibrillation. Ramsay had several stents from previous heart episodes. He had mild arteriosclerosis in his aorta. But for all purposes, his left main artery was clear."

"How did he die then, if it wasn't his heart?" Sophia voice raised half an octave higher.

"Sophia, have you ever heard of fugu?"

"No," she said. "I have not."

"It's the Japanese word for pufferfish."

"Pufferfish? As in sushi?"

"More like poisonous sushi."

"I've never heard of that." She frowned. "Sushi that can kill?" Shock registered on her face.

"Pufferfish is not the only venomous fish," Palmer said. "There are at least twelve hundred different poisonous species. They develop the toxin to protect themselves from being attacked and eaten by predators."

"Jeez." Sophia shook her head.

"Fugu, or pufferfish, carry toxins in their ovaries, intestines, and liver. A single pufferfish has enough poison to kill thirty people."

"My God," Sophia said. "Who would have known that?"

"Hardly no one. Ramsay ate fugu. His last meal. When the police released their report, they noted that there was leftover sushi found in a container on his boat. The container was marked with the letter R written in black magic marker."

"As if someone had prepared it for him and put his name on the container."

"Yes," Palmer said. "Doctor Bradshaw found it in your father's stomach. The toxicology report on your dad shows large amounts of tetrodotoxin in his blood. The fugu that your father ate contained tetrodotoxin, which is the poison that the pufferfish develops to defend itself."

"How can something that dangerous be eaten as normal food?" Sophia asked, shock still on her face.

"In Japan it's considered a delicacy. Sushi chefs have special qualifications. They go through years of training to learn how to prepare the fugu correctly, to remove the poison from the pufferfish's organs. Over the past hundred years, thousands of people, most living in Japan, have died from eating poisonous fugu."

"I did not know," Sophia exclaimed. "How horrible." She shook her head, looking down. "It must have been awful for my dad. Could he have possibly eaten the fugu by mistake? Maybe he purchased the sushi locally, in Tahoe, before heading out in his boat?"

"We don't know the answer to that yet," Palmer said. "The poison paralyzes muscles while the victim is still conscious. The victim gets dizzy, disoriented. They may get a headache, they may vomit. Over a ten-minute period, the poison attacks the lungs. They die from asphyxiation."

"My poor father. It must have been excruciating," Sophia repeated, the hurt in her eyes deep. She looked Palmer square in the eye. "Suzie Marshall owns a sushi restaurant."

"I know. That would fit in with the theory we're discussing," Palmer said. "But we don't know if she is involved. My office received the autopsy and toxicology report this morning. My gal Meghan just emailed them to me right before I met with you today."

"She is the granddaughter-in-law of the man that my grandfather stole land from. She meets Brad and marries into the family that stole her familial land. She owns a sushi restaurant; she probably knows about fugu. My father was killed by eating poisonous sushi. That kind of seals the deal for me. Way too many facts here, Palmer. Too many facts to be coincidental." As she spoke, the anger in her voice grew to a rage.

Jeez. Murder by sushi. What's next?

Palmer remained silent. But his mind was racing thousands of miles per hour. Either Brad or Suzie might be responsible for the murder of Ramsay Marshall. If true, then Sophia could be the next target. Once again, Palmer felt that he had to protect this woman. He felt an urgency to solve this, before anything happened to Sophia.

"We know that my father was murdered," Sophia said, snapping Palmer's mind back to the moment.

"If so, it could have been premeditated. We are working on it. As we speak." He paused. "You could be the next target, Sophia."

"Yes. I know," she said. "I stand to inherit half the estate. They may want me out of the way."

"Agreed."

"It scares me to death, Palmer," Sophia said. "What am I going to do?"

"I'm not going to let anything happen to you," Palmer said matter-of-factly. "I will make sure that someone is watching you 24-7."

Even if it has to be me who does the watching.

"Thank you." Sophia folded her arms across her chest. "That makes me feel a bit better. I need to talk to Martin about this. He'll know what to do. Hire a bodyguard, I think, or something like that. Maybe just stay at my house, under lock and key until this mess is resolved."

"Probably not a bad idea."

Palmer's phone buzzed with an incoming text.

"Well, well. Looks like you were right about your brother and Jojo."

"What do you mean?"

"Just heard from my man. They are having sex at Jojo's house."

"No kidding?"

"Right now."

"I knew it."

"He also thinks that Brad has Covid."

"Holy shit."

"Holy shit is right," Palmer said. "Just because the vaccine has been out for a year now doesn't mean that you can't still catch it."

"The pandemic is slowing," Sophia said. "But people still get it. The disease is still out there. Especially the delta variant. Then there's the newest strain, Omicron. But Omicron doesn't appear, at this point, to be as deadly."

"Exactly."

Palmer reached for his ice water. His hands were still shaking. Sophia rose from her seat.

"Well, I think that I've heard enough. Unless you have more." Palmer heard in her voice a mixture of fear and anger, raw emotion.

"This may be a matter for the police, Sophia," Palmer added.

"Let me talk to Martin first. Please?"

"I don't think that I can sit on this much longer. Especially if we come up with more incriminating info."

"Such as?"

"Well, suppose we find poisonous sushi in a freezer in her restaurant? Or if we find a bill or an invoice from a supplier in her books? Indicating that she purchased fugu just before your father died?"

"Can you give me a couple of days? To see what my father-in-law thinks?"

"I'll see what I can do."

"Thanks."

"That's about it," Palmer said, standing next to her. "That's enough for one day, isn't it? Like I said, I'll email you the autopsy report."

"Thanks. Martin will want to read it." She extended her hand.

Palmer extended his hand towards her, expecting a handshake, or even a fist bump. But she hugged him instead, pressing her breasts press firmly against his chest.

"I can't thank you enough for taking care of this," Sophia said. There was pain and softness in her eyes. "And for watching over me. I really appreciate it."

Palmer backed away awkwardly.

When a woman shows a man her cleavage, she knows exactly what she is doing; she knows exactly what she wants. "No problem at all," he said, shuffling his feet.

And when a woman presses her body up against a man's, the effect on the male anatomy can be immediate. Palmer turned to the side to prevent Sophia from Sophia noticing. "I expect that I'll have more news for you rather quickly."

"Thank you, Palmer."

I'm in trouble now. I'd better go talk with Becky. Soon.

He thought he might talk it over with Becky later tonight, as his dead wife appeared in his dreams almost every night.

"Talk to you soon, Palmer," Sophia said.

And I have to figure out how I'm going to keep Sophia safe.

And with that, she was gone.

11.

Brad Marshall couldn't believe his eyes. The statue of Jay Silverheels was being torn down. Gone was, arguably, the most famous American Indian in television history— Tonto, trusty sidekick to The Lone Ranger. Brad was at the entrance to the Hekawi Indian Resort and Casino. A young Asian couple, both wearing face masks, stood nearby, watching the famous statue being dismantled by Hekawi Indian construction workers.

"What's going on?" Brad asked. He was wearing his customary black outfit, a long-sleeved black golf shirt, with his black hair glued down to his head by hair gel. He smiled at the couple with his oversized front teeth. Then he coughed.

Can't shake this, whatever it is.

"He's being replaced with a statue of Sun Tzu," the Asian man said, backing away from Brad.

"Sun Tzu?" Brad asked.

"The famous Chinese general and warrior."

Brad looked at him blankly.

"You know, the military strategist who wrote the famous book *The Art of War*."

Brad's blank look remained. "Now, why would they do that? Don't they know who Tonto is?"

"I don't think so," the man continued. His female companion shook her head. "That show was on television thirty years before we were born. Besides, I read that the owners of the resort want to attract the growing Asian millennial crowd in California."

Growing Asian millennial crowd?

"Adults in their late thirties or early forties."

"I know what millennials are."

Brad looked towards the main floor of the casino.

Mostly Asians.

Entering their middle ages. Asians with money.

Crazy Rich Asians. I get it. I saw the movie.

"Bye bye, now," Brad said, peering out above a special pair of prescription glasses he wore to the casino. "Have a nice day."

The woman stared at Brad.

"Winnaa!" From far away Brad heard Lumpia. There was no mistaking that squeaky voice. His favorite dealer. Not because he liked her, but because she miscounted card counts and paid out money to people for hands that the house had won.

Gotta like a dealer that can't count cards correctly.

Brad found her table and sat at his favorite position, third base. Like many gamblers, he favored third base. From here, he could see all the cards played before him, which gave him a slight edge, he thought.

An advantage at blackjack was exactly what Brad Marshall needed.

The gambling debt that he owed the Circus Circus Las Vegas casino had grown to over five hundred thousand dollars. Last week, a supposed employee of the casino, Vito, had demanded payment. He hinted a veiled threat about what might happen to certain parts of Brad's anatomy, mainly his genitals, if he didn't pay down a chunk of the debt soon. Vito had told him Brad had one week to pay.

The problem was that Brad didn't have any money. He didn't have any of his dead father's money. Yet. Brad blamed his dead father for that.

Idiot didn't put any of his bank accounts into his living trust.

This meant that in order to get Ramsay's money, the accounts first had to clear probate, which would take six to nine months.

So much for quickly getting my hands on the moolah.

Brad heard the familiar casinos sounds, the hustle and bustle of people rushing, slots singing, roulette wheels spinning, gamblers chatting and laughing at the craps tables.

I feel right at home.

Speaking of assets, Brad was tiring of fucking his dead father's young widow. Sometimes he thought that the Viagra he had in his system 24-7 was to blame for that. Brad was always horny. Always ready to go.

You fuck them once or twice and what do you get?

A clingy, needy, horny widow.

"Where are you going now?" Jojo would ask after they had sex. Or "Why can't you hold me after?" Or "Why don't you hang around for a while, and maybe we can go out for dinner?" Or "Please don't leave yet. Let's watch a Netflix movie." She always spoke a whiny voice, refusing to let him out of her sight. And boy, could that woman talk. Seemed like she never shut up.

Doesn't she understand that I've got things to do?

Like gamble. And play golf.

Last thing I want to do is watch a romcom.

And who the fuck is Benny?

274

The guy whose name she cried out every time she had a *petite mort*—a little death, the French term for orgasm.

Sometimes, Brad thought it would be better to go home and have sex with his wife instead. Suzie, though, was not as interested in having wild sex as she was before they married. But like a good Japanese wife, she would accommodate him.

Old, reliable.

None of that old passion anywhere when they made love. It was as if she didn't give a shit.

Which was fine with Brad.

Brad ordered a Manhattan, watching the cards that Lumpia dealt. This time he was tipping the odds more in his favor. The prescription glasses were working fine. They picked up the invisible ink that he had soaked into the sleeves of his black golf shirt. When he wanted to mark a card, usually a picture card, he'd touch his sleeve, smear invisible ink on his fingertip and place it on the corner of the playing card. After he'd marked a number of cards, he had a better idea when a picture card, or brick, would be played next.

Thirty years prior, a professional gambler had marked cards using invisible ink. Eventually, he was found out and banned from the casinos. But not before he had won a fortune. So far, so good for Brad. He was aware of the security cameras overhead watching everything. He felt certain that he was getting away with it.

Easy peasy.

He was reeling in green chips. But for some reason, he couldn't taste the whiskey in his drink. His sense of taste was gone.

Gotta win big today so I can pay down some of that fucking marker.

"Winnaa!" Lumpia squeaked again, sliding more hundred dollar chips Brad's way. He tossed her a five-dollar red chip as a tip.

"Tank you, kine sir," Lumpia said.

Though the worst part of the pandemic was mostly over, Brad still found it next to impossible to get a decent tee time. The game had boomed during the pandemic, and new golfers were everywhere. Brad could not play the challenging golf course here at the resort. No available tee times. The last time he'd played the Hekawi Hills golf course, it had taken almost six hours to play an eighteen-hole round, when, prior to the pandemic, an average round of golf had taken about four hours to play.

Like Chinese water torture.

Brad liked to gamble when he golfed. He played different golf gambling games like closeies, greenies, sandies, birdies, poleskis, first in, first on, bingo, bango, bungo, nassau's, automatic presses, Cousteau's, barkies, and others. He enjoyed having lots of action going on at the same time. Kept his interest. And whenever he got the chance, which was whenever one of his playing partners was not paying attention, he cheated. He'd kick his ball out from behind trees, improve his lie, and when he could get away with it, he cheated on his score, putting down a lower score than he actually had. Cheating his way at golf and through life was Brad Marshall's modus operandi.

A young woman sat at the table in a chair next to Brad. She had magenta-dyed hair and a gold ring piercing in her left eyebrow.

"Anyone sitting here?" she asked in a pleasant voice.

Lumpia pointed to the chair.

"It's all yours, sweetheart," Brad chimed in. He did a double take on her hair.

"Thanks. Change please," she said to Lumpia, placing a hundred-dollar bill on the blackjack table. "Red chips are fine."

Great. A real player. Five-dollar chips.

At least she's easy on the eyes.

She was wearing black leggings and a short-sleeved blouse. Brad looked her up and down once again to see that she wore no makeup, but she had massive muscular arms covered in colorful sleeves of tattoos.

"What are those?" Brad asked, nodding towards her tattoos. "They look like flying pigs."

"Archangels."

"Archangels?" Brad face screwed into a question mark.

"Yes. You know, from the Bible."

"Oh. Right. What's your name? Brad asked.

"My name is Cindy," Dakota Johnson said.

"Ready to prey back jac now?" Lumpia asked.

"You must work out a lot," Brad said, ignoring their dealer.

Dakota said nothing.

"I work out, too, you know." Brad flashed his oversized toothy smile. He looked how Bugs Bunny might look when he was enamored with Pepé Le Pew.

Dakota said nothing.

"They have a gym here at the resort. Maybe we can work out together tomorrow morning. What do you say, Cindy?"

This time Dakota slowly turned her head and looked at Brad. "Don't even think about it, asshole."

"Ready to prey back jac now?" Lumpia asked again, eyeing the two of them. "Goo luc then."

"Deal the cards," Brad said, adjusting his glasses while eating crow.

12.

"Winnaa!"

"Winnaa!"

"Winnaa!"

Brad won on several straight one-thousand-dollar hands.

Easy peasy.

Lumpia dealt from two decks. No shoe. She'd been dealing from the same two decks for the past thirty minutes, which allowed Brad to mark quite a few cards. He was on a roll.

First, he doubled down against a dealer five upcard, knowing that Lumpia's hole card was a picture card. She busted. Then he hit a blackjack. Next, he stayed pat on a hard thirteen against a dealer four upcard, also knowing that Lumpia had a brick in the hole. She busted again.

Every seat at the table was taken. Lumpia was busting often, people were winning, liquor flowed. Everyone seemed happy, laughing. Brad ordered another Manhattan. Despite her rude response, it looked to Brad like Cindy was having fun too as she added to her pile of red chips.

The pit boss paid a visit. After all, the house would stand for losing money for only so long. "Having a good time here, I see." He was a balding, skinny man in his mid-fifties, with a lit cigarette dangling from thin lips. His name tag read "Burt". He handed Lumpia new cards sealed in a box. "Next shuffle," he said to Lumpia as he walked away. Brad took a quick look at the overhead security cameras.

He doesn't suspect.

Brad had another thing on his mind—what to do with his half-sister Sophia. To Brad, Sophia was a complete stranger. He could count on one hand the number of times he had seen her in his life, let alone spoken to her. No way was he going to share half of his father's fortune with her. Brad Marshall didn't give a flying fuck about his half-sister. But what was he going to do about her?

After hours of pondering, the only solution he could come up with was that Sophia had to go away.

Permanently.

But how am I going to get away with it?

I have to make it look like an accident.

But how?

"Winnaa! Agen!" Lumpia announced, pushing several green chips Brad's way.

"Buddy, don't you ever get up and leave this table?" A grizzled old guy with an unkempt beard and rheumy eyes took another gulp of his whiskey. "You're our lucky charm, Buddy."

Brad raised his Manhattan in salute.

The old guy had bad skin too. *What is that?* Skin was flaking off of his face.

Eczema?

Maybe I can make it look like a home burglary gone bad? Lots of people die from home burglaries.

But after a moment's reflection, he thought; *nah.*

With home security systems, ring systems, cameras inside and outside the house, I'd never get away with it. What if I hired some guy, some ex-con loser type to do it for me?

Nah. He'd probably fuck it up. Lead the cops right to me.

Sophia enjoyed hiking, taking long walks in the hills of the county parks, like Briones Regional Park in Martinez.

There are mountain lions in those hills. Plenty of them. Maybe one of them might drag her away?

Better yet. Maybe I can go to someone like the Tiger King, the television show, or something like that. Buy a mountain lion instead of a tiger. Say that I want the big cat as a pet. Thousands of people do that. Then I starve him, just a little. Let him loose on the trail where Sophia is hiking.

Something about that scenario reminded Brad of how Wile E. Coyote came up with those lame-brained schemes to catch the Road Runner.

How do I get the mountain lion into the park? Hire a U-Haul? How do I get him to the spot where Sophia is hiking? With no paved roads? Suppose the lion doesn't go after her? Suppose the lion goes after someone else and drags that person away instead?

Nah. Too many ways that can go sideways.

The cards turned bad, like they always did. Brad had lost some of his advantage with the new deck; he hadn't had the time to mark them. The old, rheumy-eyed whiskey drinker left the table and took his flaking facial skin and his hooting and hollering with him. Burt, the pit boss, had a smug look on this face. Cindy continued to win methodically, increasing her stack of red chips.

Wait a minute, wait a minute, wait a minute! Sophia has a swimming pool at her house, doesn't she? When I see her, she always has a good tan. It's still warm enough this time of year in California, and I bet she likes to sit by the pool. Probably no security cameras out there. I know she likes her Chardonnay. I know that much about her. Maybe I spike her wine while she's lying out by the pool. She'll fall asleep, and I'll dump her in the pool. Or maybe I get a guy to dump her in the pool? Not some ex-con loser type. Someone who won't fuck it up. Have to pay that person well though.

Maybe, just maybe.

The Asian couple that Brad had briefly talked to near the Tonto statue stopped at Brad's table.

"Wow. Look at those stacks," the man said, eyeing Brad's piles of green chips.

"I told you," the woman said triumphantly, looking at her husband.

Brad turned around.

"I told you," the woman said again, her voice animated.

"Told him what?" Brad asked.

"Honey, let's go," the man said, taking her arm. "It's not worth it."

"He's cheating! He knows which cards are coming out. That's why he's winning."

"Do what the man says, honey," Brad said, irritated. "Time to go."

"Those are special glasses," the woman said.

Lumpia kept dealing. Burt, the pit boss, was watching another blackjack table.

"What the fuck are you talking about?" Brad said. "I have bad eyes. I'm nearsighted." Brad had perfect vision.

"Those are special glasses," the woman repeated. "They can see invisible ink."

"Who the fuck are you?"

"I'm an optometrist."

Brad stared blankly at her.

"An optometrist is an eye doctor."

A look of recognition slowly replaced Brad's blank stare.

Well, now I'm screwed.

Brad's head spiraled on a swivel. First, he looked at his cards, then at his stack of chips. Then he looked from Lumpia to Burt, the pit boss, then back to his stack of chips again. He felt his face flush red.

"Color change, please." Brad pointed a finger towards Lumpia.

"Changen coror!" Lumpia yelled.

Burt walked over.

Brad gulped the last of his Manhattan. "Never mind the color change." He scooped up his chips. "I'm outta here."

13.

Brad took a quick trip to the cashier's window.

"Large bills, please," he said to the lethargic middle-aged man working the window. "I'm in a hurry." He tapped his anxious fingers on the counter, which made no difference in the speed the guy used to double-count Brad's chips and then the bills. "Thanks for nothing," Brad said, as he collected his money.

Up about fifty thousand.

Then after a moment's reflection, he decided on a fresh approach, one that many gamblers might have chosen. He headed to the sports bar.

Maybe make a bet or two on the ponies.

On the walk through the casino, he remembered the gamblers creed: *I hope that I break even today. I need the money.*

Brad stifled a laugh, then a cough. Since he'd developed this cough, he'd grown adept at stifling it. Not once did Brad think that he might have Covid, nor had he gotten the vaccination when it became available over a year ago.

Why would I?

I'm young and strong. It ain't gonna kill me.

I'm not black. I'm not old. I'm not Mexican.

With his head on a swivel, he headed towards the sports bar after stopping at one of the casino bars for another Manhattan.

Sometimes he thought he should divorce Suzie. Sex was the only thing that they had in common. They had nothing to talk about. Most days, they hardly spoke to each other. Sure, when they first married, they'd had sex every day. What newlyweds didn't? But over the past year, their sex life had shriveled, like a prune. It felt as if they were complete strangers.

There's gotta be something better out there for me.

To Brad, the grass was always greener on the other side of the fence.

Two large guys dressed in black suits and wearing earpieces in stood at the entrance to the sports bar. Bouncers.

Shit. That Asian lady eye doctor probably spilled the beans to Burt.

He ditched his prescription glasses in a trash bin, breaking them first into pieces.

Fuck the ponies.

Brad had originally planned to spend the night, so prior to playing blackjack, he had checked into the hotel. He took a quick trip up to his room, where he repacked his overnight bag, making sure that his large haul of cash was secure inside.

As he entered the elevator to return down to the lobby, a large Caucasian man wearing a silver jogging suit ambled on. The guy had to be six-foot-four and north of two hundred seventy-five pounds. He had a full black beard. About forty years old by Brad's estimates. He was as wide as a refrigerator. Muscular. Except for a beer belly, the guy could have been at one time an NFL lineman. Something about him creeped Brad out.

Brad clutched his overnight bag close to his chest.

The manhattans had taken hold. *Think I'll call him Tiny.*

As the elevator door closed, the large man pushed the emergency button.

Did he see me mark the cards? Does he work for the casino?

Brad's heart raced, his blood pressure spiking.

The guy pulled a knife. He looked at Brad and waved it menacingly.

"Did the Chinese bitch give me away?" Brad asked, sweat beading down his forehead. The guy had him trapped. "Well? Did she?"

Or had this huge guy just watched him win all that money? Maybe this was just a robbery? "Here's the money." Brad thrust the duffle towards the man.

"Vito sends his regards."

Wait. What?

This is not about the money I won? It's not about cheating at Blackjack?

"Vito told me I had another month to pay," Brad said anxiously. He took out his iPhone. "Here. Want me to call him so you can check?"

Brad didn't know who this guy was. He didn't know what to think. He didn't know what to do.

"Wait a moment, Tiny. I've got a solution."

"Who the fuck you calling Tiny?" the large man growled.

Then he slashed at Brad with the knife.

Instinctively, Brad's arm flew upwards to ward off the blow. The knife caught him on the forearm. Blood poured out as Brad crumpled to the floor.

"Please. No more. Please. I've got money," Brad pleaded, offering the bag to the man.

The big man raised his knife to slash at Brad again. "Like I said. Vito sends his regards."

A crowbar pried its way between the elevator doors. The doors sprang open and a woman with magenta-dyed hair and huge, muscular arms stood there.

"Cindy?" Brad said.

"What are you? An Easter egg?" Tiny said, looking at her hair. "This is private, sweetheart. If you know what's good for you, you'd skedaddle."

"Mind if I join the party?" Dakota said. She took a long drag on a cigarette, then crushed the stub under her foot. "I like a good time as well as anybody." She pushed a button on her smartphone. "Mind if I play some music?"

Every man wants to be a macho man

To have the kind of body always in demand.

Hey, hey, hey, hey, hey, hey!!

Macho macho man!

I gotta be a macho man

Macho macho man!

I gotta be a macho!

What the fuck?

Brad vaguely recollected the song. It had been popular before he was born. *The Village People? The all-male gay band from the seventies?*

What followed next happened so fast that later Brad had to take several minutes to piece it together. Dakota grabbed the crowbar, jammed it into Tiny's stomach, then dragged it upwards toward his arm, swatting the knife out of his hand. She slammed the crowbar against the man's left kneecap, breaking it. Brad felt sickened by the sound of the kneecap breaking; it sounded like a four-by-four piece of wood being snapped in half. The guy crumpled to the floor. Before he could hit the ground, Dakota smashed her fist into his face. Blood poured out of Tiny's mouth. He spit out several teeth.

She handled that heavy crowbar like it was a cheerleader's baton.

The entire scene took less than three seconds. The immense man lay heaped on the floor, out cold—maybe even dead. Brad didn't know.

"Cindy?" Brad sputtered. "What are you doing here?" He paused, catching his breath. "Who the fuck are you?"

"Let me look at that arm," Dakota said. "You're bleeding. You may need a tourniquet."

Brad didn't know what to think. He didn't know what to do.

Who the fuck was that guy?

Who the fuck is this woman?

And what the fuck is going on?

Brad ducked out of the elevator and scampered away.

Dakota watched him. She patted down the enormous unconscious man, looking for his ID or his phone.

Once Brad got to his car in the parking garage, he ripped the strap off his overnight bag and tied it tight across his arm above the bleeding knife wound.

Then he quickly drove away.

14.

"Revered *Baa-baa*. I bring your breakfast of gohan, miso shiru, and hot tea with lemon," Aiko had said, bowing.

By the age of five, Aiko had been taught about honor and respect from her parents. From birth she'd been indoctrinated into these Japanese beliefs.

"Thank you, my beloved child," Hana had said. "Did you know that your name, Aiko, means beloved child?"

"Yes, *Baa-baa*. You have told me before."

"Throughout your life, you must honor your family. Treat them well. It is how you earn respect. It holds great value within our community. You understand, child?

"Yes, *Baa-baa*."

"The old are wise, yet nobody really notices or pays attention to old people. You get wisdom by aging. Old ones deserve respect. Because the old die soon. When they die, the wisdom that they have gathered during their lives dies with them, but respect and honor live on," Hana had said.

Since generations in a family lived in the same house, the family bonds between children, parents, and grandparents grew strong.

When Aiko turned thirteen, she had blossomed into a curious, intelligent young girl. That year her father, Ichiro, told her of the great shame that had befallen their family. Ichiro, the firstborn, was a small-boned man with bad eyes, requiring that he wear thick-lensed glasses. He'd worked in Japanese restaurants his entire life, earning a modest living. Then, in his late forties, he had developed arthritic hands, especially in both thumbs, from all the years of chopping vegetables and meats into tiny pieces with large, sharp knives.

"Our family lands were stolen from us by the giant pale eye, Warren Ramsay," Ichiro had said. "Your honored Grandfather, Ikatsu, husband of Hana, owned those lands, and when they were taken a great dishonor was done to our family." As he spoke, he nearly spit the words out. "Then the giant man in Washington did our family and thousands of other families like ours an even greater disservice."

"Who was that, honored father?" Aiko asked.

"The round-eyed president, Franklin D. Roosevelt, signed a legal order to send us to camps. Because we were Japanese. Because of what other Japanese had done at Pearl Harbor," Ichiro explained. "They called them internment camps, but they were prisons, and your family could not leave, though they were American citizens. Your grandfather and your honored *Baa-baa* were forced to live there along with your beautiful mother, Akemi, who was just a little girl when this bad thing happened."

"They shamed our family," Aiko said.

"That is correct, beloved child." Ichiro looked off into the distance as if he were looking for more to say.

Japanese culture regarded the loss of honor as a serious thing. Centuries ago, loss of family honor was lessened by Seppuku, ritual suicide by disembowelment. The practice of hari-kari, as it as referred to by Western society, was used extensively by Japanese in World War Two. Kamikaze pilots gave their lives by dive-bombing planes into American ships. In present day Japan, suicide rates were higher than in other nations; Japanese who felt they had shamed their families committed suicide, as their ancestors had done for thousands of years. Japanese people could, somehow, reclaim family honor by committing suicide.

"Can we now get those lands back, father?" Aiko asked.

"No, child. It is now a place where many homes stand. They are called mobile homes. Owned by Warren's son, Ramsay."

"Father? How can I, a girl, return honor to our family?" Aiko had asked.

"I don't know child," Ichiro had answered. "Many years later, another American president, a large man named Ronald Reagan, signed a bill that paid damages to Japanese families who were sent away to the internment camps. Our family received ten thousand US dollars—a small pittance for lands that are now worth tens of millions."

And with that, the seed of an idea had been planted in Aiko's head.

"If our family could receive one million dollars," Aiko asked, after quickly doing math in her head. "Would that help return honor to our family?"

Ichiro's eyebrows raised.

Two years later, when Aiko was fifteen, she had blossomed into a beautiful young woman; one look from her would take the breath away from any man. As she began to learn the power she held, Aiko consulted her mother.

"Mother? I want to learn the ways of the geisha," she had said.

Akemi, a beauty herself when she was a teenager, knew the power a young woman possessed by proper training and agreed to assist her daughter. Akemi taught her all three stages of geisha with emphasis on *Maiko*, the last stage, when Aiko learned how to entertain men by dancing, singing, and playing musical instruments. She learned the proper way to prepare and serve men food and drink. She learned how to converse with men, how to keep a man's interest by asking questions, and how to stroke a man's ego.

And like many geisha who had chosen a more carnal path, Akemi taught her how to please a man; she taught Aiko how to be a *yujō* geisha, or a true courtesan.

And now, years later, Suzie—born Aiko Tanaka—was married to Brad Marshall, grandson of the Baka Gaijin, Warren Ramsay.

Foolish foreigner.

Brad and Suzie were driving to her parent's home in San Jose to celebrate the ninety-fifth birthday of Susie's revered grandmother, Hana. It was a drive that Suzie was familiar with, as she drove to her sushi restaurant, located ten minutes from her parent's home, almost daily. She wore her silver hazmat suit, which was duct taped shut at the ankles and wrists. She donned black combat boots and blue latex gloves. Since she had recently received her second Moderna Covid shot, she lost the full-faced helmet and had replaced it with two N95 surgical masks, both of which she wore over her nose and mouth.

Suzie drove, and Brad sat shotgun as he texted on his phone. He wore a long-sleeved hoodie sweatshirt, and his right arm hung by his side. He had just returned from his most recent trip. When Brad had exited the bathroom that morning, he left it littered with bloody towels and a box of butterfly clips purchased from CVS Pharmacy.

"Cut myself on a broken wineglass," he'd said to Suzie.

"How did that happen?" Suzie had asked, just to make conversation.

"Playing blackjack. This guy with bad skin won a big hand. Got excited. Smashed his glass on the table. I jumped so fast that I jammed my arm down on the broken glass. Cut myself bad."

"Why did you want me to come down to San Jose with you?" he'd asked, after a pause.

When she visited her family, Suzie normally went alone.

"*Baa-baa*'s ninety-fifth birthday is today."

"Is that so? Wow!" he'd said, feigning interest.

"She asked for you. She wants to speak to you. Who knows how much longer she will be around? Ninety-five is very old," Suzie had said.

"Okay, then. Sounds great, honey." Brad continued to feign interest.

Suzie noticed that Brad's face was flushed red, and he was sweating. "Are those clips enough? Or should we go to the doctor's office? He could look to see if you need stitches, or a clamp?"

Does he have a fever?

"Nah. I'm okay. Got the bleeding to stop."

Not quite true. Brad's arm was seeping blood. His triceps muscles were lacerated, and he couldn't straighten his arm. He needed a proper medical treatment for it to heal properly. He couldn't move the last three fingers on his right hand.

"You got your Covid vaccination, right?" Suzie asked.

"Yes," Brad lied.

"Both shots?"

"Yes," Brad lied again. "Moderna vaccine. Two shots. Hurt like hell, honey. Made me feel tired and dizzy for a day or two after."

Last thing I need is for this asshole husband of mine to bring Covid into my parents' home.

"What else have you been up to?" Suzie asked.

"You know what I've been doing, honey. The usual stuff," Brad said. "Golfing. Spent the last two days at Hekawi." Then he added, "Before that I'd been helping Jojo settle some of Dad's bank accounts and credit cards. You know the drill."

Ahh. Yes.

I know the drill.

Brad and Suzie had been married for two years. They'd dated for one year prior to Brad popping the question. Suzie's plan had come together. She would wait for Ramsay to die—after all he was old, and he'd already had several heart attacks. Suzie was patient, a Japanese trait passed down from generation to generation by the *Bushidō*, or warrior's code.

Good things come to those who wait.

She planned to file for divorce, citing any of Brad's many infidelities as the cause.

Let's see now. Long ago, I calculated the value of my family's share of the land at one million dollars. Today's worth? Twenty years later? With the land located in the

295

heart of Silicon Valley? Fifty million divided by two, then divided by two again, comes to twelve million five hundred thousand dollars.

"If our family received twelve and a half million dollars as reparation for our lands being stolen? Would that restore our family honor, revered father?" she had asked Ichiro recently, calculating her share of the settlement under California divorce law. Ichiro was now in his seventies, still working but now in his daughter's restaurant. He was still crippled by arthritis and now legally blind. His memory was not as good as it had been when he was younger.

Ichiro nodded his head in approval. "Long have I thought of how I might avenge our family's honor. I am a Tanaka, beloved daughter," Ichiro began. "I married into the Nakatomi family when I married your beautiful mother. I then learned of the great shame she carried. Because I love her so deeply, I wanted to be the person to avenge her shame. The shame that I feel is bottomless. I wanted Ramsay Marshall dead. I thought that I, Ichiro Tanaka, could make that happen."

"Father," Suzie said. "Please. There is no need to tell me this."

"Now that evil one is dead," Ichiro said. "We only have his moron of a son to deal with." He stood erect. "I am still strong."

What was honored father saying?

It is said that a Japanese man has three faces. The first face is the face that they show the world. The second face is the face he shows to friends and family. And the third and last face is the face he never shows to anyone, which is the truest reflection of who he is.

Which face is father now showing me?

"Father," Suzie replied, her voice betraying her anxiety as she regarded the frail old man. "I think it best that we plan on getting reparation."

"That would best restore our family honor. A significant sum of money. Your grandfather, Ikatsu, would feel proud. You have done well, beloved daughter."

Suzie had other problems to think about, mainly the restaurant apocalypse in northern California. Throughout the pandemic, the current governor had flip-flopped on dining restrictions. Employees were laid off. Owners of hundreds of restaurants sued the governor. Suzie held off laying off employees for as long as she could, paying them out of her savings. Her father, who would not accept wages, was the only person helping her keep the place open.

The whole world went crazy during the pandemic.

Her restaurant was open for takeout only. Indoor and outdoor dining were closed. This did not generate enough income to keep the doors open. She had Sophia, Brad's sister, to thank for talking some sense into her.

"You can't keep paying people forever," Sophia had said. "It makes no sense. When all of this is over, you can hire your people back, if they haven't found other jobs, that is."

"That makes sense," Suzie had said.

"And I can come by to help, if you'd like the help. I waited tables in college. Helped prepare meals too."

"Thanks," Suzie had said. "That'd be helpful. You're too kind."

That was good business reasoning; Suzie felt relieved that she had someone to talk to in Sophia, and she could use extra help during these tough times.

I thank the stars that my father helps also.

Divorce money would help with reopening my restaurant.

They arrived at Suzie's parents' house in San Jose, the same small home that Ikatsu and Hana had lived in, then it had been passed down to Suzie's parents. The neighborhood had many older homes. Ichiro and Akemi stood at the front door to greet them.

Before hugging her parents, Suzie first bowed to them. Her parents bowed back.

"You too skinny, Blad," Akemi said, fawning over Brad. "I'll fatten you on dumplings. Make special. Just for you." Akemi, also in her seventies, was bent over like a question mark with osteoporosis.

"Pleasant ride?" Ichiro asked Brad, while observing his limp right arm.

"Lots of traffic," Brad answered. "Like always."

Ichiro had a smile on his face. "Pleasant ride?" Ichiro repeated.

Suzie gave her father a look. "Lots of traffic on the roads, father." she repeated.

Ichiro and his wife Akemi hated Brad Marshall. But, keeping their eyes on the prize, they chose to tolerate him.

Inside, Suzie sat next to her revered grandmother, Hana, holding her hand. She felt saddened at how frail Hana's hand felt. Hana appeared shrunken, tiny almost,

298

her hair white and thinning. Her dry white scalp peeked out between the clumps of white hair. She smelled like she had bathed for a while. A purring cat sat in Hana's lap.

"Hi Grandma," Brad said, pulling up a chair and sitting in front of her. "I understand you wanted to talk to me?"

With effort, the old woman raised a hand and motioned Brad closer. She was weak. The ravages of old age had taken their toll. There was nothing wrong, however, with her voice, which was clear and strong. Brad stifled a cough. When he placed his ear close to her, she said, "Why are you such a shit to my beautiful granddaughter?"

15.

Dakota had just finished her afternoon workout, this time targeting quads.

Feels great to lift.

But, she'd thrown her back out. She moved gingerly, the result of morning squats with heavy weights. Dakota hurt herself regularly while lifting, always pushing the envelope—it was the price you paid if you wanted to have a freakishly powerful body.

Her long black hair was tied up in a bun. She had washed out the temporary magenta color. She wore a Wonder Woman sweatshirt with the ageless Amazon running, her long black hair flowing behind her, while holding her magic golden lasso of truth. Dakota had her AirPods in, listening to "Disco Inferno" by the Tramps, one of her favorites.

Zeus lay at her feet in a twin-sized mattress one would normally find in a teenager's room. The massive dog was calm.

"Odd," the veterinarian had said when Dakota picked Zeus up after having him fixed. "When we opened this morning, we found him just lying on the ground. Quiet as a church mouse."

"Unusual for Zeus. He's kind of skittish."

"He broke out of his cage. Somehow. And he was not familiar with his surroundings. Usually, a dog can get agitated by that—they get anxious, destructive. Getting into garbage, tearing things up when they're scared."

"I agree."

"And there he is, lying around, seemingly without a care in the world. He had a doggy smile on his face."

"Well," Dakota said, wondering what her massive dog had done. "I'm glad he didn't get into any trouble."

She watched as Zeus calmly rolled over on his mattress, stuck out his massive tongue and licked himself where his pair of massive balls used to be.

Can't unsee that.

At four p.m. she Face-Timed Palmer.

"Meg found you another car insurance company, Sarge," she said.

"Pardon?" Sarge said.

"You remember. All American Insurance. The company with a customer service department in India?"

"Yeah. Right."

He looks like he lost some weight.

"Good old, reliable Meg," Palmer added. "Can you believe that company?"

"Meg also wanted me to tell you we got a check from the US Government for helping in one of those Covid scams we've been working on."

"Finder's fee?" Palmer asked.

"Sort of. A bit more than that. Some guy who ran a vaccination scam. They contacted seniors, mostly via phishing emails. Promised to get them closer to the front of the list to get their vaccines. People had to provide their contact info to see if they might qualify—age, health questions, social security numbers, that sort of thing."

"Ahh."

"Threatened to withhold their social security checks if they didn't provide personal info."

"Preying on people's fears."

"Yep."

"Meg helped me on this too."

"She did, did she?" Palmer said. "She's turning into quite the little private investigator."

"She pretended to be a senior. Said she wanted to get her vaccination sooner. Filled out one of their online forms. While the form was loading, she sent their website a worm. The virus relayed info back to us. She could trace their server. From there, it wasn't too hard to find the computer and its location. Turns out, it was a guy working on a snorkeling boat, sitting on a beach in Kona, running the scam."

"How'd she know how to send a worm, Dakota?" Sarge asked, already knowing the answer.

"I might have given her a hint or two."

"A PI in the making," Palmer said proudly.

"We sent it to the FBI. Let them take it from there. The government pays a handsome fee for helping find these scammers. Some of these fuckin' leeches pose as medical providers or health department officials."

"No ethics, no morals."

There's something off in his voice.

"You okay, Sarge?"

"Yeah. I'm fine. Why do you ask?"

"Dunno." Dakota paused. "Don't you have a birthday coming up next week?"

"Yeah. Sixty."

Sixty—an age when if you didn't pay attention to your blood pressure, cholesterol, plus other things, serious health consequences could happen.

"To tell you the truth, my stomach has been bothering me," Palmer said, saying nothing of the problems he'd been having after getting his kidney stone blasted.

I'm going to keep a closer eye on him.

"So. Do you think Brad Marshall is okay?"

"No arterial spray from the knife wound on his arm," Dakota said.

"Was this guy trying to kill him? Over an unpaid gambling debt?"

"He was trying to kill him, all right. I'm not yet sure if a gambling debt was the reason."

"What do you mean?"

"ID said his name is William Smith. I'm still tracing who this guy is. Who he works for. He kept saying 'Vito sends his regards' to Marshall."

"Who's Vito?"

"Supposedly works for Circus Circus in Vegas. Brad owes them money."

"Did you take care of him?"

Dakota remained quiet while carefully choosing her words. "Neutralized."

Sarge didn't push. "Someone paid this 'William Smith' money for the hit. Follow the money, Dakota. That'll give us what we need."

She was way ahead of him. When "William Smith" lay on the ground, kneecap broken, unconscious, and bleeding from the mouth, Dakota had found his iPhone. She took out her D2-sized Pentalobe screwdriver from a kit she carried, unscrewing the back cover to the phone and removing the SIM card. Then she copied its contents onto a Magic firmware reader.

Illegal, of course, but who gives a flying fuck.

She had all the contents on his phone at her disposal—his contact list, all texts and calls that he'd sent and received. Access to his phone apps, bank account info, credit card numbers, even his Charles Schwab account information.

Easy peasy.

"One other thing, Sarge," she said. "I'm gonna take some vacation time."

"How long?"

"About a week."

"What for?"

"I located my birth mom," Dakota said, while filing down a manicured nail on her right hand. She noticed another chipped fingernail. *Must have chipped it when I punched that guy in the face.*

"That's great news, Dakota. Splendid news."

The many hours she had spent searching for her birth mother had paid off. First, Dakota had had her DNA ancestry analyzed. Through a combination of genealogical research, via firms like ancestry.com, and familial relationship searching techniques that those firms provided, a match had been produced. They identified a close DNA match, possibly an aunt, living in Boston.

My mom's sister?

Another hit showed she had a more exact DNA match with a man in Chicago.

Possibly my brother?

After contacting them and after having conversations with each, she had found that her birth mother was alive and well.

"Where is she?" Palmer asked.

"Oklahoma, Sarge."

"Have you talked with her yet?"

"Yes. She's excited to meet with me."

Dakota planned to visit her in Oklahoma City next month.

"I need you to do me a favor before you leave and when you get back," Palmer said.

"Sure, boss. What?"

"Keep tabs on Sophia Mueller for me. I'm worried that she might be next on the hit list."

"Got you. Sure thing. I can put a GPS tracer on her car before I leave? This way you'll know where she goes when she leaves her house."

"That's good."

"When I get back, I'll keep an eye on her. Make sure nothing happens to her."

"Okay. Good. Well, take all the time you need," Sarge said. "Nothing is more important than something like this. Finding your birth mom. Best of luck."

"Thanks, Sarge." Dakota made a mental note to take her passport on the trip as well.

Zeus gave his best doggy smile, rolled over, then offered her what bits and pieces he had left.

Jeez.

Dakota put in her earbuds and played "Bad Girls" by Donna Summer.

305

16.

John sat in his front yard, stomach flopping over belted shorts, watching his fifteen turtles flounder in their seven-dollar, blue plastic, Walmart-brand kiddie pool.

"Clyde? Heathcliff? Gertrude? Have you met our new friend Barney Two?" he said.

"Petula? Don't be trying to hump Barney Two just because he's the new guy."

John had figured out the correct dose of horse tranquilizer to give him the best relief from his hemorrhoid itching and pain without leaving him feeling woozy. The Banamine, however, left him with a dull headache, a constant buzzing in his head as if bumblebees were bouncing around in his skull.

"Give Barney Two a couple of days before you start humping him. Okay, Petula?" John's eyes crossed a little when the bumblebees bounced around.

"Morning, John," Henry said, as his ninety-year-old neighbor slowly pushed his stroller with the little black wheels on his daily three-hundred-yards, one-hour-long walk.

"Morning, Henry," John said, watching as his neighbor slowly shuffled his stroller six inches forward, before slowly shuffling his feet forward six inches.

"Odd that you have two turtles named Barney," Henry said, stopping to rest.

"No, Henry. His name is Barney Two."

"That's what I said. Same name as your other turtle named Barney."

"No, Henry. Barney died last month. I bought another turtle and gave him the same name."

Henry inched his stroller forward. "You're just like George Foreman."

Forgot how hard of hearing he is.

"George Foreman? The guy who makes the hamburger grill?"

"No," Henry said. "Not that one. The boxer George Foreman." Henry hacked up a green glob, spitting it on the ground. "He's got five sons. Named every one of them George."

"My new turtle is not named Barney, too, Henry. His name is Barney also, like my favorite turtle that died last month." John repeated. "I named him after him."

"Strange that you did the same thing that George Foreman did, John," Henry said, this time feeling stronger, inching his stroller one foot forward. "Giving your turtles the same name. Are you a boxing fan, John?"

In a flash, John's eyes crossed, and he felt a homicidal urge knife through him. Plus, his stomach felt a little off, and he couldn't figure out why, though he had just eaten microwaved fish for breakfast, though, because of the rank smell, he couldn't finish it all.

"Have a nice day, John." Henry said as he inched his way past John's house.

"You too, Henry," John said, fighting the urge to kill as he watched his turtles play in the pool. He returned his attention to the book he was glancing through to get his mind off of Henry.

He didn't mind that the book, *How to be a Futurist—a Dummy's Guide* by Alvin Toffler the third. Who was the grandson of the famous 1970s futurist writer.

If a futurist can give his sons and grandsons the same name, I can give my turtles the same name too.

John thought that he'd like to become a futurist. *Why not?* A futurist studied and predicted the future. Accurately. Though John had none of the advanced education and special training that a futurist might have—like having lived in different places around the world, training in systems thinking, years of writing and publishing credible works, and success at public speaking and higher education teaching—John thought that being a futurist might help him in other areas.

I could predict who will win the next Super Bowl. Even better, predict the winner of the next WWE main event wrestling match! I'll place huge bets. Win a fortune.

John was patting himself on the back for predicting that Ichiro Tanaka may have had something to do with the death of Ramsay Marshall.

He couldn't wait to tell Sarge that he had solved the case.

First, had to hide a couple of microphones and cameras at Ichiro's San Jose home.

Check.

Next, he had to listen and watch.

Check.

Next, he followed Ichiro to his daughter's sushi restaurant in San Jose, where he worked. When the restaurant closed, he broke in to hide a couple of microphones and cameras.

Check.

He listened and watched.

Check.

He watched Ichiro at the restaurant.

Check.

He watched Ichiro make fresh sushi.

Check. Check!!

Finally, he listened in when Ichiro spoke with his daughter, Suzie, that saucy little spitfire, at his house. Ichiro wanted Brad Marshall dead. Ichiro had wanted to kill Ramsay Marshall himself. He'd wanted to kill him to avenge his family's honor.

Practically a confession right there. Certainly, the motive is clear cut.

Ramsay may have gotten his favorite sushi meals from his daughter-in-law's restaurant.

It's possible. Check!

It made sense. Instantly, there were fewer bumblebees bouncing inside John's head.

I'll show Sarge. Laugh at me now, will ya? So, I thought that Bob Hope was alive at one hundred and seventeen years of age. So what? And that Hope was still ogling women in the "me too" era. I'll show Dakota. And Meg.

Go ahead. Laugh at me now.

John couldn't wait to tell Sarge.

His stomach felt better, too. A foul smell emanating from the kitchen drifted by.

I can give Barney Two the rest of the microwaved fish.

Suddenly, John caught a strange sight heading his way. An old man with a long, greying red beard approached. He wore an odd-looking hat, one that a fishing boat captain might wear, except this hat was dirtier and more ragged looking. The hat had one long black feather sticking out of it.

The man was pushing an old, beat-up baby stroller. In the stroller sat a huge dog, panting with his tongue hanging out.

"Well, hello there, John. Remember me?" The man spoke in an English accent, as if he'd played a footman in "Downton Abbey". "It's me, Jonesy."

Fuck me. Why the hell is this guy at my house?

"You remember me, don't you?"

"How could I forget?" John said. "You helped me and Sarge at the cemetery."

"Who's Sarge?" Jonesy asked.

"Palmer Doyle."

"Ahh."

"How did you get here? To my house in Tracy? Did you walk here?" John's office was twenty miles away in Dublin. The cemetery where John and Palmer had exhumed Ramsay Marshall's body was in Lafayette, about forty-five miles away.

"I have my means of transportation," Jonesy said. "I'd rather walk, though. Walking is such wonderful exercise, plus it's great for the soul. Don't you think?"

"Yeah. Sure. Whatever."

"Do you remember Mister Peabody here?" The German Shepherd looked at John, not blinking.

John stiffened. "You keep that mongrel away from me. You hear?"

It looked like something was growing out of Jonesy's beard. Mister Peabody could use a good grooming too.

Visions of Zeus attacking him just days ago spun in John's head. He broke out in a sweat. The bumblebees in his head started bouncing around double time. Since Zeus had assaulted him at the vet's office, John kept having a recurring nightmare about the giant English Mastiff. With each successive dream, Zeus grew bigger; in last night's rendition, Zeus's massive head took on the proportions of a large male African lion with a full mane. He had four-inch long, sharp canine teeth lions used to rip skin and tear away meat.

John shrunk and walked backwards towards the front door of his house.

"Keep that fucking dog away from me," he repeated.

Mister Peabody jumped out of the baby stroller and pranced next to the blue plastic pool, stuck his head in the water, and sniffed at the turtles.

"How did you find out where I live?" John asked, keeping his distance.

This guy smells like sewage.

"Now in today's world, that's really not too difficult. Is it?" There was that pretentious English accent again. Mister Peabody kept sniffing John's turtles, wagging his tail.

"What do you want? What are you doing here? Can you please keep your mangy fuckin' dog away from my turtles! And, when was the last time you took a shower?"

"Well, I told your friendly boss—Mister Doyle, that is—that I'd like to be of service to him."

"How can you do that?"

"I think I can help you with some cases that you're working on."

"Why the fuck would you do that?"

"So that I can be a private investigator. Of sorts."

"Yeah, right. Like that will ever happen."

"Quite right. I can see why a person might think that. Though, I believe that I'd excel at it." Jonesy added proudly, "And I did shower last week."

Doesn't smell like it.

"Best of luck. Now, could you leave me alone and get the fuck outta here?" John said, standing upwind.

Is that something moving around in his beard?

"If I were you," Jonesy started. "I think that'd be well worth your time to hang around the city offices."

"What the fuck are you talking about?"

"You know. City government offices. That is what I used to do when I was working."

"What the fuck would you know about that? And how would that help me?"

"Well, I used to spend quite a bit of time there myself. Back in the day." The retired superior court judge said. "A person can discover all kinds of interesting things there."

"Yeah? Like what?"

"The General Plan, the City General Land Use Map. Things like that." Jonesy smiled. "It's a happening place."

"What's a General Land Use Map?" John asked.

"Shows what land can be used for within city limits—whether land can be used for homes, businesses, commercial or industrial use, or for schools, churches. That sort of thing."

"Now why would I want to do something like that?" John asked.

A phone rang somewhere inside of Jonesy's filthy clothes. He answered, holding the device in his dirty hand.

"Well, yes. This is he," Jonesy said.

Jonesy listened thoughtfully while stroking his long beard.

"Why, yes. I see. I think I can do that. I should be able to get there sometime tomorrow afternoon. It'll take me a day to walk there," Jonesy said. "Cheerio." He ended the call.

"A friend of mine in Danville needs help with a briefing."

Help with a briefing? Take a day to walk there? Cheerio?

"Where do you live, exactly?" John asked.

"Coliseum."

"Liar. No, you don't." John answered.

"Yes, I do," Jonesy retorted.

"No, you don't. The Coliseum is in Rome," John said triumphantly.

"No, no, my dear man," Jonesy said. "Not that coliseum. The Oakland Coliseum. Up in Mount Davis,

313

where the Oakland Raiders used to play football. Before they moved to Las Vegas."

"Oh," John said, at a loss for words.

"Now. Where was I? Ah, yes. I remember. I think that I've said quite enough for now. I've been told that I talk too much." Jonesy paused. "Time to go, Mister Peabody. I'd rather not be known as a gabbler."

Quick as a cat, the German Shepherd jumped into the baby stroller, first stopping near the turtle pool to lift a leg and pee.

"Gabbler?"

"Well, you know. A blabbermouth."

Now, where did I hear that word before? Oh. Yeah. The old Honeymooners TV show. Jackie Gleason.

John noticed that the stroller was chock full of dirty cooking utensils and one grimy looking book, *The Paleo Diet Cookbook.*

"Just think about what I said," Jonesy added.

"Good fuckin' riddance," John said, gazing into the blue plastic pool to see if his turtles were any the worse for wear. Bouncing bumblebees in his head took over again. He felt fried. No more reading about how to become a futurist today.

I think I'll watch half-naked girls dance on those Instagram Tik-Tok reels, instead.

Jeez. It's been so long since I last had sex with a woman.

"You have a great day now, you hear?" Jonesy said, walking away. "Hi there, neighbor," he said to Henry as the ninety-year-old rounded the corner, slowly pushing his stroller with the little black wheels.

Grumpy Old Man by Tom Lyons

Henry stopped to give Jonesy a long look.

Part Four

"It's Jonesy's world. We all just happen to live in it with him."

1.

"Meghan picked out the flowers," Palmer said, sniffing their fragrance.

Meghan was her usual perky self this morning, Palmer had noted, when he picked up the flowers— smiling and wearing another snappy outfit, at least it seemed snappy to Palmer. She had a cute, feminine way of shaking her head and tossing her hair.

Like she took a Grace Kelly pill.

"Red roses, Becky. Your favorite."

Palmer removed the dead flowers and carefully arranged the fresh ones. Buddy lay splayed out across Becky's grave. He whined, then looked up at Palmer.

"I know pup," Palmer said. "You know Mommy's down there. Don't you?"

"What's that honey?" Palmer said. "Yes. Yes. I talked to Francesca. She's doing fine. Think I'll go visit her as soon as I wrap up a case I'm working on."

It was a beautiful fall morning in northern California. Palmer finished perfecting his floral arrangement, glancing at it once more to make sure it looked okay. Every time he visited Becky here, he could not shake the feelings of despair he'd felt at losing her.

"There you go. That should do it," Palmer said. "They smell wonderful. There're a couple of things I wanted to talk about, honey. First, I don't think that I want to go to the California foothills anymore. I want to move out of California. Get the hell out."

He paused.

"Why? Too many bad things happen in this state. Property taxes are too high. Sales taxes too. Do you know they are close to ten percent now? Ten percent! On everything you buy! Taxes on gas are ridiculous. Gas prices are stupid high. Too many people are moving into the area. Traffic is a nightmare. It's too crowded. Crazy drivers. Just this morning, this guy flew past me, driving close to one hundred. He was texting! Has a date with a funeral home soon, is my guess. And don't get me started on politics. They just voted to recall the governor."

Just thinking about all the weird stuff happening in California made Palmer grumpy.

"I was thinking about either Oregon or Idaho. What do you think about that, honey? Is that okay?" Palmer asked his dead wife. "I realize that you don't want to move away from here, but I just don't think I can take it anymore. I'll find you a delightful spot. With a splendid view. Promise."

Palmer struggled to stand, wincing in pain.

"Look at me. I'm a one-armed, half deaf old man." He looked at the grave. "No other way of looking at it." He glanced at Buddy sitting by his side. "Yes, I know. You're right. I'll go to the doctor, honey."

He felt a surge of pain in his abdomen. He had peed blood again weeks after the procedure to blast his kidney stone. He'd popped a Vicodin this morning to help with the pain.

"What's that, Becky? Yes. I hear you. Probably my prostate this time. I'll get it checked. You were a nurse. Always knew what was going on with me." Becky had always known when her needed another MRI, another X-ray, another CT scan.

"There's this lady." Palmer looked to the ground, hands in his pocket, as he shuffled his feet. "I never thought that something like this would happen, but I'm attracted to her."

He cocked his good ear towards Becky's grave.

"Yes, I know. I know that you want me to be happy. And yes, I agree with you. Enough time has passed. I miss you, honey. But I want your blessing. Before I ask this gal out. I want you to know. She's a client too. I will not ask her until her case is closed."

Oddly enough, Palmer obsessed about Sophia, about whether she cared for him. He found himself playing, in his head, an odd game of "She loves me, she loves me not" complete with pulling petals from a yellow daisy. And now, he was worried about her, concerned that someone might harm her.

Buddy's whining snapped Palmer back to the present. He nudged Palmer's hand, wanting a scratch behind his ears. Palmer obliged, then sat. "Magnificent views here, eh Becky?" He admired the view.

"Gotta go, sweetie. Buddy's right. Got work to do," Palmer finally said. "I'll see you next week, sweetheart."

Palmer and Buddy walked around gravestones and trudged back down the hill.

A visit to the doctor would have to wait. Palmer had business to attend to.

"Get this," Dakota had said during a phone call with him last week. "I have news about that big guy who attacked Brad Marshall. The one who supposedly threatened Marshall about his gambling debt."

"Yeah," Palmer had responded. "And?"

"That's not the case. He doesn't work for Circus Circus. This guy works for the owner of a garbage disposal company."

"How'd you find that out?"

"The big guy's phone records. William Smith. Remember I copied his SIM card?"

"Yep."

"Turns out the owner of the garbage disposal company is Vito Coppola. He's the man who pays the guy who knifed Brad Marshall."

"What's the connection?" Palmer had asked. "Between Brad Marshall and Vito?"

"I don't know, Sarge," Dakota had answered. "I'm working on that. His company is called Trash Kings."

Vito.

A line from the first Godfather movie flashed through Palmer's mind: *Leave the gun. Take the cannoli.*

But . . . *Trash Kings?*

Palmer knew that on the east coast, organized crime controlled the lucrative garbage disposal business. Crime bosses used a legitimate business to launder money from their illegal activities, like drugs and prostitution. Decades ago, the Mafia controlled all the garbage disposal companies in the New York metropolitan area. The garbage collection business was a cash cow.

That was New York, though. East coast stuff.

Could it be happening here in California?

All Palmer knew was that he had work to do. He had to get ready for his upcoming meeting with Vito Coppola. He also had an urge for cannoli.

2.

The grief Suzie felt was overwhelming. She couldn't stop crying.

In Japanese custom, the deceased was cremated, and the family held a ceremony every seven days for forty-nine days, seven ceremonies in all. Before Hana was cremated, Suzie's family placed a small pearl in her mouth to insure a smooth journey into the afterlife. Suzie's mom, Akemi, grieving, took care of funeral arrangements, which kept her busy and kept her mind occupied.

I miss my revered Baa-baa. She taught me so much. Her sage advice. She had learned so much over her ninety-five years. The wisdom and knowledge that she had accumulated. Now, like Hana, that wisdom and knowledge that she had learned was gone.

Thank goodness she went quickly. At ninety-five years old, she'd been frail. Her health issues had shut down her kidneys and heart.

We only just celebrated her birthday last week.

Suzie was overcome with despair.

Three days after her birthday, Hana had woken up with a fever and flu symptoms. When she was admitted to the hospital, she was diagnosed with Covid.

Just because the pandemic is mostly over doesn't mean you can't catch it. It's a virus, like the flu.

Suzie's grandmother lived for only forty-eight hours after the diagnosis.

"I don't understand it," her father, Ichiro, had said. "How did she catch Covid?"

"Did she get vaccinated?" Suzie had asked.

"No," Ichiro had answered. "Why should she? She never left the house, except to go to Yaoyo San with your mother to buy groceries," Ichiro said.

"I see," Suzie had answered, knowing full well how *Baa-baa* had caught Covid.

"She was careful at the market. She wore her mask. And she always practiced social distancing," Ichiro said. "Kept herself safe."

The part that hurt Suzie the most was that her grandmother had died alone, in the middle of the night, hooked to a ventilator. 2:04 a.m.

How scared she must have been!

How horrible that must have been for her, to die alone like that, with no one there to hold her hand and tell her that they loved her.

Just the thought of someone, anyone, let alone her revered *Baa-baa*, dying alone in the middle of the night made Suzie's entire body shiver.

My shithead husband.

That's how Hana had caught Covid.

My shithead husband.

Suzie and Brad had visited for Hana's ninety-fifth birthday just ten days prior. She'd caught Covid when Brad sat next to Hana and talked to her. He'd been coughing and hacking on the drive to her parents' house. He'd told her that he'd gotten his vaccinations. But Suzie went through his personal items in his home office, where Brad kept all his important documents.

No vaccination card.

He lied.

He had Covid. I bet he knew he had Covid.

He gave it to my grandmother.

I'd better get tested. He probably gave it to me, too.

Through her grief and despair, Suzie felt a quiet rage swell inside her. Quickly, she made her mind up. Time for *puchi fukushuu* on this *baka.*

Idiot.

3.

Bay Area Rapid Transit, or BART, is the Bay Area's version of the New York City subway system. With railway arms stretching fifty miles from San Francisco in all directions, BART offered a suitable alternative to sitting in the grid-locked traffic plaguing the Bay Area during the work week.

That morning Palmer took BART to the city to visit the Trash Kings office near the Embarcadero in downtown San Francisco.

No way I'm gonna wait at the Bay Bridge toll plaza for thirty minutes or longer.

Before he left home, he gave Buddy a bison bone.

Maybe he won't wreck the furniture.

Then he set the house alarm before he left. Dog theft had become a very huge thing during the pandemic. With most people staying home, a dog became an invaluable companion. Thieves had figured that out; the black market for stolen dogs brought in big money.

Gotta make sure Buddy is safe.

This morning when Palmer arrived at the Dublin BART station for the thirty-minute train ride, he was greeted by six BART police cars, lights flashing.

When he walked to the station, he saw what the ruckus was all about.

Homeless people, about one hundred of them who had made the heated confines of the station their home, were being herded and kicked out. Some were protesting, and they held up cardboard signs scribbled in magic marker that read:

BART is my home!

Don't take our home from us!

Where will we go to the bathroom if you kick us out of BART??

Palmer weaved through rows of wrinkled blue tarps and shopping carts filled with soiled, smelly clothes to get to the train station to catch the 8:15 to the city.

Homeless people are taking over BART stations now.

Potted palm trees surrounded one ragged tent.

An island paradise homeless park.

Palmer was reminded of the homeless situation in Venice Beach, California, where hundreds of tents were pitched on the beach boardwalk. Homeless from the entire country had moved to Venice Beach because city officials, rather than evict them, fed, clothed, and provided medical supplies to the homeless.

One homeless man, a toothless, recovering addict named Dave, had commented to the media: "I want to stay here because of the difference in the people here. I moved here from the Bronx. People are a lot ruder in New York. People in California are more laid back, that easy California style, and will you look at this!" The camera panned over the beach setting, while Dave smoked a cigarette. "You got millionaires living here, and they take care of us. Who wouldn't want to live here? It's the California dream. It's beautiful."

*So how do homeless people in other parts of the
country know about the Cadillac of all homeless
encampments in Venice Beach?*

Never mind.

*Even homeless people have iPhones. Everybody
knows everything these days. Even in New York, the word
got out about how good the homeless have it out here in
California.*

He wondered if perhaps Jonesy lived here in the
BART station. He looked but didn't see him among the
protestors. *How does he always seem to know where I'm
at? Is he tracking me?*

He spotted two homeless women, both maybe in
their mid-thirties, holding more magic-marker hand-
written signs. TV trucks had arrived, and cameras were
rolling. The homeless protest would be on this evening's
news.

Free Mr. Potato Head!

Bring back Doctor Seuss!

Several Dr. Seuss books had just been pulled from
production for having racially insensitive pictures of
Blacks and Asians, though they were first written in the
1930s. And Mister Potato Head would now be called
"Potato Head" from now on, effectively now being
"gender neutered".

*Just like last year when Aunt Jemima pancake batter
disappeared from supermarket shelves.*

Yet the song 'Wet Ass Pussy' can win song of the year.

Strange times.

And what had Jonesy been referring to when he'd told John to watch the city offices? What had he meant by that? What had he referred to with the General Plan? And the Land Use Map? Palmer had an idea what these were. A city's general plan detailed future growth concepts within a city, or county, over the next five to seven years. A land use map, part of a general plan, showed areas where residential homes could be built, where stores and businesses could operate, where industrial buildings may be built by attaching zoning codes to areas within a city's or county's sphere of influence.

Why had Jonesy mentioned that to John? Palmer didn't know, but he made a note to have someone check out the city offices in Livermore, Dublin, and Pleasanton.

Jonesy hasn't been wrong yet.

Thirty-five minutes later, Palmer stood in front of the Trash Kings building.

Trash business must be good.

Vito Coppola, however, looked more like the head of a crime family than the owner of a garbage disposal company—short, heavy, pushing sixty, with black bushy eyebrows, and a face pockmarked from a lost battle with acne in his adolescent years. When he walked, he barely hid the pain his flat feet caused him. He reminded Palmer of Abe Vigoda, the actor who'd appeared in the first Godfather movie.

"What can I do you for?" Vito asked Palmer in a heavy Brooklyn accent.

He led them into a conference room where a large man, at least six-foot-four and as wide as a refrigerator, waited. The hulking, muscular man looked like he spent most of his free time in the gym. He had a black beard only partially covered by a black face mask. Palmer got the feeling he wore it not to protect himself from Covid, but rather to partially hide his face, which was black and blue around the top of his nose and eyes.

Must be the guy that Dakota pushed his nose back into his skull.

"I'm a private investigator. Working on a case. I hoped that you'd be able to help me out."

Palmer couldn't help but wonder what the hell he was doing here. How could this guy possibly be connected to the murder of Ramsay Marshall? By poisoned sushi? It made little sense.

Have to check all the boxes.

Palmer looked at the big guy. "You don't look so good. What happened to your face?"

The large man instantly took offense. "You don't look too good yourself, old man," he said, stepping closer to Palmer menacingly.

Truth be told, Palmer didn't feel good at all, though he'd popped a pain pill on BART. His complexion had grown pallid, his skin clammy. He broke out in a sweat. That morning, he'd noticed that a couple more nose veins had burst and starred. Yesterday he had gone to the doctor. His doctor had diagnosed him with a kidney infection, fallout from having his kidney stone blasted.

"Sometimes it happens," said Doctor Lee, one of the six Doctor Lees who worked in urology at the hospital. "That's why we monitor you after procedure. Check blood and urine. But not to worry. At least you don't have sepsis."

"Sepsis?"

"Life threatening infection complication."

"I don't have sepsis?"

"No. Just an infection. We have meds for that. Clear you up no time. Don't worry."

Nowadays, they had medicines for everything.

"I need more Vicodin too," Palmer had said.

"No problemo," his doctor replied. "And by the way, you should have someone look at those veins on your nose."

The large man moved into Palmer's space.

"Leroy," Vito said quietly.

Leroy? Thought Dakota said this guy's name was William Smith, according to his ID.

Leroy took a step back, his eyes trained on Palmer.

"Yeah," Palmer said. "Back off, Leroy."

Getting off to a good start.

"Let's see if we can help this man," Vito said. "He drove a long way this morning just to talk with us."

"I took BART."

"Ahhh."

"I'm investigating the death of Ramsay Marshall," Palmer started. "I understand he owed you money."

"Nice man," Vito said. "I like Ramsay. He died?"

"Several months ago."

"Really. How'd he croak?"

329

"I'm not at liberty to say."

Croak?

"Not at liberty to say? Huh. Murdered then, I suppose?"

Palmer did not answer. "He owed you money?"

"One point two million."

"Wow. That's a very large unpaid garbage collection bill."

"Nah, that's not it. I own other companies besides Trash Kings. We do road paving, concrete work, that sort of thing."

A vision of concrete overshoes flashed through Palmer's mind.

"Last year we repaved his entire property. The mobile home place in San Jose. He'd let the streets go to hell. Hadn't done any work on them for years. We repaired the potholes—in some places, the road had settled a couple of feet down in the soil. We leveled the streets. Stuff like that."

Sounds like something Ramsay would do. Not the first owner or landlord who didn't take care of their property. A slum landlord. Work like that could easily cost a million dollars.

"Ramsay didn't pay?"

"Not yet. Said we used inferior asphalt. Whatever the fuck that is. Said we didn't repave the streets correctly." Vito was lost in thought for a moment. "Wait, a minute. I see where you're going with this. But there's nothing there. We didn't do nothing to that guy. Nothing."

"What do you mean?"

"This isn't the nineteen forties. We don't hurt people anymore."

Jeez. Did this guy just admit that he was connected to organized crime?

"We have our lawyers handle things like this," Vito continued. "We pay them a boatload of money. Put a mechanic's lien on his place. Then we take him to court."

A mechanic's lien prevented the owner from selling before the debt was settled. Plus, if the filer of the lien won the court case, a court order could remove from their bank account the defendant's money. Palmer made a mental note to have Meghan or Dakota check it out.

"This wouldn't be the first time someone sued Ramsay Marshall," Vito added.

Not the first time?

"Last week someone threatened his son, Brad Marshall," Palmer said.

Leroy shifted uneasily in his seat.

"We had nothing to do with that," Vito said. "Right, Leroy?"

"Right, boss."

Both of them are liars. Clearly, they don't know that the gal who knocked "Leroy" out works for me.

Palmer felt as if he had come to a dead end. He knew he couldn't get more info out of this guy. He'd just lie again. Vito was hiding something.

The Vicodin had begun to make Palmer feel wobbly. He didn't know what to say next.

"You like sushi, Vito?" It was all he could come up with.

"What the fuck?" said Vito. "What are you, some wise guy?"

Palmer's BART ride back to Dublin gave him time to reflect.

Both Vito and Leroy are liars. Leroy tried to murder Brad Marshall. But over a dispute about paving some roads? Because his father didn't pay the bill? That made little sense. One thing we know for sure is that Ramsay Marshall died from eating poisoned sushi. But I doubt that either Vito or Leroy have ever stepped into a sushi restaurant.

What am I missing here?

Palmer decided to run it by Dakota, who had just returned to town.

Two minds are better than one.

"How's Tiny doing?"

Palmer nearly chuckled at the first words out of her mouth.

"He's still hurting, I'd imagine," she said.

"He wore a face mask," Palmer said. "You messed him up pretty good. I'd hate to be on your bad side, kid." This time, he allowed himself a quick chuckle. "Let's recap. Ramsay was poisoned with sushi. They attacked Brad with a knife. Somehow it doesn't make much sense that Vito would be the one to take out Ramsay. What do you make of all of this?"

"You know what it sounds like to me, Sarge? Sounds like we're looking for two people here. Somebody took out Ramsay. But someone else tried to take out Brad."

That made more sense than anything Palmer could think of.

4.

The next morning, much to Palmer's delight, his urine had returned to its usual yellow color.

Hopefully, the worst is over.

He felt normal and his strength had returned, except for his left arm, which had had little strength for years.

He dry-swallowed his last Vicodin.

Gotta pick up the refill Doctor Lee prescribed.

Already this morning, he'd received several robocalls; he blocked the numbers, knowing well that the robocall computer center would simply switch the incoming call number. He'd get the same robocall pitching the same thing tomorrow morning, only this time it would appear that the call was coming from a different number.

Palmer was driving to the Ruby Hill neighborhood, an upscale development in southeast Pleasanton, winding its way through a Jack Nicklaus signature golf course. Once inside the gates, he was greeted by an immense lake, water fowl cawing and scampering about. Each house, it seemed, was a large custom home, five thousand square feet at least, on half-acre lots.

Bet each one of these puppies sells for five million plus.

As he pulled up to Sophia's home, via a large circular driveway lined with flowering roses, tulips, and bright orange poppies, he received an incoming text.

Your pending claim for $4K in Covid relief is here! Go to: tax.ref.//TREAS. Or click here on the above link!

Another Covid scam, Palmer thought, saving the text so he could forward it to the proper authorities.

It was another warm, late morning fall day in northern California. Sophia answered the door wearing a yellow floral coverup over a white two-piece bikini.

"You're early, Palmer."

"I was born early."

Palmer extended his hand, and Sophia grabbed it, but instead of shaking Palmer's hand, she pulled him in close and kissed him on the cheek.

"I was doing laps," she said, pulling away and gathering her wet blond hair into a pony. "Care to join me out back?"

She turned and led Palmer through the house towards the backyard. He couldn't take his eyes off the way her backside swayed. Her kiss had stirred something inside of him.

"Would you like a cold drink? An iced tea perhaps?"

"That'd be fine." Her kiss reminded him of fifteen years ago, when she'd kissed him as he lay wounded in the Kandahar Trauma Hospital in Afghanistan.

Palmer couldn't help but be impressed by the house. It was huge, with fifteen-foot-high coffered ceilings throughout the ground floor. The kitchen was a gourmet chef's delight. Roomy and spacious, with custom white cabinets and matching stunning grey, white, and black slab granite counters.

The rear yard backed to open space and hills dotted with orange poppies and fragrant wild mustard flowers. A black-bottomed pool and spa towards the rear of the yard were situated to take in the best views.

"This is fabulous, Sophia," Palmer said, after taking a moment to let it sink in.

"Quite the place."

Damn. If someone wanted to harm Sophia, they could easily get access from this backyard. Open space. No rear neighbors. It'd be a piece of cake to break into. Better get John on this until Dakota gets back in town.

"Thanks. Belongs to Martin. He bought it when we moved here a couple of years ago. After mom died." She paused, looking into the black pool. "I wanted to be closer to my father. As it turned out, it's also a lot closer to the MD Anderson center. All we have to do is jump on a plane."

"How did Martin make his money?" Palmer made small talk, trying to hide the fact that he was worried for her safety.

"He built homes in Stuttgart."

"Really?" Palmer remembered now that Dakota had mentioned this to him.

Home builders make a shitload of money.

"How's your stepdad doing, by the way? Is he here today?"

"No. He's at the oncologist office." Tears welled in her eyes.

"Uh oh. That doesn't sound good."

"It's not. His cancer has returned."

"I'm so sorry to hear that, Sophia."

"Thanks. I find it helps to talk about it."

Palmer remained quiet.

Those whiskey-colored eyes.

"It's spread to his colon."

"Not good."

"No. It's not."

What do you say to a person when they tell you that a loved one has cancer?

Palmer felt tongue-tied. He bowed his head. "I'm sorry, Sophia. I hope they can treat it. Doctors perform miracles these days."

"Thanks, Palmer." She moved closer. Then she tossed her head back. "Let's sit by the pool. Okay?"

"Sure thing."

Sophia handed Palmer his iced tea. She had a glass of Chardonnay.

"What was she like?"

"Who?"

"Your mother."

Palmer felt a kinship with Sophia since both of their spouses had died from Covid. He also felt comfortable around her. But since their relationship was still business, he felt he best not let that show. He tried to keep his face expressionless, neutral.

"She was a wonderful athlete. A beautiful figure skater."

"That's right. She made the German Olympic team in sixty-eight."

"Not a simple thing to do. Quite the accomplishment."

A faraway look gathered in Sophia's gaze, as if she'd gone somewhere else, her eyes looking at something in the distant hills. Then she returned and looked at Palmer. "She was a gentle soul. A wonderful mother. Wonderful person too. I miss her. She was only sixty-two when she died."

"Way too young."

"She was a broken soul after her divorce from my father. You already know how he was. He cheated on her. It took her years to get over the pain he caused her."

"You were just a child when they divorced."

"Yeah. But mom told me the stories. When I was old enough." Sophia paused for a moment, taking a sip of her wine. "Took me years to forgive him for what he did. I mean, during the divorce, he tried to cheat her out of child support and alimony. Submitted false financials to the courts. Claimed he was destitute when he was actually wealthy. He had expensive lawyers, so eventually, when the dust settled, he ended up paying her a lot less money than she was entitled to."

"Hmmph."

Sophia held Palmer's gaze.

"It'd be easy to hate him. Forgiveness is harder. But worth the effort. Took me years."

"I see." Palmer felt comfortable with her eye contact.

"He is my father, after all. And when I moved here, he was a changed man."

"How so?"

"Older. Time had made him softer, rounded out his hard edges. He loved his gardens. Liked to putter around, pull weeds, try different color and flower combos to see what looked best. That sort of thing. The gardens that Brad destroyed with his motorcycle when Ramsay refused to give him money to pay off his gambling debts."

"Yes. My father was also somewhat understanding of what an asshole he'd been when he was younger. He tried to make it up to me. We had a better relationship, more like what a father-daughter relationship should be."

"Good for you."

She flashed a smile. "Thanks."

"Speaking of your brother."

"Half-brother."

"Yes. Did you know that someone tried to kill him?"

"No. I didn't." Shock crisscrossed her face. "What happened?"

"Guy by the name of Vito Coppola. Owns a company called Trash Kings, a garbage collection company."

"What?"

"His guy, a guy named Leroy, knifed him in a casino elevator." Palmer didn't mention that his name may not have been Leroy, but William Smith.

"Why?"

"Your dad, apparently, owed Vito money. One point two million, to be exact. For work done to your dad's mobile home park."

"Do you think this guy had anything to do with my father's death?" She leaned in closer.

"Not likely. Guys like Vito do their dirty work with bullets to the back of your head. Or they slit your throat. We think he's connected to organized crime. But would they kill someone with poisonous sushi? Not likely."

"So where does that leave us?" Sophia asked. She poured herself a second glass of Chardonnay. "Would you like a drink?"

"No. Thanks."

Drink vodka at eleven in the morning? After taking a Vicodin?

Palmer remembered the last time he'd mixed vodka with his pain medicine. He'd spent the better part of an hour bent over the throne at that restaurant.

Wouldn't be the first time I felt shitty.

"Okay. I'll have that Vodka."

"With a mixer?"

"Just a twist of lemon. On the rocks."

"Be right back."

Palmer watched as she sashayed towards an outdoor fridge.

She looks great.

A minute later, she returned and handed Palmer his drink. She touched his arm.

"Convenient," Palmer said, hiding how her touch shot through him, like a bolt of lightning. "Keep all your adult beverages outdoors, and close by."

"Works for me," Sophia said.

"That leaves us with Suzie as our number one suspect," Palmer said, getting back on point. "She had motive and opportunity. Poisonous sushi as a murder weapon points us directly at her. And her father."

"Her father?" Sophia asked.

"Ichiro. He threatened to harm Brad. He also wanted to hurt Ramsay to avenge his family's honor, since Warren Ramsay stole their lands during World War Two. Ichiro works at Suzie's restaurant. He's certified and trained to handle fugu. He's a person of interest. Right in the mix."

Sophia sat back in her chair.

"I can't believe that." Her voice brimmed with raw emotion. "I've gotten to know her a little."

"How so?"

"She's had a tough go with her restaurant during the pandemic. Had to lay people off when the county shut her down. When she reopened for takeout and outdoor dining, most of her staff had already found other jobs. I helped at the restaurant. Preparing some of the simpler items on the menu—salads, miso soup, things like that. Until she could hire and train new people."

"I see. Is there anything else about her you can tell me?"

"No. Not really. She was always very sweet. I met her father once or twice. I didn't talk to him much. He seemed like the quiet type. Don't think he spoke English well."

"I talked to the Washoe County police department too," Palmer said after taking a sip of vodka.

"Washoe? Where is that?"

"Washoe is the county where your father died. On the Nevada side of Lake Tahoe. They have jurisdiction over crimes committed on that area of the lake. Since it was determined that your father was poisoned, well then, it falls in their lap to investigate the murder."

"I see. What did they have to say?"

"Not much. They have limited resources. Not the largest police department. They have two homicide investigators."

"Two?" Sophia asked. "Only two?"

"Yes. Plus, their charter is to investigate crimes committed against county residents."

"Which my father was not."

"Yes. So, we're not likely to get much help there. But if we can give them a solid case wrapped in a bow, then they'll prosecute and bring it to trial."

"So, if I'm hearing you correctly then, Palmer, you and your staff are pretty much on your own."

"Looks that way. Yes." Palmer looked around, first towards the inside of the house, then towards the expansive yard. "No bodyguard?" A worried look flashed across his face. "I thought you were going to hire someone to watch over you?"

"Martin didn't think that it was a good idea," Sophia said. "He doesn't believe that either of us are in any danger."

"Can't say that I agree with him," Palmer said. "If you'd like I can talk with him about it."

"I think I would like that. Thank you." She remained quiet for a moment, looking at the ground. "Well," Sophia then said. "I can't tell you how much I appreciate all of your efforts." She stood. "Thank you so much. I feel that sometime soon you're going to sort this out. I can't thank you enough."

After a pause, a moment of hesitation, she moved closer to him, close enough for him to smell her perfume. She put her lips close to his good ear. "You know I haven't been with a man since my husband died two years ago."

Just like that, Palmer's iron-clad resolve not to get involved with a client while working on their case flew out the window.

She kissed him. Her mouth opened. Sophia moaned. There was something frantic about the way she kissed. Palmer kissed her back. She then rested her head on his shoulder; she took his hand and led him inside the house.

As he walked into her house, his head spinning as he imagined what was about to happen, he thought about what a friend had said to him long ago, when Palmer was a young man. What he'd said had always remained with Palmer.

I have a conscience. But sometimes, the male parts of my body?

Not so much.

5.

"Mrs. Green? I'm looking at you. You wore green so you could hide from me. Didn't you? Hahah! I don't blame you. You're such a tramp. Oh, that was a good one, Mrs. Green, you monkey woman. You're lean and mean, and you know that you'd like to wrap your spikes around my . . ."

High on a hill, hidden by flowering, scented yellow gorse, sat Brad Marshall, using high-powered binoculars to watch his sister Sophia cavort about her yard wearing a white bikini. As he watched, he recited lines from his favorite movie, *Caddie Shack*, where actor Bill Murray, playing stoned greenskeeper Carl Spackler, watched women from the Bushwood Country Club tee off as he lusted over them.

Damn, she looks good in that bikini, spilling out of the top. Who wears bikinis in late October?

Thank you, global warming!

Brad had been watching Sophia from his perch for a week, searching for ideas on how to get rid of his half-sister so he could get his hands on his dead father's entire fortune.

Who's that old guy sitting by the pool with her?

That's when it hit Brad square in the face.

The outdoor fridge!

It's where she keeps her wine.

He could easily access her yard by climbing the wrought-iron fence. No neighbors around. No other houses or people who might see him. No security gate, no cameras or motion detectors. Her house was nestled in the hill in a remote location. *Just wait for a dark night, no moonlight, wear black clothes. Climb that fence, inject a poison, one that can't be traced in her dead body afterwards, through the cork and into her Chardonnay bottle with a hypodermic needle and voila!*

Nothing could be easier.

The next time she sat in her yard and went to her fridge for a glass of wine, she'd be a goner. It didn't matter when. It could be tomorrow, next week, next month. Whenever. The next time she had a glass of wine, it'd be over. And no one would be the wiser.

Now . . . what poison to use?

That might take time to figure out.

Looking through his binoculars, he watched as Sophia stood, then moved close to the old man.

He's a big guy. Looks like something is wrong with his left arm.

Brad watched as Sophia kissed him, then led him by the hand into the house.

She's gonna sleep with him?

"Damn," Brad said out loud, feeling jealous.

"Lucky guy."

Once home, he researched poisons, discovering that he could buy a dozen lethal ones with a few clicks of his mouse. At first, he thought of getting cane toad poison, remembering an obscure saying from when he was a kid: "Lick a toad once and get high. Lick a toad twice and die." But toad poison could be detected in the bloodstream. After thirty minutes of research, he ordered aconite, "the queen of poisons." Aconite, a plant-based toxin, was also known by other names: monkshood, wolfsbane, leopard's-bane, devil's helmet, and blue rocket. It came from the dark green leaves of the purple Aconitum flower, and it was extremely poisonous. In its extract form, it was clear and odorless, leaving no trace in a person's system. The only postmortem signs were those of asphyxia, or oxygen deprivation.

Once ingested, it would take two to four hours for a person to die. First, the victim would suffer gastrointestinal issues, projectile vomit and diarrhea, frothing at the mouth, and debilitating stomach cramps. Those symptoms were followed by hypotension, or low blood pressure, then difficulty breathing. Finally, the afflicted fall into a coma. Then they die.

Perfect.

It was easy to order a couple of hypodermic needles from a medical supply website.

Easy peasy.

Brad was hungry. He'd played golf this afternoon. It had taken six hours to finish since he'd been behind a group of beginners who knew nothing about pace of play and proper etiquette. He'd cheated several times by moving his ball from behind a tree and then not adding a penalty stroke when he drove his ball in the middle of a lake. He still shot ninety-four. Not good. But at least the knife wound on his arm had healed. The afternoon exercise had made him ravenous.

Browsing through his fridge, he found a container of sushi, marked with a capital B in black magic marker. B for Brad. It was delicious. He washed it down with several jiggers of scotch.

Suzie must have left it for me. Thoughtful.

His wife was visiting her parents in San Jose, helping with funeral arrangements. It had been only a couple of days since Suzie's grandmother had passed.

She probably thinks that I gave her precious Baa-baa Covid. Maybe I did, maybe I didn't. What's done is done.

I probably gave Covid to the old hag.

He expected to be slapped with divorce papers soon.

Deal with that later.

That night, conditions were perfect. Clear dark skies, no moon, cool temperature with a light breeze.

Show time.

He wanted to get this over with and jump on a plane to Vegas. After the success he'd had at the Hekawi Indian Resort and Casino playing blackjack with special glasses that allowed him to know what cards might be dealt next, Brad bought several more pair, thinking that he'd be able to hit up Vegas casinos and make a killing. That idea excited him.

Dozens of casinos on the strip. It'd be nice to make a dent in the money I owe to Circus Circus.

Brad dressed in black chinos, a black sweatshirt, and a pair of black high-top Keds. He cut eyeholes out of a black ski mask and pulled it over his head before looking in the mirror.

Perfect.

He took a flashlight and a bottle of water.

Gotta stay hydrated.

He loaded the hypo with aconite.

Brad looked like a cat burglar. If he'd had a black cape, he would have looked like Batman, or more like Wile E. Coyote dressed as Batman.

He parked his car in a Starbucks parking lot a mile away from Sophia's house, then walked into the hills behind her house. It was one in the morning.

The fun started when he scooted down the hill towards the wrought-iron fence at the rear of Sophia's yard. He didn't want to be spotted, so he didn't use a flashlight.

He didn't see the gorse, which was filled with thorns. Several ripped into his legs. Thrown off balance, he stepped directly on a thorny bush that thrust several thorns through the rubber bottoms of his Keds. He hopped around in pain, stifling a yelp.

What the fuck?

Climbing over the fence, his fingers felt stiff. Once in the yard, he hid behind a tree to assess his injuries.

Fuck me. Bleeding pretty good.

He checked the house. No lights.

Asleep.

His stomach felt upset, it made strange gurgling noises.

When he moved toward the outdoor fridge, he felt a tingling run up and down his legs. His mouth felt thick as numb, as if he'd had a shot of Novocain at the dentist's office. His legs felt heavy, like they were weighted down with weights.

What's going on? Is this all from the gorse thorns?

Then he got a woody.

Good ol' blue pill.

He'd taken one earlier in the day, half hoping that he would pair up with a random gal at the golf course and get lucky.

No such luck.

The numbness in his legs intensified. He felt paralyzed. His arms were useless; unable to move them, they hung limp against his torso.

What the fuck is happening?

Brad crapped his pants. Diarrhea. He vomited, his retching sounds carrying in the cool night air as fear gripped his mind. Stiff as an ironing board, Brad pin-balled off of expensive lawn furniture, then off a brick-faced outdoor fireplace, and finally towards Sophia's pool. He could not move his arms or legs. The hypodermic needle was still in his pocket. Drooling now, with yellow mucus flowing out of his nose, Brad danced the Zombie dance as he pin-balled about—a life-sized Wile E. Coyote dressed like Batman, hopping around, and banging into things as if someone had hit him on the head with a large boulder.

"Fook muh," he gurgled, struggling to take a breath.

Brad Marshall felt scared.

His last thought was, *What a waste of Viagra.*

Then, like a stone statue, arms pinned to his side, his hard-on very much intact, Brad Marshall toppled over and fell into Sophia's pool.

Like father, like son.

6.

Meghan and John stood near the coffee machine. Meghan, who had gotten her two Moderna vaccination shots as soon as she was eligible, was not wearing a face mask. Sharkie, who had not gotten his shots, wore his green face mask with pictures of turtles.

"Why didn't he get the vaccine?" Dakota had asked last week when she saw John in the office. "You gotta be an idiot not to get it," Dakota had added. "If you're vaccinated, not only does it reduce your chances of catching Covid, but it helps preventing passing it on to anyone else."

"I know," Meghan said. "He told me he didn't believe in them. He said that if you got the shots, you'd have frequent dreams about floating in outer space without a space suit."

"Really?"

"Yeah. And that it would feel like your mouth was full of pennies that you couldn't spit out. So, you'd have a metallic taste in your mouth as you floated around in outer space."

"Lots of stupid stuff out there on why not to get the vaccine."

"Then he added that if you float around in outer space for too long, not only do you become impotent, but you can't get an erection."

"What?"

"Something about how a man needs oxygen to get a hard-on. Since there's no oxygen in space, when you come back to earth—or in this case, when you wake up— you can't get an erection."

Sounds like Sharkie, Meghan thought.

Stupid.

Palmer walked out of his office to grab another cup of coffee. He had a spring in his step. He looked happy.

"Morning, Meg," he said. "Great coffee this morning. Thanks."

"Thanks, Sarge." Meghan smiled. She'd noticed that Palmer seemed to be floating on air for about a week now.

"And John?" Palmer said looking at John. "Great idea on bugging the Tanaka house."

"Thanks, Sarge."

"Gives Ichiro an excellent motive to get rid of Ramsay Marshall. Reclaim their family's honor. Good call."

"Thanks, Sarge," John said again, a quizzical look on his face.

They both watched as Palmer walked, skipped almost, back to his office.

"Thanks for getting donuts too, Meg," he added, taking a big bite out of a chocolate one.

"What got into him?" John asked. "He was nice to me. He paid me a compliment."

"Dunno," Meghan said.

"He usually rips me a new one," John said. "I'm always expecting him to go off and snap at me. And was he whistling when he walked back to his office? Sarge whistling, imagine that?"

"I believe he was," Meghan said.

"I don't think that I've ever seen him happy," John said. "Strange. He's not grumpy."

Meghan knew what had gotten into Palmer. Or rather, what he had gotten into.

He's sleeping with Sophia Mueller.

A woman's intuition.

He broke one of the cardinal rules. Mixing business with pleasure.

Meghan felt as if she'd been gut-punched.

Meghan and Dakota had talked just the other day.

"Got a hunch about her," she had said to Dakota. "Does she check out?"

"Clean as a whistle," Dakota had said. "I can't find any dirt on her."

"But she's only been living in the States for a couple of years," Meg had said.

Dakota looked Meghan square in the eye. "I know, but she's been clean since moving here."

Meghan and John watched as Dakota walked into the office with Zeus on a short leash.

"Morning," Dakota, her face mask-free, said cheerfully.

Nice that things are getting back to normal.

John started shaking. The color drained from his face.

"That fuckin-n-n-n' dog shouldn't be in here." He said, nervously.

"Why not?" Dakota said. "Palmer brings Buddy to the office. Doesn't he?"

"He's afraid somebody might steal Buddy. You know, with all the dog thefts going on. Because of the pandemic," Meghan said.

"Pandemic's over," John said. "Besides, who'd be d-d-d-dumb enough to nab a Malinois? He'd bite their h-h-h-head off."

"Buddy wouldn't hurt a fly," Meghan said.

Zeus sniffed the air and lunged towards John, but Dakota braced herself with both of her legs pushing against the ground and held Zeus still.

"There, there. Good boy," she said, scratching him behind his ears, his favorite. The giant dog lifted his head and drooled.

"T-t-think I'll g-g-g-go back to my-my desk now," John said, stuttering, color still drained from his face.

He held his coffee cup with both hands to stop them from shaking. He scampered off, looking like he had just swallowed a lemon. "No one is going to try and steal a three-hundred-pound fuckin' English M-M-M-Mastiff," he whispered under his breath as he left.

"What got into him?" Dakota asked.

"Dunno," Meghan said.

Zeus lifted a massive hind leg and licked himself where his gigantic balls used to be.

Palmer sat in his office, daydreaming, poking at computer keys. Buddy lay in the corner on one of the many doggy beds Palmer owned. Buddy's alert eyes never left his master's face.

"Don't look at me like that."

Buddy, as dogs do, maintained eye contact.

"I know what you're thinking, pal," he said, jokingly. "But you were there when we discussed this with Mommy. She gave me permission to date again."

Buddy's ears perked.

"I'm hoping to see her again." He thought about Sophia. *That was wonderful Palmer*, she had said after they had made love last week, as they lay naked in bed. He liked her. Rather, he was falling for her. He knew that. No denying it.

Sophia looks magnificent naked.

He kept seeing her naked in his mind's eye.

Then he found himself, once again, counting days.

Buddy is now seven. If he lives to, say, twelve—which is a long life for a Malinois—he'd have five years left.

About eighteen hundred days.

"Hoping to see Sophia again soon, Buddy. Not Mommy. We'll go see Mommy next week," he said, contentedly. "Like we always do."

Buddy stared at Palmer. He bared a smile and showed his chipped front tooth.

"Okay?"

Palmer reached over and scratched Buddy's belly until the dog's rear leg started kicking.

Meghan poked her nose through Palmer's office door. Palmer thought that she might have lost a couple of pounds. She looked great, and he noticed she was wearing another new outfit.

I will not compliment her outfit again. Not going to go down that rabbit hole. I'd be walking on eggshells the rest of the day.

"Got that info you asked for, Sarge."

Palmer noticed that her smile did not quite reach her eyes.

A Cheshire cat smile. What's up?

"Easy peasy. Thanks to the Freedom of Information Act, trial records are public domain. For a mere two dollars and fifty cents per page, you can pull full transcripts."

"Thanks, Meg."

He remembered what Vito Coppola had said to him: *This wouldn't be the first time that someone sued Ramsay Marshall.*

"Sent you an email with the links. Two different plaintiffs sued." Still with that smoky Lauren Bacall voice.

"Thanks again, Meg. Good work." He watched her as she walked away.

The first lawsuit against Ramsay Marshall had been filed in 1995 by a company called Bug-B-Gone-Termite Company Inc. Perusing the transcript, Palmer learned that the suit had been filed in the Santa Clara County Courthouse. Bug-B-Gone had alleged Ramsay owed them two hundred fifty thousand dollars for work performed. The exterior of the community center at Sunrise Mobile Home Park, the mobile home park that Ramsay Marshall had owned, was made entirely of wood. Not unusual for 1950s construction, when the center had been built.

Apparently, as the suit alleged, Marshall had neglected, for many years, to have exterior maintenance work done until a wooden pergola that stood over the community Parcheesi tables had rotted so badly that it collapsed, injuring two septuagenarians underneath, who were playing Parcheesi. An inspection, performed by Bug-B-Gone, unearthed over two hundred thousand dollars of termite infested and rotted wood. It wasn't unusual for wood that had been subjected to the weather for close to forty years to have that amount of termite damage. True to form, Ramsay had refused to pay Bug-B-Gone after they had completed the work, citing inferior workmanship, price gouging, plus not performing repairs within the contracted time period.

Bug-B-Gone promptly took him to court.

As did the two injured septuagenarians.

All three plaintiffs had won their cases.

Palmer made a note to call Bug-B-Gone, still in business in Santa Clara.

The second lawsuit was a class action filed by the residents of Sunrise Mobile Home Park in 2005. Many mobile home parks lacked access to quality water. Mobile home park water systems comprised thirteen percent of all state systems. The parks were understudied, but they housed a large portion of California's population. Once again, Ramsay's crooked ways had come to the forefront, as he often hadn't paid the water bill. The water systems had been shut off, and residents forced to make do with well ground water, which lead to health problems for some residents.

"My bath water smells like cow manure," one resident's complaint read.

"My coffee smells like dog shit," another complaint read.

And finally, the last dagger, from the oldest resident at the park, ninety-three-year-old Mrs. Edna Potter. "I saw ca-ca in the community pool."

The judge awarded the residents $1.7 million dollars in damages, handing Ramsay yet another setback.

This guy was a loser.

The judge?

Palmer did a double take.

The presiding judge for the Bug-B-Gone case was Judge Jonathon Jones. The same judge, Judge Jonathon Jones, handled the class-action suit filed by the Sunrise Mobile Park residents.

Jonesy?

Was the judge?

He Googled Jonesy's Wikipedia page again and there it was.

Judge Jonathon Jones, Superior Court, Santa Clara County, California, 1994-2006. Alameda County, California, 2006-2017.

Now Palmer didn't know what to think. He dug further into the documentation on both court cases. Turns out that Judge Jones had cited Ramsay Marshall twice for contempt of court. Once on each case. During each, Ramsay had stopped the proceedings by screaming obscenities at the plaintiffs. Jonesy had asked him to stop. When he'd refused, Jonesy had cited him for contempt, landing Ramsay in jail for the evening, in addition to a five-thousand-dollar fine for each violation. Ramsay had yelled at Jonesy during each case, vowing to "get even" and that he'd "have his revenge".

Palmer blinked.

Jonesy knew Ramsay? Ramsay had threatened Jonesy? Then Jonesy introduces himself to me. He shows up, unannounced when we exhume Ramsay's body, and he says nothing to me about all this court business? Why didn't he tell me he knew Ramsay Marshall? What's going on?

Palmer Doyle did not believe in coincidences.

He was deep in thought, Meghan had to speak louder as Palmer did not hear her the first time.

"Sarge? Did you hear me?"

"What, Meg?"

"There's a Lieutenant Taylor on the phone for you. Says he's from the Pleasanton PD." She still had a Cheshire cat's smile plastered on her face.

"I know him. Patch him through."

Taylor was a detective with the Pleasanton police department. A seasoned vet. Plus, like Palmer, he was ex-army. He was a fireplug of a man—short, square body, with no visible neck. He'd always shown professional courtesy to Palmer. Palmer didn't know why private investigators and police departments were often at odds, but he was glad this wasn't the case with Taylor. A good PI needs friends in the police department. Makes things easier.

"Dan. Good to hear from you," Palmer started. "How are you? To what do I owe the pleasure of this call?"

"Hey, Sarge," Taylor started. "Your client asked me to call you."

"Yeah. Who?"

"Let me see here." Taylor seemed to check his notes. "Old guy. Name is Martin Mueller. Name ring a bell?"

"Yes. Client of mine."

"We just pulled a body out of his swimming pool. At his house in Ruby Hill."

Palmer's heart jumped into his throat. He broke into a sweat.

Oh, my god. Please, please, don't let it be Sophia.

"Excuse me?"

"A guy. Dressed in all black with a black ski mask pulled down over his face."

Thank God.

"No ID on him. But Mr. Mueller here says that he knows him. Say's the dead guy's name is Brad Marshall. Do you know him?"

"Yes. I do. I'm on my way, Dan." Palmer's heart rate began to slow.

"Want the address?" Taylor sounded suspicious.

A slip by Palmer. He knew the address. He'd been at the house last week.

"Yes. Sorry. You took me by surprise with your call. I need the address. Thanks, Dan."

Good grief. First the info on Jonesy and now this.

He rushed to leave the office. "Where's John?" he snapped at Meghan on his way out.

"Dunno, he just left," Meg said. "He didn't say where he was going."

Palmer grumbled. He was supposed to be watching Sophia's house to make sure something like this didn't happen.

7.

On a normal day, one without traffic, the drive from Palmer's office in Dublin to the Ruby Hill development in Pleasanton took twenty minutes. Today, a Saturday, when traffic should have been lighter, when he was in a rush, the drive took an hour. Palmer felt like throwing a tantrum. His tolerance with Bay Area traffic was at its end.

It doesn't matter what day it is. Traffic is bad every day here.

Enough is enough. I've got to get the hell out of California.

On the 580 freeway heading east, traffic was almost at a standstill.

It's just not right.

Palmer then daydreamed about Sophia.

If this turns into something serious, would she be willing to move out of California with me?

That thought made him feel warm and fuzzy. He and Sophia living together in a house on acreage in southern Oregon.

Getting way too far ahead of myself here.

Who knows if she even cares for me?

Having sex once, nowadays, doesn't mean that you're ready to go pick out stainless steel appliances together.

A motorcycle behind him revved its engine, the sound surprising Palmer. He watched as the driver eased his bike between lanes, getting ready to pass cars standing still. As the biker passed the car ahead and to the left of Palmer's, a brand new Tesla, his bike clipped the Tesla's passenger side mirror and ripped it from the car. The Tesla driver, who was alone in the car, wearing a face mask, leaned on the horn.

Wait. What? Alone in a car and wearing a face mask? Why do so many people do that? What's next? Showering with a face mask on? Swimming in the ocean with a face mask on?

Palmer could hear the driver, a woman, cursing at the bike guy. The motorcycle driver, clearly at fault for clipping the Tesla, weaved in and out of cars, clearly not intending to stop. He raised his arm behind him and gave the Tesla driver the finger.

Palmer spent the last part of the drive thinking about whether to schedule a prostate biopsy.

A biopsy is invasive. You lay on a table on your belly. The doctor sticks a biopsy needle up your rectum. A spring loaded tool 'shoots' the needle into your prostate, which slices off small pieces. The procedure lasts fifteen minutes, as about two dozen prostrate slivers are sliced off. It sounds like a staple gun going off inside your arsehole. Palmer's sphincter puckered just thinking about it.

That's not the worst part. Your rectum bleeds for days. You pee and shit blood for a week and it can take anywhere from four to six weeks to heal completely.

Palmer had an Army buddy who had peed blood, and it continued for months before he went to the doctor. Stage four prostate cancer. He was dead thirteen months after the diagnosis.

Best to have it done.

When he finally arrived at Martin's house, Palmer spotted several Pleasanton police cruisers and a shiny new black Ford parked outside.

Detective's car.

Yellow crime tape outlined areas in the backyard. Martin and Sophia sat under an arbor in the shade.

Martin looked terrible. Thinner than when Palmer had seen him last. His face was pale, ashen. He offered a skeletal hand to Palmer as he leaned on a cane.

"Glad you could get here quickly." Mueller said.

If you call being stuck in traffic for an hour quick...

Sophia, a worried look on her face, sat next to Martin. She wore jeans and a bulky red sweater, her arms wrapped tightly under her chest.

Palmer wanted to hug her, to tell her that everything would be all right, that he'd take care of everything and that he'd take care of her. Her eyes seemed to plead with him, then she tilted her head towards Martin.

Palmer nodded.

She doesn't want him to know about us.

"Can I get you something to drink?" she asked. "A cup of coffee, perhaps?"

"Yes. That sounds great. Thanks," Palmer said. "Black, please."

Palmer remembered Lieutenant Dan Taylor as a fireplug of a man, but it had been several years since he had last seen him. Now the man that stood before him was fatter, stockier, as if he had subsisted solely on donuts. To Palmer, he resembled a hedgehog. Taylor, an African American, also had a lazy left eye; one eye would look right at you and the other would look at something to the right.

"Good to see you, Dan," Palmer said, extending his hand. "You're looking well." He suppressed a smirk.

"Yeah, right," Dan Taylor said, tilting his head towards a body bag near the pool. A CSI team of two, a man and a woman, worked the scene.

"Who identified the body?" Palmer asked.

"This is my crime scene, Doyle," Taylor said. "Only reason you are here is because Mister Mueller here insisted."

"Okay. No problem."

"You don't get to see anything or ask anything unless I give you the okay," Taylor added.

"I identified the body," Martin Mueller said, taking two steps forward.

"What's the matter with you, Doyle?" Taylor asked. "You look like shit. Have you looked in a mirror lately?"

Truth be told, Palmer knew that he still wasn't at his best. With the kidney stone blasting and subsequent infection, the issues with his prostate, he'd lost fifteen pounds. He'd been popping Vicodin like they were bon-bons. And he hadn't cut back on the vodka. He felt grumpy. All the time.

"With all due respect to you, Lieutenant Dan, how the fuck would you know what I look like?" Palmer said, smiling.

Lieutenant Dan Taylor's wandering eye looked further to the right and did a dozen tiny, quick circles. Then he let out a giant loud guffaw worthy of a hedgehog.

"Good one, Sarge. Good one," Taylor said, his laughter releasing the tension from the air. "You got me. Okay. I'll do you a favor. Come over here and look."

Taylor, Palmer, and Martin, with the aid of his cane, walked over to the body bag. Taylor unzipped it.

"Why he's dressed like a burglar?" Martin asked. "Dressed in black with a mask on."

"Maybe he was here to rob us?" Sophia asked, her arms still tightly wrapped around her waist.

"I can't comment. This is an active police investigation," Taylor said. "We'll have questions pending the autopsy."

"Sure. Okay. Whatever," Martin said.

"And that's not all," Taylor added. "I shouldn't be showing you this, but look."

He pulled a hypodermic needle out of a plastic bag and held it up.

"He had this in his pocket."
Palmer took a quick look around the yard.

The outdoor fridge. Where Sophia keeps her wine.

"Why would Brad want to rob us?" Sophia asked again.

"Don't be a fool, Sophie," Martin said. "He wasn't here to rob us."

He knows.

"Don't you see?" Martin added. "There's something bad in that hypo. Brad was here to kill us. Or you."

8.

High in the rafters above left field, John Babbitt peered into military-grade binoculars mounted on a tripod. He turned the tripod, searching Mount Davis on the opposite side of Oakland Coliseum.

Getting inside the Coliseum was easy. A fake ID badge certified he was a contracted bathroom maintenance specialist. In his previous job, John had removed human waste out of Porta Potties, so he was in his element - cleaning shit from bathrooms. His olive green maintenance uniform matched those worn by regular Coliseum maintenance workers. He blended right in. Plus, it was late October. The Oakland Athletics baseball team, who played home games at the Coliseum, had wrapped up their season last month. The Oakland Raiders— now the Las Vegas Raiders—no longer played football in Oakland. The Coliseum was empty. It was seven in the morning.

Mount Davis was enormous, built in 1995 to seat twenty thousand football fans.

Jeez. Steep up there.

John had to crane his neck to look up at the concrete monstrosity.

Like looking up at a mountain in the Swiss Alps.

"Find Jonesy," Palmer had told John. "Follow him. I need to know what he's doing. Where he goes."

"Okay, Sarge," John had answered. "How should I do that?"

"You're a private investigator, aren't you?" Palmer had retorted. "Figure it out. Find out where he's living and take it from there."

"I know where he lives," John had answered.

"Yeah? How?" he'd snapped back.

"He told me. Lives in a place called Mount Davis."

Palmer shook his head. "Al Davis, who used to own the Oakland Raiders, built it years ago to increase seating capacity at the Coliseum. City of Oakland let him build it in order to get the Raiders to move back to Oakland from LA, where they moved in 1982," Palmer had explained in a near growl. "It's a concrete monster. Concrete seats with no backs, concession stands that sell watered down beer, luxury box suites. That sort of thing," Palmer had added.

Okay. An old homeless guy lives in a baseball stadium.

Not unusual.

John had heard of one homeless man who'd lapped it up in a luxury suite in Al Lang stadium in St. Petersburg, Florida for over a month before a Cuban cleaning crew had found him. He'd gained access during the height of Covid, when sports were on hiatus. Not only did he steal food and alcohol, but he also broke into the sports merchandise shop and had 'borrowed' team jackets and sweatshirts to keep himself warm at night.

Another homeless man, a Vietnam War veteran who had earned a Purple Heart, had written a book detailing how he had lived in a secret apartment complete with central air and a central vacuum that he built in the now demolished Veterans Stadium in Philadelphia. That book became a best seller.

John felt good today. He'd reached a happy medium with the horse tranquilizer pills. Through trial and error, he'd discovered a workable balance: first, he'd take a quarter pill of Banamine and mix that with two large tablespoons of extra strength Pepto Bismol, then he'd wash that down with eight ounces of bicarbonate of soda. Not only did the cocktail dull the hemorrhoid pain and itching, but it left him feeling a hell of a lot less wonky.

A win-win.

John's futurist studies were going well too. He'd practically memorized the entire book, *How to be a Futurist—a Dummy's Guide* by Alvin Toffler, the third. Now he speculated he had just as good of a chance as anybody to predict what might happen in the future. The only problem was that trying to predict the future was stressful, and John broke out in a sweat and felt anxious when he thought about the future.

A tall figure with a bushy, reddish beard and a ruddy complexion appeared from under a staircase high on Mount Davis. He shuffled towards a stairwell.

Jonesy, all right. With this military-grade binoculars, it looks like he is standing right next to me.

Carrying a bath towel and a toothbrush, he was wearing a Looney Tunes themed bathrobe with a picture of Yosemite Sam on the front.

Now I remember who this guy reminds me of.

It took John over twenty minutes to navigate his way from the left-field seats and climb to the top of Mount Davis. He was breathing hard when he arrived.

Long fuckin' way up here. No wonder this Mount Davis thing was a flop.

After catching his breath, John inched his way towards a men's bathroom door. Inside, he heard running water and something that vaguely sounded like music.

Judy Garland?

He's singing in the shower.

Somewhere over the Rainbow? From the Wizard of Oz?

Knowing that Sarge's instructions were to follow Jonesy but to make sure he didn't him see him, John crept over to where Jonesy was living. He planned to take a couple of pictures and text them to Sarge. Let him know he was on the job.

He found Josey's living quarters in an abandoned luxury suite. Jonesy had furnished it with a Bunsen burner stove, a Styrofoam Igloo cooler for a refrigerator, one green plastic lawn chair, an aluminum table littered with fast food wrappers, antenna ears from an old TV (but no TV), and a tattered, navy blue sleeping bag sitting atop a wrinkled blue tarp. The place stunk to high heaven.

You would think that a retired superior court judge might have some money.

Mister Peabody stirred from inside his baby stroller.

"Get away from me, you mangy fuckin' mutt," John spat.

He couldn't trust any dog these days. But Mister Peabody wouldn't be swayed. He inched closer to John, nose to the floor.

Newspapers were scattered all over the floor.

Who the fuck reads newspapers these days?

John snapped his pictures as Mister Peabody started sniffing John's butt.

"Bad dog!" John yelled. "Bad fuckin' dog." He picked up an old newspaper from the floor, rolled it up, then feigned hitting Mister Peabody in the nose. John broke out in a cold sweat; since the incident with Zeus, he nearly seized in a panic attack every time he saw a dog.

The old German Shepherd gave him a look and walked away, tail between his legs.

He finished and left, then set up shop back in left field, watching and waiting for Jonesy to leave. He texted Palmer.

Palmer responded instantly.

Palmer: John boy? Thought I told you to keep an eye on Martin and Sophia's home?

John: You also told me to stay on Jonesy? Can't be in two places at the same time, Sarge.

Palmer: You should have kept me in the loop. I need to know where you're going. What you're working on. Capisce?

John: K Sarge. Sorry. Maybe we need to hire another PI?

Palmer: K.

"What was that all about?" John said, out loud. "I wonder if something happened."

9.

Palmer lay in a California king at the Normandy Inn in one of the tourist meccas of California, Carmel-by-the-Sea. Buddy, not taking his eyes off of Palmer, sat at the foot of the bed. Across the street, Palmer gazed out at scenic Carmel Beach and the Pacific Ocean.

Gulls flew overhead, squawking mating calls and gliding on ocean winds.

For the first time in a month, Palmer had dreamt about his dead wife, Becky. He credited his blooming romance with Sophia for not having dreamt about Becky for a while. For the first time since she'd passed, he didn't feel so alone. He couldn't remember the details of his dream, only that Becky had been alive, and that they were together, but the dream had been coupled with feelings of profound loss and sadness. Those feelings had passed as soon as he woke.

"How about we take a walk on the beach later, pup?" Palmer said. "It's a dog beach. You don't have to be on a leash. Would you like that?"

From the popular beach, looking north you'd see the tenth green of the world-famous Pebble Beach Golf Links located a couple hundred yards away.

"Won't look forward to cleaning you up after, though," Palmer added. "Covered in wet sand with your tongue hanging out in exhaustion," He mused. "I'm talking about me, pup, not you."

Carmel, Monterey, the picturesque city of Pacific Grove, and the rugged coastline of the Monterey Peninsula were some of Palmer's favorite places to visit for a quick vacation getaway. During non-commute times, it was only a ninety-minute drive from his Dublin office.

Nowadays? It could take up to five hours to navigate the eighty-mile drive if you were unfortunate enough to catch traffic during commute hours or get stuck behind an accident, as the Monterey area had become so popular that tens of thousands of tourists visited every week.

Palmer labored through his left arm exercises. First light weights, lifting and curling, then several stretches. The exercises were painful; he winced as nerve pain shot through his elbow, leaving his arm without enough strength to pick up his cell phone. He paused a moment until the nerve pain subsided. The pain made him feel grumpy.

"First, a shower and breakfast," he said. "Then we hit the beach. Okay, boy?"

Sophia came out of the bathroom, freshly showered, with a white fluffy bath towel wrapped around her.

"Hey what about me?" she teased. "I had plans for this morning too."

With that, she let the towel slide to the floor. In a modern world full of silicon, Botox, collagen, and liposuction, it was refreshing to see that Sophia was all natural.

She looks wonderful.

"How about we pick up where we left off last night?" She climbed into bed and straddled Palmer. "As I seem to remember, you didn't have any problems with this last night." She lowered herself onto him and kissed him full on the lips. "Um. That's better. Feel like getting another birthday present?"

Lucky me. Just turned sixty. Having sex twice within twelve hours with the same beautiful woman.

Sixty. He had now lived two years longer than his father had.

The heck with feeling grumpy. I'm grateful. Happy to be alive.

Good morning, Dad. Thanks for everything you did for me.

Sophia and Palmer had agreed not to let Martin know about their new relationship, their secrecy prompting a two-day getaway.

"How's he doing?" Palmer asked after they finished and lay in bed.

"Doctor gave him a treatment plan," Sophia said. "They gave him a year." Her eyes glazed over, as if she was lost in thought.

"Well," Palmer said. "Good things can happen in a year. With new treatments for cancer being developed, people go into remission often. Let's hope for the best."

She raised the comforter to cover her shoulders and nuzzled her head into Palmer's chest. "I hope you're right."

She paused before speaking again. "It's so beautiful here. I've never been to the Monterey Peninsula before."

"You haven't?" Palmer said. "How come?"

"Never really knew about it. You forget that I've only been living in California for a couple of years."

"Well, let's make it a point to come here again. Soon."

As they fell into a comfortable silence, they could hear ocean waves hitting the beach, seals bark and growl, gulls squawking overhead. They could smell the salty Pacific in the air.

"Let's," Sophia said, snuggling close. "Sounds like a plan."

He kissed her.

"After this case is over, then we can tell Martin. Okay?" Palmer asked.

"Fine with me," Sophia said. "I'd like that."

After breakfast Palmer asked, "Okay to discuss a little business?"

"Sure."

"I don't really know how to start this conversation, so I'll just blurt it out and get to the point."

Truth was that Palmer felt conflicted. Here they had just made love twice in the last twelve hours, and now it was back to business, talking about the murders of her father and half-brother. He knew he was falling for Sophia, but he didn't know how she felt about him or about this whole situation of mixing business with pleasure. One thing he knew for sure: mixing business with his personal life made him feel uncomfortable.

"Okay."

"Your brother's autopsy report came back yesterday."

"My half-brother."

"Okay. Your half-brother."

"Thank you."

"The autopsy found poisonous fish, fugu to be exact, in his stomach."

"Oh my God." Sophia covered her mouth with her hand. "He was murdered."

"Looks that way."

"Like my father," she said. "By eating poisonous sushi."

"Yes."

"Points right towards Suzie again," Sophia said.

"Yes. But why would she kill her own husband?" Palmer asked.

"My God. I can think of a dozen different reasons. I know he was cheating on her. For many women that's reason enough."

"Agreed," Palmer said. "But here's another possibility. What if she murdered him so that his half of your father's estate passed down to her?"

"Do you think that's possible?" Sophia asked, in a high-pitched voice. "She murdered my father in order restore her family's honor? Then she murders Brad to get his share of Dad's inheritance? Do you think that's possible, Palmer?"

"It's possible," Palmer started. "Remember that Suzie and her family don't know what we know about Ramsay Marshall."

"What do you mean?"

"Everyone believes that Ramsay died from a heart attack. Suzie doesn't know that we exhumed his body and performed an autopsy. She doesn't know, that we know, Ramsay died from eating poisonous fish."

"Ahh. So, if she did kill my father, she may think that no one is onto her," Sophia said, her hands moving excitedly. "She may also believe that she could get away with Brad's murder too."

"Maybe. Poisonous fish is hard to detect. You have to run the contents of a person's stomach through several tests to discover the poison. Coroners don't always do those tests."

"They wouldn't know that the person had been poisoned."

"Exactly," Palmer said. They'd conclude that the deceased had a heart attack."

"Like they did with my father."

"Yes. Remember that the Washoe County coroner did not do an autopsy on Ramsay. They concluded that since he'd already had several heart attacks, he must have had another one and didn't survive."

"I understand," Sophia said. "I agree with you. She must be after Brad's share of my father's estate. What are you thinking is the next step?"

Well, if Sophia has any concerns mixing business with pleasure, she's not showing it. She wants to know everything that I can share.

"There's something else first, before I get into that. That hypodermic needle?"

"Yes," Sophia said, elongating the word.

"It had aconite in it."

"Aconite?"

"Poison. Kills you in a couple of hours and leaves no trace in the system. Anyone investigating would think that the person died from a heart attack, as well."

"I don't think I understand, Palmer," Sophia said, her face scrunched up in confusion.

"Your stepfather, Martin, was right. Brad was there to kill you, Sophia."

"But how?" Sophia asked. "And why?" She clasped her hands together.

"I think Brad had been planning this. I think that he'd been watching you, when you were in your yard, from up on the hill behind your home. He knew that you kept drinks and wine in your outdoor refrigerator. He thought that it'd be easy to inject poison into your drinks. Your yard is private; no neighbors look in. No cameras back there. Brad thought that it'd be easy. Except he didn't think that someone would kill him first."

"My God, Palmer." Sophia folded her arms under her chest. "I don't feel safe."

"I understand. And why?" Palmer said. "That's easy. He wanted the entire inheritance. With you dead, he'd inherit it all. That's why."

"Now I'm confused," Sophia said. "And scared. I don't know what to do."

"First thing we need to do is get proof that the fugu that killed your father and Brad came from Suzie's restaurant."

"How do you do that?" Sophia asked.

"We're working on it," Palmer said.

"What do you mean?"

"We've bagged the contents of their stomachs. Ramsay's and Brad's. Now all we have to do is compare that with the fugu that may be stored in Suzie's restaurant. In a freezer, perhaps."

"How do you do that?"

"Get a search warrant," Palmer said. "We can prove probable cause. I'll go to Lieutenant Taylor tomorrow to show him what we've got and request a warrant."

"Sounds reasonable," Sophia said. "What do you think, Palmer?"

"I'm not sure yet. We need to search her restaurant, possibly go to her suppliers to verify that she bought fugu from them. Sushi restaurants get all of their raw fish from fish supply distributors."

"Sounds good."

"But if Suzie did do it, then she was probably smart enough to get rid of the evidence."

"I agree with that." Sophia said.

"But it gets more complicated."
"What do you mean?"

"We still have other suspects."
"Like who?"

"Vito Coppola for one. Unless I'm mistaken, he is the head of a crime family based in California. Your father owed him one $1.2 million. And he is the guy who sent his minion, Leroy, to rough up and knife Brad at that Indian casino last month."

"You told me about that. Could he have had anything to do with Brad's death?"

"I thought of that. But with Brad dying from poisonous sushi, that rules him out, I think. But he still may have had something to do with Ramsay's death. I'm not completely sure of that, Vito, probably had nothing to do with fugu, but I need to check all the boxes."

Buddy circled and sniffed around their room.

"Then there's this guy Jonesy," Palmer said while watching Buddy.

"Jonesy?" Sophia asked. "Who's he?"

"He's this homeless guy who was once a superior court judge in Santa Clara County."

"What?"

"Yeah. That's right. He presided over two of your father's lawsuits in Santa Clara. Cited your dad for contempt of court, twice. Your father threatened him. Then suddenly Jonesy shows up on my doorstep."

"Odd." Sophia frowned. "What would he have to do with anything?"

"I don't know yet. Got my man Sharkie on him. Just got a text from him."

"Sharkie?"

"John. You met him."

"Why do you call him Sharkie?"

"Long story, Sophie," Palmer said. Already he was calling her by a pet name. Sophie, instead of Sophia. "Best to save for another time. But John is on his tail as we speak. And don't forget Jojo."

"Jojo?" Sophia asked.

"Ramsay's third wife. The bikini barista? Brad was having an affair with her. Remember?"

"Why would you suspect her?"

"Well, perhaps she thinks that with Brad dead, she can get more money from Ramsay's estate."

"Can she do that?"

Circle and sniff. Circle and sniff. Buddy was getting serious, trying to get behind a table up against a wall. Then he pawed a closet door.

"Who knows? Who knows what her lawyers are telling her. What they may have fed her." Palmer looked at his dog. "How about we get Buddy to the beach?"

"What's he doing?" Sophia asked.

"Looking for a place to poop. He likes to poop in private. Remember?"

10.

Jonesy didn't leave his abandoned concession stand apartment in Mount Davis for the next two days.

On the third morning, John watched as Jonesy carefully lowered his baby stroller down hundreds of concrete steps towards the BART side exit ramp. Once in the parking lot, he pointed a key fob towards a parked van with a side panel sign that read, "Coliseum Security."

WTF?

Jonesy drove like a ninety-five-year-old lady. Finally, he made his way onto Interstate 880, heading south towards San Jose.

John followed, unconcerned about getting discovered by following Jonesy's car too closely. He began tapping the meridian points on his head and face with his right-hand index finger.

He'd been tinkering with the EFT, or the Emotional Freedom Technique, tapping method. He'd found about it online while trying to deal with the severe anxiety he felt whenever he was around dogs. Or around a single dog. Or even if he thought about a dog.

Tony Robbins endorses it. If it's good enough for the "Awaken the Giant Within" guru I guess I can try it.

"Decreases anxiety by a whopping forty-three percent!" Robbins claimed in ads.

You can measure anxiety by percentage points?

Sounds good to me.

John chose six easy payments of ninety-nine dollars each to download the app onto his phone, so he could rewire his brain.

First, John tapped his TOH, top of head, meridian. Then his EB, or eyebrow meridian, followed quickly by the side of his eye, under the eye, then under the nose, and finally his chin. About twenty taps to each meridian.

He still felt stressed.

Well, Tony says that it takes time. Tony knows what he's doing. I'll stay the course.

Traffic on 880 South, which had more than the usual number of potholes, had John creeping along at no faster than fourteen miles per hour.

I miss the part of Covid when there was no traffic.

John also knew that to reduce his stress, he could have sex. With a woman. For a change. A real woman, not the blow-up kind. Once upon a time, there were men and women and a man had sex with a woman. And vice versa. Straight people. Heterosexuals. A lot of that had changed.

Then there were homosexuals: gay men and lesbian women. Or homos, to John's way of thinking.

Nowadays, there were new names attached to the sexual preferences of human beings. You had your asexual, and your allosexual people. Transgender, bisexual, polyamorous, fluid, and pansexual. Binary and non-binary. Some had a condition now known as gender dysphoria, whatever the hell that meant.

Maybe if I become a transgender futurist? Maybe that will get me some tail?

I just want to have sex with an adult woman.

Why is that so difficult?

An hour later, John watched Jonesy park his car, give Mister Peabody a drink of water, put him into his stroller and walk towards the San Jose City Offices building on Santa Clara Street in downtown San Jose.

John followed from a safe distance, still following Sarge's instructions to follow Jonesy without being seen.

There were people coming in and out of the building, and as John walked up the marble entry steps, he lost sight of Jonesy.

Where did he go?

John looked right, then left, then he scratched his head before someone tapped his shoulder.

"Hi there." It was Jonesy. "What took you so long to get here? I've been waiting for you."

"You knew I was following you?"

"Of course."

Mister Peabody started sniffing. John backed up a step.

"How?"

Jonesy pulled out his iPhone and showed John a video.

"Bad dog!" John yelled in the video. "Bad fuckin' dog." John watched as he picked up an old newspaper from the floor, rolled it up, and swatted at Mister Peabody in the nose. John recognized that this had been taken a couple of days ago when he had broken into Jonesy's 'home' at the Coliseum.

"You see," Jonesy said, in his deep baritone voice. "I have a Ring system."

"Wait. What? You were watching me?" John started tapping the meridian points on his head.

Jonesy gave him a queer look.

WTF? This homeless guy is squatting in an abandoned concession stand on Mount Davis in the Oakland Coliseum, and he installs a Ring security system?

"I got it on sale. On Amazon," Jonesy said. "I've been

waiting for you. Remember, a couple of weeks ago I mentioned to you that you should hang around the city offices?"

"Yeah. We thought you meant the offices in Alameda County. You know. Dublin, Pleasanton, Livermore."

Jonesy looked to the sky and scratched his beard. "Well, I can see how you and Palmer might have been confused. I figured that I could lead you to the correct spot, like leading the mouse with a piece of cheese. Better late than never. Let's go stand here at the side of the entrance. The show is about to start."

"The show?"

"Yes. If I were you I'd get my phone out."

"What in God's name are you talking about?" John asked.

Jonesy pushed Mister Peabody's stroller, which made a mousy squeaking noise.

"Ever hear of WD-40?"

Jonesy pointed towards the entrance. Martin Mueller, hurrying with a spring in his step, came out of the building.

"You getting this?" Jonesy asked.

"Is that who I think it is?" John asked.

"It is."

Mueller was dressed in an expensive navy blue business suit. He wore dark sunglasses and carried a briefcase; he moved fluidly down the steps. No cane. He looked healthy, his complexion rosy.

"That guy doesn't look like he's sick at all," John said. "Palmer's gonna get a kick out of this!"

"A kick may not be the word I would choose, but yes,

he will."

"This guy is supposed to have stage-four cancer. Be on death's doorstep. Sarge won't believe this. There's nothing wrong with that guy," John reiterated. He started tapping, this time furiously, on different parts of his head.

"What are you doing?" Jonesy asked.

John stopped his head tapping. "Nothing."

Jonesy gave him another queer look. "Did you get it on video?"

"Yes. Of course. I'm not stupid, you know. What do you suppose he was doing in there?" John asked.

"Well, let's go have a look-see," Jonesy said. "My guess is that our first stop should be the planning department."

11.

"Holy shit!" Dakota said excitedly. "Has Sarge seen this?"

"I texted it to him," John answered. "Haven't heard back."

Dakota, John, and Meghan stood near Meghan's desk.

"Is Sarge in yet?"

"On his way," Meghan said, checking her makeup in a compact mirror.

"Why did Sarge have you follow the homeless guy?" Dakota asked.

"Dunno. When I asked, he told me to just do it, that I was on a need-to-know basis."

"That's not like Palmer," Meghan chirped. "Maybe he'll fill us in."

"How'd this Jonesy guy know about Mueller?" Dakota

asked.

"Dunno the answer to that either," John said in his squeaky voice. "Maybe because he was a Superior court judge at one time,"

"Was he lying about having cancer?"

"I don't know," John said. "Maybe he wasn't. Maybe he was just having a good day. A person can have cancer and still feel okay sometimes."

"What was he doing there?" Dakota asked.

"Now get this. According to Jonesy, he was at the planning department."

"What the hell for?" Dakota's left eyebrow arched upwards.

"Well, once we were inside, no one would tell us what he was doing there. But Jonesy said that Mueller probably was submitting a tentative map in the zoning department."

"Speak English, please," Meg complained. "What the hell is that?"

"Perhaps it has something to do with home building. Mueller was a home builder."

"Meg?" Dakota asked. "Can you approve a travel voucher for me?"

"Where to?"

"Germany."

"Germany?" John said. "What the fuck is in Germany?"

"Got a hunch."

"You're gonna fly to Europe on a hunch?"

Dakota stared down at John, then looked at Meghan. "Don't tell Sarge. Okay?"

Ten minutes later, Palmer walked in. He looked rested and relaxed, with a smile on his face.

"How was Carmel?" Meghan asked, her lips pursed.

"What?" Palmer startled. "Carmel? How'd you know I was in Carmel?"

"Palmer's got a girlfriend," John said, in a singsong voice. "Did somebody get lucky?"

Palmer shot John a look. "You itching to go back to sucking the shit outta Porta Potties for a living, John?"

John slinked back. He started tapping the top of his head.

"What the fuck are you doing?" Dakota asked.

"Nothing," John said. "Tony Robbins does this."

"Who the fuck is Tony Robbins?" Dakota asked.

John stopped his head tapping.

"Everybody knows everything. You, of all people, Palmer, should know that," John replied.

"I don't have time for this nonsense. Let's get to work."

"Coffee, Palmer?" Meghan asked, her usual perky self.

"Yes, please," he said. "Black." He looked at John. "My life, or what I do when I'm not working, is none of your business."

So much for being in a good mood.

"Be right back." Meghan rushed into the kitchen, no longer wanting to be part of this conversation.

Dakota whipped out her phone and started browsing. Then she said, "Gotta go. Later."

"What did you find out at the planning department?" Palmer asked, sipping coffee.

"Not sure what to make of it, Sarge. Wanted to shoot it by you."

Palmer took another sip. "Okay." He motioned with his head. "In my office."

Meg interrupted: "Lieutenant Taylor is on the phone for you."

"Tell him I'll call him back in ten?" Palmer asked.

"Say's it's urgent."

Palmer took the call. His eyes widened. "Okay. Okay. I'm on my way. Be there in twenty."

"What was that?" John asked.

"Hold your thoughts for later, will you, John? Ichiro Tanaka just confessed to the murder of Brad Marshall."

"Holy shit!" John said. "Okay."

"Who's Ichiro Tanaka?" Meg asked.

"Suzie Marshall's father."

12.

From behind a two-way mirror, Palmer Doyle and Lieutenant Dan Taylor watched Ichiro Tanaka, sitting in an empty room, handcuffed to a table that was bolted in the floor.

"Doesn't look like a killer, does he?" Taylor said.

"No. He doesn't."

Ichiro was short, thin, frail, and north of seventy years of age. It looked like he had trouble seeing clearly. Arthritis had bent his spine.

"He refused an attorney," Taylor said.

Palmer couldn't get used to looking at Taylor's wandering eye. He never knew what to look at. At the eye that was looking at him? Or the eye that looked off somewhere to the right?

"He's stubborn," Taylor said.

"Proud."

"Does this then make him a suspect in Ramsay Marshall's murder?"

"I'd say so. Yes."

"Okay. You want to listen in? I'm about to go in there. You know the drill."

"Yes. I appreciate you helping me out, Dan. But, if I can, I'd like to be in there with you."

"Why?"

"It would be nice to have no more surprises at this point in the case. Also, I'm interested in seeing how he reacts with the two of us in the room."

"No problem," Taylor said. "I shouldn't be doing this,

but us Army guys stick together."

Palmer's mind drifted. He and Sophia were planning a trip to Napa's wine country. Perhaps a bottle of Cabernet over a picnic lunch of prosciutto, salami, and cheese on the scenic grounds of V. Sattui winery in Saint Helena? Then maybe dinner at the famous French Laundry restaurant in Yountville? Where the current governor of California had been caught with his pants down during the pandemic by dining inside without a face mask on?

Perhaps then they would spend the night somewhere?

Since their first intimate encounter Palmer had decided, for the first time, to manscape. He had read, somewhere, that women liked it when men were shaved down there. Women had been doing it for decades. His deceased wife, Becky, waxed monthly. Even his daughter, Francesca, had started waxing when she was a teenager. Back then, Palmer didn't want to know anything about it. The thought of shaving his privates had made him shiver. And shrink. But these days? Half the men, according to a Wikipedia article, shaved their privates. In researching which shaver to purchase he read an article titled: 'A detailed look into mowing your private lawn', then he purchased the popular Manscape 4.0 because its angular design was supposed to glide carefully and uniformly around your groin, and it had teeth that protected your 'jewels' from harmful nicks.

Well, he nicked himself several times when he used his Manscape 4.0. He howled in pain like a momma cow giving birth. He used toilet paper to stop the bleeding. It was not a pretty sight, nor was it a good day.

Manscaping felt weird.

Will I ever stop bleeding down there?

But, He couldn't wait to see Sophia again.

Ichiro straightened noticeably when Lieutenant Dan and Palmer entered the room.

"You sure you don't want an attorney?" Dan asked. "You're entitled to one and I advise you to either have your attorney present, or let the court appoint one for you. Understand?"

"Yes," Ichiro said. He bowed his head.

"You were read your Miranda rights? Correct?"

"Yes." Ichiro studied Palmer.

Probably wondering who I am.

"And you understand and speak English?"

"Yes."

"All the same. I'm going to read you your rights and have you sign a waiver stating that you understand your rights and that you refused legal counsel."

"Fine."

"I'm also going to record and videotape this session. Is that okay with you, Mister Tanaka?"

"Perfectly."

When that was completed, Taylor started in: "So you confess to killing Brad Marshall?" He waited for Tanaka to reply with a verbal "yes" for the record.

"Tell me how you did it."

Ichiro Tanaka leaned in closer and spoke softly. "Mister Brad liked sushi. He had it several times a week. I simply prepared a meal for him with fugu."

"Fugu?"

"Yes. A poisonous blowfish. Considered a delicacy."

"Your English is good."

"I am American citizen. I was born and raised in San Jose."

"I see. Are you sure that you want to continue talking to me about this?"

"Yes. Very sure."

"Okay. Explain to me how you know how to poison somebody with this blowfish."

Ichiro took a long moment before answering. "Gladly. Fugu contains lethal amounts of Tetrodotoxin. A deadly poison. It's in the liver, ovaries, eyes, and skin of the fish. When you prepare it properly for normal consumption, you cut out, or cook out, the poisonous parts."

He knows how to do it.

"It doesn't kill all the time," Ichiro started. "You have to make sure that there is plenty of poison in the fish if you want to make sure that your victim dies."

"Go on," Lieutenant Dan said. Palmer couldn't tell whether Ichiro had trouble watching Taylor's wandering eye.

"The poison is a sodium channel blocker. It paralyzes the muscles while the victim stays conscious. The poisoned victim can't breathe and suffocates. Make sure that there is plenty of poison in the fish if you want to make sure that your intended victim dies."

Did he just repeat himself?

"There is no known antidote to the poison," Ichiro continued, proudly. "I marked the meal with a giant B with magic marker, so he would know it was for him. We always did that, marked the meals. I gave the meal to beautiful daughter to take home and put in the icebox for him."

Icebox?

"Beautiful daughter?"

"Yes. Aiko Tanaka," Ichiro said. "She likes to be called Suzie." Ichiro looked off in the distance, at nothing in particular. He looked to be having difficulty choosing his next words.

"She likes to be called Suzie," Ichiro repeated.

Wait. What?

"Why did you do it?" Taylor asked, clearly wanting to tie this up into a neat package for the district attorney.

Palmer expected Ichiro to dive into a speech about restoring his family honor after their lands were stolen from them during World War Two by Brad's father, Ramsay, while his family was imprisoned at an internment camp .

But Ichiro said none of that.

"He treated beautiful daughter like shit."

Huh?

"So," Taylor continued. "Brad dies just like his father. Poisonous Sushi. Did you have anything to do with Ramsay's death too?"

"What?" Ichiro said, his brows furrowed in confusion.

"You heard me," Taylor said. "You have anything to do with the death of Ramsay Marshall?"

Ichiro took his time before answering, as if he had to search his mind for the words. "Thank you." Ichiro bowed his head. "I know nothing about that. I thought that Ramsay Marshall died from a heart attack." Ichiro said. "Didn't he?"

"What?" Palmer said.

Grumpy Old Man by Tom Lyons

Dan Taylor looked at Palmer.

13.

Palmer stopped for a cup of coffee before he went back to the office. Ester was behind the counter. There was something different about her, but Palmer couldn't quite put his finger on it.

"Hi Ester. Black coffee, please?"

"Sho nough," Ester said. "Dat'll be foa nie fi."

"Here's ten. Keep the change."

Ester flashed him her pretty smile.

Palmer knew she was attractive, but somehow today she looked more voluptuous, as if she'd had some work done. Her blond hair, almost platinum in color, was tied in a bun by that ever-present dog bone.

Platinum blond hair?

"Didn't you have auburn hair last time I was here?" Palmer asked.

"Yah." Then Ester put her arm behind her head and struck what she thought was a sultry pose. "I study to be actress."

Palmer leaned towards her with his right ear. "Ahh."

I wonder if speaking English well is required.

"Don't tell me," he said. "You're channeling Jayne Mansfield."

"Who dat?" Ester said.

"Never mind."

Before her time.

"Marilyn Monroe maybe?"

Another blank stare.

395

"Lady Gaga, then?" Palmer said, exasperated.

"Na," Ester said, smiling. "Was goin more for Coortney K."

"Courtney K?" Palmer repeated.

"Kardasian."

"Ahh."

Once outside, Palmer's thoughts turned to Ichiro Tanaka. Ichiro had looked genuinely surprised when he learned that Ramsay Marshall had been murdered rather than having died from a heart attack. Palmer had believed him.

Where does that leave us now?

Palmer heard a commotion by the bank of Tesla Supercharger stations close to where he had parked his car. Shouting, screaming, blasting car horns. As he approached, Palmer saw that there were a dozen supercharging stations, every one taken except one, and it looked like two different Tesla's were trying to access the empty spot at the same time. Both owners, young men, had backed their cars into the spot trying to get to the station, but neither could, as each blocked the other car's access. Both drivers were out of their cars, shouting profanities at each other. By the sound of their voices, and by how they looked, Palmer guessed that both young men were of Middle Eastern descent.

I hope they don't have any guns on them.

I hope that it's not an Israeli and an Egyptian.

So many people owned a Tesla these days that there weren't enough charging stations to go around.

Palmer carefully watched as he approached them. He

figured he might help make peace between the two.

Out of the corner of his eye, Palmer watched as Jonesy approached the two men. He wore his captain's hat as usual, and had his broken-down stroller with Mister Peabody inside, in tow. Jonesy didn't acknowledge Palmer as he passed. Palmer could smell his stench from thirty feet away.

"Now, gentlemen," Jonesy said in his deep Queen's English booming voice. "Gentlemen. Please. There is no need to argue. Obviously, you both believe that you were here first. I suggest that instead of fighting, we flip a coin to see who gets to charge their car first. How does that sound?"

One man nodded his head. The other scrunched his face from Jonesy's stench. Jonesy's unkempt beard also stank to high heaven.

No one spoke a word. "Okay then," Jonesy said. "I'll do the honor." He reached into a pocket of his filthy army fatigues and pulled out a grimy coin. He tried to clean it on his fatigues. After a minute he said: "I apologize to everyone. Do either of you perhaps have a clean coin that I might use?"

"Clean coin?" said one of the young men.

"Yes. Please. If you don't mind," Jonesy said. "I can't make out which is heads or tails on mine. Thank you very much."

Palmer walked up: "Here you go, Jonesy." He flipped a shiny new quarter his way.

"Why, Mister Doyle," Jonesy said, excitedly. "It's a pleasure to see you, sir. To what do I owe the honor of your presence?"

"Got a couple of questions for you, if you don't mind,"

Palmer said. "That is, after you finish with these two gentlemen."

"But, of course, sir," Jonesy said. With that, he flipped the coin in the air and said to one of the young men. "One of you call it, please."

"Heads," said the taller of the two.

"Heads, it is," Jonesy said.

"Ah hah!" said the taller young man. "Praise Allah!"

The other man walked towards his Tesla, getting ready to move out of the way, muttering something about the other guy's mother and a goat. Another supercharger station had opened, so he quickly hooked up his car there.

"Now how can I be of service to you, Mister Doyle?" Jonesy said.

"How is it that you always seem to show up wherever I am?" Palmer asked.

"Oh. I don't know," Jonesy started. "My good fortune, I guess. Plus, I once mentioned to you, if you remember, that I wanted to be a member on your fine staff."

"Wanted to be?"

"Yes. Wanted to. I changed my mind. I believe I am being drawn to a higher calling." Jonesy moved in closer. Palmer turned away from his stench, leaning in with his good ear. Mister Peabody sat calmly in his baby stroller and sniffed the two of them.

"Dare I ask?"

"Well, I'd be glad to discuss this with you at a later date. Once I've decided on my future path," Jonesy said.

A future career path for a homeless, retired superior

court judge?

Palmer stifled a laugh.

"Of all the homeless encampments here in the Bay Area, why do you choose to live in the Oakland Coliseum?" Palmer asked.

I can't believe that I just said that a homeless person has many choices about where to live. Absurd. Only in California. Why not live in Venice Beach? Where homeless people from all over the country move to?

"Well, that should be obvious, isn't it?"

"Humor me."

"Are you a baseball fan, Mister Doyle?"

"Yes. Yankee fan."

"Ahhh. The New York Yankees. The Bronx Bombers. Murderer's row and Cano too." Jonesy said. "To answer your question, I'm a baseball fan. An Oakland A's fan, to be exact. Have been my entire life. Ahh, those teams in the early seventies, three straight world championships. Reggie, Bando, Campy, Catfish. Who can forget them? By living at the Coliseum, I get to go to all the home games. For free. I've even met a few of the players. Fine boys, all of them. Fine boys. Free hot dogs too."

It dawned on Palmer that Jonesy looked like the crazy fan who dressed in an A's yellow jersey, green sweatpants, a flowing faded green cape, and an A's hat with a tiny propeller sticking out of the top—the guy who walked in the stands, playing music, during the A's games encouraging fans to root for the them. He had a beard just like Jonesy's.

"You're not Banjo man?" Palmer asked. "Are you? The unofficial Oakland A's mascot."

"You mean Samuel?" Jonesy said. "I'm not. But I know

him. Plays a mean banjo, Samuel does. He stops by my place every now and then for a cold one."

Okay then.

"Why not live in Venice Beach?"

"My goodness no."

"City too crowded?"

"No. Not that. The beach is too crowded. Too many homeless people live there."

Good grief. Time to get back on track.

"Ramsay Marshall."

"Yes."

"The man whose body you helped us exhume a month ago. You've had run-ins with him before?"

"Yes, I have."

"Two court cases. He threatened you. You cited him for contempt. Why didn't you tell me that before?"

"Well, to be honest, I figured you'd find out for yourself what kind of man he was."

"That he'd get what he deserved? Is that what you're saying?"

"No. Not at all," Jonesy said. "But that somewhere down the line, justice would be served."

"So, once a judge always a judge?"

"Perhaps. Yes. Something like that. Well said, sir. Wish I had thought to say that myself."

Palmer shook his head.

I'll buy it.

"How'd you know about Martin Mueller being at the San Jose City offices? And why did you tell members of my staff to watch the city offices?"

"When I was working, I was at the offices five days a week. Lots of people go in and out. Lots of important people. With money. Lots of stuff happening there. Especially with real estate. Shakers and movers. That's where the big money is, in real estate development." Jonesy paused. "I simply pointed him in the right direction. I figured that your guy, John is his name isn't it? I figured you hired him because he's smart. I figured that he could take it from there and sort through it correctly."

"I see."

John is smart?

"But that he'd figure what out?" Palmer then asked.

"Oh. That's not for me to say. I wouldn't want to assume anything. You know what they say about people who assume?"

"No, I don't."

"People who assume make an ass. Out of you. And me."

Palmer gave him a blank stare.

Jonesy then said, "Ass-u-me. Get it now?"

"Ahh."

"Felix Unger."

"Felix Unger?" Palmer repeated.

"Yes. From the "Odd Couple" television show. In the seventies. Neil Simon wrote the original play?"

"I know who Felix Unger is, Jonesy," Palmer said. "Okay. That's all I got. Thanks for leveling with me. Do you want to tell me now why you no longer want to be a private investigator?"

"No. Sorry. But soon Mister Doyle. Soon." Jonesy grinned. "Now you take care. And may God bless."

There he goes, sounding like Red Skelton again.

Jonesy walked away, pushing Mister Peabody in the stroller.

14.

"I have good days and bad days," Martin Mueller said, after he watched the video of himself at the San Jose City offices. "Like every cancer patient."

Today, he looked to be having a bad day—frail, his complexion chalk-like. "Do you have any idea what it is like to have this awful disease?"

Palmer shook his head.

"On the good days, you feel hopeful, thankful," Martin said. "You feel you have a chance to keep living. You want to do something productive. I was having a good day that day. I remember. On my bad days, I'm not sure how many days I have left. I feel miserable on those days. Sick as a dog. Can't put one foot in front of the other. Can't keep food down. Do you know what it feels like to throw up all of your meals? You live in uncertainty and fear. Sometimes it's so bad that I want to die right then and there."

Sophia nodded slightly, her eyes cast downward.

"I can understand that," Palmer said, empathizing.

Truth was that Palmer was having a hard time focusing on work when he was around Sophia. He was enamored with her. He felt giddy when she was around, as if he didn't have a care in the world. Today, sitting next to Martin in their yard in Ruby Hill, she was wearing jeans and a loose-fitting white top. When a shapely woman wears loose-fitting clothes, a man wonders what she looks like underneath. Palmer was no different. He struggled to avert his gaze. He imagined all of her wonderful feminine curves underneath. He looked forward to going to Napa with her soon. He tried to maintain a neutral expression to not give away his feelings in front of her stepfather. Plus, as an added bonus, his privates were healing nicely; Palmer no longer walked stiffly, like he had a broom stick wedged up there somewhere.

"I was having a good day," Martin repeated, his voice no more audible than a whisper. "Plus, everybody knows that when I was living in Germany, I built homes for a living. Not a secret. I'm interested in building homes. I wanted to see what is involved here in the States. Not that I would ever get the chance to build here, you know. I just wanted to see what it takes."

Sophia said nothing. She sipped iced coffee. She didn't look at Palmer.

"Makes sense to me," Palmer said after a moment.

"But why would you have somebody follow me and video me?" Martin asked.

Palmer said nothing.

"Oh. I see. Everyone is suspect. Right, detective?"

"Something like that." Palmer decided not to say anything about Ichiro Tanaka confessing to the murder of Brad Marshall.

Not just yet.

"Well," Martin said. "I guess I understand that." He thought for a moment, his hand stroking his chin. "I agree, actually."

15.

Before returning to the office, Palmer stopped for another cup of coffee.

"You're gonna make a great octress, Ester," he said to the Tasmanian barista as he left

She narrowed her eyes in confusion.

"Err . . . I meant actress."

Ester curtsied and gave him her best Marilyn Monroe look. "Thank you," she said. "I think so too."

Palmer's head was spinning. His hands were shaking, and his right eyed twitched.

Too much caffeine.

Palmer planned to talk to Vito Coppola again. Had he received the $1.2 million settlement he was owed from Ramsay's estate? After checking and verifying with several sources, Palmer discovered that people who owed Vito money showed up missing. He had not ruled Vito out yet for Brad Marshall's murder, though Ichiro had already confessed to the crime. He hadn't ruled Vito out for Ramsay's death, though it didn't seem likely that a crime boss would off someone with poisonous fish.

Ichiro Tanaka? Old, blind, and frail. He didn't look like a killer. Something else was there too. Palmer just couldn't put his finger on it.

Jonesy? What about Jonesy? Palmer couldn't believe that the old homeless guy had anything to do with either Ramsay's or Brad's demise. He seemed harmless. He just didn't have it in him, Palmer believed. Jonesy had a good heart, though he certainly could have used help with his hygiene.

Martin Mueller? What he'd said today was believable. Good days and bad days. He looked sick today. It also made perfect sense to Palmer that a home builder would want to stay current with building guidelines, planning requirements, zoning issues, etc. Nothing unusual there.

He missed Buddy, having left him at home. "The more I learn about people," Palmer said to nobody in particular. "The more I like you, Buddy." He could picture Buddy sitting next to him in the passenger seat, wagging his tail while sticking his snout out the window.

His phone rang. It was Meg.

"There's a strange woman here. Says she wants to see you."

"Strange woman?"

"Yeah, Sarge," Meg said. "She's wearing a silver hazmat suit that's duct taped at the ankles and wrists. Black boots, latex gloves," she continued. "And get this, Sarge. She's wearing two surgical masks, one on top of the other."

"Ahh."

"Says her name is Suzie Marshall."

"On my way, Meg. Be there in fifteen."

Yep. The more I learn about people, the more I like my dog.

16.

Palmer looked astonished. In his office stood a female version of a 1950s movie scene from *Man from Outer Space*: a slight figure covered from head to toe in a silver hazmat suit and multiple face masks.

"I've been vaccinated," Palmer started. "You?"

"Of course," Suzie said. "If you haven't been vaccinated, you can still get Covid and pass it on to other people. Got my booster shot too."

"As have I. For the life of me, I can't understand why so many people are resistant to getting the vaccine. Makes no sense." Palmer paused for a moment. "Would you feel more comfortable if we sat outside and talked?"

"Yes. Thank you. Please call me Suzie."

Outside, staying six feet apart, they sat on a bench. Suzie lowered her face masks. She was pretty, Palmer thought. Thin and small-boned, with pale, almost porcelain-like, skin. Her hair was pulled black into a pony with a red band.

"How did you know about me?" Palmer asked. "Working on this case?"

"Honored father told me you visited him at the jail."

"Ahh. Yes." Palmer remembered.

"I have a confession to make," Suzie said. Her voice was soft, her tone polite and deferential.

"Okay."

"Honored father did not kill my husband. I killed him. I did it." Suzie spoke without a trace of remorse in her voice. She sat up taller in her seat, as if she was proud of it. Then she bowed her head.

"Okay." Palmer's face remained stoic. He knew better than to show the surprise he felt.

"Honored father is a very gentle man. He wouldn't hurt a fly."

"Can you explain?" he asked.

Suzie took her time, gathering her thoughts, before answering. "Honored father did not want me to lose my inheritance."

"How so?"

"Are you aware of the California slayer laws, Mister Palmer?"

"I am." Palmer said. "If you're found guilty of killing your husband, then you don't get any of the monies that may pass down from Ramsay's estate to Brad."

"Exactly," Suzie admitted. "Honored father didn't want that."

"I see." Many other questions crossed Palmer's mind. "Did Brad cheat on you? Was that why?"

"I don't care about that. He cheated all the time. Thankfully. Saved me from my wifely duties, which I couldn't bear to do much longer, anyway."

So much for the sweet, subservient housewife.

"But Ichiro knew exactly how Brad died. From poisonous sushi. How do you explain that?"

"No way he could have gotten the fugu. He didn't have the keys. Do you know how dangerous fugu is? There are requirements for keeping it safe. The Environmental Health and Safety Department inspects my restaurant four times a year. You have to keep it under lock and key in a freezer, six feet off the ground, until you are ready to prepare it."

"So?"

"Have you noticed how forgetful my father is?"

That's what I couldn't put my finger on.

"My father's memory is not what it once was."

"Alzheimer's?" Palmer asked.

"Well. He hasn't actually been to a doctor to get a proper diagnosis," Suzie said, her voice trailing off. "He's too proud to see a doctor when he doesn't think there is anything wrong with him."

He didn't look like a killer.

"He'd already lost two sets of keys to the restaurant. So, I took his keys away last year. I don't think he missed them. He never said a word about not having them. So, you see, there is no way he could have prepared a meal with poisoned fish. He didn't have access to the fugu. But I did. I prepared the meal that Brad ate. I left it in our home refrigerator for him."

Lieutenant Dan will be surprised.

"Okay," Palmer said. "We also thought that your father might have had something to do with Ramsay's death as well."

"What do you mean?"

"Well, he was killed the same way as your husband, Brad. By poisonous sushi."

"What?" Suzie said, her voice rising in pitch. "What do you mean? I thought he died from a heart attack."

She doesn't know. Just like her dad. She does not know that we exhumed Ramsay's body. No way she could have known. Back to square one. Her father had nothing to do with Ramsay's death, and neither did Suzie. Where does that leave us now?

"Well," Palmer started. "If you can, I'm going to need a list of employees at your restaurant, past and present, who might have had a set of keys and access to the freezer where you keep the fugu. Can you do that?" Palmer asked.

"Yes. Of course."

"But Suzie . . . You didn't answer my question. Why did you kill your husband?"

"Ahh. That fucking *baka yatsu*."

Japanese slang for something nasty?

"He killed my beloved *Baa-baa*."

"*Baa-baa*?"

"*Baasan*. Japanese for grandmother. He gave my *Baa-baa* Covid. Brad had it when we came to visit for her birthday. He gave it to her. He killed her. I'm sure of it. That's why I did it. If given the chance, I'd do it again. Gladly."

With that, Suzie Marshall spat on the ground. "That's what I think of Brad Marshall." The rage in her eyes confirmed the story.

"*Baka yatsu!*"

17.

"I don't know. Sometimes I feel like the lawman in *No Country for Old Men.*"

Palmer, scowling, took a swig of vodka straight from the bottle. "You know. The movie? Always one step behind the bad guys." Buddy lay splayed out on the ground over Becky's grave.

"Overmatched." He took another drink, then paused a moment to let it settle in his stomach. "You know. The guy Tommy Lee Jones played? Sheriff Bell. Know what I mean, Becky?" He spoke to his dead wife while sitting on a camping chair in front of her grave.

"Or maybe I'm just a one-armed, broken-down old alcoholic who can't hear. Old age wins."

He took a minute to look around and enjoy the serenity of the cemetery. He glanced at Buddy and said, "Bad dog!"

Buddy, knowing that tone of voice, lowered his head in guilt. Yesterday, after meeting with Suzie Marshall, Palmer had returned home to find that Buddy had chewed through the leg on Palmer's walnut coffee table in his family room. "Bad dog! You know better than that," he'd said. Buddy still looked guilty. Palmer cocked his good ear towards the ground.

"Yeah. You're right, Becky. Growing old is a privilege denied to many." He took another swig of vodka. "I'll try not to bitch. Complaining doesn't do any good."

This morning, before visiting Becky's grave, he'd received a text from Dakota. She'd broken into the MD Anderson Cancer Center's computer system.

Seems like it gets easier and easier these days to break

into sophisticated computer systems.

Dakota hadn't found any records of them ever treating Martin Mueller. Palmer's memory was excellent. He remembered exactly what Sophia had said the first time they met in his office a couple of months ago: "*Living here in California has been good. Closer to MD Anderson.*"

If Martin had never been treated at the world-famous cancer hospital, then Sophia must have known.

What does that mean? Is he or isn't he sick? Maybe the hospital's records are wrong? Did they go to another hospital? Instead? Palmer knew that some people, people who had money, would "donate" big bucks to have their names removed from all client lists. Famous people did that. Celebrities too. They didn't want the public or media to know anything about their lives. They wanted to keep their private lives private.

Who could blame them?

Maybe it was just a mistake. Or maybe he'd checked into the hospital under a different name. Palmer couldn't fathom that Sophia had anything to do with this. She had only done her best to take care of her stepfather. Palmer wanted to believe in her. He hoped they'd have a future together. Still, he also knew that he'd have to broach the subject with her when they went to Napa. He'd have to ask her straight out.

Two days ago, as Palmer had asked, Suzie had emailed him a list of people who had worked at her restaurant. Sophia's name had appeared on that list. He knew that Sophia and Suzie Marshall were friendly. Sophia had mentioned that to him when they met for a drink at Jack London Square last month. What he didn't remember right away was that Sophia, on occasion, had helped out at Suzie's restaurant. Then he remembered what Sophia had said to him: *I helped at the restaurant. Preparing some of the simpler items on the menu—salads, miso soup, things like that. Until she could hire and train new people.*

Palmer took another swig of vodka. Scratched Buddy behind his ears, his favorite. The dog's face eased from a guilty expression to relaxed. He put his paw on Palmer's arm.

"It's okay, boy. I forgive you. Gonna cost me a couple hundred to replace that table. Wish I could ding your allowance." Palmer laughed.

"Maybe I could sell the business to John. Or Dakota. Or maybe both of them might consider buying me out. Then I could move out of California."

With Sophia?

He wondered about whether John was okay. His eyes had been clouded over for days, and he'd suddenly taken to tapping his head and face constantly.

What is that all about?

Palmer took a last swig of vodka and capped the bottle. Then he rearranged the fresh flowers he had bought for Becky.

"There. That should do it," he said as he straightened himself. "How does that look, honey?"

His thoughts turned to Dakota.

Is she still visiting her mother?

18.

Sophia placed her overnight bag in the trunk of Palmer's car.

"I can't believe you haven't been to Napa. It's wonderful."

"Haven't had the chance," Sophia said. "But I've heard great things about it. I'm looking forward to this. I'm excited!"

"You look great, by the way," Palmer said.

Sophia leaned over and kissed him on the cheek.

She was wearing a short white dress, something a young woman might wear to a date on a warm summer night. Her hair fell off her shoulders. She wore little makeup, a touch of lipstick.

"I wanted to look pretty today," she said. "For you."

Palmer, his cheeks reddening, didn't know what to say.

"Why do we need to stop at your office?" Sophia asked.

Dakota had asked that everyone meet this morning. Beyond that, Palmer knew little about it. He guessed that it'd be a good time to update Sophia and Martin about Suzie Marshall's confession. It'd also be a good time to ask both Sophia and Martin questions about their recent findings.

"Staff has updates," Palmer said. "Shouldn't take long." He paused. "What about Martin?"

"Coming from his doctor's office," she offered. "He had an appointment with his oncologist. It's less than a mile from your office."

414

When they arrived, Martin was already there. He sat slumped in a chair, a cane hooked over his arm.

Meg, John, and Dakota were present. Dakota wore her workout clothes and a muscle shirt. She had new ink on her neck. She had her ear Air Pods in, blasting disco music so loud that Palmer could hear it.

"Bad girls

Talking about the sad girls

Sad girls

Talking about bad girls, yeah.

See them out on the street at night walking"

Donna Summer?

Palmer gave Dakota a look.

She lowered the volume.

John, still reluctant to get the Covid vaccination, wore his green turtle face mask. Palmer remembered asking John last month why he hadn't gotten the vaccine.

"Oh. Heavens no," John had said. "When you get the vaccine, they put a chip in you. Then they control your brain from outer space."

"Ahh."

"From a satellite," John added. "Aliens. Don't you read, Sarge?"

"Read what?"

"Buzzfeed. Mashable. Oddee," John had listed off. "You know, the big news feeds."

"I see."

"Hope you have a good reason for this, Mister Doyle," Martin Mueller said. "I'm not having a good day. Perhaps you've good news for us?"

Dakota stood. "We do," she said. "In fact, I believe we have it solved." Dakota took a clean wet cloth and walked over to Martin. With arm veins popping, she placed one powerful hand on top of his head, freezing it in place. "Young lady!" Martin said. "Just what the hell do you think you're do—"

Dakota held his head still, took the towel and dragged it across Martin's forehead. Then across his nose. Then she held up the smeared towel.

"Makeup," she said. "A natural finish concealer. He uses it to make his skin pale. Makes him look sick."

Sophia stiffened. Her face became a stone mask.

John guffawed.

Palmer sat in shock. He looked at Sophia. She did not return his gaze.

"This guy isn't sick, Sarge," Dakota continued. "He lied to you. He lied to all of us. Martin's a fraud."

The MD Anderson records were correct.

Martin tried to stand. "I don't have to sit here and listen to this. C'mon, Sophia," he added. "Let's get out of here."

Dakota put one of her muscular arms on Martin's shoulder, forcing him to stay seated. "You're not going anywhere," she said. "I'm not done yet." She walked around the table and took a seat. "That's number one. Here is number two."

Dakota handed documents to everyone, including

Sophia and Martin. Neither of them picked one up.

"Suit yourself," Dakota said. "We all know that Martin Mueller built homes when he lived in Germany. What you see before you are the fruits of his home building work. First is a court-notarized document stating that Martin Mueller had his building license revoked, in Germany, several years ago."

"Wait. What?" John said. "Why?"

"Well, put simply," Dakota said. "He built shitty houses. Shoddy workmanship. Sent out bids to contractors for electrical and plumbing work and chose the cheapest bidder. His general contractor didn't check to see if these shoddy workers did their jobs correctly. He did not build his home in accordance with building code guidelines. As a result, those contractors did shitty work. Plumbing pipes corroded and exploded in concrete slabs under the houses he built. Electrical shorts in the walls caused fires. Roofs leaked. The homeowners filed class-action lawsuits. He didn't have the money to settle. They revoked his building license and he left the country. You'll find all the information, plus several newspaper articles in your packets."

After flipping through the info, Palmer asked, "Where did you get this info, Dakota?"

"In Germany."

Palmer shot Meghan a look.

Meghan looked towards the ground, her face reddening.

Meg approved the travel voucher.

"So, he's a liar," Dakota continued. "Martin Mueller is not sick. He's a fraud. He's a crook and he's broke. His bank statements showing low balances are at the back of your package. That's why he came to the States."

"Don't. Say. One. Single. Word," Martin warned Sophia. "Not one word. My lawyers will handle this."

"I don't get it," John said. "Why'd he move to the States?"

"I'm getting to that."

Sophia had a look of cold fury on her face.

Palmer felt numb.

Just like the sheriff in No Country for Old Men. Overmatched.

"Sarge," Dakota started. "You won't like this, but it's gotta be said."

What now? But look at her. She's magnificent. Dakota. I once promised her father that I'd take care of her. But instead, she's taking care of me.

Dakota walked the room again, placing a piece of paper in front of everyone.

"What you're looking at is a marriage certificate. Notarized in 1999. I got it from the courthouse in Stuttgart, Germany. It shows that Martin Mueller and Sophia are not stepfather and stepdaughter. It states that they are husband and wife. Married over twenty years ago."

John's hand shot up to cover his mouth, his eyes springing wide open.

Meghan had a triumphant look on her face.

Palmer was gut shot. He tried not to let anything show.

Nooooooo! . . . Noooooooo!

"Not. One. Word." Martin repeated to Sophia.

Sophia looked towards the ground.

Palmer put his good memory to use.

It was all a lie. She was married to Martin when I was in the hospital in Afghanistan. When she left Afghanistan, she went home to Martin. What she'd told me about her husband, being the doctor? A cardiologist who volunteered to work in the Covid wing? A lie. That he died from Covid, like my Becky? Another lie. Why? Why? To pull me in, to sucker me in, to get me to fall for her so I'd tell her about the case. Make sure that I wasn't getting too close to the truth. It was all a lie.

What's worse is that both she and Martin were in on this together.

He saw Meghan studying his face. He felt too numb to feel the pain of Sophia's betrayal. That would come later. Now he was furious.

"So." Dakota paused. "I guess you're all wondering what all of this has to do with the death of Ramsay Marshall. John?" Dakota said, looking at Sharkie. "Care to explain?"

"Happy to," John said. "If I can draw your attention to the screen on the wall, please." John queued his computer. "Gotta give kudos to Jonesy on this. He pointed me towards the City of San Jose offices. Specifically, the planning department. What you're looking at on the screen is an application for a zoning change."

Jonesy. Again.

"The land in question is the mobile home park, Sunrise Park, owned by Ramsay Marshall. Once his estate is settled, the property passes to the beneficiaries in his trust, namely his daughter, Sophia, and his son, now deceased, Brad Marshall. Now that Brad is dead and his wife Suzie is in jail for his murder, Sophia stands to inherit the entire estate. The park is built on approximately fifty acres of land."

Martin and Sophia remained quiet.

"Presently the land is zoned R-2 to R-4," John continued.

"Which means?" Dakota prompted.

"That it's approved for low-density housing. Anywhere from two to four residential units per acre. Which basically means houses with large lots. A typical zoning for mobile home parks, where the mobile homes are all single stories and spread out."

"Thanks, John," Dakota said.

Is this the same guy who thinks that aliens put a chip in you and control your brain from outer space if you get the Covid vaccine?

"Last week, when Jonesy and I took the video of Martin leaving the city offices of San Jose . . ." John paused for a moment. "Be glad to show you the video if you want, Mister Mueller."

Martin didn't say a word.

"Anyway, he was there applying for a zoning change—something that builders, developers, and contractors often do. The one you see on the screen requests a change from the R-2 to R-4, to a denser housing zoning, specifically R-12 to R-16."

"Which means twelve to sixteen homes to the acre," Dakota explained.

"Correct. Takes a year or more to get the final approvals, but in the end most municipalities approve these changes because it means a tremendous increase of tax revenue headed their way once the project is built out."

Becky, I'm sorry that I ever said one bad thing about your brother.

"Thanks, John. Good job," Dakota said. "What's interesting here is that the request is signed by both Sophia and Martin, stating that they are the owners of the land."

"What about Brad?"

"He was already dead. They thought they'd be the sole owners. So, they filed for the zoning change." John said. "I'll turn this over to Meghan now. She has the numbers."

Meghan? Numbers?

"I've heard enough," Martin said, rising from his chair. "You'll be hearing from my attorneys. Come on, Sophia. We don't have to listen to this shit."

"Uh, uh," Dakota said, standing and moving towards him. "You're not going yet."

"I'll sue your ass off!" he screamed. "Elder abuse. I'll sue your ass off! You'll go to jail for this."

"Be my guest," Dakota replied. "Knock yourself out. Meghan?"

Meghan stood, brushing wrinkles from her blue skirt, and donned reading glasses.

"Remember, Mueller is close to broke, and he can't build homes in Germany. I believe he thought he could escape his problems in Germany and build here in America," Meghan began. "Current market value on the land for Sunrise Village is fifty million dollars, from an appraisal done last year for a refinance. If the zoning change is approved, he'd be able to build fourteen homes to the acre. Fourteen homes multiplied by fifty acres equals seven hundred home lots. Multiply that number by the price of eight hundred thousand dollars for a finished lot."

"Finished lot?" John asked.

"A finished lot is one that is leveled with all utilities at the curb. The land is ready to be built upon."

"Got it," John said. "Land is expensive in San Jose."

"You bet," Dakota added.

"The new current market value on the land is five hundred and sixty million dollars."

John whistled. "Wow. Got it. Lot of dough."

Palmer hung his head.

It's always about the money.

"That's a lot of motive." John added.

"Exactly," Dakota chimed in.

"Now get this," Meghan continued. "He didn't even have to build out the development. All he had to do was get the zoning change approved, then submit a tentative map with the city. Then the big guys, builders like KB Homes and Toll Brothers, would come knocking on his door, if the market was still hot at that point and pay him huge bucks for the development." Meghan beamed a look of pride.

"Great job, Meghan," Palmer said proudly.

Per current appraisal? Zoning changes? Tentative map? Build out the development? Current market value? When did Meghan become an expert on home building? She did a lot of homework. Looks like she maybe she wants to be a private investigator?

Sophia looked like she wanted to say something, but after a sharp look from Martin, she thought better of it.

"Doesn't prove a fucking thing," Martin said.

"We're coming to that." Dakota scowled at him.

"You've kidnapped me. Holding me against my will without cause. You're in a shitload of trouble. A shitload," Martin said.

You'd need a steak knife to cut through the tension. To Palmer, it felt like anyone could snap at any moment. He knew that if Martin Mueller were a younger man, this situation could have turned violent.

"But," Dakota started again. "In order for you to accomplish this, Ramsay Marshall had to die. Brad too. Once they died, you were free to file for the zoning change. Suzie Marshall made your job easier by taking out Brad. Bet you counted your lucky stars when that happened. Didn't you?"

"You have no proof," Martin fumed.

"We'll see," Dakota said. "This is where Sophia comes in. Both of you plotted to kill Ramsay Marshall. That's the reason Sophia befriended Suzie."

Sophia looked at Dakota with daggers in her eyes.

If looks could kill.

Who was this woman?

I missed the boat. I was busy falling in love. Love clouds your ability to see clearly.

"By befriending Suzie, Sophia ensured that she'd have the opportunity to help at Suzie's restaurant after she lost her staff. She also knew how much her father loved sushi," Dakota continued. "She gained Suzie's trust. Suzie gave her the keys, access to the fugu."

"I'll say it once again," Martin said. "You've absolutely no proof."

What kind of man is Martin Mueller? Where his plan to get rich includes murder and letting his wife sleep with another man?

"Oh, yeah?" Dakota said. "But we have this. If you will look at the screen, please."

Dakota pressed a couple of buttons on her phone.

"What are we looking at?" John asked.

"There are no security cameras at Suzie's restaurant. But there's a security system at Ramsay's and Jojo's house. Jojo was nice enough to provide us with this video feed."

Probably in Jojo's best interest to provide the footage. If Sophia is found guilty of murdering her father, then Jojo would become the sole beneficiary of Ramsay's entire estate. Being nice had nothing to do with it.

"What you're looking at is the security feed from the camera outside the front door of Ramsay's house. And here comes Sophia, walking up the steps and ringing the front doorbell of her father's home a couple of days before he died."

"She's holding a couple of containers," John said.

"I'll freeze the feed there and zoom in," Dakota said, pressing more buttons on her device. "And there you have it right there."

"What are we looking at, Dakota?" Palmer asked.

"She's carrying a takeout container of sushi that was prepared at Suzie's restaurant." She zoomed in more. "And if you look here, at the corner of the container, you can see a letter "R" written with a black magic marker."

Sophia shifted in her seat.

Her whiskey-colored eyes are ice cold.

"Here you see Ramsay open the door. After he gives her a hug, she hands the sushi to her father. It's all there on the video feed."

"So the fuck what?" Martin said.

Dakota gave him a look. "And if you look here," she said, pushing more buttons to split the screen. "Here is a shot, taken by the Washoe County Police Department at the crime scene. The photo is of the sushi container found on Ramsay's boat, after his body was recovered. Look at the two pictures, side by side."

"Haha!" John said. "It's the same container."

"Exactly. It's the same container that Sophia dropped off. The one containing the poisonous sushi. Marked with the letter R in black magic marker. R for Ramsay."

"Well, I'll be damned," Meg said.

Palmer felt stunned.

"Busted!" John said, laughing beneath his turtle face mask.

"That doesn't prove a fucking thing," Martin yelled. "All it shows is that Sophia dropped off food at her father's house. It doesn't prove that she prepared it. You've got nothing!"

"Ahh!" Sophia said suddenly. "What's the use, Martin? What's the use?"

"Sophia? Sophia! Don't say a word. Not a word!"

Palmer studied Martin's face.

He's a crook. Dishonest. A cheat. He faked having cancer. He plotted murder.

"They have all the proof they need. What's the use?"
She repeated, her voice rising in pitch. "I'm done with
this. I'm so sick and tired."

"Why don't you tell us what happened, Sophia,"
Palmer said, looking at Sophia before glancing at the
conference room door. "In your words. Get it off your
chest." He kept the anger and pain that he felt from her
betrayal out of his voice; his was a trained poker face.

Sophia stood. Her face twisted into a scowl.

"My father was a piece of shit." She almost spit out the
words. "Yeah, I killed him. I'll tell you I'm glad that I did it!
I'd do it again!"

"Sophia. Please. No," Martin pleaded.

"Shut. The. Fuck. Up. Martin," she fumed. "Why? Why?
I'll tell you why." Her eyes narrowed, her face a mixture
of rage and satisfaction.

She's crazy.

"My father tossed my mother aside like she was
nothing. Nothing! He divorced her when she got too old
for him. Too old! She was thirty-six! I was eight. Eight!"
Her eyes narrowed further. "He was rich. He had all the
money. But he cut her off. He cut us off! Cheated her. And
me! We had nothing. Nothing you hear! He wouldn't pay
child support. He refused! He cut us off! No, no. I would
not let him get away with that. I was not going to be
discarded. No, no. Nothing will stop me from getting what
I deserve. Nothing! Do you understand me? I'm entitled
to his inheritance. I will not be ignored!" Sophia was
almost screaming. Her faced had reddened, and she'd
begun hyperventilating, her chest heaving.

Hell has no fury like a woman scorned.

"So, yes. I befriended Suzie. Got in her good graces.

Made sure she trusted me. Am I not trustworthy?" she exclaimed, looking around the room, searching for agreement, with a crazed look on her face. "And I learned about poisonous fish. What a wonderful way to kill somebody. Wonderful. Very fitting that father died that way. Very fitting. Look at all the famous people throughout history who died from ingesting poison. Socrates. Cleopatra. Those Nazis—Heinrich, Himmler, Hermann Goring. It's an elegant death. Painful. A person who has been poisoned dies in agony and has no idea why they're dying. My father deserved that kind of death!"

Why did she befriend me?

Then it hit Palmer.

Sun Tzu. The Art of War.

Keep your friends close and your enemies closer.

Sophia wasn't finished. "If you hadn't exhumed my father's body and did that fucking autopsy, we wouldn't be here today," she said, looking at Palmer with daggers in her eyes. "Martin and I would be lying on a beach counting our money."

That's true. There would not have been a case. It would be confirmed that Ramsay Marshall succumbed after his fourth heart attack.

Palmer thought back to that conversation they'd had at the restaurant. When he'd told Sophia that he'd exhumed Ramsay's body and had Doctor Bradshaw perform the autopsy, she seemed surprised by the news.

She never wanted the autopsy done.

Sophia smoothed out her white dress and sat back down, a maniacal look on her face. "I killed my father. I made the poisonous sushi. In fact, I picked a piece of fugu that I thought had the most amount of poison in it. I'm glad I did it. I'd do it again." With that, she pulled out a cigarette, lit it, and took a long, deep drag. A smug look crossed her face.

Palmer felt numb.

Martin sat, resigned to his fate.

Meghan smiled.

Dakota shook her head.

John wiggled in his seat, clearly trying to get comfy despite his hemorrhoids.

"Did you get all of that, Dan?" Palmer asked, looking towards the conference room door.

"Sure did," Lieutenant Dan Taylor said, entering the room. One of his eyes looked at Palmer, the other at Martin Mueller. He held up his iPhone. "Yep. Got it all here."

"That's not admissible," Martin said quickly. "Good fucking luck with that."

"It's admissible," Palmer said. "If a confession is voluntarily given, it is admissible in court. I didn't see anyone twisting Sophia's arm. Did you?"

Martin Mueller shut his mouth.

"Time to go," Lieutenant Dan said. "Martin Mueller, Sophia Mueller, you're both under arrest for the murder of Ramsay Marshall."

Sophia gave Palmer a sideways smirk as she was handcuffed and led away.

Who is this woman?

I feel like I'm in a movie with a woman who has multiple personalities. Sybil.

How did I miss this?

Grumpy Old Man by Tom Lyons

I'm an idiot.

Does anyone ever really know what goes on inside the minds and hearts of others?

Two weeks later

Driving east with traffic light on I-580, Palmer saw no red brake lights ahead. He felt good—his withered left arm no longer felt numb, and there'd been no blood in his urine this morning.

Good times.

"What now?" he says.

Buddy, sitting shotgun, gave him a look.

"What's that?" he asked, watching a huge black cloud drift sideways in the sky ahead. "What's that Buddy? Do you know?"

Buddy stuck his head back out the window and sniffed.

He was headed to the office to take Meghan out to lunch for Administrative Professionals' Day, or what he called "secretary appreciation day". He'd put it off for the last month and figured that it was about time.

After all she has done, it's long overdue.

He wanted to ask about her plans for the future during lunch. Did she want to become a private investigator? After her work on the Mueller case, it seemed possible.

Traffic stopped. As he inched closer to the black cloud, he realized what was going on.

"Are those birds?" he asked Buddy, who watched him, eyes never leaving Palmer's face.

They were birds. Off to the side of the road lay a paneled truck. It had run off of the road and toppled over. Hundreds, if not thousands, of birds swarmed the truck. Black crows, turkey vultures, doves, pigeons, and even a red-tailed hawk all took turns diving onto the truck, squawking.

Buddy barked.

"Easy boy," Palmer said. "Easy now."

As he drove closer, he saw a sign on the side of the truck: ACME PET STORE. On the ground lay piles of bird food.

It looked like a scene out of the movie *Birds*. They were everywhere, squawking, fighting, nipping at each other to get their share of the free meal. Car drivers blared horns, some slowed, opened a window to film the scene, hoping no doubt to post this weird happening on social media so that it would go viral. Others kept leaning on their horns, yelling and cursing at those who slowed to gawk.

"Why is everybody so angry these days, Buddy?"

Buddy looked at Palmer.

"Drivers are more reckless these days. Why, pup? Aftermath of the pandemic, maybe?" Watching so many people get angry at the drop of a pin made Palmer grumpy.

No reason for it.

Palmer drove under the moving black cloud of angry birds. Buddy barked when a bird flew too close to the car, trying to snag it in his mouth.

"Tough to catch one through a closed window, boy," Palmer said. Buddy growled at the birds, bearing his chipped front tooth.

After several minutes of stop-and-go driving, he inched past the crazy scene. Next to his car, a Chevy Tahoe with a bent right fender and dents in the right passenger door, veered into his lane. The driver flew past

Palmer, nearly sideswiping him, missing by mere inches. The Tahoe driver, a young man in his twenties, was texting on his phone.

When Palmer arrived at his office, he saw that the top of his car was covered in bird poop.

Nice to know that things are getting back to normal.

Meghan looked great. She'd dressed with their luncheon in mind. She was wearing a formfitting red skirt with a low cut white blouse. A white pearl necklace drew Palmer's attention to her décolletage.

First time I've seen her dress like this.

A line from a long defunct television show flashed through Palmer's mind. In the scene, a male lawyer sees a female coworker, who normally dressed in business suits, but who dresses provocatively in the scene. He looks down her dress. "Those are new," he says. Canned audience laughter follows.

You couldn't get away with that in today's world.

He'd never say such a thing to Meghan. Instead, he said, "Wow. You look great today."

Meghan smiled, her face reddening slightly.

"Oh, Sarge." She giggled. "Coffee?"

"Sure. Hot and black, please. Pick out a restaurant?" Palmer asked.

"How about Amakara?" Meghan suggested. "I hear it's pretty good. I've got reservations."

"What kind of food do they serve?"
"Sushi."

An odd look crossed Palmer's face.

"How about a good steak?" he says. "How does that

432

sound?"

Meghan responded immediately. "Sure, Sarge. How about I call Black Angus and see if they have any openings?"

"Sounds good."

Meghan walked toward her desk, sashaying almost.

Palmer watched Meghan saunter off.

Dakota sat in John's office as Palmer and Buddy walk in.

"Couple of words with you later?" Dakota asked.

"Sure," Palmer replied. "Give me fifteen?"

"You bet, Sarge," she said.

Both watched Dakota walk away.

"John boy," Palmer said. "What you up to?"

"Just a little reading."

Even now, Palmer still found it odd to hear such a big, bald man speak in such a child-like, squeaky voice. Palmer watched John slink away from Buddy when the dog, with his tail wagging, tried to get too close. John was drinking a Red Bull; his face mask hung off his right ear.

On John's desk were dozens of books, with titles like *2030*, *After Shock*, *Mega Trends*, *Think Like a Futurist*, *The Future is Faster Than You Think*, and *Vladimir Putin—Life Coach*.

"What's going on, John? Palmer asked.

Vladimir Putin—Life Coach?

"I'm thinking of starting a side job as a futurist, boss."

"A futurist? Really?"

"Yeah. You know. Predicting the future. Think about

how much money you could make if you could predict the future—like, say, predict what might happen in the stock market." John beamed with pride. "People would pay big bucks for that. Don't you think, Sarge?"

Palmer stifled a guffaw. *This coming from the guy who thought that Bob Hope was still alive at one hundred and twenty years of age.* "You may be onto something, John boy."

"I think so. I'll advertise on TikTok, like those young girls do. They get thousands of followers. Make big bucks. I can do the same. Create a video about what might happen next week, or next month."

Palmer didn't have the heart to tell him that the reason pretty girls garnered thousands of TikTok followers was because they were gorgeous, they danced seductively, and they were half naked. No one was going to follow a TikTok video featuring a bald, fat, middle-aged man who spoke like he'd just inhaled helium from a balloon.

John didn't want to tell Palmer that the main reason he studied futurist books was because he was trying to gain an advantage with sports gambling. Win a big Super Bowl bet. Or better yet, win a huge WWE wrestling match bet.

"I need to have a little medical procedure first, Sarge. Probably need about a week off of work."

"What's the matter?"

"It's personal, boss."

"Well, it's difficult for me to okay that without knowing what's going on."

John started tapping the side of his head. "Got a little problem down there, if you know what I mean." John lowered his eyes towards his pelvic area.

"You mean you're finally getting your hemorrhoids lanced?" Palmer asked.

"You mean you know?" John asked, hanging his head.

"Everybody knows, John. Everybody knows."

Nothing is sacred anymore.

John tapped the side of his head harder and faster.

"Well, yes," Palmer said. "You can take time off."

"Thanks, boss," John said, his face redder than a McIntosh apple.

"Well, I hope you don't leave your job, John. We need you here," Palmer said. "You did great work on the Mueller case. We couldn't have done it without you."

Palmer watched as John's body swelled with pride. "I owe you, Palmer. If not for you, I'd still be cleaning Porta Potties."

A stinky picture wedged its way into Palmer's head.

"Well. You did good. You made your sister, Becky, proud. I'm sure of it."

"Gee. Thanks, Palmer," John said.

Palmer noticed that John had stopped tapping the side of his head.

Dakota sat in her office in her workout clothes, her tattooed Arnold Schwarzenegger-sized arms on display.

"Why did you go to Germany without telling me?" Palmer asked, the first question on his list.

"You wanted us to check everyone out. Didn't you?"

"Yes, I did. Everyone's a suspect until proven otherwise. I agree."

"Well," Dakota started. "I couldn't find anything here in the States. Nothing on their computers. Nothing. It's like they didn't have a past. But everyone has something in their past that they don't share."

The pain of Sophia's betrayal was still a raw wound in Palmer's heart. "You're right, of course."

"Well. Their past was in Germany. Then when I saw the video of Mueller quick-stepping down the stairs at the San Jose City offices, I figured that something was rotten."

"I see."

During the pandemic, few people got on an airplane to fly across an ocean. Palmer thought that the Mueller's probably assumed that no one would fly to Germany to check out their story. Palmer felt stupid for letting Martin Mueller take advantage of him the day he'd confronted Martin about the video.

"I have good days and bad days. Like every cancer patient," Martin had said.

How could I have been so gullible?

The answer hit him, right between the eyes. Sophia. I wanted to believe in her. I wanted a future with her.

I believed him too.

"I couldn't tell you that I went to Germany, Sarge. I couldn't risk that info getting back to Sophia. Couldn't let them know that we were getting close. Know what I mean?"

"Of course."

Palmer had finally bought a ticket to "pop across the pond" to visit his daughter, Francesca, and her partner. He'd even agreed to stay with them in their London flat. Though he hadn't been able to see Francesca's face when he'd told her this, he could feel, from across the Atlantic,

436

how happy that had made her. *It's time to accept my daughter for who she is.*

"They would have disappeared in a nanosecond. I could not let that happen," Dakota said, snapping Palmer's mind back to the present.

"I agree."

"Turns out they were planning to get out of California anyway. The police searched their house. Found plane tickets. They were going to leave the day after they were arrested."

"Really? Where? Germany?"
"Australia."

"Australia?" he repeated, his voice rising.

"Yeah. Off the grid. Once Martin had applied for the zoning change, he could have handled any other requirements that the city wanted remotely. Chances are, they would have gotten away with all of it if they had gotten on that plane."

Palmer shook his head, still processing.

"And that's not all," Dakota continued. "The police found a sushi box in their freezer marked 'PD'."

Palmer froze. A chill slowly spread through his body. "They planned to kill me."

"Looks that way," Dakota said. "Especially if you were getting too close to the truth."

"I like sushi, too." Palmer plopped down into a chair.

"Sophia probably knew that."

"Did you know they were married?" Palmer asked after a moment's pause. Realizing that Sophia and Martin had planned to kill him made him feel sad. Then angry. Then grumpy.

How that woman played me. A black widow.

"No," Dakota said. "No idea. As I read through the court transcripts on his building license, they mentioned that his Sophia may have been complicit. Just by seeing that made me dig further."

"Glad you did," Palmer said.

"You hear they were denied bail?" Dakota said.

"They're a flight risk. No way they're getting out of prison."

"I think they'll be convicted," Dakota said. "Don't you, Sarge?"

"It'll be interesting to see how their defense lawyers position this. We do have her confession on video. Tough to argue against that."

"You know, Sarge," Dakota then said. "What I can't figure out is why they hired us in the first place. All they had to do was dispose of Ramsay and Brad with the poison sushi. No one would be the wiser. It'd look like they had heart attacks. Sophia would have inherited everything. After things cooled, they could have gotten their zoning change and pocketed their five hundred and sixty million dollars and been on their merry way."

"I hear you," Palmer started. "I've given that very same question a lot of thought."

"And?"

"Best that I can come up with is this: if there was any hint of wrongdoing or if there was an autopsy on Brad Marshall, which hinted at any impropriety, then Martin and Sophia would become one of the top suspects in a heartbeat."

"Okay."

"I think their plan was to deflect attention from

themselves. Work with a reputable investigations firm, then we come up completely clean on our efforts."

"That part is true," Dakota said. "At least at first look."

Palmer continued. "They wanted people to think that they were working to find the killer, or killers. That looks completely different." He took a sip of coffee. "And they wanted to keep their enemies close. Namely us. They could keep tabs on what was happening. Now, that's plausible. Isn't it?"

"I think so."

"I think so, too." Palmer tilted his head to the side. "You know, I promised your father, Jimmy, that I'd take care of you. Turns out, Dakota, that's not the case. You're taking care of me. You're taking care of a grumpy old man. Thank you for that."

"That's okay, Sarge," Dakota said. "You don't owe me anything. I owe you."

"You owe me?"

"Yeah. You knew of my conviction for identity theft before you hired me. Didn't you?"

"Well . . ." Palmer started to reply, measuring his words.

"Yet you hired me anyway. You gave me a chance. I want to thank you for that. Like I said, you don't owe my anything. I owe you, Palmer Doyle."

Meghan stopped by and refilled Palmer's coffee cup.

"Thanks, Meg," Palmer said. "Ready to leave?"

"Yes," Meghan said before leaving to freshen her face.

"You going to be here a while?" Palmer asked Dakota.

"Yes."

"Mind if I leave Buddy while we go to lunch?"

"Sure thing, Sarge."

"What's next on your list, Dakota?"

"Stop ransomware attacks. You remember the Colonial Pipeline attack. Don't you?"

"I do."

Ransomware hackers, supposedly based in Russia, had broken into Colonial Pipeline's workers' computers, planted a worm, gained access to their network, and shut down their computer systems. The attack affected half of the East Coast's fuel supply, which drove up gasoline prices and created shortages for half the country. Top officials at Colonial had paid the hackers $4.4 million for the computer key codes to disable the computer virus. The attack had struck a nerve throughout the entire country. No company was safe from this kind of computer attack.

"This kind of stuff is right up your alley. Isn't it?"

"It is," Dakota said proudly.

My own Lisbeth Salander.

Black Angus was located in the same shopping center as Palmer's favorite coffee shop, the same center where the Tesla Supercharger stations were located. No one seemed to be fighting over charging stations today, but all twelve stations were being used.

Walking towards the restaurant, Palmer spotted a German Shepherd circling in a vacant lot nearby.

Mister Peabody.

He watched as the dog circled and sniffed, circled and sniffed. Endlessly. After several minutes of circling and sniffing, Mister Peabody squatted.

Just like Buddy. Takes forever to do his business.

When Mister Peabody finished, he kicked up dirt with his rear legs. Jonesy appeared, poop bag in hand.

Palmer walked over. "Got a second, Jonesy?" He asked. "I've been looking for you. I'd like to have a word."

"But of course, Mister Doyle. Of course." Jonesy leaned over to pick up Mister Peabody's poop. "And who, may I ask, is this lovely lass you have with you this fine day?"

"Meghan, this is my friend Jonesy."

Meghan looked at Jonesy, struggling to keep the revulsion she felt off of her face. After getting a whiff, her face scrunched.

"Jonesy, this is my secretary, Meghan."

"Secretary? I see. I see."

"We're having lunch," Palmer added as way of explanation. "For secretary's day."

"I see," Jonesy said, stroking his filthy beard, which tobacco spittle had dripped into. "Fine day it is for lunch. Isn't it?"

Meghan threw up a little in her mouth.

"I wanted to thank you for all of your help," Palmer started. "We would not have been able to solve the Mueller case without you."

"'T'was nothing at all. I was glad to be of service," Jonesy said, motioning with the fully loaded poop bag. "Glad to be of service. It's what I live for." Then he added: "Case is good?"

"Yes," Palmer started. "The Mueller's are in jail. Bail was revoked."

"I'm not surprised."

Then, speaking to Meghan, Palmer said, "Jonesy is a retired superior court judge, you know."

Meghan's face twisted into something unrecognizable.

"Suzie Marshall is also in jail for the murder of her husband. First-degree murder. Though, her attorneys are claiming that he abused her."

"I see," Jonesy said. "That complicates matters."

"It does. A woman in California who admitted to killing her abusive husband was just set free. Turns out, he'd been abusing her for years. Jury found her innocent."

"There are many cases like that. We'll have to see how it plays out," Jonesy said, looking over his shoulder for a trash can to deposit Mister Peabody's poop. "Tricky little devils, those defense attorneys. You never know what they have up their sleeves."

"I wanted to ask you," Palmer started. "Do you still want to be a private investigator? If you do, I might have something that might interest you."

"Well, thank you so much, Mister Doyle. Thank you. That means the world to me, coming from you. But goodness, no. I don't want to be a private investigator anymore. I'm going to become a psychologist," Jonesy said.

Palmer and Meghan passed a stunned look between them.

Jonesy continued, his weathered face animated. "The pandemic has opened all sorts of opportunities in the field of counseling. I took an Instagram course."

An Instagram course on how to be a shrink?

"Our society has a great need for trained counselors. A great need. People have been locked up for so long during the pandemic, and they feel depressed," Jonesy continued. "People are angry. Full of rage. Look at all the awful incidents of violence on planes? Mostly because people refuse to wear face masks. Fights break out. Passengers subdue and zip tie unruly people. Pilots divert the flights and police arrest the guilty when they land."

Palmer and Meghan remained silent.

"And don't get me started on what happens in grocery stores. At checkout lines," Jonesy continued. "Why, just last week a man shot a Safeway store grocery clerk. Simply because she had asked him to put on his face mask. It's madness, I tell you. Madness. There's gun violence everywhere. People are getting shot, left and right. Last Fourth of July weekend, over two hundred people were shot and killed across our country. On the Fourth of July! It's supposed to be a happy day, a national holiday. Well, it's not a happy day anymore. It's a violent day. It's a real pressure cooker out there."

"I agree," Palmer finally said.

"The need for me to help is real. There is a shitload of fucked-up people out there in this world. I have one more Instagram course to finish, and then I get my license."

An Instagram course to be a licensed psychologist?

"Ahhh," Palmer said. "Well, Jonesy, I wish you the best of luck." He took Meghan's arm. "We have to go. Just got beeped. Our table is ready."

"Well, I'm sure that I'll be seeing you around, Mister Doyle. It has been my great pleasure getting to know you."

"My pleasure too, Jonesy."

"Nice to meet you, too, Meghan. You take care. And may God bless."

Once inside and seated, Meghan wasted little time before ordering a glass of Chardonnay. She looked happy, a smile spreading across her freckled face. Palmer couldn't remember if he'd ever been this close to her at the office.

She's pretty.

Palmer was no dummy. He knew she had been attracted to him for quite some time.

The pain he felt from the entire episode with Sophia still felt raw. It would take time before he felt like getting involved with a woman again.

I'm old enough to be her father.

He also realized that May-December relationships frequently flourished; many younger women were attracted to older men. And older men? Seemed like they were always attracted to a young, pretty woman. What red-blooded man wouldn't be? Palmer didn't think there was anything bad, or lecherous, about being attracted to a younger woman.

We were made to procreate.

Men are wired, by biology, to be attracted to women of

child-bearing age. The birds and the bees.

"Thanks so much for lunch, Palmer," Meghan said, flashing her megawatt smile his way. "I really appreciate it."

"My fault for not doing it sooner," he said. "By the way, that was a great job you did two weeks ago with the Mueller's. You'd make a good private investigator."

Meghan giggled. The chardonnay was loosening her up.

"So," Palmer asked. "Are you thinking that you'd like to be an investigator?"

Meghan leaned closer, bending over the table so Palmer could get a good look at her cleavage.

Palmer accepted her invitation.

Meghan watched Palmer watch her.

"Not really," Meghan said with a twinkle in her eye. She flashed a mischievous smile. She spoke in her sultry Lauren Bacall voice.

"I have something entirely different in mind."

Palmer tilted his head, a semblance of a smirk crossed his lips. Then he smiled.

Good thing I'm manscaped!

About the author

Tom Lyons has been writing for over forty years and is the author of four previous books. The Complete Realtor – 2007, Putt like a Tour Professional – 2010, Family, AKA, Shark in the Water – 2014, Psychopath Chronicles – 2015.

Grumpy Old Man is his fifth novel and is also the first in the Grumpy Old Man Trilogy. He lives in Northern California, close to his children and grandchildren, with his wife Amelia and their rescue Lab, Buddy.

When he is not working on Book Two of the Grumpy Old Man Trilogy you can find him with his wife, with their kids and grandkids, or walking his dog, or playing golf.

Special Sneak Preview

Grumpy Old Man 2
A Palmer Doyle P.I.
Suspense novel
To be published Mid-2023

1.

Madison Thomas was not your normal eighteen-year-old-young woman.

First, she was drop dead gorgeous; tall, long legged, thin-waisted with a shapely bosom. She had been well versed, at a young age, of getting exactly what she wanted from men by flashing her smile, or offering a full-lipped pouty face, or by batting her almond-shaped blue eyes, which hinted towards Asian blood somewhere in her lineage.

Madison was fully aware of the power that she held over men, and she was not shy about using it. Of course, it didn't hurt that her father, or rather her step-father, was the most powerful man in the State, namely the current governor of California, Gordon Thomas III.

She was on her way to meet her 'boy toy of the month' for one of their frequent under the sheet's acrobatics afternoon; Madison having been sexually active for years now. She'd do anything to get out of the Governor's mansion in Sacramento and get away from her step-father and step-mother. She was now an adult; plus, she felt that her step-parents were just plain stupid. Her birth mother had married Gordon two years after her real father had died, back when Gordon was a young promising San Francisco District Attorney, before he got into politics. Then her mom died too. To make things worse for her, she absolutely hated her step-father's current wife, Brittany.

She pushed a button on her iPhone and her red Tesla model S started remotely.

Like many young people who had their heads constantly buried in their phones, and in a hurry to get naked with PJ, a sophomore at Cal State Davis, a computer science major no less, Madison failed to notice two men, sitting in a newer Black Escalade, following close behind.

2.

The only thing that was better than having one dog, Palmer Doyle thought, was having two dogs. Buddy, his eight-year-old rescue Malinois, quietly sat in the bow of Palmer's fishing boat. Izzy girl, an active four-year-old rescue Black Lab, anxiously paced back and forth, looking for an opening when Palmer was not looking so she could jump in the lake.

Like people, Palmer thought, every dog was unique. Buddy and Izzy girl could not have been more different. Where Buddy was chill; he loved to lie down and sleep and relax Izzy girl was a fireball of energy, schizoid almost, in constant motion, darting this way then that way, seemingly always stressed. Buddy would take his good old time going to potty. He'd circle and sniff, circle and sniff, endlessly, before selecting a spot to do his business; he still liked to poop in private. Izzy girl emptied her system the second she got outside, in a constant rush to pee and poop. Whereas Buddy peed, on average, maybe twice a day, Izzy girl would squat twenty times a day. Sometimes when her bladder was empty, she'd still try to pee, but nothing would come out.

"Ah. Better." Palmer said as he took a sip of black coffee. He refitted his hook with a fresh worm; he cast with his right arm, towards deep water. "Peace and quiet."

Las Vaqueros, a man-made lake a quarter mile wide and two miles long, sat between golden hills just northeast of Livermore, California.

Wearing smelly dirty fishing clothes that were unwashed, for a while, Palmer felt a nibble. Now sixty-two years old, Palmer Doyle was six feet tall. Lanky with long arms and gigantic hands, he walked with an athletic gait. Had a full head of grey hair. He had bushy eyebrows that needed trimming. Palmer had a prominent nose, reminiscent of Jimmy Durante, the actor/comedian from the mid-twentieth century whose nickname was 'The Schnozzola'. Except that Palmer's nose was flat against his face, like a boxer who had lost too many fights and was starred with burst veins from one too many Grey Goose's on the rocks. Palmer was now a little droopy in the face, wrinkled, his neck a turkey jowl. His knees crackled in pain until taking several steps. His withered left arm, injured in a bomb explosion while serving in Afghanistan in the US Army almost twenty years ago, throbbed this morning and hung limp by his side. The fingers on his left hand were gnarled, crooked, like branches on an old oak tree.

His oversized prostrate seemed to grow larger every day.

He had to pee.

Felt like he always had to pee.

"Got a big one here, boys," he said to his dogs as he set the hook and let the fish take line. "Hand me the fishing net, will you? He added; Buddy had a puzzled look on his face, Izzy girl tilted her head. Palmer laughed and reached for the net.

The air quality on this warm August morning was unhealthy; his iPhone noted the index at 275, in the purple zone with only the maroon zone being worse; an AQI of 275 was unhealthy where the risk of serious health effects was increased for everyone. To the northeast, the Caldor fire raged in the South Lake Tahoe area. Southeast of the Caldor fire, the Tamarack fire was only 10% contained; it had already consumed over two hundred thousand acres. Winds carried clouds of ash and soot over the East Bay where it settled down like an end of days apocalypse. Though it was nine in the morning, the sun hid behind the red smoke clouds that rose thousands of feet into the sky. Most of the San Francisco Bay Area lay under these enormous clouds of smoke. The fire smell choked Palmer, his heart skipped a beat as he tried to breathe. Together the land mass area affected and destroyed by fires in California this year alone was larger than the area of the New England States, Massachusetts, Connecticut, Rhode Island, Vermont and New Hampshire. Combined.

Drought. Global warming.

Welcome to California.

This morning, however, Palmer was not feeling grumpy. No, not today. He'd just put a deposit on a five acre ranch high in the Cascade Range in Oregon. Away from everything and everybody. He hoped to move there in about sixty days, right after escrow closed on his private investigation firm, Palmer International, which he had just sold. It'd be just him, his wife Becky, Buddy and Izzy girl. Exactly what he wanted.

I'm finally getting out of California.

Becky will be very happy.

The fish, a three pounder at least, put up a fight but Palmer finally netted him, took a picture, then removed the unbarbed hook. Buddy sat in the boat's bow, showed a chipped front tooth he broke while trying to chew a rock. Izzy girl wagged her tail furiously, sniffed the fish, a wide mouth bass, then licked it. The bass thrashed in Palmer's hand, refusing to give up; to Palmer, it then seemed that the fish looked around and saw clouds of soot and ash overhead. When Palmer threw him back into the water, he thought he heard the bass cough.

3.

Miguel and Hector Ybarra, brothers only one year apart in age, could not have been more different. As infants, their fifteen-year-old mother dropped them over a border fence near San Ysidro, the most southern city in California, with a note attached to Hector, who had just turned two. The note contained the address of the boy's grandparents who lived in San Ysidro. Tata, who worked in landscape maintenance, was mean to the boys; after all, it wasn't his idea to raise the grandkids and Nana, who always wanted more kids and treated the boys well, cleaned houses.

Nana, who liked American television shows, gave the boys nicknames. Her favorite show was–*The Cisco Kid*–a popular show in the '50's where the Cisco Kid, a lady's man, and his faithful sidekick, Pancho, roamed the Mexican countryside riding Palomino ponies while joking, laughing, taking care of the bad guys and helping the poor and downtrodden. A Mexican Robin Hood. At the end of each show they'd joke with each other and say in their high-pitched voices:

"Hey Cisco!"

"Hey Pancho!"

Then they'd ride off into the sunset.

Mick became the Cisco Kid and Hector, who liked to eat a lot, was the short portly Pancho.

Growing up, Hector liked fast food best. His favorite was a Burger King Whopper with cheese. Washed it down with warm Coca Cola. He'd never consider a MacDonald's double cheeseburger. Or something from Carl's Junior or Wendy's. Only a Burger King Whopper with cheese would do.

Mick, a workout fiend, started lifting weights when he was ten. By thirteen, he was muscle bound. Hector would never workout or lift any kind of weight. Hector didn't like to exercise, except to bend an elbow to either down a Modelo, or woof down a Whopper. One day, when the boys stole Grape Slurpees from their local Mexican food market and got caught by the owner, Mick tried to scale an eight-foot fence in order to get away; he slipped and landed squarely on his noggin. There was a loud crack. He felt dizzy for days. He couldn't tell Tata or Nana what happened; God forbid that they'd find out what the boys were up to. Plus, there was no money for him to go to the hospital, or to a doctor.

Mick hadn't been able to move his head or neck much since then and he was now twenty-five. He had a frozen neck. Both had been in the States now for over twenty years, neither had a green card or a work visa. Both were illegal immigrants.

Mick figured he'd heal his neck by lifting heavier weights. His neck, now shaped more like a comma, held his head low on his shoulders as if it was not strong enough to support his head's weight. When he wanted to turn his head, he had to turn and move his entire body, starting with his feet. Kind of like a robot from the 1960s. And if he tried to turn his head without first turning his body, it felt like he'd stuck his neck into a 220 volt electrical socket. Electrocuted.

Both Mick and Hector had dropped out of school in 10th grade, but their academic skills were lower than high school level. Mick's reading and speaking skills were at the 4th grade level, Hector's were lower. Both were a couple of fries short of a Big Mac meal.

Mick was driving the boss's black Escalade, making sure that Madison Thomas didn't know she was being followed. He sipped a Modelo.

Like she'd noticed anything besides what was on her phone.

"Man, she's pretty." Hector said, munching on potato chips. "I'd do her. Know what I mean, bro?" Mick had a stoic look on his face. "You think she's pretty, bro?"

Mick said nothing. He kept his eyes on the red Tesla. "We got a job to do." Mick finally said. They looked like brothers; both had black greasy long hair, dark eyes, and similar south of the border complexions.

"Would you do her, bro?" Hector said again. "Bet you'd do her." He ate more chips, some falling from the corner of his mouth. His eyes teared up. "Man, my allergies are bad today, bro. My eyes are burning." Hector looked at the sky. "What happened to the sun, man? Do you see that? The sun is red, bro. The sky is full of red stuff."

"Do I look like a fuckin' meteorologist to you, Hector? Do I?"

"Man, I wish you were that Mexican weather girl. What's her name?"

"Yanet Garcia." Mick said. "She's on Mexican TV. Every day."

"Yeah." Hector said. "Yanet Garcia. She wears those short tight dresses while she's doing the weather. She is smokin' man. Hair in a ponytail. Got an outstanding ass, man. Outstanding." Hector put the potato chips down. "You got any eye drops bro?" He asked.

"We got a job to do." Mick repeated. "You got the duct tape?"

"I ain't got no stinkin' duct tape." Hector said. "I thought you brought the duct tape."

"You told me you'd bring the duct tape man."

"Ah, bro. I never said such a thing."

"Did too."

"Did not."

"Did too." Veins popped in Mick's right temple.

Both men went quiet.

"Ah. Man. How we gonna do this without duct tape?"

"I saw some black electrical tape in the trunk." Hector added. "We improvise."

Mick tried to turn his head but couldn't. "Ahh Pancho. It'll be okay."

"Ahh, Cisco." Hector said, laughing. "Electrical tape should work too." Then he coughed.

4.

As Palmer entered the freeway, the morning alternating traffic light was on. He pulled close behind a late model white BMW. When the light turned green, the car ahead of him didn't move. The light quickly turned red. Palmer's car didn't move. Buddy sat in the shotgun seat, his head contentedly out the window, sniffing. Izzy girl, sitting in the back seat, ran back and forth to both rear seat windows, eager to see what was going on.

"You're a real spaz." Palmer said. "You know Izzy. Don't you?"

The dog tilted her head as if trying to listen better.

When the light turned green again, the BMW still didn't move. Palmer leaned on his horn. "C'mon man!" he yelled. "There're other people in this world beside you numb nuts."

The BMW pulled out. Slowly. Got into the right-hand lane and sped up to 40 MPH. In a 65 MPH zone.

Palmer moved over a lane and passed him, giving the driver a dirty look as he did.

Asian.

Chinese?

The driver had to be at least ninety years old. Wispy white hair that ran down the back of his neck. He had this pained expression on his face. His face looked contorted, both hands firmly on the steering wheel, as if he were in the middle of a severe gastro-intestinal issue.

To Palmer's way of thinking, Chinese were not the best drivers. Many did not have a valid California driver's licenses, which was mandatory in order to drive in California. Most had a Chinese driver's license, which did not contain one word of English on them. While driving, whenever there was some kind of issue, be it a traffic violation, or driving well below the posted speed limit, or some kind of traffic accident, dollars to donuts, a Chinese driver was involved in many of these.

Not that Palmer Doyle had any kind of issue with Chinese people. It was just that there were so damn many of them living in California. Why, in the San Gabriel Valley area, near Los Angeles, you could drive for miles down a major thoroughfare without seeing one sign in English. Chinese made up over 80% of the population in the valley there. The same thing was happening to the San Francisco East Bay Area. First, Chinese moved, in large numbers, to cities like San Jose, Santa Clara, and Milpitas. Then slowly they worked their way north, into Fremont, then Pleasanton, Dublin, San Ramon and finally into Livermore. Already, in Dublin, where Palmer's office was located, Chinese business signs were popping up everywhere.

The Asians he knew were polite, well educated, well spoken, and good citizens. It was just that there were so damn many of them. In California, there were, perhaps, 20 million Caucasians living there. With 1.4 Billion Chinese living in China they outnumbered the California Caucasians by 150 to 1. And it seems like in recent years all those Chinese discovered how wonderful it was to live in California with its glorious weather, and thousands of great things to see and do.

Palmer just wished that the ones who lived here in California knew how to drive a car correctly.

And Chinese were not the only Asians that were changing the ethnicity of the state. Add in another 3+ billion Asians who lived in either India, Japan, South Korea, the Philippines, Taiwan, Vietnam, or others and you'd get the general idea of what was happening. Asians outnumbered the Caucasians 1500 to 1. The great ethnicity shift in California had already happened. It just had to play out over the coming years. It was unstoppable.

And that's not counting the 15 million Mexicans that already lived in California, millions of them here illegally, as well.

Palmer had just finished reading the United States Census report for 2020 that had been released by the Government. In the last census, in 2010, approximately 70% of the US population was Caucasian. Now, ten years later, Caucasians accounted for only 58% of the population in the US, with Asians being the fastest growing minority in the nation. Caucasians living in California were now only 39% of the population according to the census. These facts supported Palmer's long held belief about how the ethnicity of California was transforming.

People liked living among their own kind. That's been going on in America forever. Most major cities had names for the areas where people of the same ethnicity lived, gathered, and practiced their religions. Chinatown, Little Saigon, Little Italy, Germantown. Nothing wrong with that. Birds of a feather flock together.

Palmer Doyle had nothing against all the Chinese, Indians, and all the other Asian people who lived in California. He just didn't want to live amongst them. He wanted to live among his own kind. Caucasians. Nothing wrong with that, either. Asians are taking over California and there is nothing anyone can do to stop it.

Can't wait to move to Oregon.

There was no wind, the air quality had not improved, the sky was a hazy red color and the mid-morning summer sun was a dim red bulb in the sky. To Palmer, it felt like he was driving on the surface of Mars. Traffic on Freeway 580 West was at a standstill. Palmer crept along at four miles per hour. It'd take over an hour to travel the six miles from West Livermore to his office in Dublin.

The sad part? I'm getting used to this.

And talk about cost of living? California has the highest housing costs in the nation, the highest prices on gasoline and utilities. And if you want to live in the State that has the highest taxes, then California is the place for you. Property taxes are through the roof. Then you have estate taxes, trust taxes, inheritance taxes, county, city, and municipality taxes. You're taxed on your home utilities, gasoline for your car and liquor. Then you have the State Income Tax. And then you pay a 10% sales tax on everything that you buy in California. From groceries, to appliances, to cars and boats, to lawn and garden furniture and for the topsoil, fertilizer, and grass you buy for your lawns. You're taxed on the water you used to water your lawn and you're taxed on the lawnmower you buy to mow your lawn. They tax people in California on everything.

Multiple that 10% sales tax by approximately 30 million working adults in the State buying goods and services around the clock 24/7, 365 days a year, and it adds up to a pretty penny. No wonder the State's bank accounts total billions of dollars. The State of California is doing very well. California is very rich. The latest estimate was that California had over twenty-six-BILLION-dollars in the bank.

And what do we do with that surplus of billions of dollars, Palmer thought, while dodging another freeway pothole? Do we widen and add freeways? Do we fix the f'ing potholes?

Potholes go unfixed for years.

Do we plan and develop new infrastructure to better accommodate the population increase in the state? Such as modernize the schools? Add new schools? Pay teachers more money for the invaluable service that they render the State's children? Add new State parks? Add State run lakes for boating, fishing and recreation? Do we add more roads? Wider roads? More freeways that are desperately needed? Do we finally address and take care of the State's incredibly enormous homeless problem?

Palmer knew that the answer to most of these questions was a resounding no.

Like Doctor Evil from the Austin Powers movies.

NNNNOOOOOOOOOOO!

Instead, one of things that the Governor of California implemented was to give older illegal aliens free medical coverage.

Wait.

What??

Let me see if I got this straight, Palmer thought when he read that one.

First, hundreds of thousands of Mexicans climb a border fence, or swim across a river, and enter the state illegally. Then they stay here, illegally, for years while not getting a work permit visa or green card. They earn money. They pay ZERO taxes. Over the course of their entire life. Then we reward that criminal behavior by giving them free health care?

And we, the taxpayers, foot that bill? From tax dollars we've paid the state over the years?

How is that fair to me? To anyone in California who has paid their fair share of taxes over the years.

I don't want to pay one red nickel towards that.

Time to take my dogs and oversized prostrate and move out.

Oregon, here we come Becky.

Traffic eased, Palmer sped up to twenty miles per hour. An older Honda Civic, with a dented rear right fender and no rear bumper, driven by a young guy who didn't look old enough to drive a tricycle, let alone an automobile, cut Palmer off.

Palmer slammed the brakes. Within two seconds, traffic stopped again and Palmer now followed the inexperienced driver in the beat-up car. Palmer gave him plenty of room.

Wonder how your car got so banged up, dude?

5.

Palmer loved a good cup of coffee. Most days he drank four to five cups. Black, no cream or sugar. All that caffeine made his right eye twitch and his hands shake, even his bad left hand. To make sure that no one saw his hands shaking, he'd stick them in his pants pockets while talking with somebody. Coffee, however, was his second favorite beverage, vodka being his favorite, preferably with lime juice and triple sec, which made for a tasty vodka gimlet.

Two of those stopped the twitching in his eye and the shaking of his hands. Last night he'd downed three vodka gimlets; he felt pretty good this morning. Nothing was twitching or shaking.

He stopped at his favorite local coffee house, in a strip mall in Dublin, before heading to his office.

The parking lot was crowded. Palmer had to circle in the lot several times before a spot opened up. He looked towards a bank of Tesla Superchargers in the lot's rear. Several blue tarps were strung together nearby. As were a couple of shopping carts, each filled with dirty, soiled clothes that he thought smelled like raw sewage, even from a distance.

Homeless.

The homeless situation in California was getting worse. By some experts count, there now were over one-hundred-and-fifty-thousand-homeless people living in California. And counting, as many homeless in other states moved to California, namely to cities like Venice Beach, where the locals fed, clothed, and offered medical care to homeless people who pitched tents on the beach, to take advantage of the great weather.

Who wouldn't want to move to Venice Beach California, if they could mooch off the locals and live on the beach. For free?

The state had spent over four-point-eight-billion-dollars over the past three years to ease the homeless situation in the state. They built tiny homes, thousands of them, each only one-hundred-and-fifty-square-foot large, at the cost of eighty-thousand-per-tiny-home, to help get homeless people off the streets. The programs included rent help, so people would not be evicted, and foreclosure prevention, with the same goal in mind.

Keep people in their homes so they don't take to the streets.

All that did, when the word got out about all the perks offered by the State of California, was to create an influx of homeless people from other states, tens of thousands of them moving to California.

Homeless never had it so good.

Inspecting the blue tarps near the banks of Tesla Superchargers, Palmer noticed that someone, probably a talented and educated homeless guy, had jury-rigged electrical wires that ran from one of the Tesla chargers to inside one of the blue tarp tents. He heard a soft humming sound coming from the tents.

With the AQI still hovering in the 275 range and the blood red sun warming the smoke filled air, Palmer stifled a laugh. Then a cough.

Probably an air conditioner. Or an air purifier. Or both.

Smart.

Ester, Palmer's favorite barista, who was from Tasmania, was working the counter inside. A bone held her hair, dyed a vibrant purple, in place, and from the looks of it, it appeared to be a chicken thigh bone.

"Ey, Mista Doyle." Ester said. "Yo usul?"

"Yes, Ester. Coffee and a blueberry muffin. Make sure the coffee is extra hot?"

Palmer had been coming here for a couple of years now; he understood Ester's unique brand of English.

"Sur ting. Dat'll b eye twi fi."

Ester was an attractive young woman. Her hair was naturally auburn, not purple, and she was studying to be an actress. Though Palmer guessed that if she was to get a part in a movie or TV show, that it would be a non-speaking role.

"Eight twenty-five?" Palmer asked.

"Ya."

Palmer handed over a ten. "Keep the change."

"Tanks!" Ester said cheerfully.

Driving to his office, while sipping coffee, Palmer dreaded what he had to do next. Thinking about it made his mouth dry up; it felt like he couldn't swallow. He had to tell his staff that he'd sold the business. He knew that, to a person, they'd each be unhappy. That he'd might have to deal with their anger, their sadness. Just thinking about what was going to happen next made Palmer Doyle feel very sad.

6.

"How'd' you get your lips to look so pouty?" Maggie asked. "A filler? Get stuck with a needle?'

"No." Madison answered. "I used a lip-plumping gloss."

"Just a plumping gloss?"

"Then I rubbed a little cinnamon in." Madison continued. "The cinnamon acts as a irritant that helps plump lips. Then you apply a darker lipstick underneath, a lighter color on top. And voila!"

"Well. You look great, Mad." Maggie said. "Gonna drive the boys positively wild." Then she giggled.

"That's the idea." Madison said, giggling too. She turned her face from side to side, while holding her phone above her head to give Maggie the full effect. Madison had perfect facial bone structure, high cheekbones like a runway model, a strong jaw, long straight black hair which fell loosely off her shoulders.

"You should be an influencer, girlfriend." Maggie then said. "You're a natural. You'd make a fortune."

"I thought about it." Madison said. "But I don't need the money. Besides. It seems like a lot of work."

"Yeah. Right. You got Daddy's money." Maggie said.

"Why don't you do it Mags?" Madison then said. "I can prep you with all the stuff you'll need."

"Naw." Maggie then said. "I'm not nearly as beautiful as you. I couldn't get as many followers."

The drive from the Governor's mansion in Sacramento to her boyfriend BJ's dorm at UC Davis took thirty minutes. So, Madison decided to FaceTime her bestie on the way.

"I love makeup." Madison offered. "Use Kylie Jenner's makeup only. One of her lip kits. They're clean and vegan." Madison added. Her red lipstick matched the color of her car.

"I do too." Maggie added. "Pan down. I want to see your outfit."

"K!"

"K!"

Though Madison was driving westbound on Interstate 80 doing seventy-five-miles-per-hour, she took one hand off the steering wheel and pointed the phone's camera towards her, then raised it up and down.

"You ho!" Maggie said, who, like Madison, was eighteen years old. "Those shorts barely cover your ass! And that top? Very chic. And tight. Love the cleavage. Leaves nothing to the imagination."

Madison wore the short-shorts favored by young women that only young women can get away wearing.

"You don't think it's too slutty?" Madison asked, her voice a high-pitched question mark.

"No. It's perfect. Says come fuck me now."

"That's what I'm going for." Madison said, looking at her phone to make sure that it framed correctly her in the middle so that Maggie saw the full picture.

"PJ is gonna to rip those clothes off of you in a nano-second and throw you down on the bed."

"That's the idea." Madison said, giggling. "This girl is hangry! Got waxed yesterday."

Both young women giggled.

Her Tesla swerved from lane to lane. Cars behind her gave her ample space, or they moved over a lane before they sped past her.

"Is he good in bed?"

"Working on that."

"Whatca mean?"

"He's a premie."

"A premie.?"

"Yeah. You know. Can't help himself. Like most young guys."

"Excellent." Maggie said. "Working on that stuff. Call me later. I want details."

"K." Madison said.

"K!" Maggie said, giggling.

Madison ended the call; she whistled as she looked in the rear-view mirror, applied more lip gloss while she was driving, neglecting to engage the Tesla's auto drive feature.

Madison Thomas's biological father, passed away when she was six years old. She had vivid memories of him. His musky masculine smell when she sat in his lap; she felt content, happy, protected and safe. Her mother married Gordon Thomas III when she was eight. Two years later, while driving in the usual heavy traffic on the Bay Bridge, her mom, inexplicably, lost control of the car, bounced off a center divider, flipped the car and broke her neck. She had just turned thirty-two.

Madison had been sitting in the back seat and, somehow, she escaped unharmed. Physically, at least. She would carry the emotional scar from that day to the end of her life.

So, both of Madison's natural parents were dead when Gordon married Brittany Collins two years later, just as Madison was entering puberty.

Brittany gave birth to two kids; Lily, now three, and Kevin, almost two. Brittany completed ignored Madison, as if she didn't exist. Instead, she gave all of her attention and time to her two youngsters. Her step-father Gordon did the same thing, ignoring her, as he was one-hundred percent wrapped up in his burgeoning political career. Some even said that he had intentions of running for even higher office someday, perhaps even a run for President of the United States.

To Madison, it seemed, her new step-mother just plain resented her. Seemed like all she did was criticize Madison. She was constantly in a bad mood, it seemed, when Madison was around; she was always angry, mad, and yelled at her frequently. There were no motherly talks between her and Brittany. She didn't help with Madison's school work nor did she take any interest in Madison's life. No discussions about Madison's approaching womanhood, no talks about what to expect about puberty, menstruation, how to deal with it, nothing at all about the birds and the bees. Brittany couldn't care less. Sometimes, Brittany would purposely avoid Madison while they were both at home, not wanting to see, or talk, to her, leaving Madison to figure everything out by herself.

Then, almost overnight, Madison blossomed into a stunning, beautiful young woman. A young woman that could be discovered by some bespectacled middle-aged man at the local malt shop, like Lana Turner, or plucked from a crowded inner city front doorstep, like Rosario Dawson, and then transformed into a supermodel, or movie star. One time, when he thought she wasn't looking, Madison even caught her step-dad giving her the old male gaze.

She'd been pretty much on her own since she was fourteen; she'd come and go as she pleased; no one cared where she was, or who she was with, or what she was doing, or what time she came home. The freedom suited her well; it made her feel happy.

The smoke shrouded midday red sun was hot by the time she pulled into the student parking lot at UC Davis. Madison checked her lipstick and makeup again before getting out of her car. She pulled her top lower, checked to see how much cleavage she was showing, wanting to make it very clear to PJ just what she wanted. Then she coughed, she covered her mouth with a tissue.

Suddenly, she was accosted from behind. Rough strong hands pinned her arms to her side. "What are you doing?" Madison screamed. "Are you crazy? Do you know who I am?" then she added: "I have money. I can pay you."

The man spoke, his voice Mexican tinged. "You can't fellate your way out of this situation, darlin'." He tightened his grip, flung her around like a rag doll until she stopped fighting.

"That's better," he said. "We good now."

Another muscular hand clamped over her mouth. Rough hands. Madison felt terrified. She tried to scream. Her screams were muffled. Then a second man was in front of her, a red bandana covering most of his face. Madison struggled. She tried to kick at them. But the men were strong. The second man placed a white cloth over her nose and mouth, held it firmly in place. Seconds later, Madison felt herself drifting off. Her body relaxed and went limp.

7.

Short, portly Hector secured Madison's hands and feet with black tape. "Man, I told you to bring duct tape, Mick." He said. "I told you."

"Did not."

"Did too."

"Did not." Veins popped in Mick's right temple.

"I'm not gonna fight with you, Mick." Hector said, tightening the tape. Then he secured a porous, black cloth bag over her head. "Securing this bitch would be a lot easier with duct tape."

Hector liked to fight. The problem was he was not very good at it. He wasn't athletic, he had zero boxing, or wrestling skills; he'd spent much of his youth getting beat up by kids who were smaller and younger than he was. "Your face has fucked up a lot of closed fists." Mick would say, reminding Hector just how bad of a fighter he was.

"Ahh, Cisco!" Hector would then say, laughing along with his brother.

Hector then wondered what it would feel like if he had sex with the beautiful young woman, or with Yanet Garcia, the beautiful Mexican weathergirl.

"Hey!" Mick yelled. "Don't be so rough with her. She's just a little girl. Boss said not to hurt her."

"Ahh, Cisco. I'm not hurting her. Quicker we get her in the Escalade, the better. Less chance we'll be seen. Ahh, man, look at that."

"What?" Mick asked.

"She peed her pants."

"Ahh, Pancho. What the fuck did you expect? You didn't have to be so rough. Let me carry her. I'm stronger than you."

With that, and favoring his bad neck, Mick cradled Madison, who was in a chloroform sleep, in his powerful arms and gently laid her in the back seat of their car.

"Hey Bro? How does a young girl like this get to drive a Tesla?" Hector then asked.

"Her father has money, Bro." Mick said. "Remember, that's why we're doing this."

"Let's go to Burger King." Hector then announced, changing the subject. "I'm starving, bro. Okay Cisco?"

"Ahh Pancho. Is okay." Mick said.

Made in the USA
Monee, IL
25 January 2022

89820084R00260